The steep mountain walls slipped by with dizzying speed as the *Benwoi* broke the sound barrier. The whining of the strained engines grew louder. The forward shield began to overheat, causing a slight blur to the forward screen, further impeding H'Roo's ability to navigate.

Andrea turned to see the rear screen that showed great plumes of snow shaken from the t⸻d mountainsides. The so⸻⸻ s wake. She rehearsed ⸻ would quickly turn ve⸻

Brigon watc⸻ ⸻howed the *Benwoi*'s ⸻. Two hundred miles ⸻ out of ground sensor r⸻

Fal'Dar reported, "Twelve hundred miles per hour."

They accelerated steadily. Mercifully, the valley widened. Then the mountains suddenly disappeared, leaving an open tundra: flat, white, and desolate. Andrea looked twice, thinking that perhaps the screen had malfunctioned.

H'Roo fought the ship's tendency to climb, yet he was ever mindful that to put the nose down for a split second would be his last mistake. "Are we clear?"

Brigon looked at his charts, then announced, "You are clear of ground radar. You can go vertical."

With a series of commands, H'Roo turned the nose up, withdrew the *Benwoi*'s wings, and engaged the dampener. He paused, allowing the shipboard computer to recalculate a short hop under FTL drive—a mere two parsecs in the opposite direction of the Cor Fleet. He said under his breath, "Assuming we don't fly through a star, we ought to be all right." Then he pushed the throttle to FTL drive. Instantly, they passed from ballistic speed to total blackness. The forward screen automatically switched to a virtual display.

Andrea turned to Brigon, whose eyes were glued to the forward screen and the image of stars traversing space. He didn't know that the images were a cartographic device, not real light. Brigon didn't understand the physics of space travel yet. Andrea unfastened her straps, leaned over and patted Brigon on the arm. "Welcome to my world."

TENEBREA RISING

BOOK THREE OF THE TENEBREA TRILOGY

ROXANN DAWSON
AND
DANIEL GRAHAM

POCKET BOOKS
New York   London   Toronto   Sydney   Singapore

This book is a work of fiction. Names, characters, places and incidents are products of the authors' imagination or are used fictiously. Any resemblance to actual events or locales or persons, living or dead, is entirely coincidental.

An *Original* Publication of POCKET BOOKS

POCKET BOOKS, a division of Simon & Schuster, Inc.
1230 Avenue of the Americas, New York, NY 10020

Copyright © 2002 by Bill Fawcett & Associates, Inc.

ISBN: 0-671-03611-4

First Pocket Books printing November 2002

10 9 8 7 6 5 4 3 2 1

For information regarding special discounts for bulk purchases, please contact Simon & Schuster Special Sales at 1-800-456-6798 or business@simonandschuster.com.

Front cover illustration by Jim Burns

Printed in the U.S.A.

To our first and best teachers:
Richard and Rosalie Caballero;
Daniel and Ruth Graham

We thank Fiona Lee, Tina Steele, Maura Valis Lint, and Diane Bellomo for their thoughtful insights into character, plot, and theme as well as their keen eye for detail.

TENEBREA RISING

chapter 1

Hal K'Rin—headman of the Rin Clan, leader of the Tenebrea—stepped from his dusty concrete shed into the prison yard. His bones and joints ached, having absorbed the cold from the concrete floor where he'd slept. He squinted at the Klamdara sun that would soon heat this desolate repository of traitors. The yellow orb peered over the stone walls, casting long shadows. K'Rin shielded his sore eyes, pressing his thick hand to his forehead.

At the base of the wall, Feld Jo'Orom's ossified body lay on a pallet, his eye sockets staring up, the once bright rings beneath his eyes turned slate gray. A thin shroud of red dust covered the black and gray uniform of the Tenebrea. Jo'Orom's jaw was agape, his dried lips peeled back, showing yellow teeth. The prison commandant, D'Cru, had ordered the body prominently displayed to intimidate the prisoners.

K'Rin closed his eyes and remembered Jo'Orom alive, training the young Tenebrea to serve the Rin Clan, to fight and survive. He missed Jo'Orom's good counsel as much as his companionship. In his mind, K'Rin addressed the image of Jo'Orom: *How did I get us into this awful situation?*

K'Rin's memories stirred Jo'Orom's voice that answered predictably, with the same admonition: *Hal K'Rin, you may look into your past, but don't stare.*

I can't help but stare, K'Rin thought. *I started us down this path. My father warned the council about clone manufacturing in the Cor Ordinate system, and the council ruined him. I formed the Tenebrea with your help to monitor the Ordinate—and to vindicate my father. I infected you, old friend, with the Quazel Protein that killed you. I infected all of us, and I can't undo what I've done. Instead of vindicating my father and saving Jod, I have managed only to lead us all to this prison.*

K'Rin gazed upon Jo'Orom's body. K'Rin had infected himself and his Tenebrea with the protein to ensure discipline, assuming that he'd always have the Quazel enzyme to administer or withhold—the ultimate guarantor of loyalty. Now, he was ashamed of his cynicism. The Tenebrea were as loyal as ever—perhaps more so, since their brotherhood was now nailed to mutual suffering, a suffering he'd caused. He regretted his arrogance, his vain assumption that he'd always have the enzyme—that he needed it at all.

And K'Rin was embarrassed for misreading his enemies on the Jod Council. *I believed Pl'Don and the council would look at the physical evidence and see the dangers inherent in the Cor Ordinate's cloning program.*

K'Rin glanced down to observe a sightless notsig beetle trying to climb over his frayed boot: stymied yet stubborn. It clawed at the dust with its hind feet, reaching the sole of his boot with forelegs. Feathery antennae tried to make sense of the obstacle, too close to the problem to have perspective. *My boot might as well be a mountain. The council and the Fleet are as blind as this notsig beetle.* K'Rin lifted his boot and let the beetle shuffle ahead in the dust, resuming its straight path apparently to nowhere. He raised the heel of his boot to crush the beetle, but a thought prevented him: *This beetle's blindness is natural; the council's blindness is culpable.*

I tried to make them see. I sent the Tenebrea throughout the galaxy to track the Cor Ordinate's ability to use clones as a weapon. I set into motion the events that drew Andrea Flores into this conflict . . .

K'Rin turned his thoughts to Andrea Flores, the Terran woman he had brought into his Tenebrea. He had sent her to Cor to spy, to find hard evidence of the Ordinate's intentions. Not only did she get the evidence, she exceeded her goal by triggering a clone insurrection, indeed, leading an assault into the Cor capital city, Sarhn. Andrea's improvisation, although fateful, amused him. *And you, Andrea, you certainly stirred the stinging Z'la creeper's nest. At least you're safe.* K'Rin whispered hoarsely, hoping his thought might reach out into the stars, "Find your way home, Andrea. Go back to Earth and live."

Pairs of languorous Jod marines stood in patches of shade, their weapons draped over their thick shoulders. Instead of helmets, they wore loose caps to cover their pale, hairless heads. The guards engaged in conversation, trying to fight the tedium of Klamdara isolation. They kept one wary eye watching their own officers. More than the prisoners, they feared opprobrium. A season earlier, they feared the Tenebrea, K'Rin's own guard.

The guards utterly ignored the once formidable K'Rin, once an admiral in the Jod Fleet, now condemned for treason by the Council of Elders and the council's leader Hal Pl'Don.

Treason? K'Rin chaffed. *Hal Pl'Don and the council are traitors—or worse, they are fools.* K'Rin had long believed that the Ordinate, a human species transported to the Cor system, would eventually challenge the Jod with clone armies. The council admonished him to respect Cor neutrality, but he was, after all, the Chief of Offworld Intelligence. Andrea's raid into Sarhn forced the conflict into the open. *Then I most certainly blundered. I assumed that Pl'Don would put Jod's security ahead of his enmity toward the Rin Clan. I was so wrong, but what could I have done differently?*

K'Rin felt a trickle of blood spill from his nose. A drop of the dark red fell at his feet, leaving a black pock in the dust. He raised a bloodstained cloth to wipe his upper lip.

K'Rin turned his thoughts to the present. *The Quazel Protein is slowly turning us to stone: killing us. How ironic. The odds for escape are terrible. The odds of surviving another sixty days are worse.*

K'Rin hoped he might still lead them off Klamdara and to a cache of enzyme aboard the freighter *Kam-Gi*. His Tenebrea believed he would succeed—somehow. He must. If the battle turned against them, they would fight to the death. K'Rin promised that he would not order a retreat. If they did not succeed in freeing themselves from Klamdara by the strength of their arms, then death would free them from the torment of the Quazel Protein.

K'Rin was acutely aware of his own symptoms. His joints ached. He was reduced to hoarse whispers as his larynx stiffened, making all speech painful. So far, his vision remained unimpaired, but he knew that myopia was beginning to affect some of his warriors.

K'Rin walked among the small huts. Small groups of Tenebrea stood at attention at the rickety doors as K'Rin passed. He read the twinge of pain in their faces as they forced themselves erect out of respect for his rank. He looked each of his afflicted warriors in the eye, saying nothing.

Words were painful; therefore, every word spoken had purpose. The Tenebrea longed to hear one word: *Attack!*

Their uniforms were frayed about the collars. Their sleeves were stained with their own blood wiped from their upper lips.

Their prison diet had reduced them to sleek animals. Their uniforms hung loose on their large bones. Their eyes were sunken into their hairless faces. The rings beneath their eyes—each ring denoting a decade of life—appeared darker. Even the bright yellow ring of childhood had turned a dark amber. *The Quazel poisoning* . . .

Despite their wan appearance, the Tenebrea were still physically strong. K'Rin saw the sinewy strength in their arms and legs, less supple for sure, but eager to strike. His warriors paced the prison yard like hungry carnivores, disciplined yet impatient. They held their heads up, watching the inattentive guards, occasionally glancing back at K'Rin—always waiting for the word. Every warrior knew that with the arrival of the next supply ship they would escape Klamdara or die trying. With a look, K'Rin told them: *Soon. We'll take them soon.*

A younger Jod walked stiffly to catch K'Rin. He croaked, "Sir, staff meeting."

K'Rin nodded and followed Kip into a concrete building. The room was bare of furniture. The four officers sat on their haunches in a semicircle waiting for K'Rin. The walls were streaked with rust leaching from the iron-rich sands used in the mortar. Bal'Don and a handful of younger officers started to rise, when K'Rin preempted them. "Sit."

K'Rin hunkered down, eye level with his staff. He turned to the oldest in the group, Bal'Don, and hoarsely asked, "Supply ship?"

Bal'Don shook his head and croaked, "Delayed."

Kip, Bal'Don, and the rest of the staff knew the explanation that they pieced together from snatches of information gleaned from the guards. The Jod Fleet was standing down for a diplomatic show of goodwill for the Cor Ordinate government. Consequently, Fleet logistics churned in disarray, and Klamdara was a low priority in the present scheme of things. Cor's ministers would soon visit Jod, inspect the Jod Fleet, and begin diplomatic relations. Recently, the Klamdara commandant, D'Cru, had taunted K'Rin, claiming that Jod was about to open a new epoch of peace—a peace that K'Rin had tried to sabotage.

K'Rin envisioned the Jod Fleet in synchronous orbit above the capital city of Heptar waiting like sitting ducks for the Cor Ordinate. *Another bitter irony, although not my fault.* K'Rin believed in the iron Law of Unexpected Result. His own humiliation and incarceration on Klamdara was a case in point. He believed the Cor Ordinate would not come for the expected peace; rather, they'd come to destroy the Fleet and thereby decapitate Jod: galactic war. And he, having prepared his whole life to defend Jod, would miss the battle—another unintended result.

K'Rin asked, "Weapons?"

Bal'Don nodded solemnly. "All." He reached into his black tunic and withdrew a metal phalange, a blunt rusted rod scraped to a ragged point on the concrete floors, tapered to a serviceable point. He handed the weapon to K'Rin. "Yours."

"Thank you." K'Rin peeled open the breast flap on his tunic and hid the weapon. "Soon," he reiterated his promise.

Andrea watched her warm breath disappear into the bitter cold of Cor's winter. She stood at the mouth of a cave, refuge of the wilderness clones, looking into the rapid onset of night. The steep volcanic mountains cast long shadows. She felt like one looking up from a deep pit. The last tint of indigo disappeared into a pitch-black sky shimmering with stars. Cor's waxing moon cast a pale light over the snow. Tall snow-laden pines stood like slump-shouldered giants guarding the entrance of the cave.

She stood in the moonlight. Her brown eyes glistened. The dry cold bit her cheeks, adding a tinge of red to her olive skin. The cave's humid thermals blew at her neck. She shrugged and tightened her parka, tucking her straight black hair into her upturned collar. She adjusted her harness. Her heavy pack and a pair of snubbed snowshoes lay at her feet.

On the trail winding between trees and rock, a dozen wilderness clones packed three sleds. The first sled held rifles, bundled like wood and lying on heavy sacks of ammunition. The clones cinched the leather straps hard, anticipating a fast and rugged march to the *Benwoi*, now repaired, and ready for deep space travel.

Andrea looked at the multitude of stars. One of the distant specks of white lost in the jumble of the crisp sky was the Jod sun. Somewhere in the Jod system was the prison planet, Klamdara. There, K'Rin and her comrades, the Tenebrea, were incarcerated, waiting to die from Quazel poisoning. She knew that Brigon's small company of wilderness clones—just thirty-five combatants—was the only slim hope to save K'Rin. And K'Rin was the only—and slimmer—hope for saving the starving and persecuted clones here on planet Cor. Andrea was not optimistic. However, her pessimism was irrelevant. They had no other option except to flee the immediate conflict and merely postpone the inevitable. The NewGen clones were due to hatch in large numbers shortly. The scales of military power would soon tilt permanently in favor of the Cor Ordinate. And the Ordinate were pitiless. Time was short.

"Andrea." She heard her name echo from the cave walls.

"Here," she answered. Andrea's lips were dark, almost purple from the cold.

H'Roo Parh followed her voice and found her. He wore the gray and black uniform of the Tenebrea, and carried a bulging rucksack. He also carried a bulky parka in the crook of his arm. H'Roo was tall for a Jod and less thick than most. He said, "Brigon sends word that we leave in ten minutes. I spoke with Eric. He was at the infirmary helping Dr. Carai take care of Tara."

"He was?" The news pleased Andrea, who only yesterday had belittled Eric for not showing more concern for his wounded mate. Andrea asked, "How is Tara?"

"The bleeding from her arm has almost stopped. Dr. Carai thinks he can save her eye." H'Roo drew a line on his own face where Tara had suffered a gash. "The left side of her face may suffer some paralysis—nerve damage. These clones have only the most primitive medical tools. Carai can't regenerate the nerve or eliminate the scar without the proper tools. He doesn't even have a surgical laser: he had to cut off her frostbitten toes with a blade." H'Roo grimaced at the thought. "If we could get Tara to Jod, we could build her a new arm. Carai will do the best he can here."

Andrea looked up in disbelief. "Carai is staying?"

H'Roo nodded. "Yes."

Andrea looked around and lowered her voice to a whisper. "H'Roo, these clones are starving to death. His chances are better with us on the *Benwoi*."

"He'd rather take his chances with the clones." H'Roo put on his parka and pulled the hood over his hairless scalp. His small delicate ears were bluish from the cold.

Andrea glanced back. The dim artificial light in the cave sparked her brown eyes. "Did he say why?"

"He doesn't want to go back into K'Rin's service—especially back to Yuseat. He said, K'Rin can rebuild the Yuseat Lab and manufacture the enzyme without him." H'Roo patted his rucksack. "We have eight hundred doses of enzyme right here. Carai will reduce the raw crown gall into more enzyme while we are away."

Andrea nodded knowingly. "Just as well. Carai is no warrior. His biggest challenge is going to be keeping these clones from eating him—thin though he is."

H'Roo pulled his hood closer over his hairless head and pink ears. "Dr. Carai is articulate. Sentient beings don't eat creatures smarter than themselves."

Andrea chuckled lowly. "Happens all the time."

H'Roo pursed his thin lips in disgust and carried his precious rucksack to a sled. The fresh snow crunched beneath his large boots. Andrea watched from a distance as he gesticulated, trying to make the sled master understand the critical importance of the enzyme. The clone nodded indifferently and strapped the medicine down with the same care shown any sack of ammunition. H'Roo found the other four Jod and they stood together, stamping their feet trying to keep warm.

A female clone, Chana, led a large group of clone warriors from the cave shadows. She bent at the waist under her heavy load: two backpacks and a pair of new carbines slung over her shoulder. She paused briefly to stand by Andrea. The shorter, thick-waisted clone looked up at Andrea with a slow smile. Raising an eyebrow, Chana said, "I'm coming, too. I guess Brigon needs me after all."

Or you need Brigon . . . Andrea said nothing. Rather, she looked down into Chana's upturned eyes, deep chestnut-brown eyes. Sad eyes. Chana had full lips on a large mouth set in a square jaw. Her facial bones about the eyes were exaggerated due to months of malnutrition. Her straight black hair, oily from lack of bathing, showed a couple streaks of premature gray. She wore her parka loosely open. Andrea saw that Chana wore body armor, picked from a dead Cor soldier.

Brigon had planned to leave Chana behind, but he had not anticipated his heavy losses at the South Mountain ambush. Brigon still would have left Chana behind, except that Andrea insisted that they take at least thirty-five experienced fighters to Klamdara. Chana could fight. She trudged away to the sleds where she unshouldered her burden.

Andrea watched. Chana was a strong woman: broad shoulders and hips, a thick waist, yet all muscle. She had a stubborn strength—not athletic, but enduring. She had braided her black hair to make herself more attractive. At the nape of her neck was a simple mark, a tattoo visible only when her hair was set up. The tattoo was the shape of an eye, burnt orange in color. She helped the others adjust the loads, and in short order, the sleds were secure.

Eric reluctantly followed Chana's group to the sleds. He gave Andrea a perfunctory glance. He had wanted to stay behind with his mate, Tara. He didn't know why. Grievously wounded, having lost her arm, Tara was no longer functional. Her wounds unsettled him. As a clone, he didn't know to behave around a clone bereft of her functions. Andrea knew Eric's predicament: he did not understand raw pity and he sensed this missing quality in himself. The Artrix seemed better suited. On a more practical point, Eric wanted to stay behind to organize the clones in Brigon's absence. But Eric acceded to Brigon's loose authority. Brigon needed Eric's fighting skills on Klamdara, and he didn't trust Eric to manage the clones' affairs in his stead.

Andrea felt a hand on her shoulder. Her first reflex was to resist the touch. Then Brigon's voice said, "Walk with me to the head of the column."

Andrea relaxed at the sound of his voice. "Oh, it's you," she said as a way of apologizing for pulling away.

Brigon pulled at his tawny beard and raised his eyebrows as if to respond, *Who else?* "Tell your friend, H'Roo, to join us. We have yet to figure out how to get off Cor without being intercepted."

Admiral Brulk held a model of a J-Class attack ship in his hand. In gold leaf, the ship's hull number J-480 reflected the soft light from his desk lamp. The Cor Ordinate had not commissioned a military vessel for almost a hundred years. He refurbished the Lynx Colony shipyard just two years ago. He considered the design and manufacture of J-Class ships a marvel, second only to the design and manufacture of the NewGen clones. He mused: *the Lynx shipyard met their goal. My plan is coming together* . . . He carefully set the model on the glass shelf with other trophies of his career.

The rest of Brulk's office was dimly lit. Through the large plate-glass windows, an insipid evening twilight muddled in. Fresh snow sat on the windowsill, softening the right angles of the otherwise stark room. A stack of reports sat unread on his desk.

Most of the Cor Security Ministry staff had ended their day and gone home to their families. Admiral Brulk didn't have a family, which was just as well as far as he was concerned. Brulk wore his dark blue battle uniform. Five gold pips on his collar indicated his rank. His short military hair, fading brown, was speckled liberally with gray. Otherwise, he looked like an aggressive young man in his uniform. Brulk felt fresh despite his recent space travel. His body was still on Lynx Colony time. He planned to return soon, so he felt no need to adjust his biorhythms.

He consulted his daily schedule: *6:40 P.M. Dr. Sandrom, 7:05 Lt. Botchi.* The brass clock on his wall showed 6:39. He set the thin screen aside, then aligned three crystal paperweights on the top of his desk. *Just so,* he thought. He smoothed his hands over his clean desk—clear except for the silver tray and tea setting. He pulled the cozy off the white porcelain pot and poured two cups.

Dr. Sandrom walked into the room. Without looking up, Brulk commented, "Doctor Sandrom, punctual as ever."

Sandrom bowed slightly. Sandrom looked old and frail, with thinning white hair and neatly trimmed goatee. His crisp blue eyes mirrored his vigorous intellect. Behind Sandrom stood two large young figures, identical in complexion, mousy brown hair, and physique. They wore simple uniforms. Both stood six foot five inches tall: powerful arms and legs. They stood with their backs to a bookshelf, seemingly disinterested. Sandrom motioned to the pair. "Admiral, I brought you two NewGens that you can use for demonstrations—to the council, to the citizens, whomever. By giving them a simple command, I can transfer them to your control. You can put these two to work right away."

Brulk looked up. "Excellent. Are we still on schedule at Qurush?"

"Yes." Sandrom smiled and took his seat. "I accelerated the schedule as you asked."

Admiral Brulk rose halfway from his seat. Reaching across his desk, he handed Sandrom a cup of tea. He said, "Thank you for making the journey to see me on such short notice. I want to get down to Qurush to see you work, but I have so much to do: the final details at Lynx and—" Brulk grumbled, "—keeping the Prefect and her ministers informed."

"A short hop from Qurush—" Sandrom returned the courtesy, "—much shorter than your trip from the Lynx Colony."

Brulk furled his brow and thought: *True, I should be with the fleet instead of spending time holding Madame Prefect's hand.* He said, "I wanted to go over some last-minute details before I leave for Jod."

"Yes, Admiral." Dr. Sandrom pulled a small data card from his pocket to take notes. Sandrom carefully intimated, "I heard the rumor that Sarhn faces organized resistance from some renegade old-order clones. Frankly, I was alarmed to hear that the first fifty New-Gens I sent to Sarhn were destroyed in a skirmish. Did our NewGens not perform to specification?"

Brulk pursed his lips and suppressed his anger: "Your NewGens performed precisely to specification. Unfortunately, the officer in charge did not. We will not waste any more of your valuable commodity, I assure you."

Sandrom nodded somberly. "A pity to lose those fifty, but soon you'll have more than enough NewGens."

Brulk lifted the porcelain teapot and offered to refill Sandrom's cup. "Excellent. I'll hold you to your word." Brulk wagged a finger in a friendly way. "Your NewGen technology will change the history of Cor and the galaxy."

Sandrom smiled and leaned forward with his cup and saucer to catch the steaming amber liquid. "You give me too much credit. The concept was yours. I am just your technician."

Brulk cut the mutual admiration short, asking bluntly, "How soon can you run the Qurush facility using only NewGen labor?"

Sandrom looked up from his tea and smiled as if anticipating the question. He set his cup down on the side table, allowing a dramatic pause before his answer. His blue eyes sparked with his triumphant news. "Eight weeks. We are hatching about ten New-Gens per day now. We are training those hatchlings to run the Qurush facility, and with the increased labor we can increase production to one hundred per day. Already we have plans laid to expand the facility. With access to the boundless resources of the ocean, and expanding NewGen labor, I see no limit to the number of NewGens we can produce. However, we do need more computing power."

Brulk reached out and grabbed Sandrom's thin hand and pressed it between his two beefy hands. "And you shall have it!" Brulk got up and posed a question delicately. "Dr. Sandrom, how soon can we relocate Qurush's civilian population and make Qurush a military facility?"

"Why?"

Brulk paused. A shadow quickly passed over his face until he realized the question came from his stalwart supporter. Then, he brightened. He said frankly, "I must delicately manage conflicting priorities on the council. To be blunt, the less our civilians know about Qurush's capacity, the better. Do not share any of your records."

"I'll do as you say, Admiral Brulk. How shall I explain this secretiveness to other Ordinate scientists?"

Brulk was annoyed by the question. "You tell them nothing. We need the NewGens for security as we cancel the old-order clones. Unfortunately, most of the civilian population wants the NewGens brought into service to prop up their standard of living, and too many in our government agree with the civilians. The government seems to think we can make this transition without inconveniencing anyone. They don't realize that we must secure our frontiers before we can improve our standard of living. Some sacrifice is necessary to ensure our future. We Ordinate are in a struggle for our very survival."

"I agree with you. I'll tell them nothing."

Brulk forced a smile. He oscillated between demanding agreement and disdaining yes-men. "I cannot be distracted by petty competition for resources. I need the Qurush facility secured from our own people because I need the Qurush output to remain secret. So I want the civilians relocated before the facility begins high-volume production."

Dr. Sandrom nodded solemnly. "I understand completely."

Brulk added, "A few days from now, I'll lead 480 J-Class ships to the Jod system. The Jod government expects that we come to negotiate an arrangement brokered by the Chelle. However, such an arrangement would place us within the Jod hegemony as part of their damnable Alliance." Brulk's eyes widened as he leaned down to share his triumph with Dr. Sandrom. "The Jod have assembled all their capital ships in one place as a gesture of goodwill and to demonstrate their might. The Chelle assure us that they are lined up as if for a parade. They won't be able to use their starboard or port weapons without hitting each other. Our ships, piloted by *your* NewGens, will fly right through their defenses with quark torpedoes. The Jod do not expect an attack. Nor will they expect that our pilots are NewGens, obediently emulating themselves as they fire their weapons at point-blank range."

Dr. Sandrom congratulated Brulk. "An excellent trade. We can build J-Class ships and hatch NewGen pilots much faster than the Jod can rebuild their Fleet. I commend you, Admiral Brulk. Your strategy is pure genius."

Before Admiral Brulk could accept Sandrom's compliment, a middle-aged woman wearing the tan duty uniform entered the room. Without apologizing for the intrusion, she said, "Sir, Lt. Botchi is here as you requested."

Brulk turned slowly. His countenance fell into a storm of deep-seated anger, but he willed himself to an equivocal humor. "Send him in. Then, you go home."

"Thank you, sir." The woman left. Sandrom also got up to leave.

Brulk then turned to Sandrom and said in a low voice, "Please stay. You might find this interview interesting. This is the officer who wasted your fifty NewGens."

A moment later, a young officer walked into the room and paused to let his eyes adjust to the shadowy light. Despite the cool dry air, perspiration beaded on the young man's upper lip. His eyes settled on Brulk.

Brulk's voice was cold but polite. "Botchi, I brought you here to explain your fiasco in the South Mountains."

Botchi's voice cracked, "I can explain."

Brulk stepped closer to the younger officer. "As I recall, I told you not to become engaged. I told you to use all other means to investigate the crash site, and not to use troops, didn't I?"

"Sir, we had reason to believe the crashed ship was the *Benwoi*. We had to be sure they had not seen our fleet assembling at Lynx." Lt. Botchi refused to allow Brulk to put the entire disaster on his shoulders. "Sir, you approved the mission."

"I did not approve such a fiasco. How dare you suggest otherwise?"

"We were ambushed, sir, by large numbers. We had no idea . . ."

Brulk interrupted Botchi's weak protest. "You lost a third of Sarhn's security troops: one hundred twenty-four dead, fifty-two wounded. You lost all the NewGens. Is that correct?"

"Yes, sir." Botchi lowered his eyes.

Brulk asked coldly, "Why didn't you die with your men? Why are you here? Why are standing in my office without a scratch, reporting to me that you lost your entire command?" Brulk didn't give Botchi time to answer: the implication was that Botchi was a coward.

Botchi's cheeks reddened at the suggestion. He glanced at Dr. Sandrom, who witnessed this humiliating rebuke.

Brulk snapped another question. "And ships? How many losses?"

"Two gunships and one hovercraft."

"You . . ." Brulk checked his wrath. He took a deep breath. "So we must assume that the wilderness clones now have the weapons and ammunition from the two gunships. Our garrison force is roughly cut in half, and why? Because you did not follow my orders! You had to risk everything to satisfy your curiosity."

"Sir," Botchi defended himself, "I believed that the wreckage in the valley was the *Benwoi*, stolen by the Terran female."

"I don't give a damn what you *believe*; I gave you orders. The *Benwoi* is of no consequence—not then, not now!" Brulk stepped forward, causing Botchi to retreat.

Brulk's words stung Botchi and he lowered his eyes for the first time. He murmured, "We had no idea the wilderness clones had such numbers and weapons. When we get more NewGens, I'll take a regiment in and clean out the valley."

"No!" Brulk yelled, losing his composure. His jaw muscles tightened. "Let the winter kill them. My plan is to contain them and starve them—not to engage them. Not to agitate them into armed conflict! Don't you understand? Even now, the clones outnumber us ten thousand to one. We are at the most dangerous crossroad of Cor's history. We must simultaneously neutralize the Jod Alliance and replace the old-order technology with NewGens. And you would jeopardize everything—my life's work—because you *believe*," he said the word mockingly, "that you must personally confirm an insignificant crash site."

"I understand, sir. I won't let . . ."

"No, you don't understand!" Brulk wagged his finger in Botchi's face. "You shall conduct no operations in the wilderness until I return from Jod. You shall keep all our assets inside Sarhn to protect our strategic resources from any threat from either the precinct or wilderness clones. Is that perfectly clear? You are not to take a single soldier outside that wall." Brulk pointed through his window. "Not until I return to give you explicit direction."

Botchi raised his eyes and said, "But, sir, with all due respect, what if you do not return?"

Brulk dropped his arms at his side and studied Botchi for a minute. Then, he shook his head slowly and turned to Dr. Sandrom. He asked softly, "Would you please transfer control of the two NewGens to me now?"

The white-haired doctor rose from his cushioned seat. "Yes, Admiral Brulk." He turned to the pair of NewGens standing in the shadows. He made a hand signal directing four fingers of his left hand to his mouth and the four fingers of his right hand toward Brulk. He said, "Accept Brulk commands." The two NewGens turned their heads in unison to face Brulk.

Realizing that he now had control, Brulk spoke directly to the two NewGen clones. "Take Lt. Botchi into the courtyard and kill him."

chapter 2

Brigon's wilderness clones settled in the *Benwoi*'s narrow cargo bay. They huddled together on the floor braced against the walls as if they were in an oxcart. They grinned nervously as they gawked at the inside of the ship. Andrea smiled: *They have no idea.* She left the cargo bay after instructing the four bemused Jod from the Yuseat Lab. "Explain space flight to these flatlanders." Wrinkling her nose she added, "And as soon as we're well underway, run them through the electrostatic shower, and show them how to wash their clothes."

Andrea returned to the bridge. She found H'Roo Parh at the controls of the *Benwoi*. Brigon sat in the navigator's chair, silently watching H'Roo run through the preflight checks.

H'Roo accidentally toggled the bridge lights off, then on again. His neck showed a tinge of orange. Andrea prodded, "Are you nervous?"

"It shows?" H'Roo put his hand to his neck. He muttered, "Are you sure you want me to pilot?"

"Better you than me," Andrea nodded, offering no

other clue as to her doubts. H'Roo damaged the ship when they landed on Cor, but frankly, she was amazed that he managed to land in that violent snowstorm. Either H'Roo was good enough, or he was lucky enough: she didn't care which.

H'Roo added, "You know that we'll burn up the forward shield if we try a low-altitude jump."

Andrea looked up from her console. "We don't have a choice. We have to fly below the Cor ground radar until we're out of cannon range. Let's not second-guess ourselves now. Besides, we know that the *Benwoi*'s forward shields aren't worth much against gunnery. We're just an armed merchant. We might as well use the shields to help us sneak out; they're no good in a stand-up fight."

"Right." Then H'Roo announced through all commpanels, "Everybody strap yourselves into a seat or a berth. This is going to be," H'Roo looked at Andrea and smiled feebly, "exciting." He engaged the engines and lifted the *Benwoi* straight up, sloughing off a thick blanket of snow.

Absent the snow's weight, the *Benwoi* rose with a jerk until H'Roo stabilized. A few excited exclamations rose from the passengers. H'Roo turned to Andrea and smiled sheepishly.

Brigon, who sat next to Andrea, looked at her with wide eyes, bracing himself in his chair. Neither he nor any of his wilderness clones had ever flown before. The sudden vertical movements and the momentary weightlessness startled him, like slipping on ice, and a mischievous smile lifted his mustache.

Then H'Roo accelerated quickly forward, keeping the *Benwoi* just several hundred feet above the rocky valley floor. He kept his hand on the steering ball and his eye glued to the forward screen. He accelerated up the valley, banking right and left trying to match the twists and turns in the steep volcanic walls of rock and ice. Always the alarms beeped, alerting him that he was flying too close to the ground, too fast for conditions. "Turn off that racket!" H'Roo commanded.

A fellow Jod, Fal'Dar, complied. The sheer mountain walls slipped by with dizzying speed as the *Benwoi* broke the sound barrier. The whining of the strained engines grew louder. The forward shield began to overheat, causing a slight blur to the forward screen, further impeding H'Roo's ability to navigate.

Andrea turned to see the rear screen showing great plumes of snow shaken from the trees and mountainsides. The *Benwoi*'s sonic boom left avalanches in its wake. She rehearsed the plan in her mind. Soon, they would quickly turn vertical and jump into space.

Speed was their best security. Cor sensors would at best get one blip of data marking their ascent. The chances were remote that the Cor would see or analyze a random speck in their data. Even so, with only one data point, the Cor could not calculate direction or speed. Andrea knew that returning would be far more difficult. Jumping into a void undetected would be relatively easy compared to jumping onto a planet's surface.

Brigon watched the interactive charts that showed the *Benwoi*'s location relative to Cor terrain. Two hundred miles farther and they would be well out of ground sensor range.

Fal'Dar reported, "Twelve hundred miles per hour."

They accelerated steadily. Mercifully, the valley widened. Then the mountains suddenly disappeared, leaving an open tundra: flat, white, and desolate. Andrea looked twice, thinking that perhaps the screen had malfunctioned.

H'Roo fought the ship's tendency to climb, yet he was ever mindful that to put the nose down for a split second would be his last mistake. "Are we clear?"

Brigon looked at his charts, then announced, "You are clear of ground radar. You can go vertical."

With a series of commands, H'Roo turned the nose up, withdrew the *Benwoi*'s wings, and engaged the dampener. He paused, allowing the shipboard computer to recalculate a short hop under FTL drive—a mere two parsecs in the opposite direction of the Cor Fleet. He said under his breath, "Assuming we don't fly through a star, we ought to be all right." Then he pushed the throttle to FTL drive. Instantly, they passed from ballistic speed to total blackness. The forward screen automatically switched to a virtual display.

Andrea turned to Brigon, whose eyes were glued to the forward screen and the image of stars traversing space. He didn't know that the images were a cartographic device, not real light. Brigon didn't understand the physics of space travel yet. Andrea unfastened her straps, leaned over and patted Brigon on the arm. "Welcome to my world."

The Madame Prefect of Cor stormed into Brulk's office. She was pale, suddenly looking her age. Although her yellowing hair was meticulously swept off her high forehead, her waist jacket was awkwardly cross-buttoned. She was the picture of ragged self-control strained to the breaking point. Her hand agitated as she pointed an accusing finger. Her voice shook with anger as she demanded, "Admiral Brulk! What is the meaning of this outrage?"

Brulk turned slowly from his window and rebuked her with a look. He already knew what was sticking in her craw. The night before, he watched the two NewGens grab Botchi, who struggled helplessly. The entire Ministry echoed with the doomed man's protest, then desperate pleadings. He recalled that he was mildly amused when Botchi wet himself as the NewGens hauled him away. He remembered noticing that the few office workers on the night shift went to their windows to see the cause of the tumult.

The unnaturally strong NewGens held Botchi fast as he tried to thrash his way free. Pointless. The large clones stopped in the middle of the Ministry courtyard in the dim flickering light of ornamental gas lamps. Then, one of the NewGens simply twisted Botchi's head with a sudden jerk. The snap was audible as Botchi's voice stifled in a short, shrill gasp. The NewGens dropped Botchi's limp body in the snow, belly down. Botchi's face stared up at the gas lamp, his eyes locked and his mouth misaligned. The serenity of the courtyard returned.

Brulk answered the Prefect with a simple question. "Lieutenant Botchi, does he concern you?"

The Prefect stammered, "Of course . . . *of course!* How could you let those . . . *those* . . . creatures . . . kill that young officer? The people are almost hysterical, having seen a pair of clones snap a security officer's neck. Already the alarm is up that the NewGens are dangerous."

Brulk raised an eyebrow and offered the Prefect a thin smile. "Those *creatures* simply obeyed my orders. If the good citizens want something to fear, let them fear me, not the NewGens. As for Botchi, he had become a liability, a distraction." Brulk's voice was smooth. "Madame Prefect, we are about to engage in a galactic war of history-bending proportions."

"You *cannot* summarily execute Cor Ordinate officers." The Prefect's cheeks turned crimson as she pounded one small fist into the palm of her hand.

"Yes I can, and I did." Brulk smirked. "I think a stark lesson in military discipline is most appropriate just now. I suggest you leave military matters to me for the time being."

"The government will not tolerate any usurpation of its authority by you." The passion in her voice rose with each syllable.

It already has, Brulk smiled. Madame Prefect was in effect the government, and the fact that she referred to government in the third person indicated an erosion of her will. He stepped from his desk and walked up to her. Without asking, he began to fix the buttons on her jacket. His thick fingers deftly worked the first mother-of-pearl button at her thin neck.

The Prefect stiffened at his touch. She started to recoil, then stopped. Brulk watched her eyes and saw her flashing anger chill, then turn to a pale, low-grade fear. He smiled coolly and said, "If you disapprove of my methods, you may, of course, relieve me."

Brulk corrected another button, while looking directly into her widening eyes. "And I, in return, will leave Sarhn to the mercy of half a million clones starving outside the Sarhn city walls. Of course, the security forces that I lead will fail to understand your motives if you relieve me. They, as do I, want to believe that the government—that *your* government, Madame Prefect—appreciates their efforts, especially when the risks are so great. There, your jacket is straight." He tugged gently down on the lower hem of her jacket.

The Prefect lowered her eyes. She felt her jacket buttons with her fingertips as if the buttons were too hot to hold. The conviction in her voice was gone. She said, "I cannot let you flout the law."

Brulk returned to his desk. "I believe the Law of Self-Preservation trumps your government's artificial ordinances. I cannot let anyone or anything undermine my mission now. I don't think you truly appreciate the risk of maintaining the *status quo*. If we do not immediately remove the Jod Fleet from the military equation, the Jod will aid the old-order clones. The old-order clones, who still outnumber us ten thousand to one, will overrun the Ordinate, and life as we know it will cease. It's a little late to get squeamish, Madame Prefect."

She stood silently and glared. The color began to return to her cheeks.

Then Brulk flashed a charming smile that showed his straight teeth. "Let's not quarrel, Madame Prefect. Let's simply agree that I shall run military operations as I see fit, and you can run civilian affairs as you see fit. But understand this, until I destroy the Jod Fleet, I cannot tolerate interference. Our survival is at stake."

Madame Prefect merely nodded, turned, and left Brulk's office.

*   *   *

As far as they could tell, the *Benwoi* had escaped Cor undetected. The experienced among the Yuseat crew settled into the tedium of a three-week flight. But the wilderness clones, surrounded for the first time with all the trappings of space travel, immediately indulged their innate curiosity, pestering the Jod with questions and trying their hand at the many technical amenities. Brigon planned to spend most of his hours on the bridge, learning the consoles for each position.

Andrea found her few belongings still stored in the locker in the narrow captain's cabin. She looked in the small round shaving mirror stuck to the wall above a tiny sink. She hardly knew the woman looking back at her. She had to pause to do the calculation: she was now twenty-seven—no, twenty-eight years old. Andrea leaned forward to get a close look in the confining mirror. Same straight nose, high cheekbones. Her face was thinner than she remembered. Same slight bow in her lips. Could it be that her lips were thinner as well?

But the eyes were somehow different. *How*, she wondered, *had her eyes changed over the years?* Her wide, happy eyes had looked innocently on the world as a child, then lovingly on her husband Steve and daughter Glendon. Her eyes had changed forever by what they saw. Experience, like a grinding wheel, cut away their simplicity, leaving a hundred facets that confused and diffused the light. Her eyes dimmed—almost to black—when they saw Steve and Glendon murdered by the Cor Hunter Team.

Now the eyes in the mirror narrowed even as the memory presented itself. *Steve, Glendon, I'll make them pay.* A wicked smile crossed her lips. *You should have seen what Tara and I did to the Ordinate's Clone Welfare Institute—we burned it down. If we get K'Rin out of Klamdara, we can wreck their world like they wrecked ours.*

Andrea saw her lips move in the mirror and worried for a moment that she might be overheard talking to herself. She turned away and sat on her bunk to compose herself, but a second wave of memories collided with her present. The clone Eric plagued her vision like a living ghost of Steve, a mystery now solved. She saw the DNA match that proved that her husband Steve, as a small child, was a refugee clone on Earth, a clone built from the same genetic code as Eric. Andrea ran her hands tightly through her black hair, trying to press the images back.

She groaned quietly. *What is K'Rin's involvement?* She learned that K'Rin helped the child Steve escape from Cor more than twenty years ago—helped him and his refugee foster parents settle outside Baltimore. While tracking an Earth-bound Ordinate Hunter Team, K'Rin discovered Eric, a refugee clone. He immediately recognized Eric as Steve's genetic double, and he correctly surmised that the Hunters who were after Eric might find Steve instead. K'Rin did not arrive at Baltimore in time, and the Hunters murdered Steve.

She believed K'Rin. A voice in her head told her, *All words! Trust your eyes!* But her eyes had not seen the objective truth.

Andrea heard a soft noise behind. She turned and found Brigon standing in the narrow doorway to her cabin. "How long have you been standing there?" she demanded.

Brigon excused himself. "Just this second; your

door was open." Brigon's hair was a shade lighter, dry, with a bit of curl. His cheeks were slightly sunburned, making his beard appear yellow.

"I see you took a shower."

"In hot water. I pulled rank." Brigon grinned. He stretched out his arms to show his faded tan shirt. "Washed my clothes, too." He stepped into Andrea's cabin, letting the door close behind him. He looked around the crowded space. "Two beds." He pointed to the upper berth.

Andrea bit her lip and wagged her head. "This cabin serves as the captain and first mate's quarters."

Brigon winked at her and smiled. "You can be the captain. I'll be the first mate."

Andrea forced herself to look peeved, but a thin smile betrayed her.

Brigon sat on the lower berth and observed, "Comfortable. I like it."

Andrea leaned back against a desk. "Then I'll gather my gear and leave."

Brigon protested, "No, stay. Stay. Give me one good reason why we shouldn't share a room."

Andrea's smile disappeared as she said, "Okay. I'll give you two." She bent down and took Brigon's face in her hands. She pressed his full beard into his cheeks as she looked into his dark gray eyes and pressed a soft kiss on his lips.

Brigon reached out to pull himself into Andrea's arms and prolong the kiss. Raising himself, he banged his head against the metal of the upper berth. "Ow!" He blinked away the pain.

Andrea leaned back on the bunk, propped on her elbows. She said, "Reason number one: we must not be a distraction for each other—not now, not on

Klamdara. Reason number two: you really ought to live with your people if you are going to lead them into battle. My father taught me that."

"Your father?" Brigon stood up rubbing the top of his head. His face was red from pain and disappointment. He asked bluntly, "Was that a kiss or just a lesson?"

Andrea smiled wryly. "Why? Did you learn anything?"

Brigon reached down and grabbed a fistful of Andrea's tunic. He pulled her off the bunk, kissing her on the mouth, then set her down slowly. Her brown eyes flashed, but she didn't speak. Brigon walked halfway to the door and turned, saying, "I learned plenty. Did you?"

In the evening sky above Heptar on Jod, a new constellation appeared. Seven new lights shone bright through the deep violet twilight when most stars did not yet appear. The seven Jod dreadnoughts, the largest war machines ever created, stood in a synchronous orbit directly overhead. Smaller lights spread before them: cruisers, and heavy destroyers.

The citizens of Heptar pointed to the sky. They took pride in their invincible Fleet that had procured peace and commensurate prosperity for Jod. Never had the Fleet been assembled in one place, and even the most hard-bitten campaigner's heart swelled with pride.

The head of the Jod Council, Hal Pl'Don, stood on his garden balcony watching the sky get darker and his ships glow brighter. He still wore the robes of his office. The heavy gold chain of office hung about his neck. His day had been long—indeed hectic with the preparations to receive the Cor Ordinate delegation. But his labors were rewarding, and Pl'Don felt as fresh as the moment he first opened his eyes. All his careful plans slipped effortlessly together like tongue and groove, each piece reinforcing the next. The Chelle ambassador just confirmed that the Cor Delegation would arrive on schedule according to the agreed protocol. Soon he would have the Cor Ordinate safely in the Alliance where he could manage their ambitions. However, at present, he had one more decision to make today.

Behind Pl'Don, a Jod wearing the black Tenebrea uniform sat on a stone bench. The soldier looked down at his hands, kneading the pain out of the stiff joints. He was a dark contrast to the sunburst of yellow jasmine clinging to the wall behind him. The scars on his face and neck were a swirl of dark purple streaked with red veins. The facial wound looked like bleeding wax. A faint blue light on his pain collar blinked, indicating that he needed to refill the collar with more neural blockers. Tamor-Kyl grumbled to himself. Then he spoke aloud. "You must let me interrogate K'Rin my own way. He knows where I can find the enzyme. I delivered him to you. Now you must deliver him to me."

Pl'Don turned to face Tamor. He frowned at Tamor's demanding tone. Yet he understood the desperate nature of Tamor's condition. Tamor, like all the Tenebrea, carried the Quazel Protein in his body. Without the corresponding enzyme, the protein would quite literally turn him into a fossil—an excruciating way to die. On the other hand, the Quazel Protein-enzyme combination doubled one's life span and greatly increased one's vitality. This potential was not lost on Pl'Don. He, too, felt the cold hand of old age tugging at his sleeve. Pl'Don said, "I've changed my mind."

Tamor looked up with a glimmer of hope.

Pl'Don folded his soft hands and looked down at the disfigured soldier. "After the Cor Ordinate delegation signs the peace accord with us, I can be more flexible in your case. My standing in the council and as First Among Equals with the clans will be assured. I need fear no resistance from Hal K'Rin's supporters. Therefore, I will allow you to use whatever means necessary to break K'Rin and discover his secret. But not before."

"Thank you." Tamor stood up slowly, reacting slightly to the pain in his knees. "Within the month, I'll have the enzyme. You, too, shall have the secret of a long life."

"One word of caution." Pl'Don stepped closer to speak softly to Tamor's twisted face. "When you get hold of the information, make sure that you and I are the only two *living* persons with that knowledge."

The right side of Tamor's mouth screwed up into a grin that exposed yellow teeth and bleeding gums. "I understand your meaning exactly. Hal K'Rin will not survive the interrogation."

chapter 3

Aboard the *Benwoi*, the wilderness clones were good passengers. They had simple needs. They followed instructions without complaint. They drank hot tea constantly, but otherwise seemed disinterested in the food stores—eating only when Brigon returned from the bridge to announce a meal. When the Yuseat Jod tired of explaining ship technology, the clones amused themselves in conversation, although their conversations were more thoughtful silence than banter. They played a simple game, moving polished colored pebbles around a dimpled surface.

Andrea clearly admired the clones' simplicity. These most unlikely space travelers were as comfortable in the belly of the *Benwoi* as they were in their caves. Yesterday, she had wondered aloud if they had felt at home everywhere because they had no home.

If that was so, then Brigon was not like the clones. He felt restless. Already, he missed the panorama of his mountains. He had thought outer space would provide the ultimate panoramic view—how wrong. He found space travel oppressively claustrophobic, especially in the crowded *Benwoi*. Plus, he had a difficult time acclimating to the artificial days and nights. He began the habit of wandering the deck during the artificial night. During the solitude of the sleep cycle, he could pace the empty companion deck for exercise and collect his thoughts.

At present he paced the companionway that ran up and down the spine of the *Benwoi*, and he contemplated Andrea. Eric stepped from the galley into Brigon's path, causing a minor collision, sloshing Eric's hot tea on both of them.

"Excuse me," Brigon apologized.

Eric responded with a peevish look, then walked back into the galley to refill his mug. Brigon followed him in. He asked, "What do you know about Andrea?"

Eric was surprised at the question. "Who wants to know?"

"I do."

"She doesn't confide in me. We don't get along." Eric leaned against the bulkhead and let Brigon speak.

"That's what I want to talk about: why she doesn't like you. I know part of the story. I know that her husband, Steve Dewinter, left Cor as a premature clone— an experiment or something. You were made from the same genetic code; so you look identical to him. His adopted parents flee Cor and K'Rin settles them on Earth. Steve grew up never knowing his origins. He marries Andrea. Later, you escape Cor as a renegade after starting the Underground with your mate, Tara, right?"

"Right." Eric crossed his arms over his chest. "You seem to have your facts right."

"The Cor Hunters pursued you. You sought asylum in the Jod system—"

"I was looking for help," Eric corrected Brigon.

Brigon nodded, "You linked up with K'Rin."

"Not quite. He took me prisoner and interrogated me for three months, if you call that linking up."

"So the Hunters looked for you on Earth and killed Dewinter, thinking that they'd killed you."

Eric looked down the corridor to ensure that they were alone. He said, "That's about all there is."

Brigon looked into Eric's eyes. "Are you sure that's all you know?"

"If you've got a point to make, you'd better make it now." Eric faced Brigon directly. His voice was steady but measured, almost belligerent.

Brigon glared at Eric and thought, *No wonder Andrea dislikes you.*

Eric seemed to read Brigon's mind. He said, "Listen, Brigon. I don't owe Andrea a thing. I look like her dead husband—yes. Can I help that? No. She doesn't like me because I look like her dead husband—fine. She doesn't like me because I don't act like her dead husband—fine. She doesn't like the way I treat my own mate. None of her business. Frankly, I don't know what you see in her."

Brigon pursed his lips and shook his head to deflect the question.

"Well? What *do* you see in her?" Eric goaded.

"Why don't you just go about your business." Brigon turned his shoulder to let Eric pass.

Eric countered, "You started this conversation." Then he leaned forward and spoke in a restrained but belligerent voice. "Don't you see what this is all about? She doesn't care about us. She's still trying to avenge her family by punishing the Cor Ordinate. Frankly, I don't care about her intentions, because she's helping our cause. But don't forget, Brigon, you are just a means to her ends." With that statement, Eric took his mug of tea and brushed by Brigon, disappearing down the corridor leading to the bridge.

H'Roo's three-legged course to the Jod system allowed an approach from the thinly patrolled Artrix frontier. The circuitous route added six standard days to their journey. He explained that the Artrix were notoriously lackadaisical with their flight plans, but equally nonthreatening. "Nobody pays much attention to the Artrix. A small merchant-class ship, ostensibly from Artrix, can slip into Jod without notice."

As much as they wanted a quick trip, Brigon and Andrea accepted the detour. The *Benwoi* was militarily weak. Andrea said, "If you can't fix it, flaunt it. We look like a merchant. We'll act like a merchant. Maybe everyone will treat us like a merchant."

H'Roo brought the navigational display to the forward screen and interpreted the backward-counting chronometer. "We come out of FTL in the Jod system in seventeen days, two hours. Then we have about twenty hours at kinetic speed to reach Klamdara."

Brigon stroked his beard. "Then what?"

Andrea looked at H'Roo. "H'Roo, you don't look too confident."

H'Roo scratched his neck as it turned slightly gray—a display of low-level angst. "There is a lot we don't know about Klamdara, the opposing force, the . . . well, lots of important details."

Andrea raised one of her dark eyebrows, and cuffed H'Roo on the shoulder, "You know the most about Klamdara. Just teach us what you know. The rest we'll learn when we get there."

Brigon grumbled, "I don't like going into a fight knowing less than my opponent."

H'Roo shook his head apologetically. "What I can teach you is recollection and speculation. I'll research what I can." He raised a hand as if to surrender. "I'll give you a briefing soon."

For the next three cycles, H'Roo collected every scrap of data about Klamdara to augment his sketchy memory. He researched the *Benwoi*'s library where he found geological and meteorological surveys of Klamdara. Fortunately, the library included copious navigational data on how to arrive and land at the only occupied and operational site on Klamdara, the fortress prison. What he needed was a picture of the prison or even a detailed map. Neither existed in the scant *Benwoi* files.

So H'Roo relied on his memory of books. As a boy he read the tales of recalcitrant clansmen exiled to Klamdara. He read fictional accounts of their rescues. He recalled an old pen-and-ink drawing of the fortress still imprinted as a childhood memory.

H'Roo tried to re-create the images. He drafted pictures of the Klamdara prison fortress: a giant maw in a sandstone cliff—the cave, perhaps exaggerated in his boyish imagination. However, he remembered distinctly that the Klamdara caves were two hundred feet high at the opening, and cut straight back into the sandstone. At the entrance to the cave he drew a forty-foot wall, anchored to the natural walls of the cave. At the front of the wall, he drew a pit filled with menacing spikes. The solitary gate of the ancient fortress was made of iron.

Noting the overhang of the cliff, H'Roo surmised that any comm link or long-range cannon must be outside the wall—perhaps fifty or more feet away—to provide line-of-sight transmissions, and adequate fields of fire. The fortress landing pad must likewise be outside the gate.

H'Roo had no way of knowing the layout of the Klamdara prison, so he guessed. He guessed that the landing pad would be nearest the gate. He drew a long-range cannon to the right, then a laser comm link and parabolic antenna to the left. He closed his eyes and shook his head. H'Roo was painfully uncomfortable with this glaring imprecision.

The bridge was packed with wilderness clones sitting cross-legged on the floor. They came for H'Roo's briefing. H'Roo stepped over and around the spectators to pin his ink drawings to the wall insulation. Andrea, Brigon, and Eric stood. They studied the drawings. Eric pointed to the inconsistencies in scale, then muttered to himself, "I suppose it's better than nothing."

"I heard that." Andrea thought H'Roo was actually quite talented at freehand drawing. "If you can do better . . ." She turned to H'Roo and said, "We're ready."

H'Roo stood next to his drawings and said, "I'll tell you what I know about the planet and the fortress. Later, we can discuss a concept of opera-

tions." He pointed to a chart with some data.
"Klamdara is mostly sand and iron ore. The planet
is slightly smaller than Cor, just as Jod is slightly
larger. It rotates quickly, with a decided wobble.
Millions of years ago when Klamdara had oceans,
the tides were a hundred feet high, crashing in and
out twice daily." H'Roo pointed to his picture of
the large overhang above the Klamdara prison.
"The cliffs stretch for a hundred miles or more
where the tides beat the red rock. The prison is at
the southernmost tip, near a great fissure. The tides
carved out a cave, a huge gaping gouge in the
cliff—nothing like the narrow lava tube caves on
Cor."

"What happened to the oceans?"

"No one knows." H'Roo shrugged his shoulders.
"Klamdara has huge underground aquifers: the
water is alkaline. We Jod need to treat the well water
to make it potable. Any other questions?"

H'Roo waited a moment. "In those early days, our
ancestors managed about the Jod system with crude
chemical rocketry. They established a colony on Klamdara and began mining iron ore. In fact, Klamdara, in
the old Jod language, means iron anvil. When the mining gave out, we turned Klamdara into a penal institu-
tion."

H'Roo stepped around one of the seated clones—
"Excuse me"—in front of a picture of the fortress
wall. The wall looked like a high dam running across
the mouth of the yawning cave. "Now here," he
pointed at the sketch, "I'm speculating, based on
what I know about Jod fort construction. Klamdara
is a point defense. The standard marine point
defense has five elements: shore-to-ship communica-

tions, long-range cannon, landing facility, power source, and of course, the garrison. Because of the cliff's overhang, we can assume that the cannon, comm-link landing pad, and solar power supply will be outside the wall."

"Lucky for us," Brigon added.

"Yes," H'Roo turned to Brigon. "I can say with some certitude that we are going to need four fire teams."

"Explain."

"We need to instantly isolate Klamdara from the Fleet, which means we need to cut their comms and keep their ships on the ground. We must control the cannon. And of course, we need to get into the garrison. How, I don't know yet."

Brigon nodded, "I'll organize four teams. If we move slowly, our wilderness cloaks provide near-perfect camouflage. We can get close to our targets undetected, then attack simultaneously. Stealth and speed of execution are key."

H'Roo nodded, then added, "I suggest you attach one of our Yuseat Jod with each of your teams."

Andrea asked, "You want to spilt up Fal'Dar and his guys?"

"They can help each team anticipate Jod tactics and behavior. It's just a suggestion. The first casualty of any firefight is the plan. I'd put Fal'Dar on the team going into the garrison. Put Ti'Maj with the team going after the comm link. Put Bir-Tod with the team going after the landing pad and the surface transports. Zu'Pah knows something about long-range cannon."

"Speaking about the long-range cannon," Eric asked, "how are we even going to land on Klamdara?

They'll see us coming for days. I don't see how stealth or speed of execution can help us."

"Eric is right." H'Roo folded his hands and pressed them to his lips. "If they even suspect we're hostile they'll shoot first and sift the debris for answers. Our Jod cannon can hit anything we can detect, and we can sense to a meter's accuracy objects the size of a ship out to—let's say—eighty thousand miles or more."

"Then we'd better come from their blind side," Eric said.

"Easier said than done." Fal'Dar sat in the navigator's chair. "At some point, they'll get a fix on us with a space buoy. We'd need to come in on full throttle to dive below their horizon. That kind of maneuver will put them on alert. Then we dare not show ourselves above the horizon again."

Brigon asked, "Then, how far must we land from the Klamdara fortress?"

Fal'Dar stroked a few keys to bring up a full-screen visual of the planet. He had already oriented the chart to show the coordinates of the Klamdara fortress, just ten degrees north of the equator. "Circumference is 67,273 kilometers at the equator."

"Calculate distance to horizon," Eric said impatiently.

Fal'Dar chafed at the condescension in Eric's voice. "From what height?" he asked in a tone to assure Eric that he knew his job better than any upstart clone.

H'Roo piled on. "Good point, Fal'Dar. A typical configuration—the cannon yoke is probably no more than fourteen feet off the ground."

Fal'Dar deftly tapped the keys and answered,

"Distance to horizon is 39.5 kilometers, assuming the terrain is flat."

H'Roo added, "And we must make that assumption."

Andrea interjected, "Damn, I wanted to get closer. How soon will they know our landing site?"

H'Roo smirked, "In about one second—a standard picket set of overhead sensors will spot our ship from the time we enter the gravity well until we touch down. You can bet your life that within fifteen minutes of touchdown you'll have two companies' assault troops all over the *Benwoi*. We need to pick a good spot to land, then get as far from the ship as possible."

Brigon asked, "You sure about that?"

"Positive." H'Roo glanced at Andrea. "Standard procedures."

Fal'Dar and Ti'Maj stood on a makeshift platform in the center of the crowded cargo bay. They wore nothing but loose undergarments that tied at the waist with a drawstring. Each held a blade. They had offered themselves as training aids. The assembled clones watched with murmuring curiosity. Fal'Dar raised his thick arm over his head to command attention. "Today, my colleague Ti'Maj and I shall teach you the most efficient way to kill Jod."

The cargo bay fell silent. The near-naked Jod stood still. The clone Eric stood in the front row. The subject matter obviously appealed to him—the science of killing. Fal'Dar looked down at Eric's cold eyes and he wondered at the prudence of satisfying the deadly curiosity dwelling behind those eyes.

Fal'Dar stiffened. He remembered when his

instructor Feld Jo'Orom gave the same class years ago. But this class was different. Jo'Orom taught Jod how to kill other species, or when necessary, a fellow Jod. However, Fal'Dar was about to teach an inferior species—cloned humans—how to kill Jod. He felt a traitor to his race, but H'Roo's orders were explicit. Besides, his brother was one of the captives, and if he died, Mother would never forgive either one of them. Fal'Dar feared few things. His mother's wrath was one of them.

Fal'Dar used Ti'Maj as a training aid. Practically devoid of adipose tissue, Ti'Maj showed superb muscle definition. His Jod arms and legs were almost identical to the human physique, just shorter and thicker. The flesh above the abdomen and the back above the waist showed a crisscross of sinews and muscle.

Fal'Dar tapped Ti'Maj on the chest. Fal'Dar explained, "We don't have ribs as you do. We have four curved plates of bone hinged at four seams. Jod body armor particularly protects these seams. Therefore, you cannot drive a blade into a Jod chest: an ax perhaps, a heavy spear, but not a light blade." He slapped Ti'Maj on the chest and the sound was like one slapping a block of polished marble.

"I recommend that you kill the Jod at a distance. Your larger rifles shall prove effective, especially your faster rounds. Our torsos are especially susceptible to hypostatic shock, which, by the way, is the principal killing effect of our handlance. Therefore, you may target us—I mean the Jod—by aiming mid-torso. Jod body armor is designed to stop energy weapons and blades. Your crude rifles will be a rude shock. Any questions?"

The clones looked at each other warily, then at the Jod without saying a word.

"Very well." Fal'Dar reiterated, "The best attack is from a distance. However, if you get into close combat with the Jod regulars, you need to strike at the neck or the gut." He threw a quick punch at Ti'Maj's throat, stopping a centimeter from contact.

Then Ti'Maj spoke. "Do not underestimate the Jod's ability in hand fighting. Our arms may be shorter than yours by as much as four inches, but the Jod know how to parry a blow. And we are stronger than you are. You do not want to trade blows with a Jod marine. You will not get up again."

The clones knew that Ti'Maj was not indulging in a boast. Several of them had seen these Tenebrea fight the NewGens at the South Mountain ambush. They saw the Jod's skill and strength firsthand. Indeed, one purpose of this demonstration—according to Brigon—was to assure his men that Jod were in fact as mortal as humans.

Ti'Maj continued. "If you do engage a Jod marine in hand fighting, I recommend you use your superior agility to sidestep a Jod attack; then pivot around behind the Jod, thus—" On cue, Fal'Dar lunged. Ti'Maj used his inside arm to deflect the blow as he stepped through. He now stood behind Fal'Dar to the right. He continued the simulation by pulling a punch aimed where Fal'Dar's back tapered to the waist. Both froze in a pose for all to see. "Here, you plunge your blade deep into the vitals. If you are lucky enough to slice the pancreas, your victim will fall to the ground, unable to continue the fight. He is finished."

Eric raised his voice, "Like canceled? He gives up?"

Fal'Dar scowled, "When mortally wounded, the Jod typically goes into shock. We consider death an honorable affair, personal, and most of us will not thrash about in our final seconds trying to change some immutable outcome. You should never equate a Jod's death with a clone being canceled."

Eric shrugged his shoulders. "I still don't see the difference."

Andrea stood in the galley, waiting for the dispenser to fill her glass mug with black gaval. The dispenser issued an apology on the screen: *Water Low*. She sighed. The *Benwoi's* environmental suite did not anticipate a complement of thirty-five persons for such a long voyage. The water recycling struggled during the early hours of the daily duty cycle.

The one female clone, Chana, stepped into the galley with two empty mugs and queued behind Andrea at the dispenser. Andrea did not turn, but acknowledged her presence by saying, "Dispenser is slow again."

Chana answered, "That's all right. I've got time."

Andrea watched the thin trickle dribble into her cup. She purposefully watched the machine and not Chana.

Chana broke the awkward silence. "Do you think it was wise sending Brigon back to sleep with us?"

Andrea answered flatly, "Yes."

"I wouldn't have." Chana spoke as if she were discussing her preference for sugar in her tea.

Andrea took her mug before the dispenser finished, letting the last dribbles fall into the stainless steel drain. Chana blocked her way, not out of any belligerence. The galley was narrow.

Andrea looked at Chana's slow smile and said, "Listen, I'm sorry if I've upset any of your plans."

Chana stifled a bitter laugh. "Don't feel sorry for me. I can see why he prefers you to me. Don't look surprised—Brigon told me as much."

"When?" Andrea instantly regretted asking the question: first because she didn't really want the answer, and second, because she didn't want to prolong this conversation.

"I had just fled the precincts and arrived at the caves, half dead from starvation. My mate did in fact die on the march."

"How?" Andrea suddenly felt obliged to listen.

"He had been feeding me his rations—I didn't know till it was too late."

"I'm sorry."

Chana raised an eyebrow, questioning Andrea's sincerity. She continued, "The rest of us found the caves and Brigon took me—took all of us in. He was unattached so I made myself available to him."

Andrea thought, *Any port in a storm* . . . Her disapproval showed. Chana's mate starved to death to keep her alive. And by the time she had eaten enough to shake the pangs of hunger, she had likewise shed her attachment to her dead mate. Yet Andrea sensed that Chana was, in her own way, consistent. She sensed in this female clone a strong sense of monogamy, offset by a stronger streak of practicality—the two dimensions of a monolithic love. *Remarkably shallow? Or does it take greater depth of soul to exfoliate the past?*

Chana laughed with a note of derision, saying, "He told me he was waiting for a Terran female who promised to return by the spring. Well, I'm patient and I know how promises are, so I stayed in his company, but—" Chana shrugged, "—you returned. Now that I've seen you two together, I must say, I'm touched by the irony: I want Brigon, Brigon wants you, and you don't know what you want." Chana reached around Andrea to put one of her mugs in the dispenser. " 'Scuse, please."

Andrea turned sideways to trade places with Chana. She didn't try to contradict the clone. The issues affecting her life were far more complicated than Chana could understand.

Chana watched the slow dribble of tea and spoke without looking back at Andrea. "It's not so bad wanting something you can't have. I want this dispenser to speed up, but then I know that in the long run, it doesn't matter. In a few months, I'll get over Brigon. He'll get over you. And you still won't know what you want." Turning she said, "So I feel sorry for you. You don't feel sorry for me."

The repetitive briefings and training stopped as the *Benwoi* powered down to kinetic speed. Immediately the screens dumped their virtual images and live data appeared. The computer digested a flood of incoming data, analyzing star patterns and calculating a fix. The screen showed and the machine's virtual voice announced: *Course correction for Klamdara: adjust two points starboard and ascend three points. Eighteen hours, fifty-two minutes on present course to enter Klamdara gravity well.*

H'Roo turned to Eric and asked, "Are your tactical screens up?'

"Yes." Eric poked at a couple of keys. "No ships within sensor range."

"Emissions control," H'Roo commanded.

Eric poked another set of keys. "Done. Scanners down; passive collectors up. All emitters powered down."

H'Roo spun around in his chair to face Andrea and Brigon. "Eighteen hours. . . ."

"I'll run the teams through their final paces, check equipment." Brigon turned to leave when the screen flashed and then emitted a high-pitched *ping*.

Andrea asked, "What was that?"

H'Roo left his chair and leaned over Eric to study the console. His neck tinged as he said, "A deep space buoy. The Jod know we're here."

"But they don't know *who* we are."

Another flash and another *ping*. H'Roo looked up and said, "No, they can't discern particular life signs at this range. They just know that we're a ship with crew on a heading for Klamdara. You can bet they'll have their cannon tracking us as soon as we get into range."

H'Roo looked over Fal'Dar's shoulder at the navigational plot. He turned to Andrea and said, "We must change course. We've got to find a way in without them seeing . . ."

Brigon interrupted. "I assume those *pings* mean that they've already seen us. Anyway, where are we going to hide out here in space? You know they've got those—what did you call it?"

"A buoy," Andrea helped him.

"—those buoys out here. If they've got one, they've got more," Brigon pointed to the screen. Instead, he posited another solution. "Let's tell them we're coming."

H'Roo reared back "This is not a time for sarcasm . . ."

"I'm serious."

Andrea prompted Brigon. "What's your idea? Lie to the Jod on Klamdara? As soon as they discover your lie, they'll fire."

Brigon grinned. His eyes cut about the room, then fixed on Andrea. "Lie? Oh, no. We tell them the truth. We hail Klamdara. We tell them I'm a renegade clone in a stolen Cor merchant ship that I barely know how to operate. I seek Jod protection. I must land immediately." Brigon turned to H'Roo and said, "However they scan the ship, however they analyze my voice, they'll only corroborate my statements."

H'Roo's countenance brightened as he grasped the simple genius of the ploy. "You're right. At the very least, they'll want to take the *Benwoi* intact. They may want to take you prisoner as a trophy to present to the Cor Ordinate."

Andrea paused to consider the Jod reaction on Klamdara. "We still don't want to land at their front door. We can land just over the horizon. They'll send a unit out to investigate."

Brigon nodded. He was already considering the landing. "The *Benwoi* will draw them like bees to honey." His eyes narrowed. "Whatever we kill in the desert, we won't have to kill at the fortress."

In the austere command post at Klamdara, the duty officer logged the contact registered by the buoy. He tapped on a glass divider that separated him from his lone co-worker and asked, "Sir, are we expecting a supply ship this week?"

"Not that I know of. Headquarters was adamant that we would *not* get resupplied until *after* their big show on Heptar." The sleepy Jod marine looked at his screen, his face glazed by the boredom of six months of seeing nothing. "Could be a meteor . . ."

The technician shook his head as he looked at the contact data. "Well, I think headquarters changed their minds. This contact has an engine." The technician saved his log entry, then leaned back in his chair. "However, it's too small to be a Jod supply ship."

Then, a faint transmission startled him: *Hello?*

"What?" He pressed his earphones to the sides of his hairless head. *Hello? We're looking for the planet Jod.*

The sleepy Jod sat straight in his chair. "What's out there?"

"An unscheduled contact—" The technician sighed with resignation. "I'll notify the commandant."

Five minutes later, Commandant D'Cru hurried into the room. Wrested from his leisure in his quarters, he frowned at the inconvenience of the intrusion. He fastened his tunic as he walked. For once his slight limp didn't slow him. He asked, "How far out are they?"

"Ten hours—depends on their speed. We just have the one buoy contact."

D'Cru marched in behind the Jod technician and stopped. The faint hail repeated: *Hello? Hello? I don't know how to receive messages—only send. I'm Brigon, a clone from the planet Cor. We stole this Cor Ordinate ship to escape. We're lost. We seek asylum in the Jod system. Please help!*

"Send a return hail. Send our coordinates and tell them to land at our site."

The technician looked up, confused by the order. "Sir, the clone says he doesn't know how to receive?"

D'Cru frowned. "Send the message anyway—all frequencies." Aside, he muttered, "Stupid clone, he doesn't even know what buttons to push."

The technician complied, but a moment later, they got an almost identical message: *Hello? Hello? I don't know how to receive messages—only send. . . .*

D'Cru pointed out the obvious to his staff. "Whoever he is, he thinks he's landing on the planet Jod. He *is* lost. He'll probably burn on entry. Here are my orders: extend sensors to track that ship. Wake Hept Ben'Toor. Tell him to assemble his company. *If* that amateur out there manages to set his ship down on his own, I want Ben'Toor to capture the ship and its crew."

"Yes, sir." The technician ran out of the command post, energized by this wrinkle in the routine.

The second technician asked, "Sir, do you want me to continue our hail?"

"Yes. Put it on auto-repeat." D'Cru shook his head in disgust. "I'm going back to my quarters. Don't wake me unless they manage to land in one piece."

chapter 4

A hush hung over the crowded bridge of the *Benwoi* as Brigon finished transmitting his hail to the Klamdara garrison. Eric looked up from his console and grinned. "They're transmitting landing instructions. Brigon, you fooled them; they think we're a bunch of dim-witted renegade clones."

Chana leaned into Brigon and put her arm around his neck and said, "We'll disabuse them of that soon enough, eh?" Brigon patted Chana's hand and shrugged her arm from his shoulder.

Sitting in the pilot's chair, H'Roo cautioned, "Brigon, take everybody aft and check your gear. Fal'Dar, you make sure the enzyme gets off the ship. Eric, I want you to monitor the surface for any sign of a power surge—specifically the loading of the long-range cannon with an energy bolt. Andrea, plot us a steep entry on the far side of Klamdara." Without another word, the crew turned to their duties.

Klamdara continued its scans, but the cannon remained quiet. Consequently, H'Roo piloted the

Benwoi with greater confidence. He dove the *Benwoi* into the Klamdara atmosphere and ran the ship below the horizon, out of the cannon's line of sight.

Klamdara's ocher surface was a monotonous blur on the screen. H'Roo followed the only terrain feature, a deep fissure, a rip in the planet's surface. H'Roo flew less than five hundred feet off the flat ground. Andrea watched their plot and warned, "Terrain rises ahead."

As she spoke, H'Roo saw spikes of rock protruding through the otherwise flat surface. Andrea added, "We'd better stay on this side of those rocks—any closer and the Jod can acquire us."

"I'm putting her down," H'Roo acknowledged, pulling back on the throttle and turning the *Benwoi*. He set the *Benwoi* on a flat rock. The ship listed onto the expediently repaired landing gear—a reminder of H'Roo's landing on Cor. He lowered the exit ramp, then left his chair to put on his battle gear. Everybody on the bridge had their battle gear on or assembled in small piles. Each pile had a wilderness cloak. Fal'Dar appeared at the hatch with a light stick and a rucksack filled with the precious enzyme. He announced, "We're ready below."

As rehearsed, Eric and H'Roo powered down all systems. The ship turned black as night. Jerky beams of handheld light illuminated the bridge and the corridors. Andrea called to everyone around, "Go! Go! Go!" She wore her battle harness and carried a rifle. "The Klamdara marines will be here in minutes."

Throughout the ship, men barked orders and exhorted each other to greater speed. Brigon stood at the ramp and counted the wilderness clones as they left. H'Roo stepped onto the ramp and he announced, "Thirty-five. Everyone's out!"

Andrea and H'Roo hustled down the ramp, leaving the dark ship for the stark sunshine. H'Roo pulled a small wrench from his belt. He began to remove a thick plate from the *Benwoi's* hot skin. He touched the ship's skin and branded himself. *"Damn!"* H'Roo wrapped a rag around his hands and gingerly turned the wrench, changing hands that began to blister from the heat. But the pain was incidental to the risk of being caught in the open.

The alloy plate fell to the ground with a thud. H'Roo reached in with his fingers wrapped in the rag. He pressed a lever and the ramp closed, sealing the ship. He plucked a data cube from the circuitry. "They'll have to cut their way in without this data cube."

Andrea stepped away from the ship and quickly surveyed the terrain: *A good place to fight.* Red rock poked though the barren soil, rising at angles that defied gravity. The rocks rose like cathedral spires, weatherworn and striped with an occasional band of green quartz. Crags and crevices opened like doors and windows, offering excellent fields of fire for an ambush.

In contrast to the rocks, the killing zone was naked. The soil was compact, hard-baked mud like tiles broken into irregular shapes. Apparently, Klamdara benefited from an occasional deluge, an instantaneous shallow lake—a liquid tease that spilled, soaked, and evaporated away. Andrea looked around. In the distance she saw desolation. The scorching heat blurred the horizon. With the aid of binoculars, she saw an occasional giant tree, great hulks of spreading branches with feathery blue-green leaves. These monsters stood eighty feet tall, uncannily lush for the surrounding terrain. *Aquifers.*

Brigon quickly organized his people. He gave Chana a comm-disk and sent her with twenty clones to the red rocks. They instinctively walked in a careful single file over the dusty ground to the nearest rocks. By stepping in each other's footprints they masked their numbers. Eric mimicked their discipline. In the rocks, they found natural berms, then pulled their wilderness cloaks over their bodies. They disappeared from view. A keen eye might spot the end of a rifle barrel in a shadow.

Following Andrea's orders, Fal'Dar and the other Tenebrea climbed into the higher rocks. She gave them strict orders not to use their Jod weapons but rely on the seemingly primitive rifles.

The clone Ariko stood by with his six sharpshooters with long air rifles. He held three satchel bombs slung over his shoulder. He interrupted Brigon and Andrea, asking, "Where do you want us?"

Brigon pointed behind the *Benwoi*, "There's a shallow cut in the ground about fifty meters on the other side of the ship. Set up there—twenty meters apart. When the Jod come, they'll converge on the *Benwoi*. You'll open fire and drive them toward the red rocks. Give me one of your satchels."

Ariko handed Brigon a twelve-pound sack of explosives. Brigon said, "They'll probably land over there." He turned and pointed to a flat piece of ground. "I'm going to lie there, cloaked, ready to toss the satchel into their ship. If they land closer to you, you must toss a satchel into their ship. We must cripple their ship in a matter of seconds. I expect this ambush to last less than two minutes." Brigon understood the storm of violence he would rain down on the unsuspecting Jod.

Ariko smiled. "My pleasure." He marched his men in the direction of the rocks following the thin path in the dust. All footprints led to the mouth of the ambush's killing zone. Ariko turned his column in a long circle to backtrack to their position behind the *Benwoi*.

The last two in the open were Andrea and Brigon. He asked, "How many do you think they'll send?"

Andrea looked at the horizon in the direction of Klamdara. The parched land blurred into the white sky. The sun stood high. Not a breath of air stirred the dust. "They'll come in company strength—a hundred marines." She did not take her eyes off the horizon.

Brigon watched Ariko's men disappear under their cloaks. "If the Jod marines are anything like the Ordinate, they won't fight well when they can't see their enemy. One sniper can stop them in the open. Thirty-five rifles can cut them to pieces. Do you want any prisoners?" Brigon asked as if it were one of life's little preferences.

Andrea answered, "No." Her face turned grim and the corners of her mouth tightened as she said, "We can't take them with us, and we can't let them warn the others."

"I understand," Brigon said. "You'd better hunker down in the rocks. You'll cover me, won't you?" he smiled.

Andrea set her jaw and nodded. "Of course I will." Then Brigon took his satchel and went alone to his position where he guessed the marines would land their craft.

Andrea ran to take her position in the rocks. She lay prone on the reverse slope of a smooth rock. Her wilderness cloak hid her completely. The heat caused her to sweat profusely, a minor irritation except for the drops that spilled over her eyebrows into her eyes. Slowly, she wiped her face. She knew that movement mitigated the effect of the cloak.

From her perch Andrea watched Brigon stand in the open ground, defiantly inviting the Klamdara marines to their ambush. All around was barren silence and red sandstone. The *Benwoi* listed in the foreground like a crippled sheep, tethered to coax the tiger from the jungle.

Then Brigon yelled his final instructions to the hidden assembly. "Remember! I fire the first shot! Nobody uses a comm-disk until the firing starts."

Then Andrea watched Brigon squat and disappear beneath his cloak. She noticed the almost imperceptible opening and a pair of searching eyes.

The whine of turbines arrived long before the bulky Jod transport. The ship cruised casually at a thousand feet, pausing above the parked *Benwoi*. The transport had the bulbous nose typical of Jod ship design, with a flat belly and humpback. Propelled by eight large turbines, the transport was easily twice the size of the *Benwoi*.

Andrea watched from her hiding place. The transport hovered in place for a long two minutes. It slipped from side to side as if peeking behind rocks. The caution of the Jod commander was apparent. Andrea knew that as long as she and the clones remained perfectly still, the wilderness cloaks would conceal them.

Finally the transport extended five short landing legs and began its descent. Andrea extrapolated the spot where the transport would touch down. *Oh, no! The Jod are landing too far away—neither Brigon nor Ariko can reach them with a satchel bomb.*

The cautious Jod were landing a safe one hundred meters behind the *Benwoi*. Andrea quickly evaluated the Jod tactics. Did they suspect anything? Perhaps they did not want to disturb the soil and any tracks with their prop wash. Then her speculation of tactics collapsed under a terrible reality: the Jod would land with Brigon between them and the *Benwoi*. Her pulse quickened. *They'll trip over him. Brigon might get a few, but they'll take him for sure.*

Andrea fingered the comm-disk in her pocket, but remembered that Brigon had turned his off as well. Plus, keying a comm-disk might give away the whole ambush and put Brigon in a worse situation. Besides, Brigon would see as well as she that he was going to be in the way of the Jod stampede when they exited their transport. She swallowed hard. *I can't help him.*

The transport lowered itself gracefully. The whine hurt her ears and the prop wash raised a dense cloud of dust that blew all the way to their positions in the rocks. Andrea thought she saw Brigon stand, wrestling with his cloak in the artificial gale, but the dust blew into her eyes, blinding her momentarily. She opened her eyes again and saw the transport on the ground with the engines spinning down. The dust cloud settled slowly. Her eyes teared, washing away the particles of grit.

Two ramps—port and starboard—dropped to the ground with a thud. Jod marines poured out with their weapons raised to their eyes. The hundred heavily armed marines formed a wide circle around their transport, each facing outward. They wore khaki chest armor over their khaki uniforms. Their helmets fitted tightly with a thick face shield that hid their eyes. The officer, a Hept, sauntered down the ramp, watching with approval his marines' execution of the drill. He looked at a handheld screen, then up at the rock formations, and back at the thin screen. *He's got a topocard display.* Andrea knew from the look on the officer's face—nonchalant self-satisfaction—that in his mind, this little clone hunt in the desert was merely an opportunity to train his troops. She wondered how many clone rifles were aimed at the Hept's heart.

On the Hept's command, three Jod ran to the *Benwoi*. They carried a box—some electronics unknown to Andrea. They pasted a sensor to the *Benwoi's* skin and a technician studied a scope. The third pointed to the clone tracks leading to the rocks. He called back his findings. "Sir! The ship is either from Cor or Earth. The crew abandoned her." He pointed directly at Andrea. "Their tracks lead to those rocks."

The Hept called back with a question. "How many?"

The Jod bent over, inspecting the footprints in the dust. He stood and called back, "Five. Maybe eight."

Andrea heard this latest addition to their other fatal mistakes. She felt a professional calm.

The officer raised a comm-disk to his lips and said aloud, "Hept Ben'Toor . . .The unidentified ship is intact and abandoned . . . Yes, sir, could be Earth design. Or Cor, we don't know. Five, maybe eight in the crew. Yes, sir. They're probably hiding in the rocks. We'll find them and bring them in for interrogation."

The officer clipped his comm-disk onto his shoulder harness. He tucked the topocard under his arm, then stepped to the front of his men. He raised his voice and said, "Well done. You may stand at ease."

The marines stood up and directed their attention to their leader. "We've got to track down a handful of lost clones before they hurt themselves out here." A low chorus of chuckles rose from the ranks.

Brigon lay as still as death beneath his cloak. He did not even dare raise a slit to peer through. The three Jod that ran to the *Benwoi* had passed him less than five meters away. He felt the vibration in the ground from their boots—or perhaps it was his imagination; perhaps he felt his own racing pulse. But he knew they had passed too close for comfort.

Now Brigon heard the clank of equipment and the crunch of dried dirt just a few feet away as the marines stood. He felt as if a hundred rifles were pointed at his head. He heard the officer speak to the men, and he only hoped that the men had the proper discipline to keep their eyes forward and not on the ground where he huddled. His chest rested on the satchel.

Hiding under his cloak, Brigon relied mostly on sound. He desperately wanted to see his situation, but he dared not raise his head. He had run toward the transport under cover of the dust cloud. So he didn't even know his exact position relative to his own people or to the Jod transport. He could not, therefore, calculate how many seconds to set the timer on the satchel bomb. A drop of sweat trickled down his nose and fell in the blackness to the ground.

He heard approaching footsteps. The three Jod who had run to the *Benwoi* were jogging back to the loose circle of marines. Was it the black, the heat, his fear, or did the footsteps just sound closer?

He felt the toe of a heavy boot catch under his ribs and the collapse of a heavy Jod sprawled over him—tripped! Brigon quickly threw his cloak aside and shoved his pistol into the Jod's gut and fired two rounds. His shots triggered the ambush.

Instantly, the thirty-four other rifles spit a hail of bullets. A third of the Jod marines fell to the ground with mortal wounds. The Jod officer spun around, hammered backward by the lethal projectiles that clawed chunks of his flesh from his torso. Brigon imagined those mortal wounds on himself. He heard bullets whizzing by his ears. He grabbed the Jod he had just slain and used him like he might use a log to shield himself from his own troops' fire. He fumbled his comm link into his hand and yelled, "I'm in the middle of this shit storm. Watch your aim!"

As a crass rejoinder, a bullet whizzed by, cutting a nick in Brigon's harness. He hid behind the Jod corpse and protected the satchel with his own flesh. He thought, *I'm going to be killed by my own men . . .* His grim speculation became poignantly real as he heard the transport's turbines start.

The Jod marines fired blindly at the muzzle flashes among the rocks. Their lasers raked the rocks, spitting up chips of scorched sandstone. The Jod tried to suppress the rain of bullets. However, their fire was as ineffective as the clones' bullets were deadly. They hollered contradictory instructions at each other. Some advanced toward the rocks, trained as they were to assault through an ambush. Others hunkered down on the ground in a pointless effort to hide. The transport's turbines began to kick up dust, adding to the wild confusion. Thirty seconds had changed a mundane exercise into a bloodbath.

Andrea frantically searched the chaos to spot Brigon. The Jod fell like grass before a blade. *There!* She spotted Brigon rising from behind a bullet-pocked corpse. *Thank God, you're alive.* He crouched low, hustling the satchel bomb toward the transport. She saw the dirt jump around him as bullets gouged chunks of dirt.

The Jod marines began to crawl backward to the transport, their only escape from the carnage. Andrea watched carefully for any Jod marine that noticed Brigon. She saw one marine turn and raise his laser rifle—she fired a short burst. Another, and another. Brigon held the satchel over his head and ran into the dust cloud blown by the transport's turbines.

Andrea held her breath.

The explosion shook the ground. Loose rock tumbled onto Andrea's shoulders. One of the transport's eight turbines flew at her; she ducked as it flew over her head, smashing onto the rocks. The ball of fire blew its burning breath over her. Hot debris rained down, clattering. Rifle and laser fire, silenced for a moment, returned sporadically. The killing zone was completely obscured by dust. "Brigon!" Andrea called at the top of her lungs. But the explosion boomed louder than her cry.

The laser fire fell quiet. Soon, the rifle reports subsided. The clones cautiously left their positions. The dust cleared and Andrea saw the wreckage of the transport. She ran down to the killing zone, stepping over the bodies of the Jod marines. She ignored the dying, moaning lowly as they slipped into glassy-eyed shock. The transport lay broken in two with a large black scar in the middle. Andrea stepped through the smoldering wreckage. "Brigon!"

She found his cloak lying on the ground with a large scorch burn in the middle. The bodies nearby were charred from the blast. She found a smaller badly burned corpse lying facedown in the dirt. With dread, she pushed the broken and charred body over. The flesh was ripped away from the face: the corpse grinned back and glared through sightless eye sockets. She had to look twice before a sense of relief displaced her anguish. *A Jod—not Brigon.*

Then she saw Brigon some fifty feet away. He was on his hands and knees. He was clearly dazed, unable to stand. Andrea ran to him. She dropped her rifle by his side. She fell to her knees and began inspecting Brigon for wounds. He held his head in his hands and did not react to her touch.

"Brigon?" she prompted him. "Are you wounded?"

Brigon didn't answer.

She grabbed his shoulders and turned him around to see for herself. His dark gray eyes wandered around in their sockets. *He's just regained consciousness*, she thought. *The blast knocked him out cold.* Brigon's face was seared. The left side of his beard had burned to a stubble, leaving a sickening smell and gray ash. Andrea shook him. "Can you see me?"

Brigon didn't answer. He could not focus his eyes. He groped a handful of her harness to steady himself. Slowly his eyes stopped swimming and settled on her. Then a pained smile appeared on his lips.

"Answer me," Andrea commanded.

Brigon shook his head. "I can't hear you. My ears are still ringing; I'm dizzy." He winced, but he sounded strong.

Andrea grabbed his harness and pulled Brigon toward her and kissed him on the lips. He tasted of dirt, creosote, and sweat.

A gunshot jerked Andrea back to her tactical mind. She turned and saw a scuffle. Fal'Dar and his three Yuseat companions shoved a pair of clones backward. H'Roo Parh stood in their midst dumbfounded. Without a word, Andrea jumped to her feet and ran into the fracas. "What's going on?" She grabbed Fal'Dar and spun the bulky Jod around.

His neck was purple with rage. His eyes blazed. He could barely speak through his anger. "This clone bastard just murdered one of our wounded marines." Fal'Dar brandished his weapon at one of the clones who didn't budge. Andrea snatched the rifle from Fal'Dar and dropped the clip. She knew by the weight that Fal'Dar had not fired any rounds during the short battle with the Jod marines. She snatched Bir-Tod's rifle and ejected the clip: again, two maybe three rounds spent. *Our wounded marines?* Andrea understood: the Yuseat Jod were reluctant to spill Jod blood.

She called loudly, "Mat H'Roo Parh!" She enunciated H'Roo's rank for effect. "Get these four

Tenebrea out of here." She pointed at Fal'Dar and his three comrades.

H'Roo approached Andrea, pulling her aside. Pointing at one of the wounded marines, he said, "We can tie them up."

"I'll think about it." She lowered her eyes. She didn't want H'Roo to detect the hardness of her purpose or the insincerity of her statement.

"Very well." H'Roo gathered the four Yuseat Jod and led them away behind the rocks.

Andrea waited until they were out of sight, then asked Chana, "How many of the Jod marines are still alive?"

Chana pointed across the remains of the battle and said, "Only three." She left Andrea with that bit of data and went to help Brigon.

Andrea looked around the field and saw the Jod bodies littering the ground. The parched dirt drank their blood—the only moisture to wet the ground in months or years. The wilderness clones scurried around, taking lasers, rifles, and handlances from the dead Jod and filling their packs with the heavy and lethal booty. Near the wreckage of the transport, three Jod marines huddled together, young two-ringers, scared and ashamed. A half dozen clones had rifles pointed at their faces.

Andrea hesitated to give the inevitable and unfortunate order. She turned and looked back at the rocks. She knew H'Roo was calming his comrades with some assurance of Andrea's humanity. Her humanity? She wondered what advantage was gained by killing the survivors. The advantage of killing the three Jod marines was marginal, but the success or failure of their mission would be determined at the margin. *They know who we are—Tenebrea, augmented with clones from Cor. They know our strength; they know about the wilderness cloak. Left alive, they'd know that we left on foot and in which direction. We don't have much going for us in this mission except that we know slightly more about the garrison than they know about us. Nevertheless, would the rest of the garrison be any less alert if we permitted these three captives to live to tell the particulars?* Andrea wished K'Rin were here to make this hard decision.

When she turned, she saw Eric standing behind the clones with his large pistol drawn. He had already decided the marines' fate and in rapid succession he executed them with shots to the head. Three loud cracks echoed from the rock walls. Eric put his pistol away and stepped over the marines he'd just dispatched. He marched by Andrea and said, "You were hesitating. Besides, it'll be better if he hates me instead of hating you."

"Who?" Andrea looked at the three young marines slumped together in the dust. She didn't know whether to thank Eric or despise him.

"Your friend, H'Roo Parh." Eric kept walking toward the red rocks.

In the distance they heard the whine of turbines. Reinforcements. The clones scattered for the rocks. Andrea paused long enough to snatch the topocard lying next to the dead Hept, sprawled facedown in the blood-soaked dirt. A light recon ship appeared overhead as the last of the clones ducked out of sight. It lingered for a moment, then sped away.

* * *

D'Cru stood before a large screen looking at digitized images taken by the reconnaissance craft. Superimposed on the images were notations. He saw the broken transport and the large black stain amidships. Scattered around were the hundred bodies of the Ben'Toor's company, each body personalized with notation of name and rank. "Who did this?" D'Cru asked.

The pilot of the reconnaissance craft, still wearing his flight suit, pointed to the image, "Sir, look here." He zoomed and enhanced a picture of three clones in full stride, running toward the rocks. The unkempt runners did not wear uniforms. The pilot muttered, "Terrans or Ordinate clones; not Jod."

D'Cru squinted at the picture. "Obviously, they are not clones seeking asylum on Jod." He wondered aloud: "A rescue attempt?"

An officer answered, "K'Rin does have friends among the Terrans. I hear that he spent much time in the Terran system. However, the wounds," he pointed to the pockmarked bodies of the Jod lying on the blood-soaked ground, "are consistent with either Terran or Ordinate weaponry. Perhaps K'Rin was closer to the Cor Ordinate clones than we thought."

"Five to eight clone laborers? Slaughter a marine company!" D'Cru spun around and berated the idea. "I doubt that. Whoever set this ambush is a professional. I'll bet the Terrans may have a hand in this outrage. I suspect K'Rin may have been working both sides of the Alliance."

"Then, we ought to interrogate K'Rin immediately."

"No!" D'Cru countermanded the officer firmly. "A

waste of time. K'Rin would learn more than we would in such an interrogation. However, I want you to alert the high command and increase the guard. Report any unusual behavior to me immediately. Quietly set up the heavy lasers on the wall." Turning his attention back to the images, he commanded, "Now, show me their ship."

The reconnaissance pilot complied. A hundred meters to the left of the carnage stood an intact ship: a merchant-class vessel. To D'Cru's eyes, the ship looked like Terran construction. However, D'Cru lacked firsthand knowledge. An officer asked, "Sir, do you want us to destroy the ship before they can get away?"

D'Cru's eyes squinted at the ship. "They aren't trying to get away. They will come to us, and they won't come by ship. They know we can shoot down a ship at will. They'll come over land. Put up constant aerial reconnaissance. Concentrate on the valley approach. Do *not* put out foot patrols."

The officer interrupted, "How are we going to retrieve the bodies?"

D'Cru sneered at the suggestion. "I am not going to send another hundred marines out there to replicate Ben'Toor's blunder. We'll kill the Terrans first, then police our dead later. That's an order."

"Yes, sir."

D'Cru turned his attention back to the screen. "As for the Terran ship, I want positive identification. Send the council at Heptar a full report and a picture of that ship. If the Terrans have sent a special forces unit to rescue K'Rin, the council needs to know immediately."

"Sir." The junior officer asked tentatively, "When I

send the report, do you wish that I request reinforcements from the Fleet?"

D'Cru looked at the images of the carnage: a hundred dead Jod marines sprawled around the burnt hulk of a transport. "These Terrans will not catch me in the open as they did Ben'Toor. Just make the report. Assure the council that I will not allow this handful of Terrans to escape."

chapter 5

The clones gathered in a deep slot in the red rocks. They clung to the shade, unaccustomed as they were to the blistering Klamdara sun. They busily checked their equipment and reloaded their weapons. They curiously examined some of the captured weapons: lasers. They worked with purpose, knowing that they must begin their march quickly, but they managed to squeeze some comfort from the moment. They passed water around. Their spirits were high: they had suffered no casualties.

Brigon sat in their midst. Chana used a sharp knife to carefully scrape away his burned and lopsided beard, exposing a square jaw and slight cleft to his chin.

Andrea sat alone on a rock studying the topocard, plotting a route to the Klamdara prison. A shadow covered the screen. She looked up and saw H'Roo frowning at the clones' ebullient mood. He said bitterly, "Eric didn't need to kill those three prisoners."

"If he hadn't dispatched them, I would have." Andrea looked at H'Roo, then back at the topocard.

"I don't believe it." H'Roo's face contradicted his words.

Andrea looked up with cold eyes. "Believe it." Then, with clinical detachment, she added, "You need to remind yourself and the others—" she motioned toward Fal'Dar, "that the Jod marines at the Klamdara garrison are, without the slightest compunction, watching K'Rin and the Tenebrea die a cruel death. We cannot save K'Rin and the Tenebrea without killing more Jod. Do you dispute that fact?"

"No." H'Roo looked past Andrea. Fifty feet away, isolated by their anger, Fal'Dar and his companions burned with resentment.

Andrea marked her place on the topocard with her finger, then looked up at H'Roo. "I know they can fight well—they beat a squad of NewGens in close fighting during the South Mountain ambush. But they froze today. Are they going to be all right tomorrow? We can leave them behind with the ship if necessary."

H'Roo frowned. "You don't understand. They weren't trained to kill Jod. We were trained to kill an enemy that more resembles you and those clones, Cor Ordinate Hunters."

Andrea raised an eyebrow. "I understand perfectly." Andrea didn't have any instant wisdom to impart. She knew the difficulty in training a decent human being to kill other human beings. Why should it be any different for another species? Even the Terran armed services abandoned the antiseptic round targets for silhouettes or even color images of the foe. She had killed hundreds of imaginary humans as part of her training, precisely to inure her toward pulling the trigger and killing one of her own. She didn't have time to ponder whether the Jod psyche would withstand the initial shock of fratricide. She said, "Somehow, *you've* got to convince Fal'Dar, Bir-Tod, Ti'Maj, and Zu'Pah that the Jod marines in the garrison are the enemy now."

"How?" H'Roo glanced over at the other four Tenebrea watching him.

Andrea spoke quietly. "Perhaps you'd better start by convincing yourself."

H'Roo's neck flushed at the suggestion. Andrea stood, shouldered her backpack, and then said, "We're leaving in two minutes. You ought to remind them that *we* asked Brigon to get involved in *our* rescue operation." She motioned to Brigon and the others. With few words, the clones formed a column and followed Andrea deeper into the rocks.

A sleek reconnaissance craft hovered onto the landing apron outside the Klamdara fortress. While the turbine blades spun down, two sturdy ground crew swapped a fresh energy cell into the belly of the craft. Up on the fortress walls, in the oppressive afternoon heat, armed marines watched through lowered face shields.

The pilot stepped onto the short wing and jumped to the ground. His helmet was in the crook of his arm and he was pale. His replacement walked across the apron, asking, "See anything out there?"

"Yeah. I saw plenty." The bedraggled pilot lowered his eyes. "I saw a lot of our friends lying dead in the desert sun." His neck darkened for a moment as he fought his emotion. Looking up, the tired pilot said, "However, I didn't see a sign of the attackers: not visual, not infrared, not radar, not moving target indicator—nothing. I think they're waiting for us, hiding in the rocks. They want us to come to them piecemeal."

"Don't worry, we'll find them. We'll burn them." The fresh pilot started toward the small craft.

The older pilot held out an arm to block the way. He advised, "Don't fly too close to the rocks. And keep your channel open to our cannon crew." He motioned toward the laser cannon mounted above a small blockhouse to the left of the landing apron. "Our boys have orders to shoot first and ask questions later. They're a bit jumpy."

"Understood."

Andrea led the column north through rugged terrain. She pressed hard, wanting to put as much distance between her and the *Benwoi* as fast as possible. She marched in long, quick strides where the ground allowed sure footing. Always, she kept her eye at the horizon looking for reconnaissance flights. Periodically, she heard the whine of their turbines; each hour the turbines sounded closer. *The Jod are carefully widening their search.*

Brigon grabbed her arm and turned Andrea around. His hair was wet and clung to his scalp: his face wilted and flushed. He panted, "The heat. My people are used to ice and snow. We need time to acclimate to this heat."

Andrea looked back over the column and saw the uncomplaining misery. The column immediately used the pause, collapsing into small bits of shade. They didn't cloak themselves and the message to Andrea was clear: *the clones would rather fight the*

Jod marines than the heat. They can survive more Jod: they can't survive more heat. Andrea turned to Brigon and said, "We planned to march to the fortress in one day."

"Then we'd better modify our plans." Brigon took a drink from his water bag. He looked up at the blazing sun and said, "When we get to the Klamdara fortress, we'll have a long hot day's work with no rest. We'll need to work cloaked. We can't afford heat casualties. I say we take an extra day or two getting to the fortress. We can rest during the afternoon and travel at night."

In the distance, the whine of turbines reminded everyone of the Jod marines. Up and down the column, the clones nervously loosened their cloaks, preparing to hide themselves. Andrea wiped the sweat from her brow. "I don't like it. The longer we stay out here arguing, the more likely they'll spot us."

With mounting frustration, Brigon said, "Then let's go argue someplace else."

Andrea stood up and straightened her harness. "That's not a half-bad idea, Brigon."

"What?" He was hot and annoyed.

Andrea pulled out the topocard. "Not a bad idea at all. We're going to make a detour, where I doubt they'll search for us. Follow me." She stepped away and the others followed. Andrea turned abruptly west, facing the source of their torment, the Klamdara sun. She took the column down an escarpment strewn with sandstone monuments: pillars and slabs of stone tossed violently and worn patiently. Imbedded in the rocks were millions of fossils: spiral shells, bivalves, and long-legged prawns, some as small as her fingernail, others larger than herself.

The downhill trek was slow. Backpacks made the marchers top-heavy and they carefully trod on loose slag. Around them, the rocks radiated heat. Even the shade lost its appeal. Andrea walked fifty meters ahead of the column, trying to find the easier path.

Two hours later, Andrea stopped. She consulted the topocard and confirmed her position. She found what she was looking for, the deep fissure that they'd seen from the air as they flew in. Andrea stood on higher ground and surveyed the ragged gash in the planet: the wound of a monstrous temblor several thousand years ago. She paused to look down as Brigon and Eric caught up with her. The ragged gash ranged from twenty-five to two hundred meters across. The walls were vertical sandstone with vegetation clinging to the sides, daring to poke green tufts into the Klamdara sunlight. The pungent odor of sulfur rose to offend. The heat rising from the fissure was moist instead of dry.

Brigon shifted the weight on his back as he said, "What are you thinking?"

"This fissure meanders toward the fortress, ends in the high ground to the west of the fortress." Andrea showed Brigon the topocard. "They'll keep looking for us on the eastward side of this fault line. They won't think for a second that we can cross that—" She pointed at the dark yawning crack in the ground, "—so we shall. Always take the harder route to confound the enemy."

"This is an *impossible* route." Brigon looked over the edge.

"Good. I'm counting on the Klamdara Jod to share your opinion." Andrea looked back at the column. H'Roo and the other Tenebrea stood in the

rear. "Then the Jod will be thoroughly confounded."
She walked ahead, studying the fissure.

They found a narrower stretch of the chasm. The
steam from thermal vents kept the canyon lush with
vegetation, while beyond the lip of the canyon the
vegetation faded to scrub, brambles, and cacti living
on the residual moisture wafted by slight breezes.
"We cross here," Andrea announced.

"Cross here how?" Brigon peered over the edge.
Thick vegetation created an awning, impenetrable to
the eyes. Spindly branches raised fleshy leaves skyward. A snarl of green vines choked the trees.
Epiphytes and parasitic plants added another layer
and some floral color to the dense vegetation.

Brigon hurled a heavy rock over the side. The
assembly listened to the rock crash quickly through
broad leaves and branches until all the sound
ceased. They waited for the defining crash of rock
against rock, but silence disappointed them. Brigon
turned to Andrea and said, "I don't think we can
climb to the bottom, then out again. We need to
stretch a line across."

Ariko stepped forward and volunteered, "We have
plenty of line."

Brigon rubbed the stubble on his chin, what was
left of his beard. He looked into the chasm and the
vegetation. "I'll take it across."

Andrea sloughed her pack and set her rifle down.
Then she grabbed a short length of line from her
pack and began tying it through her legs and around
her waist, making an expedient rappelling seat. "I'm
lighter than any of you. I might be able to work my
way through the branches." She snapped a metal
D-ring at her waist, then took the end of Brigon's

long half-inch-thick line. "I'll need you and," she looked around the cluster of clones, "Eric, come here. I need you and Brigon to belay the line."

Eric cocked his head and asked, "Are you sure you want to do this?"

Andrea discouraged the chatter. "We've got to hurry." She dug into her pack and removed a thin pair of black gloves that she put on. She checked her belt, her knife, and comm-disk, then said, "You two feed me line and belay. When I tug, you feed me slack." She handed back the thick coil of line to Brigon and Eric. "Get everyone else out of sight of the Jod recon."

Andrea lowered herself over the edge of the cliff and through the leaf canopy. She sat in her rappel seat with her feet planted against crumbling sandstone and a rust-red fern. She jerked the line then felt the corresponding slack.

She felt the water vapor as thick as steam. Sulfur burned her nostrils. Although she had yet to exert herself, she found breathing difficult.

Inside the chasm lay another world. Branches rose from fleshy trunks and spread like plumage— great wide feathery ferns, violently lush, shimmering. Vines draped over spreading limbs like a verdant veil. One vine of variegated green and yellow leaves provided a petticoat of vegetation decorated with pale violet flowers. The suspended forest was a curtain of green, seamless, with not so much as a footpath into the verdant fabric.

The canopy of leaves allowed pinholes of light. Small circles of white light danced on her long legs, like so many tiny Klamdara suns. She looked below and saw tough branches stretching out to the wall, then arching up toward the light. Beneath the branches, shadows swallowed the last bits of light. She strained to see into the infinite black. She ripped a handful of the leaves and let them flutter out of sight. *Nothingness. All this life, and below is nothingness . . .*

Andrea gave two quick tugs on the line, beckoning slack. She carefully lowered herself into the branches and tested her weight. Hanging from one springy branch, she rested her feet on another and slowly distributed her weight from the line to the branches. The branches sagged badly but held.

As she inched her way out from the ledge, the scrawny tree limbs sagged more, lowering her closer to the black. The belay line dragged against the branches, but Andrea welcomed the nuisance resistance, because it reminded her that Brigon's strong arms held her.

Snap! The limb beneath her feet broke. Andrea clung to the overhead branch that bent like a willow bearing her weight. She felt the belay line tighten at her waist. "I'm okay!" she hollered up. The belay slacked, but only tentatively.

Andrea hung in the air until she found another branch to grab. She swung her feet to it and gingerly transferred her weight. Sweat dripped down her face and she breathed heavily. Inch by inch she progressed from the wall and toward thinner branches, always sagging deeper into the shadows.

Then she saw dead air. Space. Ten feet of naked air between her and the branches protruding from the opposite wall. *Now what?* she thought. She looked back at the treacherous path she'd taken through the branches, many of which were strained or cracked from her trip out. Would they support her on the way back?

A hidden voice from above asked, "Are you stuck?"

Andrea looked at the ten feet of space. *Damn tease.* She inched closer and heard the faint crackling of the branches. She inched back quickly. She called up, "I've got to swing myself to a branch."

Brigon's voice echoed back. "Don't, Andrea. It's not worth it. We'll bring you back."

Andrea called back with an outrageous lie. "Nothing to it. Give me about twenty feet of slack." She tugged the line twice. The line went limp in her hand, and she felt precariously alone.

She carefully climbed higher. She held a piece of the slack line in her teeth as she used one hand to unfasten the line from her waist. When she felt the line fall from her waist, her knees almost gave out. *Don't look down.* The branches shook and she realized that she was nervously adding to the tremors. *Take a deep breath.* She extended her reach, balancing all her weight on a flimsy branch below. *Stop shaking.* With the tips of her fingers she gathered in three good-size branches, bundled them together, and put a clove hitch around them. She used her knife to trim the twigs away.

Twenty feet of slack fell down, reaching into the shadows. Andrea took the end, tying a large loop that she slipped under her arms. *There.* She tugged on the rope, then hand over hand she lowered herself like a spider from a single thread. *Suspended in blackness.* She could reach nothing solid. She was a pendulum stuck motionless.

Andrea pulled herself up to offset her weight from the line and she began to swing. Like a child, she used her legs to grow tiny arcs into larger ones, shifted her weight slightly to set up a harmonic adding to the amplitude of each arc: four inches became eight inches; eight inches became two feet.

She lost count of the swings; rather, she watched the far branches come within reach. Not content to catch the tips, Andrea swung harder to throw herself into more substantial branches that might support her weight. *Crackle!* She heard the branches breaking under the strain. With one last arc she reached out, almost horizontal. She grabbed a set of branches and hauled herself in. The branches above broke and snapped under her weight. She frantically grappled her way in—falling and climbing at the same time—clinging to anything that could support her. Twigs scratched her neck and face.

All motion stopped. She paused to catch her breath. She felt her heart pounding against her ribs. Andrea righted herself and stood on the far side branches. She took a deep breath to calm the shaking in her hands, then yelled back triumphantly, "I made it!" They'd crossed the hardest ten feet she'd ever traveled. "Give me slack."

Brigon's voice didn't seem any farther, as he replied with a question, "Nothing to it?"

Andrea didn't answer. She shook her end of the line sending undulations to loosen the clove hitch: the natural spring in the branches helped to yank the clove hitch apart. She was soon free to work her way to the far cliff.

Having traversed the branches, the vertical sandstone walls presented little challenge and she quickly pulled herself into the fresh air. She sat with her legs apart on the ground to catch her breath. Her shadow was long. High above, thin wisps of clouds glowed orange. A pair of bright planets—one most probably Jod itself—peered through the purple sky. The Klamdara heat waned. Her uniform, wet with perspiration, felt cool in the dry air. She tied her end of rope around a smooth boulder. She peeled off her gloves and said, "After we cross, we can rest a couple of hours."

Across the chasm, Brigon stood with his hands on his hips. Andrea saw the admiration in his eyes. She told herself she didn't want his admiration, but she could not help but smile. Eric had already secured his end of the line and called the others to begin traversing the rope bridge.

K'Rin sat in the shade by his concrete cell. He bunched his knees to his chin, then stretched them on the ground, reaching forward to touch his toes, slowly exercising his stiff joints. Stretching exercises did not alleviate the pain of Quazel poisoning but did slow the ossification of the limbs. He exhaled deeply, stifling the groan that welled up in his chest. He looked across the broad yard and saw Jo'Orom's body laid on a table, blasphemy to any Jod with a sense of piety. Yet D'Cru forbid burial; instead, he displayed Jo'Orom's body to taunt the Tenebrea and remind them of the horror of Quazel poisoning. D'Cru hoped that the Tenebrea would turn on K'Rin and extract the secret of the whereabouts of the enzyme. K'Rin's temper rose at the thought.

Walking slowly across the dusty yard, a young Tenebrea, Har'Got, approached. His otherwise boyish face was slightly misshapen from a broken nose and the constant wince of pain. A raw stump, where his right hand had been, protruded from a frayed and burned sleeve. K'Rin stopped his exercises as Har'Got approached.

K'Rin remembered the day they arrived at Klamdara. Crowing over his security, D'Cru asked this young Tenebrea—at the time K'Rin had forgotten the youth's name—to attempt to climb the ancient wall that was generously pocked with handholds. K'Rin's eyes narrowed as he remembered the rest. The wall had a touch-sensitive field—invisible. When Har'Got's hand touched the wall, no sound, no light alerted the guards. Instead, a pair of cutting lasers flashed, slicing the hand at the wrist. K'Rin grit his teeth. *Another reason to kill D'Cru.*

K'Rin could see excitement in Har'Got's eyes. K'Rin nodded a greeting.

Conserving his voice, Har'Got whispered, "Guards doubled."

K'Rin looked around the corner of the concrete wall he sat against. He quickly counted the Jod marines standing around the prison gate and on the wall in foursomes. He asked, "Why?"

"Don't know."

"What—" K'Rin winced and forced the word, "—happened?"

"Full load transport gone." Har'Got mimicked flight with his good hand. "Desert. Crashed. All hundred dead."

K'Rin sat up. "Implausible." He swallowed to lubricate his larynx. He had years as a stick pilot. He had flown transports, so he knew that the sturdy transport could auto-glide to a hard landing with all engines off.

Har'Got nodded. He held up three fingers. "Recon flights all day. Change crews. Up again."

K'Rin pondered the news. *They are looking for someone who doesn't want to be found. They've doubled the guard.* K'Rin brushed away a crust of blood from his upper lip. "Pass the word. Be ready."

The Heptar Palace, seat of the Jod government, was thick with activity. The titular heads of the clans converged to witness Hal Pl'Don's triumph. These old Jod wore their ceremonial garb and wandered the halls with little to do but watch the preparations for the Cor Ordinate delegation. The palace staff worked feverishly, festooning the halls with fresh flowers and radiant silk. Workers polished the ten thousand large panes of cut crystal built into the platinum grid: the great dome arching above the mall that connected the principal Heptar buildings. In the kitchens, the Jod chefs practiced meals delightful to the human palate. In seventy-two hours the small army of workers would disappear and the sumptuous rooms would remain as if conjured by Pl'Don's munificence.

As Pl'Don explained to the council, "The Ordinate will witness the blessings of peace: surplus best given to culture, surplus we can share with our friends." Pointing skyward through the glistening dome, he made reference to the Fleet above. "And in case our capability for hospitality fails to move them, I'm sure our capability for hostility shall."

The roomful of dignitaries applauded discretely.

Tamor-Kyl approached from behind the small crowd. He wore his black uniform with his face shield down to hide his disfigurement and the pain collar.

Pl'Don soured as Tamor approached. Without a word, he turned and retreated to a quiet side room where Tamor followed.

Tamor shut the door behind them. Pl'Don said, "This interruption had better be important—not another one of your little tantrums."

Tamor did not respond to Pl'Don's gibe, but simply thrust a message into the soft hands decorated with jeweled rings. Tamor quickly told the contents. "The *Benwoi* has landed on Klamdara."

Pl'Don held the message to his eyes, suddenly interested in the content. Tamor continued, "Andrea Flores is there, I'm sure."

Pl'Don dragged his finger over some text. "—massacred a company of Jod marines," Pl'Don read incredulously, then set the message aside on his desk.

"Don't you see?" Tamor's mind fixated on the *Benwoi* and Andrea. "The Quazel enzyme: Andrea must have brought a supply. She's going to try to save K'Rin. I've already sent a reply message ordering D'Cru to hold the *Benwoi*—undamaged. I shall leave immediately for Klamdara aboard the *Tyker*. I can set foot on Klamdara in thirty-six hours."

Pl'Don raised a cautionary hand. "Be careful."

"Careful?" Tamor raised his face shield to expose his gnarled face turning gray with advancing Quazel poisoning. "I have nothing to lose. Besides, I shall enjoy killing Andrea Flores. She is responsible for this." He pointed to the scars on his face.

Pl'Don winced with restrained disgust. "Let's hope you can soon neutralize the effect of the Quazel Protein." He motioned for Tamor to lower his face shield to hide the disagreeable sight of a liv-

ing death. "In the meantime," he said, "tell no one. If
you bring back the enzyme, you shall enjoy a very
special place in my government. Our surgeons can
restore you to health, and I shall rule for a hundred
years with you as my chief of staff."

Tamor lowered the face shield and said, "I'll bring
back the enzyme, you can count on it."

chapter 6

D'Cru stood on the ramparts of the fortress with his binoculars to his face. His walking stick rested against his chest. He scanned the dark rocks and barren fields. The Klamdara sun remained below the horizon but the dim light contrasted with the soft black humps that would soon blaze into ragged red rocks.

Floodlights illuminated the base of the wall, the landing apron, and the laser cannon. Ground radar swept the fields trying to detect movement. The marines had laid trip wires in a semicircle stretching out from the wall. The two reconnaissance craft continued to stay aloft, searching; the omnipresent whining of the turbines began to grate the nerves. D'Cru and his men had slept little that night. Already the rumors of Ben'Toor's disaster had infected the Jod garrison. The hidden enemy swelled in number and ferocity as the rank and file Jod speculated: *the attack comes at night; the attack comes at dawn.*

But the attack didn't come, and they waited.

Just after sunup, the *Tyker*'s shuttle landed. Commander Tamor-Kyl stepped out and walked to the fortress gate as if he were paying a courtesy call. D'Cru called down from the rampart, "You had better send your shuttle away to safety and bring yourself inside the walls."

Tamor-Kyl looked up with disdain, then signaled his pilot to take the shuttle away.

The Klamdara nights were as cold as the days were hot. Brigon's wilderness clones traveled all night using only the ambient light of the stars. Sweat soaked and tired, they suffered the chill but did not complain. Brigon spoke for all of them when he said through chattering teeth, "This will teach me to complain about the heat." Without a moon for light, the Klamdara nights were particularly dark. The column trudged along blindly. Many of the clones bruised their shins and ankles on the rocks. Everyone was anxious to have this fight over.

Just as they were beginning to despair of the cold and the dark, the Klamdara sun rose rapidly. The warmth reenergized the marchers. The light gave them back their sight, revealing a stark change in topography. Andrea stopped the column. She pulled out her topocard to get her bearings. They stood at the base of a large cliff that rose four hundred feet and stretched from left to right as far as the eye could see. The rosy light illuminated the red sandstone wall, sculpted by a millennia of waves and polished by wind. To her right, the chasm seemed to fall in on itself, leaving a trough of loose slag instead of the deep gash.

H'Roo walked from the rear to the head of the

column. "We're close." He pointed east and said, "The fortress is in a huge cave cut into this cliff." As if to confirm his announcement, the whine of reconnaissance craft came from the east on the other side of a rock ridge.

Brigon commanded, "Cloak!"

The column ducked and covered. Andrea spoke to Brigon who sat nearby. "The higher pitch from the Doppler effect means that the craft is coming this way." The whine grew louder, almost overhead, then quickly abated into a semitone lower, then the whine stopped. Andrea announced, "All clear." She added, "That craft just landed at the fortress on the other side of this ridge." She left her cloak draped around her neck as she looked at the topocard. "About eight hundred meters, maybe less."

Everyone shrunk at the news as if they were being watched. Brigon grabbed the first clone nearby and whispered, "Send Chana and Eric forward for a leaders' recon. H'Roo, you come, too."

The five leaders inched their way up a shallow incline. Near the top, they all cloaked. Andrea was the first to take a look. Her dark eyes peered from a fold in the cloak as she studied the terrain. She had read the topocard correctly. From their position, the fortress wall was barely eight hundred meters away. The rising sun tended to spotlight the fortress walls. *Good*, she thought. *We can approach the fortress along the base of the cliff, practically in their blind spot.*

Brigon looked through binoculars, carefully keeping the lenses in the shade of his cloak to avoid reflecting glare. He spoke first, cataloging what he saw, "A mining pit—two thousand meters east of the gate. Abandoned mining equipment. Closer in, a solar-panel farm. Then a landing pad. Two small utility hovercraft, and behind them a larger ship. Communications dish. Bunker with large laser cannon. One gate. Firing positions every twenty meters along the top of the wall. Appears to have large metal spikes at the base of the wall."

Eric's muffled voice admitted, "H'Roo, the layout is just as you described."

H'Roo replied, "I'm more relieved than you know."

Cloaked, they surveyed the fortress in silence, soaking in details that might later mean life or death. The sun baked the face of the cliff that overshadowed the fortress. The deep cave stretched its massive ledge over the fortress wall. They watched a reconnaissance craft land, refuel, and fly up the valley for more fruitless reconnaissance. Then a larger ship took off from the landing pad. A gray ship with sloping stabilizers turned straight up and quickly disappeared. Andrea prompted H'Roo, "That bird was too small to be a supply ship and too big for a utility craft."

"A captain's gig from a light cruiser." H'Roo looked at Andrea and nodded with assurance. "At least it's not a gig from a dreadnought."

H'Roo borrowed the binoculars to study the fortress wall. He pointed out the surface radar and the heavy lasers on the wall. They turned to Brigon for refinements to the plan.

Brigon quickly decided. "Okay. Andrea, H'Roo, and I will take twenty men to the gate. We'll be the main assault party." Aside to H'Roo, he said, "I'm going to split your Jod: two with us, two with Eric. Is that going to be a problem?"

H'Roo shook his head. "They know what they have to do."

Brigon nodded. "Chana, you take Ariko's snipers to the stumpy rocks facing the gate. They'll have a range of five hundred meters."

Chana whispered, "They can hit an egg at that range."

"I want them to take out the gunners on the wall."

"Then what?" Chana asked without taking her eyes off the fortress gate.

"Well, then you come in and join the party. I figure we'll have lovely fighting all up and down the wall." Brigon made an expansive gesture with his arms.

Chana smiled broadly showing her white teeth. "Promise?"

Brigon said, "Keep your comm-disk on receive only. Don't key the disk unless you see something we can't. Also, you watch our backs. They may have foot patrols out there."

"Understood." Chana clipped the comm-disk to her harness.

Brigon handed the second comm-disk to Andrea. Then, he turned to his right. "Eric, that leaves you two a fire team of five, including the two Jod. You'll need the Jod to cut the fiber optic cable to the deep space transmitter, as you simultaneously take the laser cannon."

H'Roo interrupted, "Remember, Eric, the cannon controls are in the bunker. Per doctrine, the marines change the crew on every watch—every six hours, midnight, six, noon, and six. When they open the door, you blast your way in. If they button up with you on the outside, you'll never get in. Nobody can cut their way into that bunker—nobody."

Brigon looked up at the sun. "We can time our assault around the noon watch." He ducked down and pulled the cloak from his face. He lay on his stomach, looked up, and grinned at Andrea. "I think broad daylight is the perfect time to assault an impenetrable fortress, don't you?" he asked dryly.

Andrea didn't smile, but Chana laughed. Brigon added seriously, "We have four hours to crawl into position under cloaks."

"A hot four hours." Eric scratched the black stubble growing on his chin.

"Just remember, when you move, the cloak image blurs. Move slowly, so they can't see you, their radar can't track you. If you move quickly, they'll kill you." Brigon tapped Eric on the shoulder and said, "Now listen carefully. You need to be sure that the rest of us are in position, because you're going to start this fight." Turning back to Chana, he said, "As soon as you hear Eric's gunfire, take down the wall gunners."

"Got it."

Turning back to Eric, he said, "You take that cannon and tear a hole through the gate. We're counting on you." Then Brigon turned to Andrea. "Then we go in. I figure we run as fast as we can until we run into your Tenebrea friends. We can carry in more than a hundred weapons in our packs. H'Roo will have the enzyme. Then we'll find out if your K'Rin and his troops are everything you say."

The late-morning heat was especially oppressive. The three replacement cannon gunners obediently put on their body armor and helmets, although they left the straps loose. Soon they would be inside the concrete blockhouse and they would strip themselves of the hot, burdensome gear.

They stepped through the short portal, a small door built into the main gate, into the bright sunlight. "Weapons." The senior marine reminded the others flatly of their orders to maintain tactical readiness.

"Yeah, yeah . . ." The disgruntled marines discounted the cautionary word. Nevertheless, they unholstered their handlances as they walked the two hundred paces to the bunker. One of them added, "Hey, Feld, you managed to pull us the hottest shift again."

The senior Jod ignored the chafing, hoping the irritation—his subordinates' banter—would stop if he left it alone. He had long ago relaxed discipline that seemed like an unpleasant artifice that just created friction in his little unit that sat shift after shift in the cannon bunker. Besides, they were due to rotate off this miserable rock in sixty days. Now, the ambush of Ben'Toor's company reinstilled his sense of dread, but he found he could not instantly restore the discipline that had atrophied.

The banter continued. "The Feld is *incommunicado* today." The loquacious marine talked as he walked. "Did you bring the T'aitu cubes?"

"Yeah. Did you bring some money this time?"

In a low threatening voice, the Feld demanded, "Quiet, you two. You'll get us all in trouble. D'Cru is probably watching from the wall. Save the chatter for the bunker."

The two junior marines exchanged a look of

bemusement but obeyed. They walked the same path
to the bunker that they had walked every day since
they arrived on Klamdara for what they considered
their captivity. What did they ever do to deserve an
assignment on this rock?

They arrived at the door and the senior Jod
knocked. A voice inside complained, "You're late."

"We're right on time."

The door opened. A young Jod face emerged,
pointing to a chronometer on his wrist. "You're a
minute late."

"Oh, bite a rock."

Then the senior Jod felt a dull poke in the back of
his neck. He turned and saw the concrete wall of the
bunker shift, assuming a spectral shape. An arm protruded from the swirling image. The hand held a
crude black metal object. It all happened so fast. He
heard three loud bangs and bits of flesh and bone
splashed by him as his comrades reeled backward.
Then he saw the face beneath the shroud: a human
face attached to the arm that held the odd weapon
to his face. He instinctively grabbed for the black
weapon, but too late. A flash, a searing pain, and the
hollow noise inside his head were his last aware-
ness.

Andrea hunkered down between the fortress wall
and the rusty iron spikes in the dry moat. She felt
Brigon's back pressed against hers. She heard the
first shot. She saw the red spray and the splatter of
brains on the bunker. Through the tiny fold in her
cloak she saw Eric's team dispatch the rest of the
cannon crew and toss their bodies into the dust. At
the same time, she saw a Jod emerge from a cloak

near the large deep-space antenna dish and fire a laser blast to cut the line.

A moment later, she heard dull thuds and the muffled groan of wounded above. Ariko's snipers struck down the laser gunners. She looked up in time to see a body falling, shrieking as it fell, not from the rifle wound but in expectation of the iron spikes. She winced as the body impaled itself, shuddering for a moment as if tormented by an unreachable itch. She felt her stomach turn and she forced herself to look away.

Brigon poked her and pointed. "The cannon!"

Andrea saw the heavy cannon slowly turn toward the fortress wall. Slowly the barrel lowered, then stuck. Twice the barrel raised and lowered to a loud and grinding halt. *Damn!* Eric could not lower the barrel enough to blast open the gate. Andrea saw their careful plan evaporate into thin air.

Jod marines returned to the walls and turned their lasers against the bunker. Pointless. Eric's crew was safely buttoned inside. The marines simply delivered themselves to Ariko's rifles.

Then the big cannon barrel raised and fired, raking the stone overhang above the fortress. The laser blasted the sandstone roof of the cave. Shards of rock fell inside the wall, crushing defenders. Brigon hollered, "If he shoots that cannon over us, we're in trouble."

"He won't," Andrea hollered back.

"Well, then what in hell does he think he's doing?" Brigon's antipathy toward Eric was obvious in his voice.

"He's opening the gate." Andrea smiled at Eric's improvisation. "He's forcing them to come out to him."

*   *   *

Inside the fortress, K'Rin sprung to his feet. He drew his crude blade, and held it over his head. The pain was inconsequential compared to his joy. "Now!" he yelled hoarsely. And although his throat throbbed, he cried, "Free yourselves!"

All the Tenebrea drew their homemade knives and rushed forward with K'Rin. The handful of guards patrolling the huts fired into the black mass of Tenebrea. Several fell with mortal wounds only to get up and continue the charge: one with an arm hanging loosely, another tripping over his entrails.

In moments, the Tenebrea overpowered their two dozen guards. K'Rin jumped a marine who raised his laser rifle, jabbing his spike through the ear hole in the helmet, killing the hapless marine instantly. He grabbed the laser rifle and tossed it to a comrade who fired at the advancing marines who formed ranks beneath the wall.

Then a blast of cannon scorched the cave ceiling above and the rock rained down. Two Tenebrea were crushed instantly by heavy shards of red rock. "Back!" K'Rin yelled. "Back!" He pulled his men backward behind the curtain of falling stone that separated them from the marines. Jagged stones splashed around them, injuring the men in the forward ranks.

Bal'Don ran to K'Rin. "Must attack through."

K'Rin grabbed Bal'Don's tunic and shook him. "No! We conform to *her* plan."

"Whose?"

"Andrea. Out there." K'Rin laughed out loud through the pain in his throat. "Glorious chaos! Gather men; take cover. Prepare. Assault the armory on my command."

"Yes," Bal'Don ran back to gather the others.

*   *   *

Andrea heard the heavy gears of the main gate. The locking pins grated, adding to the cacophony of laser blasts, exploding rock, and shrieks of pain. The massive iron shield began to rise, slowly—painfully slowly. Andrea peeked around the corner and saw scores of feet, anxiously shuffling. Several marines lay prone with their weapons bristling for the first light behind the gate. Some fired blindly. Andrea retreated to safety round her corner.

"You all right?" Brigon asked.

"Yes." She caught her breath. "I count fifty marines."

"We'll let them run past us to the cannon bunker. Then we all run in blasting. Got that?"

Muffled voices behind confirmed. H'Roo spoke from under his cloak. "Do you think Eric will stop dropping rock when we get inside?"

Andrea answered, "We'll know soon enough."

With a great yell, a company of marines charged out the gate toward the cannon bunker. Andrea saw several fall to a volley from Ariko's long-range rifles.

"Now!" Andrea grabbed the folds of her cloak in her arm and ran to the gate. She fired her pistol as she ran, knocking down a marine with each shot. Brigon, his men, and H'Roo poured in with her. They likewise fired rapidly at anything wearing a khaki uniform.

Inside, Andrea saw company formations of Jod marines by the barracks, hugging close to the walls to avoid the cataract of falling rock. Marines lay atop the wall, out of Ariko's sight. They held rifles pointed inside—pointed at the Tenebrea's flimsy huts, scant cover for a barrage of laser fire. *The Tenebrea are mobilized*, she thought. "Run through the rocks!" she cried. *Our only chance is to reach them and arm them.*

A large stone, half her size, landed beside her with a ground-shaking thud. It didn't matter. Survival was at best random.

A clone to her left fell beneath a rock, his skull crushed. She ran. With her peripheral vision she saw Brigon bypass her with H'Roo alongside him, ducking as if a bowed head might save him.

Through the torrent of rock they scampered into the huts and into the arms of the Tenebrea. Andrea tossed her backpack at them, and yelled, "Weapons! Arm yourselves."

The other clones likewise tossed their backpacks at the Tenebrea, who quickly passed out the heavy pistols and carbines. Unfamiliar with kinetic-kill weapons, they nevertheless understood the trigger mechanism and the business end of the weapons.

Andrea turned and saw four clones lying dead in the growing pile of rubble. Suddenly, the laser cannon stopped. The last chunks of rock fell. The perimeter lights blinked off. *The marines cut the power.*

Then she heard K'Rin's voice from the opposite side of the huts: "Clear those walls!"

The Tenebrea swarmed out of their hiding places laying down deadly fire with their newfound weapons. The Jod marines returned fire but without the same accuracy. In seconds the Tenebrea silenced all the lasers firing from the top of the walls.

The large courtyard became an orgy of hand-to-hand fighting. The Tenebrea aggressively drove the Jod marines backward, crowding them in a herd for slaughter.

Andrea called above the din, "H'Roo. Come with me."

H'Roo unshouldered his rucksack of enzyme and tossed it into one of the huts. Then he followed Andrea through the chaos to a set of steps leading to the walls. Andrea stepped over bodies, shoving others over the ledge as she plowed her way to the vacant laser guns. She pulled her comm-disk from her harness and said, "Chana, Ariko, come back to me."

Chana's voice replied, "Speak."

"We're on the wall above the gate. Don't shoot."

"Understood. We're coming in."

Andrea shoved a dead gunner who lay slumped over his laser gun. She looked over the wall and saw a horde of marines trying to break down the door to the bunker. The bunker was scarred and pocked with a thousand laser burns. *Eric, that crazy sonofabitch, is still alive.* She smiled at her own, seemingly irrational, impulse to save him. *Must be all the excitement—or maybe I am insane.* Andrea turned the laser gun on the marines and cut through them like a scythe. The howls rose with the smell of burning flesh. The marines scattered. Some ran back to the fortress. Others ran behind the bunker where they exposed their backs to Ariko's sharpshooters.

H'Roo stood at her back with an automatic rifle firing down into the prison yard, carefully picking targets from the melee.

Tamor-Kyl and Commandant D'Cru stood at the window of the command post watching the destruction of the marine regiment. With great ferocity, the

Tenebrea surrounded the far greater number of
marines and pressed them back against their barracks' walls. They slashed with their crude knives
and fired their pistols at the periphery, pushing the
dying marines backward, using their bodies as a
shield. The Tenebrea ignored their many wounds.
They were slick with their own blood mingled with
the blood of their foe. They closed like a great crimson jaw upon the marines.

The wilderness clones withdrew from the hand
fighting and set themselves on the high places—the
walls, the roofs. From sheltered positions, they fired
into the pack. They sniped at the few marines who
escaped the Tenebrea's pincer. D'Cru's regiment had
disintegrated into panic.

D'Cru was horrified by the slaughter. Tamor-Kyl
felt an odd pride in his former comrades. But he was
now bereft of honor, and he was doomed to die
from Quazel poisoning. He would never ask for
K'Rin's pity. His life was ruined, and he knew it. All
his misfortune—even his own treacherous conduct—could be laid at the feet of the Terran female
that K'Rin brought into the Tenebrea's ranks. K'Rin
had adulterated the brotherhood by recruiting her—
even worse by promoting her. *And the sacrilege of
adopting her into his clan!* That K'Rin favored the
Terran over his own kind was an insult no Jod
should have to bear. *I am justified,* he thought. *She
set this ruinous course of events; she ruined all my
nobler ambitions.*

Tamor felt the rippled flesh on the side of his face.
His fingers rested on his pain management collar.
He glowered at the mayhem below. He looked for
one person in the confusion, the object of his hate.

His eyes settled on the two figures atop the wall. *Andrea, I see you now.* Tamor-Kyl drew his weapon and started for the door.

"Don't unseal the door!" D'Cru hollered. He tried to stand in Tamor's way.

Tamor pushed the commandant aside and threatened him with his handlance.

"Do you really think we can escape?" D'Cru asked hopefully.

"For me there is no escape." Tamor pulled the lever to break the seal. He sneered at D'Cru's sudden paleness; then he rushed out.

Andrea fired the laser until she burned out the crystal. H'Roo soon thereafter ran out of bullets. For the moment, they hunkered down and rested. They surveyed the prison yard and could see that the Tenebrea had won the day. The only unknown was whether the marines would fight to the last combatant or surrender. Their numbers were soon to be less than the surviving Tenebrea.

Andrea spotted a uniformed Tenebrea walking stiff-legged across the prison yard toward them. *Odd?* The lone Tenebrea wore a fresh black and gray uniform with helmet and faceplate. She nudged H'Roo, "Who in the hell is that?"

"I don't know." H'Roo raised himself to get a better look. The uniformed Tenebrea jerked a handlance from his utility belt and without breaking stride, raised it and fired. The energy bolt hit the wall next to H'Roo splashing particles of rock. H'Roo ducked, then grabbed Andrea's arm and pulled her down beside him. He and Andrea sat side by side with their backs to the masonry.

Andrea knew. "It's Tamor-Kyl." Her nostrils flared. "That backstabber."

"He's coming for you." H'Roo's neck flared with anger. "We don't have a weapon."

Andrea reached into her belt and drew her knife and held it up to her face. H'Roo objected, "You can't be serious, a knife against a handlance?"

"You got a better idea?" Andrea challenged. She held the blade over her head using the polished titanium as a mirror. "Tamor is coming up the steps." She looked into H'Roo's wide eyes and said, "Goodbye." With a quick leap Andrea vaulted over the ledge and through the air. She aimed her accelerating body toward the lower stairs and Tamor.

Tamor raised his handlance and fired. The bolt grazed her side with a numbing sting but did nothing to slow her descent. She slammed into Tamor with her feet, knocking him backward, knocking the handlance from his grip. They fell—no, flew—down the steps. As they tumbled over each other, Andrea raked Tamor with her blade, opening a gash on his thigh. They sprawled onto the hard dirt and gravel below. Tamor's helmet rolled away, exposing his scars. "I'll kill you," he sputtered as he rolled onto his side. The blow to his chest completely knocked the breath out of him and he gasped for air. The cut on his thigh hobbled him as he struggled to his feet.

Andrea was stunned by the handlance and the fall. Her knees buckled as she tried to stand. Her side was sticky from the burn. But she stood, buttressed by an anger that overwhelmed the pain. She felt drunk—tingling from the handlance—yet alert. The hideous face before her represented all the pain that had plagued her life. *I swear I'll inflict pain for pain.*

Slowly the two found their footing. Tamor looked in vain for the handlance, then drew his knife. "I'll kill you for everything you've done to me."

Andrea saw the pain collar and Tamor's stiff movements. *He's got the Quazel hardening. He'll be slow.* She held her knife forward and waited for Tamor's move. He lunged. She sidestepped him, spinning by, dragging her knife across Tamor's back. Her blade was red with his blood. She showed the wet blade to him. She beckoned, "Come get some more, traitor." *Pain for pain.*

Tamor arched his back and cringed at the deep wound. He roared and slashed at her. She passed under his intended blow and swept his leg. How easily she could have driven her knife into his heart, but she didn't. Andrea cut a broad gash across Tamor's chest, opening another flow of blood.

He staggered to his feet, raised his knife, and threw himself at Andrea. She flattened Tamor with an ax kick, then attacked, swiping him across the abdomen with a deep gash. Tamor rose to his knees, dazed, a piece of his pink gut protruding through the wound. Andrea kicked his knife away. Tamor-Kyl was now helpless.

Andrea moved in for a last attack. She grabbed Tamor, and held her knife to his throat. Tamor spit in her face.

Andrea let the spittle run down her cheek. "Tamor," she said, "you need to learn how to control your anger." Then she used her blade to break the latch on the pain collar. She wrenched the collar away, holding it out of Tamor's reach. She jerked the electrodes and doping tubes from the back of his neck and threw the gangly apparatus across the prison yard. Tamor howled in anguish. Mortally wounded, he dragged himself through the dirt to retrieve his collar.

H'Roo caught up with her. He looked wide-eyed at Tamor, then at Andrea. He pointed at Tamor writhing in the dirt, pitifully fumbling with his pain collar. "Why?" he asked.

Andrea suddenly felt empty. She didn't like her own explanation, so she evaded the question. "I don't know."

chapter 7

The fighting stopped. The prison yard quieted. K'Rin had given up looking for D'Cru—assuming the old bastard's body lay in the jumbled pile at the base of the wall. *A small disappointment . . .*

He spotted a Tenebrea caught in the rubble, crushed by the rock ripped from the overhang. The young warrior was badly broken. K'Rin knelt beside him, making shade for the young Tenebrea's face, that he might open his eyes without pain. K'Rin lifted a heavy slab of sandstone from the soldier's chest. The injury was massive. *He's in deep shock, almost dead.* K'Rin decided not to call for help, not to trouble the soldier with any pointless heroics that would only distract the mind from the weighty matters of death.

K'Rin watched the light leave the young soldier's eyes. He whispered into the dying Tenebrea's ear. "You're free."

The youth simply blinked to assure K'Rin that he understood. Then he closed his eyes forever. K'Rin looked upon the dead Tenebrea and thought how sweet this victory was—how unexpected and sweet. Kip had already given him the cold statistics: forty-two Tenebrea dead, now forty-three; one hundred and seventy-seven Jod marines surrendered, the rest dead or escaped into the Klamdara wilderness.

"Sir." H'Roo Parh stood behind K'Rin, waiting respectfully but impatiently. "I need your arm for a moment. The enzyme injection."

"Has everyone else had their dose?"

"Yes, sir. As you ordered, you are last." H'Roo opened K'Rin's tunic, then pressed the injector to the leathery skin. "You'll start feeling the effects by morning. In a week, you'll feel good as new." He refastened K'Rin's tunic.

"Thank you, Mat H'Roo. Where is Andrea?"

H'Roo pointed across the prison yard. Andrea worked in a huddle of wilderness clones, tending to their wounded. "She sends her regards."

K'Rin felt his throat. Already he felt some relief with the enzyme. K'Rin mused, "Her *regards?* Tell her to come here at once and greet me—no. Belay that order." He looked at Andrea stooped over some hidden figure. She was helping others of her species lift one of their wounded. Her tunic was open and her harness hung loose about her shoulders. Her black hair was pulled tightly back. Her cheeks were dirty from sweat and dust. She worked with the gentleness of a mother hovering over a sick child. K'Rin said softly, "Let her be."

H'Roo packed his medical supplies into his ruck-sack and lingered, waiting to be dismissed.

K'Rin asked, "Clone casualties?"

"We recruited thirty of their fighters from Cor. They lost nine dead. That man on the ground will before sundown make the number ten."

"Is the wounded man Andrea's friend?"

"No, sir. Just a clone."

K'Rin looked around the yard. His men were already separating the Tenebrea dead into one neat row. They pressed the marine prisoners to haul their dead out the fortress gate. The clones merely lay where they fell. *Curious* . . . .

"Sir," H'Roo interrupted again.

"Yes?" K'Rin's eyes remained fixed on Andrea.

H'Roo breached protocol by laying his hand on K'Rin's shoulder to get his attention, "Sir? You have some urgent decisions to make. We need to get you off Klamdara. We need to get you to the safety of your clan. I'm afraid your worst predictions are coming true."

K'Rin took his eyes off a dead clone sprawled in the dust, alone. He focused on H'Roo. "Be specific."

"As we left Cor, we detected a large fleet of nearly five hundred craft, assembled and ready to depart. They are probably under way as we speak. Sir, the capital ships of the Jod Fleet are clustered above Heptar, standing down for Pl'Don's welcoming ceremony."

K'Rin's countenance fell. "Pl'Don is a fool. We must warn the Fleet."

"That will be difficult. No one will believe us. Pl'Don removed all your kin from operational command." H'Roo became agitated. "The other clans accept the verdict that you are a traitor. Sir, we can get you and about half the Tenebrea out of here on the *Benwoi*. After the Cor attacks, after your detractors are gone, then we can try to rebuild."

"Nevertheless, we must warn the Fleet." K'Rin cleared his raspy throat. He ordered, "Repair the deep-space comms. Open channel to Fleet Head-quarters. Tell them what you saw. Leave my name out of it—you're right: they've judged me. So, make them believe you. Make them disperse the Fleet! They must. Now, hurry."

H'Roo paused before speaking his mind. "You know Pl'Don will send a division of infantry to lock you back into your cage. I'll prepare the *Benwoi* to evacuate you."

K'Rin's eyes narrowed. "No. I'll stay with my Tenebrea."

"Yes, sir." H'Roo bowed and left. He climbed the stairs to the Klamdara command center.

From the dark command center, H'Roo sent repair teams to restore power and long-haul communications. Soon, lights returned and screens flickered. H'Roo looked at the hash of static on the comms console. *Come on, Fal'Dar, splice the cable . . .* The quiet bothered him. He turned the volume dial higher to hear the raw static. The communications cable also carried all the data from the fort's sensors, those passive sensors that monitored the wall and the deep-space sensors tied to the communications suite. Until they repaired the cable, Klamdara was deaf, dumb, and blind.

He walked impatiently around looking at the equipment. The room was tidy, almost antiseptic, except for a strong wooden staff propped against the wall and a tunic bearing commandant insignia draped over a chair. Small chrome plaques labeled the old mechanical systems. Ancient toggles made of brass operated the main gate. *This is a museum . . .* He saw a new panel of switches with a red plaque:

Front Wall Antipersonnel Device. The switch was in the *on* position.

An old map table sat in the corner of the room, retooled to accept modern displays. Along the interior wall, there stood a row of polished wood cabinets—antiques. H'Roo ran his fingers on the polished honey-tone wood. Each cabinet door had a small silver lock and handle with a shiny key neatly placed in the keyhole—all but one. Curious, H'Roo opened the cabinet door.

He saw an older, wide-eyed Jod wedged uncomfortably in the narrow space. H'Roo backed away and pulled his handlance from his belt.

"I surrender!" The harried Jod struggled to raise his hands and stepped out of the cabinet.

"Turn around." H'Roo pushed the Jod against the wall. Holding the handlance in the small of the prisoner's back, he frisked him for weapons. Nothing. He roughly turned his prisoner around to face him. "You must be the commandant." H'Roo motioned toward the empty tunic.

His prisoner, D'Cru, remained silent. The dull static from the comm suite stopped. Screens displaying the deep-space sensors flickered to life, and H'Roo saw that the computer began an auto-sequence, scanning for incoming message traffic.

H'Roo waved D'Cru to the middle of the room. "Put on your uniform."

D'Cru reluctantly did as H'Roo ordered. He watched the handlance in H'Roo's hand. H'Roo pointed to the open door. "Now go downstairs and give yourself to the first Tenebrea you see."

"No."

"Then, I'll shoot you where you stand." H'Roo

pointed his handlance at D'Cru's face. D'Cru blanched, his neck turned a brighter shade of pale green, and he left the room.

H'Roo heard the footsteps fade down the steps. Then he heard a repetitious hail: *This is the* Tyker. *Please respond. This is the* Tyker . . .

H'Roo sat down before the console and switched on the screen. He saw a display pinpointing the source of the transmission: fifty-four thousand miles up in a parking orbit. The *Tyker*'s shields were down and weapons cold. H'Roo transmitted a short message. "*Tyker*, stand by for broadcast transmission."

Then H'Roo switched the channel to a broadcast on all channels to the Jod Fleet. He took a deep breath and held his finger on the transmission key. "Attention all commands. My name is H'Roo from the Clan Parh. I have been to the planet Cor. The Cor Ordinate has launched a fleet of attack craft. You must disperse the dreadnoughts and take defensive measures. You must prepare to defend yourselves from a fleet of approximately five hundred small suicide craft piloted by clones. Reconfigure your ships' armaments for close assault."

After a moment of silence, a perplexed voice replied, "This is the first officer of the *Tyker*. Let me speak with Commander Tamor-Kyl."

H'Roo pressed the transmission key again, "Tamor-Kyl is dead. Return to Heptar and persuade the Fleet to defend itself." H'Roo glanced at the screen. The *Tyker*'s shields rose and it accelerated to a higher orbit out of range of Klamdara's big cannon.

Prudent enough. H'Roo switched off the comms. He smiled ruefully, knowing that he had most likely thrown away his only opportunity to escape. *The Fleet will notify the council. The council will order a dreadnought plus a marine division to destroy us. The Fleet will obey the council. We will spend the next two days preparing to defend ourselves from an onslaught of infantry. Three days from now, I'll be with my ancestors.*

K'Rin personally carried the ossified body of Feld Jo'Orom and laid him beside the other Tenebrea dead. The dry husk, which was Jo'Orom's emaciated body, almost floated in his arms, it was so light. K'Rin looked at his old friend to whom he spoke in silent thoughts: *You deserve better than a common burial. We will build a great pyre for you, although you are light as ashes now.* Jo'Orom lay stiff as a warped board with his jaw frozen in a last gasp for air. K'Rin looked at the faces of the Tenebrea killed that afternoon: their eyes closed, their mouths politely shut, their hands folded on their still chests. Compared to Jo'Orom's face frozen in agony, these newly dead lay in peace.

K'Rin's private moment was disturbed by a brief scuffle behind him. He turned. Two burly Tenebrea shoved D'Cru forward, saying, "We found." D'Cru stood a mere arm's length away.

A crowd of Tenebrea formed a large semicircle. K'Rin took his eyes off D'Cru just long enough to inspect the many onlookers. Andrea stood among the Tenebrea, watching with intense interest. A handful of the clones quit their work to watch the inevitable struggle. Only one of the Tenebrea spoke, Har'Got, who said, "Feed him to the wall." Har'Got pointed with the stump that had been his hand.

K'Rin set his jaw and said for all to hear, "Fortune is kind." He pulled his fabricated knife from his belt. The blade was rough-hewn and shiny. The point was chipped from the long day's fight. The handle of tightly wound strips of cloth was wet. As K'Rin gripped the blade tightly, red residue squeezed through his fingers. "You, Pel D'Cru, die on the end of my knife."

"I'm unarmed," D'Cru protested. "I surrendered." He stood erect, confident in his rights.

K'Rin cocked his head to the side to examine D'Cru. "Where were you during battle, coward?"

D'Cru stiffened at the insult. "You are just a bunch of assassins and traitors."

K'Rin saw the fear building in D'Cru's eyes. He wanted to beat D'Cru, not simply execute him. "Give him blade."

Kip stepped forward, "Sir. The risk . . ."

K'Rin shoved Kip back to the semicircle. "You can kill him if I don't." He turned and faced D'Cru.

Har'Got reached into his belt for his crude knife. He threw the knife to D'Cru; it stuck in the ground between D'Cru's legs. "Feed. To the wall!"

D'Cru looked down at the knife, then fixed his eyes on K'Rin. "I'm no fool. I'll give you no provocation to kill me. We—" he pointed to the other marine prisoners sitting on the ground near the barracks. "We are prisoners of war. Moreover, we are Jod citizens."

K'Rin stepped closer holding his knife at his side. D'Cru backed up, staying out of K'Rin's reach. "You make some good points." K'Rin crowded D'Cru who stepped backward. As D'Cru's eyes widened with fear, K'Rin's narrowed with cold determination. "Citizens . . . like Jo'Orom?"

They stepped off the hard-packed courtyard into some soft dirt that made D'Cru stumble. "That was Tamor-Kyl's doing." He recovered his stance, and K'Rin stepped closer.

K'Rin softened his voice and allowed compassion to exude from his eyes—even a hint of an ironic smile. He reached out and put his hand on D'Cru's shoulder. "I understand the pressures of command: I do." He felt the shivers in D'Cru's body. D'Cru licked his dry lips and whispered, "Please don't kill me."

K'Rin slowly shoved the long blade into D'Cru's gut angling the thrust up behind the chestplate and into a lung. D'Cru exhaled and his eyes bulged. With a second push, using the palm of his hand, K'Rin buried his knife completely inside D'Cru's belly. D'Cru stepped back stiffly. He tried to probe the hole in his stomach with his fingers, delicately, like one trying to remove a splinter without causing more pain. Worry clouded his face, and he coughed a red spray.

Then K'Rin grabbed D'Cru by the shoulders, turned him around and shoved him with all his might into the prison wall. D'Cru hit the wall flat. His own invention, his antipersonnel device, sensed the breach in the field and triggered the automatic laser cannon that fired instantly with a loud buzz and the hiss of blistering flesh, the lasers burning away everything within three inches of the wall surface.

Then silence. D'Cru fell like a tree, backward. His face, his hands, chest and knees sliced away. K'Rin stood over the corpse and saw nothing but smoldering flesh and entrails. In the background he heard Har'Got's familiar voice. "Thank you, Hal K'Rin."

*　　　*　　　*

Evening fell on Klamdara. The heat abated. H'Roo Parh, Chana, and a squad of Tenebrea took one of the Jod hovercraft for aerial reconnaissance. Bal'Don met them at the landing pad when they returned. The squad members left the small craft, each carrying a heavy bundle of wood.

H'Roo reported, "We saw a dozen or so Jod marines fleeing south through the badlands."

Bal'Don asked, "Intercept?" His voice rasped the word.

"No, sir. They were no threat." H'Roo remembered their lethargic plod, most of them wounded or helping other wounded. The small cluster cast one long shadow. They didn't scatter when he flew over them; they merely looked skyward, perhaps inviting H'Roo to finish their misery. The other Tenebrea saw their jailers and prepared to unleash the hovercraft's small cannon. He remembered his surprise when Chana intervened, saying, *Let them be.*

Bal'Don showed no sign of emotion to H'Roo's answer. He gestured with his hand: *Continue.*

H'Roo said, "The *Benwoi* is where we left her. The dead Jod still surround her." H'Roo pointed to the squad, carrying the armloads of wood. "I stopped by the forested chasm, about five miles southwest. The trees are thin, but the wood is hard. We can gather wood for pyres."

Bal'Don nodded somberly, "Later. Tonight, rest. Tomorrow, prepare defense." Bal'Don swallowed hard. "The dead must wait."

Bal'Don followed H'Roo into the prison yard to see the weary Tenebrea sitting in small groups. Already they had distributed the wood to build small fires. They didn't need the heat; rather, they needed the modicum of cheerfulness and light. They ate their first substantial meal since their captivity. But they ate sparingly. Their stomachs had shrunk. Their throats still felt raw from the Quazel hardening. But the Tenebrea were in good spirits. They flexed their arms and legs, arched their backs and kneaded their hands: the enzyme had begun to cure. H'Roo found an empty place at one of the fires. He sat cross-legged on the ground and shared in the communal plate.

In the dancing shadows, the captured Jod marines huddled together, tethered to one another. They would not eat tonight.

In a separate circle, Chana and the clones mimicked the Tenebrea by building a crackling fire. However, they ate their dinner with loud conversation, reliving the day's events. So absorbed were they in their noisy and moody recollections that they were unaware of their isolation.

In the command center above the empty barracks, K'Rin sat privately with Andrea and Brigon. They sat at a small wooden table. A simple meal of flat bread and cheeses sat before them. K'Rin reached for the glass pitcher of cold water. He ate a mouthful of cheese and immediately washed it down with sips of water. Apologizing, he said, "Swallow hard. But much better." K'Rin tore a piece of the bread and handed it to Brigon, "Repay?"

Brigon accepted the bread, and offered a nod of respect that Andrea had taught him. Brigon had washed his face and combed his oily hair back, his tawny hair looking more like rust. His callused hands were clean: again, Andrea's tutelage. A bruise on his cheek showed through the thick stubble on his face. His ear was swollen. However, Brigon spoke, not as a hireling, but as a man come to collect a just debt. "We need food—a million rations immediately and then three hundred thousand each month until we can harvest a crop."

K'Rin listened impassively, then acknowledged with a nod and a word: "Food."

Brigon continued, "We need tactical communications."

"Comm-disks." K'Rin swallowed.

"We need weapons to arm twenty thousand fighters. We prefer rifles to your energy weapons."

"Difficult." K'Rin looked at Andrea, then said to Brigon, "So many *ifs*." He pointed skyward. "Dreadnought comes. I have nothing here. Take Andrea, your people. Escape."

Brigon set the piece of bread down on the table beside his empty white china plate. He repeated himself, "I came for food, tactical comms, and weapons, not your gratitude."

Andrea bristled, "Brigon!"

K'Rin lowered his eyes. He strained his voice. "I made promises; took oaths—some twisted out of shape." He looked at Andrea briefly. "Don't want more failures. I answer carefully." He looked at Brigon and swallowed to ease the pain in his throat. "I promise: first one million rations I get are yours. Comm-disks yours. First twenty thousand small arms I get are yours. You say where."

"Fair enough."

K'Rin swallowed hard. "Also, I give you deep-space comm. You report. You request. Can you hinder Cor shipbuilding?"

Andrea reached across the table and touched K'Rin's sleeve. "I'm afraid the Cor shipyard is at a colony on Lynx."

K'Rin swallowed. "I don't know Lynx."

Brigon interjected, "Lynx is the fifth planet from Cor's sun. You Jod must neutralize the Lynx factory. We can't."

K'Rin nodded. "We talk strategy later." K'Rin massaged his sore throat with his right hand. He swallowed and said, "Brigon, leave us, please. Must talk to Andrea. Alone."

Andrea stood with Brigon. "Sir, you need to rest and let the enzyme work."

"No." K'Rin waved her down. "Sit. Little time left. Must speak with you."

Brigon hesitated, then left. K'Rin waited, then resumed his seat. "Sit." He filled his glass with water and drank. "I feel the enzyme." K'Rin abruptly changed his tack. "Cousin, must talk to you about husband."

Andrea calmly reassured K'Rin. "I know all about Steve, and Eric, and you." She was glad to spare K'Rin the discomfort of speaking.

Her admission startled K'Rin. "How?"

"I took the *Benwoi* to Earth. I matched Eric's DNA with Steve's records, then got the truth from the Dewinters." Almost as an aside, she mentioned, "A Cor Ordinate Hunter team must have tracked me to Earth. They obliterated the Dewinters' house, killing the old couple inside."

K'Rin lowered his eyes somberly. "What did they tell you?"

"That you brought the Dewinters to Earth when they were refugees from Cor." Andrea smiled acerbically. "I put the pieces together. Now I understand why you wouldn't tell me the whole truth."

K'Rin prodded nervously, "What truth?"

"Steve was a prototype clone—an experiment." Andrea forced herself to tell the story without showing emotion. "Instead of canceling him at the end of the experiment, Mrs. Dewinter and her husband took Steve and fled Cor. You settled them on Earth, near Baltimore. Almost twenty years later, when you were attempting to intercept a Hunter Team operating in the Terran system, you made a detour to investigate another runaway. You found a clone, Eric—Steve's genetic double. You knew that the Hunters would mistake Steve for Eric."

K'Rin acknowledged. "True."

Andrea took a deep breath to finish. "So you raced back to Earth, but too late. The Hunters murdered Steve. And you feel that your unauthorized detour makes you responsible for Steve and Glendon's deaths." Andrea's mouth was tight as she recalled the painful facts. "I think you could have told the truth sooner and saved me a lot of heartache."

"Is that all?" K'Rin looked sad.

"Yes. Is there more I don't know?" Andrea leaned forward. Her jaw tensed.

"It's just that . . . I am responsible, and. . . ." K'Rin paused. He didn't finish his thought but reiterated, "I am responsible."

Andrea relaxed and shook her head. "The Cor Ordinate are responsible. Your error had neither malice nor intent. I must apologize to you for all the times I held you suspect, for all the times I distrusted you, and for the insults I said to you at the Yuseat Lab."

K'Rin looked across the table at Andrea's full eyes. *How often we get the facts right and the conclusions wrong.*

K'Rin looked at his folded hands on the table. Without looking up at Andrea's face, he said softly, "When I saw you cradling your murdered husband and daughter in your arms that day at the Harbor, my life changed forever—perhaps, in some ways changed as profoundly as yours." He thought, *We probably won't live to see two more sunrises. Then, the truth won't matter. She seems content, more at peace than I've ever seen her before. Let things be.*

"Changed how?" she asked.

K'Rin smiled sadly and closed his eyes, "I'm not sure. I haven't finished the change, yet."

Admiral Xi'Don entered Hal Pl'Don's office unannounced. He found Pl'Don rehearsing a short speech he planned to give to the Madame Prefect of Cor. Pl'Don's wife, Falhal R'Oueu, sat in a comfortable chair and listened. She was poised to offer a suggestion when Xi'Don entered. "Cousin!" the old admiral interrupted. Xi'Don did not allow time for anyone to complain about his breach of protocol as he blurted out the news. "K'Rin is loose!"

Pl'Don turned slowly. His neck flared purple for an instant. Then he quickly regained his composure. Pl'Don wore his saffron robe of state. His gold necklace and badge of his rank were draped over his round shoulders. "What did you say?"

Xi'Don repeated, "K'Rin is loose. With some outside help, he overthrew the Klamdara garrison."

"The Rin Clan?" Pl'Don fumed.

R'Oueu stood from her chair, straightened her

gown, and prepared to leave the room. She appeared startled by the abrupt intrusion; however, she had calmed herself in the time she needed to stand.

"Excuse me, madam." Xi'Don tried to repair his bad manners. "I didn't see you."

"You didn't look," R'Oueu answered coolly. "I shall wait for you gentlemen to finish your business."

"Stay," Pl'Don commanded respectfully. "I may need your advice."

Instead of protesting and having her way, R'Oueu obediently returned to her seat. Her eyes sparked with interest, yet she made her face a study of passive disinterest. Pl'Don knew his wife and spotted the contradiction. He set his rolled parchment, his welcoming speech, on his desk. He repeated his question, "Is this the work of the Rin Clan?"

Xi'Don furrowed his brow. "We don't know for sure who helped K'Rin. We do know that one small merchant ship registered to the Cor Ordinate, the *Benwoi*, is involved. According to the *Tyker*'s logs, reports indicated that the *Benwoi* crew was only eight renegade clones."

"Unlikely, if the rest is true." Pl'Don shook his head and asked through clenched teeth, "And what does Commander Tamor-Kyl say about these reports?"

"Tamor-Kyl is dead," Xi'Don reported without emotion. "He was on the surface during the attack."

Calmly Pl'Don asked Xi'Don, "How do you know this?"

"One of K'Rin's household guard, a H'Roo Pahr, sent a message to the Fleet by way of the *Tyker* orbiting Klamdara at the time."

Pl'Don sneered, "Seeking allies, was he? K'Rin

thinks he can effect a coup, does he? As you now see, I was prescient when I removed all the Rin from the Fleet. K'Rin's coup attempt is already a failure." He looked at R'Oueu to gauge her reaction. She was stone-faced.

Xi'Don took a deep breath. "Cousin, his message was simple."

"Go on."

"H'Roo Parh claimed to be an eyewitness—claims he was on the planet Cor, saw the Cor Ordinate assembling a fleet of small ships to attack us."

Pl'Don wrinkled his nose. "The Pahr have always sided with the Rin. I don't believe it."

"The message simply warns the Fleet to disperse—not a bad precaution. Sir, we are extremely vulnerable at present. In our present parade formation, five of our dreadnoughts cannot use their port or starboard cannons. We are so close that our shields would create harmonic rifts, canceling our only passive defense. Sir, the Admiralty staff recommends that we err on the side of caution and disperse into a more tactically sound formation."

Pl'Don folded his hands with his fingertips together. "K'Rin is persistent: I'll give him that. Clever, too. If we take K'Rin's precautionary advice, the Cor Ordinate will come into our system and find us in a tactical mode—*precisely what we promised we would not do!* They will turn and flee back to Cor, and we will have the war that K'Rin has wished on us. K'Rin knows this. He knows that war discredits me and empowers him. If we break our promise with the Cor now, we lose everything." He turned to his wife and baited her, "Isn't that right, my dear?"

R'Oueu cut her eyes away. Her smooth scalp

wrinkled at the brow, and she pressed her purplish lips tightly together.

Xi'Don asked, "What shall I tell the Admiralty?"

Pl'Don pointed his finger to the ceiling. "If any ship moves an inch, raises a shield, or powers its weapons, I will personally court-martial the captain of that ship and recommend life imprisonment."

Xi'Don bowed slightly to indicate his concurrence, or at least obedience. "And what shall I do with Hal K'Rin?"

Pl'Don made a sour face hearing K'Rin's rank restored. "I want him dead. Send one—*just one*—of the dreadnoughts to Klamdara. That much I can explain away to the Cor Ordinate. Blast him and his Tenebrea out of existence."

"Cousin," Xi'Don contradicted Pl'Don. "The Klamdara fortress lies beneath a solid rock shield and they have a Class IV long-range cannon. We cannot trade blows with them."

Pl'Don waved his arms in exasperation. "I'm not a military man. You handle the details, but kill him, do you hear me? I want that warmongering pretender dead. I want his atoms scattered across Klamdara." Pl'Don's voice cracked with emotion. "I don't want any half measures: no surrender, no negotiation. Before the Cor delegation leaves, I want to assure them that we have eliminated the last resistance to a lasting peace. You shall bring me news of K'Rin's death within seventy-two hours, understood?"

"Yes, cousin. We shall need to use marines."

"Then send a whole division." Pl'Don shook a fist at Xi'Don. "Send your most trustworthy captain, someone who will carry out my orders without compunction. I want K'Rin dead!"

"Would you like me to personally go to Klamdara?"

Pl'Don thought for a moment. "No. I'm afraid K'Rin may have infected the senior officers with his lies. I want you to personally oversee the discipline of the Fleet. The Ordinate arrive late tomorrow. You make it known that the slightest deviation from my orders is treasonous. You will immediately relieve any officer who even suggests a deviation from our stated intent to the Cor. If necessary, you may execute the malefactor on the spot."

Xi'Don bowed slightly and excused himself. "I'll send the *Kopshir* commanded by T'Pan-Cru."

Pl'Don approved. "T'Pan is kin to Commandant D'Cru. Good choice."

When the door closed behind Xi'Don, Pl'Don turned to his wife. "You don't seem very disturbed by the news."

"I am," she contradicted him. The soft light of a wall sconce lit her face. "K'Rin's message disturbs me greatly." She sat straight in her chair.

"Really? I think you are disturbed because I am going to kill K'Rin this time."

Annoyed at the prodding, R'Oueu answered, "I always knew one of you would eventually kill the other."

Pl'Don prodded. "I see. Then, you are just disappointed in the outcome."

"Don't insult me: I am your wife." R'Oueu rose. She spoke with cold reserve. "However, I believe K'Rin's message. He is not such a fool as to notify you of his escape unless his concern for Jod was greater than his concern for his own safety. He did not liberate himself just to annoy you, husband. I believe him. I believe that the Cor Ordinate intend to attack as he says. You are making a grave mistake. Your blind jealousy will ruin everything."

In fury, Pl'Don raised a fist to strike R'Oueu. She stood and glared back, contemptuously, daring him to disgrace himself by putting a mark on his wife. His neck flared red and he cursed his wife with a string of epithets ending, "Get out! Get out!"

R'Oueu left quickly—decisively. At her nearby apartment, she quietly gathered a purse of jewels that she might use for money. She dressed in warm, practical clothes, then walked out of Heptar. She descended the obsidian butte. Carrying her purse and a simple blanket roll, she walked through the city and straight for the mountains. Lost in the foothills, she found the fresh water springs she had visited as a girl, when she and the young K'Rin had talked of marriage—back when the old Rin was First Among Equals on the council, long ago when she was happy.

K'Rin brought his staff together in the Klamdara command center. He invited Andrea, Brigon, and Eric as well. He opened the short meeting saying, "The dreadnought *Kopshir* is stationed on the other side of Klamdara. They landed a reinforced division. Tomorrow that division will descend on us with air, mobile cannon, and infantry. We have a good defensive position and a big gun, but I won't lie to you: our chances are slim."

K'Rin walked over to Andrea and Brigon. "We owe you our lives. You two can still escape with your friends. You might get away in the *Benwoi* and escape to Earth."

Brigon listened impassively. Andrea replied, "I'm staying. You are the only family I have left."

"You honor me." K'Rin shut his eyes for a moment.

Brigon looked around the room and said, "Then I'm staying, too. I'm used to bad odds."

Andrea grabbed Brigon by the arm. "No. You should go."

"Not a chance." Brigon smiled wryly. "I've got too much invested here. The admiral owes me a million rations and twenty thousand rifles. And you—you just owe me."

K'Rin pressed the agenda forward, "Then let's make our plans." He unfurled a paper map of the area.

At dawn, Andrea stood atop the wall and looked over the plain. She, like the others, had worked through the night improving gun placements, laying aiming stakes, and buttressing their fortifications. She saw Eric enter the laser cannon bunker, now *his* cannon. He had managed to jerry-rig the delicate aiming mechanism to allow the cannon to fire at ground targets.

Looking down from the wall, she saw all the Klamdara marines: dead and prisoners alike, tied hand and foot to the iron stakes below the wall. All wore helmets with face shields down. Both the dead and the living stood still. But the living held their heads up watching the skies. The dead dropped their chins to their chests in their eternal repose.

K'Rin disliked Brigon's solution for handling the prisoners. Brigon's argument, however, was solid: "We can't spare men to guard the prisoners inside the fortress. We can't simply turn them loose outside the fortress." H'Roo was even more appalled about Brigon's barbaric plan to prop the Jod dead onto the iron stakes, but Brigon rebuffed him: *The dead are certainly past caring. And maybe they'll cause the infantry to hesitate.*

To Andrea's right and left, the wall was lined with Tenebrea and clones interspersed with rifles. Even the wounded took a position. She counted their numbers: one hundred seventy-eight against a marine division of ten thousand. *Fifty-six to one.* Even K'Rin and Bal'-Don bore rifles near the center of the wall. K'Rin had said, "There won't be a lot of management required for this fight, just kill everything you see. They will use mass and shock to ferret us out."

Mass and shock. Andrea looked over the horizon. *Expect a race to the wall with land cruisers and infantry combined. Expect gunships to fly at us at 200 miles per hour. Expect gel flame.* Andrea looked down the encasement at the Jod tied to the iron stakes. *Poor bastards.*

H'Roo stood at the slot next to her. "Andrea," he vied for her attention.

"Yes, H'Roo?" She kept her eyes forward.

"What do you want to do when we get out of here?"

"Haven't given the matter much thought," she answered. "Have you?"

"I'm going back to Gyre to see my mother. You know what my father told me just before he died?"

"No, I can't imagine." Andrea had never heard H'Roo talk about his father before. However, she remembered H'Roo's mother, the formidable matriarch of the Parh clan.

"I had just started my second ring—about fourteen years old." H'Roo translated biological time for Andrea. "My father was sick, dying, it turns out. Knowing my interest in military matters and my supreme ennui for business, he told me: *Son, stay away from the Fleet. You'll just get yourself killed. And you won't make any money.*"

Andrea kept her eye on the horizon but smiled wanly. "Well, he was right about the money, but I think he'll forgive you if you prove him wrong on the first point. I don't think my father ever forgave me for not joining the service." She rested her chin on the battlement. "And look at me now."

"He'd be proud of you now."

"He died in the Patagonian revolt . . ." Andrea saw three columns of billowing dust sprouting like mushrooms on the horizon. "Here they come!"

Three gunships hovered above advancing columns. With parade precision, the columns spread into a broad front. Twenty landcruisers rumbled to the front and innumerable men dotted the desert. Then she saw a carefully orchestrated flash from every weapon out there and she felt the heavy Klamdara wall tremble from the impact of so much directed energy. She blinked, then saw the mass racing across the desert at them. The gunships broke away, leading the charge. K'Rin's voice yelled above the din. "Hold your fire until they come in range!"

The long-range cannon was the first to answer the assault. Crimson blasts chewed up the desert floor. Eric missed with his first shots, but he learned quickly. He found his range on the advancing cruisers that carefully maintained a precise hundred-meter distance between them, greatly compensating for his meager gunnery skills. He began killing the enemy from left to right.

The gunships raked the walls with laser fire. The Tenebrea returned concentrated rifle fire, downing one of the gunships. *Gel flame!* A cry erupted along the wall. The Tenebrea ducked down and pressed themselves against the wall. The two surviving gunships disgorged round bombs that splashed at the base of the wall, some bounding over the wall into the unoccupied fortress. A blistering heat rose at Andrea's face and behind her back. She could not see through the black smoke. She winced as she heard a pitiful wail from the prisoners below.

The space above Heptar was quiet. The two Jod moons were thin parallel crescents. Hanging in synchronous orbit, six dreadnoughts slipped through the vacuum like a string of pearls, their bows pointed toward the multicolored planet below. The dreadnoughts were pod-shaped, with a bulbous bow and truncated aft. Their hulls were smooth except for the underbelly where landing bays jutted down like a marsupial's pouch. Most of the portholes were dark as the crews enjoyed a festive shore leave in Heptar below. In attendance to the six sleeping behemoths, a score of equally drowsy cruisers and destroyers lay in ranks, according to their class.

Xi'Don solved his problem of maintaining command and control by enforcing an invitation to an officers' call. *All admirals and ships' captains plus senior staff shall by order of the council attend a reception in Pl'Don's private garden. The reception honors Hal Pl'Don, the Fleet, and the forthcoming*

Peace. One ship's captain demurred and Xi'Don relieved him of command on the spot. Xi'Don remained on the flagship the *Lijstar* to superintend the remaining duty officers spread throughout the Fleet.

The remaining duty officers—the unlucky ones—left aboard the idle dreadnoughts listened to the open transmission of the conflict developing forty million miles away. The captain of the *Kopshir* had a reputation for brutal efficiency—in this case punishing efficiently. The *Kopshir* and her attached division would avenge the humiliating loss of the Klamdara garrison. To a man, they wished that their ship had been pulled from the line to fight at Klamdara—not so much because they craved a good fight, but because the stagnation of the standdown was driving many of the officers and crew crazy with boredom.

chapter 8

Admiral Brulk stood at the bridge of his command ship, waiting for the final minutes to count down. His virtual display showed the spread of his J-Class attack ships grouped in eighty squadrons of five ships. His staff had practiced for this moment in simulators a thousand times. The NewGen clones piloting the attack ships were programmed throughout their incubation to recognize the seams in the Jod defenses, attack the power plants, and inflict the greatest damage—all data supplied by the Chelle.

Brulk's pulse quickened. *Less than a minute*. He reminded his bridge, "When we leave FTL drive for kinetics, maintain attack speed. I want an immediate count of our attack ships. Arm their quark torpedoes."

"Sir," the operations officer acknowledged. "We resume kinetic speeds in three . . . two . . . one."

The foreword screen blinked once, then showed the planet Jod looming toward them. The Jod Fleet seemed small at such a distance, but Brulk understood that the mere fact that he could see the ships attested to their incredible size. In front and below, Brulk saw his swarm of attack craft.

"All ships accounted for. All systems armed."

Brulk calmly gave the word. "Attack." He opened his mind to record everything about the moment. *For this I was born.*

Brulk's command ship slowed to watch the assault from a safe distance. "Magnify screen twenty times." He sat down in his chair and folded his hands in his lap. Before him his attack craft swarmed like hornets attacking lumbering beasts. In a moment he'd see them chew huge holes with their quark torpedoes fired at point-blank range.

Xi'Don sat in the captain's chair of the *Lijstar*, nervously watching the tactical displays. He got up to pace the floor, only to sit down again. He spoke to no one and gruffly dismissed the yeoman who offered him a light supper.

Lieutenants milled about the bridge trying to stay out of the way. They didn't know the Admiralty Chief of Staff, nor did they care to meet him in his present state of mind.

The tactical screen lit up. He saw the larger registration, Brulk's ship, and his first thought was one of relief: *Better early than late . . . at least they're here.* He reached over to his console to send a notice to the council at Heptar, when he saw hundreds of small unidentified blips, more than he could count. They formed a cloud of data on the screen—unidentified J-Class attack ships—moving with reckless speed toward the Fleet. Estimated arrival fourteen seconds. Xi'Don's heart sank. He pressed the broadcast button: "Battle stations! Battle stations! Shields up! Everyone get under way!"

Even as he spoke, Xi'Don already knew the futility of his order. *The senior officers are absent—ordered to Pl'Don's reception. The ensigns won't know what to do. The skeleton crews can't react fast enough. Nobody could react fast enough.* He saw one of the J-Class ships collide into the dreadnought *Zat-Mar* with a blinding flash, tearing a gaping hole. A second Cor ship flew inside the terrible wound, creating an explosion in the heart of the ship. The blast shoved the giant sideways, crashing slowly into a neighboring dreadnought. Xi'Don's own ship shuddered from multiple explosions. The lights on the bridge flickered and dimmed.

Xi'Don turned to his screen and saw a small black ship hurtling at him, obviously with no intent of turning to avoid the imminent collision.

Oil lanterns illuminated the roof garden. The lights of Heptar sparkled below. Sumptuous tables offered every delicacy known to Jod. Waiters carried trays of wine and liquor, offering glasses to the guests. The civilians drank. The uniformed guests stonily refused.

Pl'Don beamed with hospitality for the assembled brass. "This is a beautiful night, isn't it? Not a cloud to obstruct our view of the Fleet."

Captain Ter'Gem looked up and replied stiffly, "Yes, sir."

"I see you and your colleagues are particularly abstemious tonight." Pl'Don held his glass in front of the captain's face. "Tonight is a cause for celebration." Pl'Don sipped his amber wine. "Good wine."

"I'm not thirsty, sir. Will you excuse me?" Captain Ter'Gem bowed slightly.

"No, I don't excuse you, Captain." Pl'Don's voice turned to ice. "I will dismiss you when I am through with our conversation, not before."

"I apologize." Ter'Gem stood woodenly. He looked at the night sky. "Protocol has always been a failing of mine, so my wife tells me."

"Where is your wife?" Pl'Don asked.

"She is probably just rising from her sleep on the other side of Jod. We have a small villa on the coast of Izimar. Where is your wife, Falhal R'Oueu?"

Pl'Don handed his empty glass to a passing waiter and said with practiced indifference, "She's not feeling well tonight."

Ter'Gem plucked a full glass from the waiter's tray. "A pity. I'll drink to her improved health." Ter'Gem sipped the wine.

Suddenly the garden became light as day. Ter'Gem looked up at the blinding light in the sky, a flash of blue brilliance. The civilians in the crowd gasped in admiration of the show and began to applaud tastefully.

A gravelly voice in the back rebuked the crowd, "You idiots! That was my ship. That was the *Lijstar*!"

The heavens blazed with many silent flashes. Blue rings expanded suddenly, wavered and collapsed. The uniformed guests ran for the stairs. "To our ships!"

Ter'Gem stood and watched. Excited officers jostled him as they ran past. He said bitterly, "It will be over before they reach the bottom of the stairs." Tears began to run down his cheeks, reflecting the flashes of light. Without turning to look at Pl'Don he said, "You vain fool. Hal K'Rin was right. We are ruined."

Pl'Don staggered back with each flash. "Impossible." He muttered, "It can't be." Pl'Don turned and ran into the palace.

Ter'Gem's aide bumped into Pl'Don on his way to Ter'Gem's side. Out of breath, the aide asked, "Your orders, Captain?"

Ter'Gem bowed his head not in protocol but in grief. "Send a message. Recall the dreadnought *Kopshir*. Inform Captain T'Pan."

"Any orders for Captain T'Pan?" The flashes reflected in the excited aide's wide eyes.

"No. Just tell him what you've seen tonight. The *Kopshir* is our last dreadnought."

The aide ran away, and Ter'Gem found himself alone in the garden. He found a tray of full glasses, then sat down on a wooden bench and began drinking. Looking up, he saw a huge multicolored ball of flame slashing the night sky from east to west. A crippled dreadnought came streaking through the atmosphere. The ball exploded, creating a rain of fire that disappeared over the horizon.

After an eternity of thirty seconds, the billowing black smoke cleared. Andrea peeked over the parapet for a glimpse and immediately ducked, just in time to avoid a barrage of energy bolts that battered the wall. She looked at H'Roo squatting on his haunches with his back to the wall. He said, in his typically sardonic tone, "You take the five hundred on the right."

She took a deep breath, then rose to her firing slot and began picking targets. All along the wall the

Tenebrea fired with fatalistic abandon. They decimated the wave of infantry storming the wall. But hundreds more reached the wall. She saw the landcruisers, all twenty, burning as hulks. Eric, with his cannon, had managed to slow the second echelon.

A grappling hook flew over Andrea's left shoulder and purchased a grip in the stone. She drew her handlance while continuing her rifle fire. A soldier in full body armor pulled himself onto the wall, still holding onto the thin line. Andrea fired with her handlance into his chest with minimal effect. The soldier slipped but recovered his balance. Andrea drew her dagger and thrust it into his midsection, shoving him with all her might from the wall.

She saw him fall into the charred remains of the prisoners tied to the iron stakes below. With a glance she saw that the first wave of attackers was broken. The withering fire ended, and the Tenebrea frantically checked for gaps in their line.

Below, the dead and wounded cluttered the base of the wall. Whereas the infantry had abandoned their attempt to breach the wall, they continued to attack the bunker in order to silence the long-range cannon. She saw one soldier stick a plastic shape-charge to the bunker door and run away, only to fall to the fire from the wall. The blast seemed superfluous in the storm of violence. But when the smoke cleared, she saw that the blast had reduced the thick concrete to a web of reinforcing bar.

Eric! Andrea saw Eric stumble from the bunker door, disoriented. He fell facedown in the dirt. He tried to crawl, but collapsed. She saw the second wave, two hundred meters away, running and firing on the move.

"H'Roo!" she called as she put on her gloves.

"What?"

"Give me your handlance and cover me."

"Why?" H'Roo threw her his handlance, which she stuffed in her belt.

She grabbed the line from the grappling hook and jumped over the wall. "Open the small door at the gate in one minute." She rappelled to the ground in two bounds. Her hands were blistered from the friction, but she dismissed the pain as irrelevant. She ran, crouched low like a hunted deer to Eric.

Gunfire rang in her ears. The smell of gunpowder and death was too familiar. The chaos, the fear, the violence . . . She felt disoriented. She dropped to her knees over the injured man. *Steve?* Andrea turned him over. *You're alive. You didn't leave me.*

She tried to shake him into consciousness. "Steve. Wake up. Steve! They're coming!"

Andrea looked around at the familiar scene. She saw the blue sky and water at the Baltimore Harbor, and the people scattering at the sound of gunfire. The brick steps led up from the pier to the cafe. The Hunters' other victims lay bleeding on the ground. She quickly assessed her options. She dragged Steve backward to a shallow moat by the iron stakes. Her head throbbed with confusion.

Cor Hunters! She saw the pitiless eyes and the cruel faces. *I won't let them get you.* Crouching over Steve and Glendon, she fired, shattering one Hunter's face. Again she fired as the Hunters came, one after another. They fell before her. She wounded another Hunter who lunged for her. She dispatched him with her knife, driving it into the Hunter's neck. *Come on, you bastards. I'll kill you all!* Andrea dropped another Hunter with a handlance blast. He struggled to his feet and she fired again, hitting the Hunter in the face.

She called, "Steve! I'm sorry! There are too many of them!" Andrea fired frantically at the horde running at her. *Hopeless.* Andrea covered Steve with her body, draping her arm over him like a wing and holding his unconscious body to her breast. She whispered, "At least we'll die together . . . ."

But suddenly the horde stopped. They turned and retreated as fast as they had come. A voice from the wall yelled, "Cease fire! Cease fire!"

Andrea looked up, surprised to be alive. She saw K'Rin standing on the wall looking down at her with sad eyes. His aide, Kip, was speaking. All too familiar. But K'Rin was not standing with the backdrop of tall buildings behind him. Andrea looked around, confused. *A dream?* The Harbor was gone. The fortress wall was ragged with damage. Behind her, in the distance, the Jod infantry withdrew.

H'Roo opened the small door at the gate and called her name, "Andrea!" H'Roo's voice was a mix of rebuke and concern. Standing over her, he said quietly, "Andrea, you nearly got yourself killed for a clone. We can't replace you."

"A clone?" Andrea looked at the man lying beneath her. She looked at the dead infantry lying around her: not Cor Hunters but Jod infantry. She muttered in disappointment, "Eric." But even as she muttered his name, she rebuked herself. *My Steve was a clone—a person. No less.*

Eric opened his eyes, then winced in pain. She saw the burns and shrapnel wounds on his body.

His shredded tunic was wet with blood. Looking up, she said, "H'Roo, help me get him inside."

H'Roo ran to Andrea and helped her carry Eric into the fort. H'Roo told her the news: "The Cor Ordinate attacked the Jod Fleet above Heptar. The *Kopshir* recalled its forces. We have no damage assessment. Communications to Heptar are quiet."

Andrea was interested only in the problem lying in her hands. "Get some water and bandages. Get someone here to close these wounds." She pointed at Eric. H'Roo obeyed.

Andrea took her knife and began cutting away Eric's tunic. She sliced it from the neck to the waist, exposing a dozen oozing wounds. She felt the lumps where shards of concrete lay buried in his flesh. Eric's eyes opened. He saw the knife cutting above his chest and he raised an arm to stop Andrea. He muttered, "Stop."

"It's okay. I'm helping you." Andrea began cutting away the sleeve on his left arm, tearing away the cloth from the shoulder to the wrist. Eric struggled, trying to resist.

Andrea firmly pinned his shoulder to the ground. But she said tenderly, "We've got to see the extent of your wounds." She thought, *He's delirious. He thinks I'm trying to kill him.*

Eric was too weak to struggle. He groaned and turned his head aside to look away, pathetically resigned to his fate. Andrea finished cutting the length of the sleeve to the wrist and lay the wet cloth open. His arm was thick with glutinous blood. Then, she saw a curious mark on the underside of his wrist: circle within a circle—a tattoo. *I've seen that mark before: a bright yellow disk with blue halo—on a man's wrist. Many clones wore tattoos to distinguish themselves: Tara's gull wing, Eric's concentric rings yellow in blue.*

Andrea remembered. She'd seen the mark on Cor computers—the execute key. *And—* Andrea felt dizzy. She crouched on all fours as the flood of memories assailed her: that day at Baltimore Harbor. She heard Steve's voice: *Andi.* She watched Steve lead Glendon up the steps, all smiles. Steve picks at an acrylic mark on his wrist and says, *Did you see that street vendor pestering us? The one with the purple hair—slapped this stupid tattoo on my wrist, then tried to hustle me for two slips.*

Andrea backed away from Eric. Still on her hands and knees she looked at the ground. *A yellow disk with a blue halo. Not an accident.* Andrea felt dizzy, trying to put the pieces together. *The clown at the harbor marked Steve with Eric's mark. Only one reason—to mark Steve for the Hunters—to make sure that they killed him instead of Eric. Who knew? Who else knew Eric's mark? Who else could profit from Steve's murder?*

She felt her chest tighten, she could barely breathe. She looked at Eric lying on the ground with his distinguishing mark, looking feebly back at her.

Tears of rage welled up in her eyes. Every nerve in her body burned. She whispered, "K'Rin knew." She spun around looking at the Tenebrea and the clones milling about the prison yard. K'Rin stood atop the wall, giving orders to Bal'Don. She stood and yelled over the din, "K'Rin!" The venom in her voice stopped all activity, and every eye turned to her. She pointed up to him and yelled with murderous intent. "You bastard!"

Tears poured down her cheeks as she started walking toward the object of her wrath. She unsheathed her blade. The Tenebrea gathered around to stare at this aberrant display.

Kip ran through the prison yard to see what had happened. He took one look at Eric, then at Andrea. He ordered soldiers to form a barrier at the foot of the steps.

Andrea pointed her knife at K'Rin and challenged him. "You coward! Come face me. You killed my husband! You set him up."

No one else made a sound. Brigon and H'Roo ran to Andrea from opposite directions, but she marched deliberately toward the steps with fury in her face.

H'Roo got between her and the steps. "Andrea, you mustn't . . ."

"Out of my way, Jod." She slashed at him with her blade, opening a shallow cut across his chest. H'Roo did not defend himself but backed away. He ran to Brigon, "You've got to stop her. The Tenebrea will not let her near K'Rin. She's a dead woman if she tries. Here . . ." H'Roo pressed the *Benwoi*'s data cubes into Brigon's hands. "Take her to the Terran system. I'll find you somehow. Trust me."

"K'Rin!" Andrea's voice echoed from the cave ceiling.

K'Rin started down the steps. His face was ashen. A throng of Tenebrea closed ranks around him. They brandished their weapons, waiting for a command. But K'Rin said nothing.

"You killed my husband and my baby. Then you used me, you lying bastard!" Andrea's voice was choked with anger. She shuddered with rage. "Come down here and let me cut your heart out and show you how small it is." Her tears blurred her vision and she wiped them away on her sleeve.

Still, K'Rin said nothing. His nervous soldiers waited. Bal'Don asked, "Sir, your orders." K'Rin stood silent. Kip remonstrated, "Sir, she threatened your life. We must take her out before she harms you."

Brigon stepped in front of Andrea. "Let's get out of here." He grabbed her arm and she wrestled herself free and brandished her weapon at him.

Brigon ignored the threatening blade, stepped in and grabbed her arms. He looked into her wet eyes and whispered, "Don't throw yourself away. Not today, Andrea. Not today."

Andrea looked at Brigon. Her heart was broken with grief—a grief that made her rage impotent. Brigon and his surviving wilderness clones huddled around her and ushered her toward the Klamdara gate. Andrea resisted. Chana, Ariko, and the others spoke to her. "Come with us. We'll help you make things right."

At the iron gate, she turned around and said bitterly, "You are a dead man. I'll come back for you, K'Rin. But the next time we meet, I'll kill you. If it's the last thing I do, I'll kill you." Andrea dropped her knife to the ground, with the Triskelion Crest of the Rin Clan facing up.

Kip said angrily, "Sir, we must finish her. She is a serious threat to your person. You heard her. Give me the word and I'll slay her."

The small band of clones followed Andrea and Brigon through the small door in the iron gate. K'Rin said, "No Tenebrea shall harm Andrea."

"But, sir!" Kip protested, "she threatened to kill you."

K'Rin told him in stark terms, "Leave her alone. If Andrea Flores really wanted me dead, I would be dead." He raised his voice for all his Tenebrea to hear, "I forbid any of you to lift a finger to harm Andrea Flores. I owe her my life and my honor, as do you."

chapter 9

The Tenebrea stood in a long row on a flat plot of ground near the deep chasm. Away from the battleground, the fortress Klamdara looked austere but serene. The red cliffs rose majestically toward a deep blue sky. Yet every Tenebrea standing knew that more strife awaited in their future than lay in their past. They learned that they owed their sudden reprieve—the *Kopshir*'s surprised flight—to the attack on the Fleet above Heptar. Word of the Fleet's destruction left them feeling more vulnerable than ever.

K'Rin passed a torch to the youngest Tenebrea. The young warrior's tunic was torn, his pants frayed at the ankles. A rugged sheath and hand-fabricated knife hung on his belt where in happier times he had worn the ceremonial dagger of the Rin Clan. But he stood erect, unperturbed by his deprivation. He carried the torch down the long line of Tenebrea standing shoulder to shoulder according to rank. They faced a massive pyre of hardwood, gathered and stacked eight feet high, a trapezoidal base tapering to a table—more like an altar.

On the pyre lay the Tenebrea dead, shoulder to shoulder in their ragged uniforms. Interspersed among the Tenebrea—by K'Rin's order—were the slain clones. K'Rin had answered the muted protests, especially Kip's, by saying: *They joined our ranks in death.*

H'Roo disapproved, but said nothing.

The young Tenebrea marched along the pyre lighting stacks of kindling that burst into bright yellow flame. Then he returned to his end of the long row.

In minutes the flames roared twenty feet in the air without much smoke. The only breeze on Klamdara's surface was the intense draw from the fire. The living Tenebrea stood for the ritual hour facing the searing heat. The pyre crumpled in on itself, sending a shower of sparks into the air.

K'Rin gave the order to retire, and the Tenebrea marched slowly back to the fortress.

Waiting on the landing pad were six shuttles. Five bore the insignia of the dreadnought *Kopshir*. One heralded from the *Tyker*.

The shuttle crews stood around gawking at the carnage that lay around the fort and in the fields. K'Rin approached the ranking officer Captain T'Pan-Cru, who saluted. K'Rin returned the salute, asking, "Are we now fighting for the same side?"

"Yes, Admiral." T'Pan took his first look at the carnage strewn about the field. "My compliments to your Tenebrea."

K'Rin said, "It isn't good for your troops to see this killing ground." He motioned to the bodies strewn on the field.

"Perhaps it is good, Admiral K'Rin, that they see

your handiwork displayed so graphically. They will need confidence in your ability, not your affection," T'Pan spoke stiffly. He stood taller than K'Rin. He had a square face with defined temples, an equine nose, high cheekbones, and a large jaw. His eyes were dark green, a rarity among the Jod. "Where is my uncle, Commandant D'Cru? I could not find his body among the dead."

K'Rin pointed at the gate. "What's left of him is near the inside wall. He is the cadaver missing hands and face."

"Are you sure?"

"Yes, Captain. I killed Pel D'Cru." K'Rin paused to study T'Pan's reaction. "You'll find my knife still buried in his gut." K'Rin chose his words specifically to provoke T'Pan.

T'Pan's face hardened. "I will spare my mother the details of her brother's death." Then he observed, "You resent me for attacking you and your household guard, don't you?"

K'Rin smiled inwardly. *He won't be provoked easily.* "You followed your orders as you saw fit."

"Nor do I resent that you did your duty—as you saw fit." T'Pan cleared his throat. "You were right about the Cor Ordinate, of course. You risked your new freedom in a last attempt to warn the Fleet. Every officer out there—" T'Pan raised his eyes to the sky, "trusts you to put the Fleet's welfare above your own."

"Do you trust me?" K'Rin asked. "We may end up fighting side by side."

T'Pan smiled bitterly. "I trust both your judgment and your ability. I even trust your motives." T'Pan demurred slightly and stated as fact, "I doubt we'll be fighting side by side."

K'Rin took T'Pan's comment as a rebuff. "We may have little choice in the matter. The Fleet will need all the experience we have."

T'Pan looked down and shook his head ruefully, "More than you think, sir. I arrived at Heptar too late to participate in the battle. Not only did the Cor Ordinate burn all our capital ships, they attacked Heptar. We scoured the ruins and found few survivors. The council no longer exists. Hal Pl'Don, all the council, most of the assembly, and the entire Admiralty were killed in the Cor raid on Heptar. You are the ranking Hal in the system. You, sir, are the surviving senior officer in the Fleet, and you are at present the government of Jod."

K'Rin looked up at the taller T'Pan with incredulity. "What did you say? How bad was the destruction at Heptar?"

"Admiral, the Cor raid reduced the government and military facilities to rubble. Civilian casualties exceed three hundred thousand."

K'Rin furrowed his brow. "That would account for every soul in Heptar."

"You will soon see for yourself, Heptar is a total ruin. The Cor's quark torpedoes cut hundred-meter bowls of mass and created an overpressure and blast that flattened the city. The old stone structures blew apart like chaff in a hurricane. Sir, even the obsidian butte that was the foundation of the palace is chewed to pieces."

K'Rin held up his finger to pause T'Pan's report. He thought, *Of course. We would never use quark weapons—too volatile, too dangerous to have aboard a capital ship. The slightest slip and the whole ship and crew is destroyed. But the Cor have disposable ships and disposable crews. They can use this horrific technology.* K'Rin asked, "Do we have any contact with Heptar at all?"

"None. We lost our central operations and intelligence centers. We are for the moment deaf, dumb, and blind. All we have are sketchy reports from our small patrol ships and the merchant marine. I have already sent word to outlying commands to route all ops and intel traffic to the *Kopshir*."

"Good." K'Rin pursed his lips.

"Meanwhile, the civilians on Jod and throughout the colonies are in a panic. We even hear unsubstantiated rumors of Chelle incursions along the frontier."

"You can bet the Chelle had a hand in this whole affair." K'Rin looked at the ground. So much of the solace of his vindication evaporated with each report of the Jod's stinging defeat.

T'Pan squared his shoulders and faced K'Rin. "I wish to speak on a related matter. May I be frank?"

How can he be more frank than he already has? K'Rin looked at the taller officer concealing his own wonderment. Three days earlier they competed in a death struggle. K'Rin knew that T'Pan with his heavier cannon and superior force would have prevailed had he not abandoned the field to race back to Jod. K'Rin looked over the hills and saw the rising smoke from the funeral pyre burning itself out. He saw the dead Jod infantry lying about, contorted. K'Rin looked at T'Pan again. *Is this how we do it? We clear the field like we would a chessboard. We write off the battles like a game; enmities become a mutual experience from which we build alliances. But I cannot hate T'Pan if he will not hate me.* "Yes, Captain. Speak your mind."

"I will completely understand if you relieve me from the *Kopshir*. If I were in your place, I would have misgivings about Pel D'Cru's nephew. Therefore, I expect that you will staff all your ships with officers from the Rin Clan—especially my *Kopshir*, your only dreadnought in service." He paused and waited for K'Rin's response.

"A practical consideration for certain." K'Rin looked back into T'Pan's dark green eyes. The four rings beneath the eyes glistened, supposedly a sign of a passionate nature.

T'Pan's neck brightened with an orange tinge of anxiety. He said, "Sir, I am neither sentimental, nor political. I can serve you as well as I served Hal Pl'Don, because I serve my ship and my crew first. Please do not retire me to the surface. Give me a fighting ship, a destroyer even."

K'Rin pursed his lips and looked at the two shuttles aligned on the landing pad. The compact captain's gig bore the markings for the *Kopshir* and the name T'Pan-Cru. The *Tyker*'s shuttle was nameless. K'Rin needed time to think. "I shall consider your request."

"Thank you. I can ask nothing more." T'Pan's neck resumed a calmer color.

"In the meantime," K'Rin changed the subject, "we must go immediately to Heptar, to assess our situation and reconstitute the government. I'll travel aboard the *Tyker*. Transport the Tenebrea on the *Kopshir*. And, Captain T'Pan . . . ."

"Yes, sir."

"Leave a burial detail behind."

On his return to the Cor system, Brulk felt naked, almost lonely without the ships and NewGens he'd spent in his dazzling raid. He passed a thin picket on the Cor frontier: a handful of light cruisers and a dozen other aging ships. Most of the older security vessels no longer had operational FTL drives. Nevertheless, Brulk consented to deploy them with the cruisers just to humor the Madame Prefect. Fortunately, the Jod had no idea that the Cor Ordinate was disadvantaged in military space vessels, especially in large capital ships.

Brulk smiled at his own success. *I have made capital ships obsolete.* His raid had forever changed the paradigm of space engagements. Expendable crews in small attack ships would determine space battles in the future—not long-range gunnery and shields.

Brulk made a brief detour to the Lynx Colony to inspect the shipyard. He had left with four hundred eighty J-Class craft and he returned with none. He landed his command craft between the Lynx shipbuilding and munitions factories. Four new J-Class craft stood on the tarmac in the dim artificial light. He saw hundreds of large men moving material or welding seams. The men had identical good looks, strong and self-assured NewGen clones. They didn't pause their work to acknowledge Admiral Brulk's arrival.

However, the handful of Cor Ordinate citizens rushed to him to confirm the official announcements from Sarhn. The plant supervisor effused, "Admiral Brulk, you honor us by visiting us first."

"I came to thank you personally."

The supervisor was a thin man with intense eyes and wild hair. His affect was a sharp contrast to Brulk's military bearing. He was a scientist, now a manager and engineer with a sense of the great events swirling around his work. He, like Brulk, understood that small Cor stood alone against the combined strength of the Alliance. With technology and bold execution, they had triumphed. His contribution to the success added to his euphoria. The supervisor asked ebulliently, "Is it true? Did we win so completely?"

Brulk stood beneath a light hanging from a long wire. He nodded with a reserved smile. "Yes. Discounting a few minor unresolved issues, we can say the operation was a complete success." Brulk held his smile in place as well as his misgivings. *The seventh dreadnought—where was it? Where is it now?* Brulk said, "Your ships performed perfectly. In fact, we had enough to spare to assault their capital city."

The supervisor grinned, "Sir, your strategy!"

Brulk interrupted, almost rudely. "We haven't time for self-congratulation—not yet." He asked, "How are the NewGens working in your assembly plant?"

"Better than I could have hoped. They work longer shifts and make fewer mistakes. If you can procure the raw materials for us, I can, with a few modifications to the assembly line, double the output of J-Class attack ships. You can count on six, perhaps eight, ships per week."

"Good. Eight ships is a good start. You'll have everything you need. If you give me ten ships per week, you—more than any other citizen of Cor—will ensure our success, and I promise that you and your staff shall have the credit."

The supervisor blushed. "You are too generous."

"I don't think so." Brulk finally allowed his plaster

smile to soften. "Never forget, we are in a war now. We need munitions as fast as Lynx can supply them."

Brulk stayed at the factory for two hours. He let the supervisor lead him through a cursory inspection, and then he took a light meal with the staff, but his appetite left him. On the brief trip to Sarhn, he tried in vain to sleep. Was he nervous? Brulk dismissed the notion. His nerves were as steady as ever. *No, the problem*, he surmised, *is the caliber of people around me. Frail human nature is a curse. If they are marginally competent, they lack spine.* He found the fawning of the factory supervisor distasteful. *What if the attack had failed? Then the fault would have been my strategy, not his ships.* Brulk considered the silent NewGens less fickle, therefore, more reliable. He studied the Lynx supervisor and concluded, *I can replace you.*

As they approached Cor, Brulk groomed himself with extra care. He expected a crowd to greet him. He wore a clean, pressed shirt buttoned to the neck—no collar. His tunic was crisp and bore only his rank at his sleeves—no other insignia. He wanted to understate his military status because he fully intended to extend his authority over much of Cor's civil life for the next two years. The decapitation strike at Jod was just the beginning. He was no fool. He must anticipate a counter strike. He must condition the civilians to take a blow and keep their nerve.

As they made their slow, dramatic descent, Brulk stood on the bridge and looked over the landscape. From horizon to horizon, he saw clear, blue sky. The distant ocean was a darker blue with isolated specks of white ice drifting. The land was deep in snow and the ice-covered Sarhn River snaked white on white through the flatlands, dumping a muddy trace into the clean salt water. *The spring thaw has begun,* he thought. In the background, the familiar snow-covered mountains rose in their saw-toothed ranks.

Beneath him, Sarhn sparkled. Even the ruins of the Clone Welfare Institute lay hidden beneath deep snow, as if Nature had with the wave of her hand erased all the ugliness from Brulk's world. Outside Sarhn's walls the forest wore the heavy snow like a shawl, a rich pattern of dark green and white. The forest acted as a privet hedge, hiding the ugly clone precincts, now ghostly still. A few thin spirals of steam wafted from utilities: food processing, water, and power plants. He nodded approvingly at the dearth of activity. He had never seen the precincts so clean, now rid of the old-order clones. *The old-order clones are almost gone. The Jod are vanquished.*

The pilot landed Brulk's ship with a slight jar: unpropitious, but quickly ignored. Brulk stepped onto the ramp from the ship to thunderous applause. He waved as he thought, *They can't begin to contemplate what I've done.* The sun felt warm against his face. He breathed in the crisp fresh air— cool but not the biting cold that had gripped Sarhn for these long months. He noticed the rivulets streaming from the piles of snow. Fate had given him fair winds for his homecoming.

Brulk paused at the top of the ramp to see and be seen. Across the tarmac, a large crowd of civilians erupted into another round of cheers. A band played the Cor anthem. Brulk saw the thinned ranks of the Sarhn security troops in formation. Outnumbering the Cor security troops, a battalion of NewGen stood impassively in a triangular phalanx waiting for orders. Brulk approved. He looked to the dignitaries and saw Dr. Sandrom smiling back, a smile that communicated exactly what Brulk wanted to know: *The NewGens are shipping to Sarhn in greater numbers. NewGen production at Qurush remains on schedule.*

The Madame Prefect stood in a celebratory blue suit. Her lips were dark red; her cheeks flushed from the sunlight and high spirits. *She is useful: she may stay. I need a barrier between me and the populace the way a doctor wears gloves when operating on a patient.* The other members of the cabinet wore more somber outfits. The portly Minister of Support Services, Master Grundig, wore a long coat that hung from his shoulders with all the buttons undone. The spindly Minister of the Economy applauded anemically. All of them wore phony smiles. Brulk could almost smell their apprehension in the cold air. *They must go. They know it, too. Just a matter of time. How sweet it will be to have them sidle up to me and whisper their confidences, before I discharge them one by one. This present government is just a pusillanimous compromise.*

Brulk took his first step down the ramp when a sight caught his eye. An old-order clone in a thin green jumpsuit and a ratty sweater stood listlessly at the edge of the crowd. Brulk looked around and counted more green jumpsuits. The old-order clones appeared well-fed. Brulk felt his temper rising. He looked at Grundig and knew immediately what had happened. As soon as he'd left Cor, Grundig countermanded his orders regarding the precinct clones. To appease the grumbling civilians, Grundig let more clone labor into the city and increased their rations.

Grundig, you disgust me. Brulk caught himself glaring at the fat minister with the large jowls and squinty eyes. Brulk swallowed his anger. He would not spoil this historic moment. Grundig could wait for his wrath.

Then he looked again at the old-order clones. Brulk had to admit that they appeared as docile as ever. A certain ambivalence settled over him. *Perhaps I ought to allow the civilians to keep some semblance of normalcy. Content civilians are less likely to side with the cabinet ministers—more likely to give me a free hand.*

Brulk believed that the transition from old-order to NewGen clones required that he temporarily wrest power from the ministers. *The ministers will resist, of course, but their only weapon is the populace. My primary weapon is the NewGen clone. If the ministers complain to the people about their lost enfranchisement, I'm safe. If they rally the people over food shortages, I'm imperiled. But time is my ally now. I can be patient. Soon enough, Dr. Sandrom's NewGens will arrive in sufficient numbers to provide services as well as security.*

He surveyed the thousands of faces before him. His eyes finally settled on the phalanx of NewGens, who failed to make eye contact with him. They stood mute and void of emotion, indifferent to the martial music and pageantry. Fair-skinned, handsome faces, with a distant gaze—a soulless intelligence that he admired: Brulk realized that in the end, these NewGen clones were his only reliable allies.

The *Tyker* slowed to kinetic speed. Bits of flotsam splashed off the *Tyker*'s shields with bursts of light—debris from the battle. K'Rin stood before the large forward screen and looked stoically at the ruins of the mightiest armed force in the galaxy's history.

Space tugs labored to steady the giant hulks in orbit. A dozen boxy craft darted nimbly about the flagship *Lijstar* that tumbled slowly end over end, a cadaver performing somersaults. A quark torpedo had cut a deep gauge in her bridge; another gutted her amidships at engineering. K'Rin thought, *The Cor knew exactly where to fire their weapons.*

Civilian salvage barges worked around the hulks. These spiderlike craft had cylinder torsos from which spindly cranes, arms, and hoses snatched debris. They shone bright lights into the ships' deep wounds. Laborers wearing hardsuits worked in the artificial light searching for survivors.

Who arranged this rescue and salvage operation? K'Rin wondered. The Jod central government and the Fleet headquarters were completely annihilated. These tugs and salvage barges were here on the initiative of some lower echelon. K'Rin felt the first warm blush of confidence: *We might win this war yet.*

Suddenly, the behemoth *Kopshir* slipped between him and the sprawling wreckage. The *Tyker*'s forward screen announced a hail, then presented

Captain T'Pan's image and his voice. "Admiral K'Rin. The clans are gathering in the fields near Heptar. We must shuttle to the surface and reconstitute the government and the Fleet high command. I will transport all your comrades down for the ceremony."

K'Rin acknowledged, "Thank you."

T'Pan then asked, "Sir, my staff can provide a clean Fleet dress uniform, beige, with admiral's collar and sleeves."

K'Rin looked at his tattered clothes. His tunic was scorched and torn. It hung loosely on him. His trousers were frayed at the knees. His boots were worn to brown leather about the heels and toes. He looked like a rag picker, not the new ruler of the Jod Empire. K'Rin answered, "I prefer to wear this old black and gray uniform."

Somewhat embarrassed, T'Pan suggested, "No offense, sir, but you really ought to have a change of clothes. Appearances, you know . . . I wish I knew where to find a fresh black dress uniform."

Appearances. K'Rin was ready to dismiss the idea as spit and polish when he heard an old voice from a memory. He heard Jo'Orom's voice admonishing a cadet pilot for failing to repair a small tear in his flight suit—admonishing a young K'Rin. Jo'Orom's nose was an inch from his. The bluster in the Feld's voice was gone. This advice was personal. Jo'Orom told him, *If you look like you're beaten, you'll start to think that you're beaten; then you'll behave like you're beaten. Thereafter, you're useless—to me, to yourself, and to your people.*

"Captain T'Pan," K'Rin looked up at the screen and the larger-than-life image, "Send a shuttle to the

Tenebrea Academy on the coast. I'm sure your people can find our black cadet uniforms."

The evening sun on Jod was blood red, caused by the tons of dust and ash blasted into the atmosphere by the Cor's quark torpedoes. In the plains near the irrigation ditches, multicolored tents sprouted randomly like mushrooms. Larger clans had larger, more garish tents that heralded their city, region, or profession. The rich, mercantile Parh Clan from the city Gyre set up a pavilion of tents: white with gold filigree. Some of the tents reflected the clans' predominance in a profession. The Bar Clan, agri- and aquaculturalists, had tents of azure and chartreuse. The Rin Clan, whose profession was war, had modest tents of dark indigo—almost black. Pennants fluttered in the occasional breeze.

The Don Clan was noticeably absent. Angry rumors floated about that the Don Clan was hiding from the opprobrium they deserved for this disaster brought about by their headman, Hal Pl'Don. But the truth was simpler. Heptar was the Dons' ancestral city: they were now dead, their atoms scattered into the atmosphere contributing to the red sunsets.

The denizens of the tent city were as somber as their tents were festive. Many had searched vainly in the Heptar ruins for their kin, but the Cor weapons vaporized whole buildings. They found few bodies to mourn or bury. They gathered around a platform built in front of the Rin tents. Each cluster of clansmen gathered around a satin flag. The flags hung limp.

A small rustic table stood in the middle of the platform. On the table was a gilt replica of the necklace worn most recently by Hal Pl'Don, the badge of office for the First Among Equals on the council. The lonely, inanimate necklace was an invitation to any chief of any clan to accept the burdens that the necklace represented—the burdens and the awesome power of governing the Jod system. The crowd watched the necklace in silence.

The Jod constitution called for an election of assemblymen from each clan—invariably the chief of each clan. The assembly of clan chiefs selected from its ranks the Council of Twelve, and the council selected from its elite body the First Among Equals. The whole constitutional process might last six months to a year—two years in times of chaos or implacable clan rivalry.

Now, the constitution, like Heptar, was ashes. The Jod instinctively fell back to tradition—the old way of choosing the national leader from the clans. The strongest clan chief elected himself by putting on the necklace. Any challenge had to be proffered at the moment of self-election, else the wearer ruled unchallenged for one year. The crowd was as silent as the necklace on the table.

K'Rin stepped from his small hexagonal tent into the waning sunlight. His plain cadet uniform was comfortably loose and clean, with a cadet's gray piping on the collar. The civilians would not notice the incongruity of admiral's rank sewn onto a cadet uniform.

He glanced over the dour crowd. Instinct told him that some still believed he, K'Rin, had a hand in the disaster, but they were afraid to publicly vent their suspicions. He saw a tiny contingent of Artrix and Terran diplomats, hastily assembled to witness this unorthodox transition of power in the most powerful member of the Alliance. The Chelle were conspicuously absent.

His Tenebrea stood on his left. Some had scrounged newer boots, but most looked battered. Still, no one doubted that this small core of elite warriors could cut a swath of destruction. H'Roo Parh looked particularly fit. Standing next to H'Roo was a human: unmistakable, the dark hair among so many hairless scalps. The eyes play tricks. K'Rin looked twice to be sure the human was not Andrea. Instead, he saw Eric the clone wearing a bone knitter on his arm.

To his right, K'Rin saw T'Pan's officers standing in their pressed tan uniforms. In the thick muddle of strangers, K'Rin saw one familiar face, Hal Bal'Youn, the only other surviving clan head chief, his old ally.

K'Rin stepped onto the platform and without ceremony, picked up the necklace and put it over his head. He paused to look at the chaos before him. Most of the faces were pained and confused, the faces of young Jod, many of them unceremoniously promoted to fill the voids, snatched from comfortable lives and prematurely yoked with responsibility. In the older faces, he saw plenty of ill will and suspicion, but still no challenge. No applause. No cheers. The abruptness of Hal K'Rin's ascension added to the sense of calamity. At the same time, his ascension restored calm. He thought, *I can't concern myself with their opinion of me*. The crowd left, quietly murmuring.

K'Rin retired to his tent. At the entrance, he stiff-armed Kip who presumed to join him. He ordered, "Tell H'Roo Parh I want to see him at once."

"I can send a clerk to find H'Roo, and we can . . ."

"No," K'Rin interrupted curtly. "Tend to this matter yourself. Make sure that H'Roo and I are not disturbed."

Kip's countenance fell, denied his share in this moment of triumph. "Yes, sir." Kip turned abruptly and left to run his first errand as an aide to Jod's ruler—an insignificant, tedious task.

Inside the hexagonal tent, K'Rin sat on a small folding stool at a small writing desk. A bright lantern hung from the center pole to illuminate the white satin lining of the small enclosure. A black lacquered tray with a blue porcelain teapot and two simple cups occupied most of his writing desk. He poured two cups of the pale yellow tea and waited. Steam rose and disappeared in the shadows above the lantern.

Cool evening air followed H'Roo Parh as he entered the tent. K'Rin beckoned him to a second folding stool. "Come. Sit next to me."

H'Roo obeyed. He sat cross-legged on the low stool. His black uniform still bore the slice across the chest. His white undergarment showed the stain of his own blood. K'Rin nudged a cup of tea across the black tray. "H'Roo Parh, I have a problem, and only you can help me."

H'Roo sat silently with his hands folded in his lap. His pale face shone bright under the lantern, while K'Rin remained in the shadow of the tent pole.

After an uncomfortable pause, K'Rin continued, "We need to open a front on Cor to slow down their mobilization. I need Brigon's clones to fight the Ordinate. The link to Brigon is Andrea. And the link to Andrea is you. You know where Andrea Flores is, don't you?"

H'Roo skirted the question. "She believes you killed her husband and child."

"I am responsible, if that's what you mean." K'Rin set his cup on the tray. He waited a moment for H'Roo to reply. H'Roo's silence was an indictment.

K'Rin explained, "At the time, I considered Steve Dewinter just a clone, as expendable as any other clone. I've seen how you behave toward clones—I doubt you would have given Dewinter any greater consideration."

H'Roo sat stone-faced. "I'm not sure I would have sacrificed him."

K'Rin grabbed the word. "It seemed far better to sacrifice one clone than to jeopardize the future of Jod. I chose to keep Eric, a valuable intelligence asset, and instead, I delivered Steve Dewinter to the Cor Hunters. You'd have made the same choice."

"With all due respect, do not presume my ethics."

"Don't be impertinent. Neither of us have time for such nonsense." K'Rin took another sip of tea, setting his cup down impatiently. "Listen, H'Roo, nothing is as simple as it looks. At Klamdara, do you recall the pain written on Andrea's face when she discerned the truth about me—that I had a hand in her husband and child's death?"

"Yes."

"I had seen that look once before, at Baltimore Harbor, when Andrea realized that her husband and child were dead. I remember that morning too well. I was moved to pity, but it was the pity that one feels for a wounded animal—not guilt. Guilt came later. I brought Andrea aboard the *Tyker* to attempt to repair some of the damage I'd caused her. Then, I brought her to Jod. I remember asking you to watch over her. Remember?"

H'Roo nodded. His jaw was set.

"When you first met Andrea, did you accept her as an equal, or were you just curious and sympathetic?"

H'Roo sat tight-lipped, refusing to answer.

"Right, you found her fascinating. So did I." K'Rin nodded and accepted H'Roo's silence as affirmation. "Maybe, even exotic. Nevertheless, she was human, and as we've been taught from our youth, she was, therefore, less than a Jod. Conventional wisdom is that Andrea is closer to the animals than to us Jod. Frankly, when I first brought her into the Tenebrea, I thought her behavior confirmed the fact that she was an animal."

H'Roo made a sarcastic observation. "Tamor-Kyl wondered why you brought an animal into your clan; you made her kin."

K'Rin lowered his eyes. "Leave Tamor-Kyl's treachery out of this. At first, her adoption was expedient—for both of us really. I used her according to my purpose. I needed eyes and ears on the planet Cor. After all, she could go places a Jod couldn't."

H'Roo accused, "You didn't think she'd survive the mission, did you?"

"I knew the mission to Cor was a risk, but I did want her to come back to make a report, after all." K'Rin sloshed some of his tea in his saucer. Annoyed at his own clumsiness, he set the cup and saucer down.

H'Roo pressed, "Sir, I've seen you more concerned about recovering a probe."

A flash of anger crossed K'Rin's face. "I thought

she was useful—expendable, like her husband Steve. Listen, H'Roo, when it comes to the survival of the Jod, I'm expendable; you're expendable."

"But that's a choice *we* make. Andrea is not an animal to be used by you or anyone." H'Roo's simple declaration bit with an edge of hostility.

K'Rin's countenance didn't change. "I agree with you now—but I did not then. I changed my mind about her—gradually. When she returned from Cor. I saw her courage, tenacity, and loyalty: I had the uncomfortable realization that she is a better Jod than I am. Whereas adopting Andrea had been at first cynical, I became glad that she was part of my clan. Why?" K'Rin raised his empty hands and answered his own question. "Because Andrea . . ." K'Rin looked into the steam rising from his tea and he paused, unable to find words. "On Klamdara, I tried to tell her the truth."

"Why didn't you?"

"I rationalized that I was keeping a painful and useless memory from her. I fully expected we would die together on Klamdara. Why burden her with the truth?"

"Why should any of us burden ourselves with the truth?" H'Roo raised his voice.

K'Rin pushed the cup of tea toward H'Roo. "Don't be rude: drink your tea." K'Rin furrowed his brow. "While I was on Klamdara, slowly turning into stone, I resigned myself to death. A thousand times, I rehearsed telling her the truth, believing I would never have the opportunity. Then she saved us; I tried to tell her, but I faltered. I wasn't afraid that she'd kill me. I was afraid that she'd hate me. I never feared her anger, but over time I came to fear her hate. And therein lies the final proof that she is my equal or better. What Jod wants the approval of an animal? We may fear claw and fang, but we do not fear an animal's opprobrium. Why? Because an animal is incapable of hate. Or love. H'Roo, I tried to have this conversation with Andrea at Klamdara, but I missed my last chance. And fate so typically dropped the truth in her lap at a most inopportune moment."

"Why are you telling me all this?"

"I need you to contact Andrea. I intend to make good on my promise to Andrea and Brigon. I promised to send rations and weapons to the clones."

"I can deliver the supplies to Cor."

"I prefer that Andrea and Brigon return to Cor." K'Rin fingered the heavy gold necklace that sparkled in the lantern light. "I . . . I hope . . . I *want* to reconcile with Andrea. I can't undo the damage I caused her, but I can help her move forward."

H'Roo bristled. "No offense intended, but it appears that you are using Andrea again."

K'Rin raised an eyebrow and accepted the rebuke. "Self-interest and goodwill are not mutually exclusive as so many believe. Why don't you let Andrea decide what she wants to do? I think she and Brigon will not abandon their friends on Cor. I think they will accept my help, as tainted as it is."

"She has no reason to trust you, now." H'Roo offered his clinical opinion.

K'Rin chafed. Raising his voice to a harsh whisper, he said, "I realize that! Nevertheless, I'm going to keep my promise to her and Brigon. Do you have a better idea?"

Silence.

"So," K'Rin wrote quickly on a sheet of paper, "here are your orders. Take the *Tyker*. Pick your own crew. You don't need to tell me or anyone else where you're going. Find Andrea. Offer her the rations and the weapons. You will give them a deep-space burst transmitter and maintain couriers on the Cor frontier. Andrea must be able to contact us even if we can't contact her. Procure two million rations and twenty-five thousand weapons. I want you to plan a small raid against Cor with the objective of inserting the *Benwoi* and delivering their supplies. In addition, you must cripple the Cor shipbuilding on Lynx. H'Roo, this is your chance to command your first combat mission."

K'Rin looked up to get H'Roo's reaction. H'Roo sat mute. K'Rin ignored the younger Jod's misgivings and said, "Depleted as we are, we cannot afford to send a larger force to the Cor system—not while the Chelle are menacing our frontiers. After you return, you will remain my liaison with Andrea. You will manage our ground campaign on Cor."

H'Roo said, "What if she doesn't accept?"

"I haven't considered that possibility." K'Rin folded the paper and handed it to H'Roo.

H'Roo stood to leave. As he reached the tent opening, K'Rin stopped him, said, "One more thing."

"Yes, sir." H'Roo turned slowly.

"You are, hereby, promoted to the rank of commander, as is Andrea Flores. Be sure to tell her." K'Rin stood beneath the lantern, exaggerating the shadow that fell across his face. His eyes glowed like cooling embers.

H'Roo shook his head. He looked at K'Rin

standing alone by the center pole in the small tent. "I seriously doubt that she will care."

"Tell her anyway." K'Rin followed H'Roo out of the tent, annoyed but resigned at H'Roo's lack of enthusiasm. As H'Roo stepped past a pair of guards, he called after him, "H'Roo. You underestimate Andrea. I may have used her badly in the past, but I never underestimated her."

H'Roo nodded with perfunctory courtesy, and left.

K'Rin watched H'Roo disappear into the night shadows between two billowing tents. The pair of Jod moons cast a soft pale light over the encampment. Jod wearing the tan Fleet uniforms moved briskly about. Civilians clustered nearby waiting for K'Rin to hold his first audience.

He wanted to communicate to them: *It's late. Go home.* He feared that the clans would use this sudden change of power to press old grievances and resurrect grudges—problems that he had no interest in solving. Judging by their garments, he saw many of his clan's allies, many of whom suffered to some extent during Pl'Don's tenure. They would feel entitled to retribution. And the backdrop of all this opportunity to settle old scores was the shabby remains of the once great obsidian butte and the ruins of Heptar, pummeled and tossed from its perch. He wanted to direct these plaintiffs to the rubble and tell them: *Collect your debts from Hal Pl'Don if you can find him, but leave me alone.* A sudden sensation of loneliness enveloped him.

He turned to reenter his tent when a lone figure stepped from a shadow by the entrance. She wore a heavy, dusty cape. Creases indicated that she'd slept in the robe. *A survivor.* A hood shielded her eyes from the sun and hid her face. On her feet she wore thick sandals with gold braid ties. *A rich survivor. From the Clan Don?* he wondered. The woman stood silently and watched, waiting for an invitation.

K'Rin walked closer for a better look. "Who are you?"

Two delicate hands decked with jewels pulled back the hood. K'Rin recognized the face. He whispered, "R'Oueu."

"Yes, K'Rin." Her face was pale and lovely in the moonlight. Although she wore no makeup, her wide eyes appeared bright as ever. A thin layer of ocher dust clung to her embroidered azure and gold gown. The gown gathered above her waist and fell in rumpled pleats.

For twenty-five years he had disciplined himself not to wonder how he'd react if he found her alone. She was married, after all. *Now, she is a widow.* K'Rin's first impulse was to fall back on simple manners. He started to offer condolences, but he didn't see any trace of sadness in her face. All the other survivors were ashen, stunned, in shock. But she had the look of triumph. K'Rin was confused, and retreated, saying, "I presumed you had died during the attack."

R'Oueu looked over K'Rin's shoulder toward the ruins. "Whereas my husband did not believe your warning about the attack, I did. I fled immediately to the hills. I came here to say thank you."

"Then my warning was not completely in vain. I am—" K'Rin grappled with the words: *still in love with you? Affectionate? Disappointed? Hurt?* "I am very happy that you survived."

R'Oueu looked K'Rin in the eye. She offered him a quizzical smile. She said, "You said once that I had the gift for self-preservation, that I was, above all else, a survivor."

"I meant it as a compliment."

"And I took it as such."

K'Rin studied R'Oueu. He hadn't seen her for twenty-five years, and then from a distance. She still had the thin, dark lips and wry smile that he had loved as a young man. Her scalp was tight—not a distinguishing characteristic, but K'Rin did not like loose scalps on women. He knew her gentle voice and her active wide-set eyes. He caught himself staring. "It's been a long time—I don't mean to stare."

"I don't mind."

"You are still beautiful."

"I'm filthy."

I could at least offer her a bath. K'Rin wanted to invite R'Oueu into his tent, but banished the thought. *There are enough rumors swirling around the camp without me appearing to court Pl'Don's widow.* He asked, "What are your plans?"

"I have family in the north. I'll stay with them."

K'Rin remembered when they were young and the plans they had made. But he'd been a bachelor so long that he'd forgotten how to talk with R'Oueu. She seemed at once familiar and strange, comfortably desirable and exotic. He lowered his eyes. "I really don't know what to say. I wish our lives might have been different, but I guess we are both stuck with our regrets."

R'Oueu reached out with her delicate hand and pressed it against K'Rin's chest. She raised her voice, disputing K'Rin's assertion. Her neck blushed with the first sign of passion that she allowed. "What regrets? My family matched me with Pl'Don after the Rin Clan fell from power."

"But we—"

"Made promises?" R'Oueu interrupted derisively. "We were children, K'Rin. Just children. I don't regret honoring my family. I don't regret fulfilling my station. I survived. I survived thirty-five years of marriage to Pl'Don. I shared his bed when necessary. I listened to his carping, his relentless ego. I endured boredom that you can't imagine. I sat at table with him among his sycophants, where I served as decoration, like any bowl of fruit." She pressed K'Rin back. "But I survived. Now he's dead, and I'm free. I am not going to spend the rest of my life nursing regrets, real or imagined. Neither of us need that distraction."

K'Rin stood silently, a collage of thoughts racing through his mind. *Her captivity was much longer, perhaps more bitter than mine.* He was still confused, so he repeated himself, "I'm very happy that you survived."

R'Oueu put her hood on and prepared to leave. "I'm going north to live with my cousins. I'll be waiting." She turned and walked away. At the corner of the tent she turned to see if K'Rin was still watching. He was.

Safely in the Terran system, the *Benwoi* rested on Phobos at a small ice-mining operation. Barely fifteen miles in diameter, the oblong Phobos had negligible gravity and no atmosphere, but little Phobos masked the *Benwoi*'s mass.

Andrea sat in the navigator's chair. She gazed at the red surface of Mars—angry Mars. She wore a plain one-piece suit, a dusky tan that clashed with her olive skin. Her black hair fell loose upon her shoulders. The scowl on her face was as cold as Phobos. In her lap she held the tunic of her black uniform. In her right hand she held her ceremonial dagger and the razor-sharp titanium blade. With her thumb, she felt the shoulder flash, the dark gray field and the black silk letters spelling *Tenebrea*. She was dismayed by her reluctance to slice the word from her uniform. *Why?*

What could those arched letters mean to her now? She wedged the edge of the titanium blade between the tunic cloth and the stiff flash. One swipe at the threads and the symbol would chafe away. She thought, *H'Roo wears the Tenebrea flash. Gem-Bar wore it. Jo'Orom wore it. Fal'Dar . . . and K'Rin.* She gripped the cloth tightly in her hand and muttered, "I should cut away K'Rin's flash, not mine." She put her blade away without disfiguring her uniform.

As she stood, she found Brigon standing behind her. "How long have you been standing there?" she accused.

Brigon answered indirectly with an affirmative nod. "I see that you saved yourself the trouble of sewing it back on."

"What do you know about the Tenebrea?"

"I don't know them, but I know you well enough. You'll wear that scar on your shoulder for the rest of your life, and you'll wear the Tenebrea flash." Brigon's face clouded into disapproval.

* * *

Cohabiting the moon Phobos with the miners was awkward at best. The miners were a grungy crew of Terrans, making a fortune in wages with no way to spend it. Andrea explained to the miners that the *Benwoi* needed to make a few repairs. The half dozen miners eagerly believed her and extended hospitality, as much as possible given their skimpy supplies. They were glad for any company to break the monotony of filling ice barges bound for Earth's moon. They offered homemade alcohol. In return, the clones aboard the *Benwoi* traded some of their dry rations.

The miners shared their data feed, an old high-frequency system from Mars, which provided some entertainment and let Andrea and Brigon track the news—most of which was the sudden conflict in the Jod system.

Despite Jod efforts to mask the damage, the news leaked. Andrea listened intently and interpreted the news for Brigon. The Jod Fleet was crippled, having lost most of its capital ships. The Jod government was annihilated by Cor's decapitation strike against the ancient city of Heptar. A former head of security, recently exonerated—Andrea bit her lip at that choice of words—took plenary control of the Jod system. The Chelle declared war on the Jod, citing violations of the Alliance Treaty. Furthermore, the Chelle claimed swift victories as the Jod military withdrew from its frontiers. Both Earth and Artrix protested Chelle's armed intervention, but nothing more than a protest. The Chelle promised to respect Earth and Artrix's boundaries. The promise came with enough loopholes as to become a burden.

Unlike the clones, Andrea avoided the company of the miners. She spent her hours on the bridge, seated at the starboard porthole looking at the black void, the stars, and the surface of Mars. She saw the ice caps, the canyons, the ragged plains, and the monstrous volcano, Olympus Mons. She catalogued the geographical sites, trying to keep her mind off K'Rin, trying to reign in her imagination—all the pathetic *what ifs* plaguing her from her past and the useless speculations dangling before her in her uncertain future.

Brigon walked onto the bridge followed by Chana. He turned and curtly asked Chana to leave. Chana's cheeks burned as she retreated down the corridor. Then Brigon turned his attention to Andrea, who sat brooding by the window. He looked around the bridge to ensure that he was alone with Andrea, then said, "We can't stay here much longer."

Andrea looked at Mars looming overhead. She didn't answer.

"I said, we can't stay here much longer."

"I heard you," Andrea snubbed him. She turned back to her window. "Phobos is so small, the horizon falls away like a cliff. Like standing on a cliff. . . ."

"Andrea, we need to make a decision. We're using up our power just running the artificial gravity and the environmental suite."

"You ought to seek asylum on Earth."

Brigon stood behind her chair. He scratched his chin through his thickening beard. He was annoyed that Andrea spoke with her back to him. Nevertheless, he put his hand on her shoulder and said, "That's not an option."

"Why? It's pointless to go back to Cor without food, weapons, and Jod support."

Brigon squatted to be eye level with Andrea. "Look at me." Andrea slowly turned her brooding eyes to his. He said, "I told you before. When H'Roo gave me the data cubes for the *Benwoi*, he told me to wait in the Terran system. He said he'd find us. Perhaps he can still get us the supplies. I believe him."

"You were never too eager to believe H'Roo before."

"I believe what I see. H'Roo has your best interest at heart. He will help us."

"Help you? I think you mean *use us*. Don't you see? The Jod have little regard for species other than themselves, and even less for copies. We are just useful," Andrea snapped.

"He's fond of you. He knows your situation. He'll come."

"I am a curiosity—nothing more. He won't come."

Brigon leaned over her. He was angry. He grabbed her shoulder and said, "For most of my life—especially after my mother died—I was a loner. I never had a friend as good as you have in H'Roo."

"If you want your rations and weapons so bad, dump me on Earth. You can go back to Jod and pick up your supplies." Andrea tried to jerk her shoulder away, but Brigon tightened his grip.

"It's not my supplies I'm worried about. In a few months, you'll need that Quazel enzyme. You've got to get back to Cor, where Dr. Carai can give you the enzyme—or you've got to get in touch with H'Roo. He'll get you the enzyme. What do you want to do?"

Andrea spoke through tight, almost purple lips. "I want you to put me on Jod with a wilderness cloak."

Brigon pushed her away. "Don't aggravate me." He left the bridge, muttering.

chapter 10

Winter on Cor receded. The heavy snows began to melt during the longer days, only to freeze at night. Streams swelled with water, tinged green with minerals, and the air smelled heavy with the anticipation of new life and the whiff of putrefaction. Tara wore her parka open as she limped down a path thick with slush. She held a short walking stick in her good hand, which she used to poke at chunks of ice. She needed these brief escapes from the caves and the abundance of suffering. The incessant coughing of the sick and dying echoed from the walls, berating her. She needed the quiet and fresh air.

Dr. Carai walked by her side. The spry old Artrix wore footgear with the toes cut out, and he wore loose trousers. Furred as he was, he did not need a coat. They walked to a private grove of hornbeam trees with pale bark and black buds on spindly branches. Tara led the way to a bright patch of sunshine, where she basked in the warm light. The wide scar that bifurcated her pretty face turned a deep rose as her face absorbed the sun. She said, "Brigon, Eric, and Andrea should have returned by now."

"Perhaps they are just delayed," Dr. Carai affirmed in his wheezy voice.

Tara rubbed the side of her face with her stubby arm. "No, I am afraid Eric is dead. Andrea, and Brigon, too. It was a slim hope—finding and saving the Jod leader, then procuring his aid."

Dr. Carai shook the wet snow that caught between his toes. "I will miss them."

A proper response, but Tara noted Carai's lack of emotion. But she measured her own depth of feeling and found herself shallow. *Why?* Simple—her situation was just as grim. The wilderness clones were exhausted. They had run out of provisions. The snow provided plenty of water, but food was beyond scarce. The only consolation was that they had fewer mouths to feed. Starvation, disease, and accident thinned their numbers. The precinct clones had stopped coming. Indeed, she heard stories that life had recently improved for the remaining precinct clones.

The wilderness clones had begun scavenging through the valley, completely disregarding the threat of Cor Ordinate attacks. Fortunately, the valley remained quiet, unmolested. The practiced wariness of the clones evaporated as their hunger increased. Now, all seemed willing to expose themselves in the effort to scrounge food by gleaning, trapping, and fishing. Tara looked around and saw muddy trails snaking through the valley like so many signposts pointing the way to their lair.

Tara said, "Dr. Carai, look at the trails. The Ordinate must know exactly where we are; yet, they do not attack. Why don't they finish us?"

Carai replied, "Perhaps they are letting the winter finish us."

"The Ordinate are correct. If we wait here, we'll all starve to death. We've got to find some food. I know of only one place to look." She shifted the walking stick, trapping it against her body with the stump of her right arm. She reached into her pocket and pulled out a tattered paper, the picture of Eric she carried. She spoke to the picture, "Even if you're still alive, I can't wait for you, not now, not here." She folded his picture and stuffed it back into her chest pocket.

Carai stepped closer. "So you've made up your mind, have you?"

"Yes. We march back to the precincts. I know the labyrinth of tunnels quarried beneath the city. At the worst, we can defend ourselves better there than we can here."

"How do you know we can find food there? The precinct clones fled because they were starving."

She shrugged her shoulders. "We can glean something from the fields. But . . ."

"But what?" Carai coaxed her.

Tara smiled dangerously. She raised her eyebrow, split in two by the scar. With her good hand she grabbed Carai's arm and drew him to her. She spoke softly but emphatically. "We won't stop at the precincts. The food is in Sarhn. We need to take Sarhn."

Dr. Carai stiffened, but Tara pulled him harder. "Listen to me. We still have the weapons we scavenged from the South Mountain ambush. We have thousands of people willing to fight now. We must capture Sarhn. Inside Sarhn, they have enough warehoused grain to get us through the rest of the winter. We can destroy the local security forces. In the spring, our people can cultivate the land again. You," she shook Carai, "you can access their labs and begin work on our progeny."

Carai shook his head. His pale mustache flexed as he grimaced. "Too many unknowns. For instance, how can thousands of us walk back to your precincts without being attacked? I would like to be more positive about the outcome."

Tara laughed. "I for one am happy not to know the outcome. But I'm sure of one thing—outside help isn't coming. If we want to be free of the Ordinate, we must free ourselves." Her face changed as quickly as a sudden storm. She shook her stump at Carai. "We're not dead yet! We can mend our own future. We can beat the Cor. How many Cor do you think are willing to fight today?"

"They have defenses—you told me about the sonic barrier at the base of the wall. They have better weapons and better organization. What do we have?" Carai protested mildly, raising objections for Tara to bat down.

Her twisted smile made her face look even thinner and wilder. "We have nothing—nothing to lose. And that, Dr. Carai, gives us the advantage. If we can get past their technology, we can erase the Cor from our lives. Then, we'll hunker down and live as long as we can."

Dr. Carai shut his wide eyes and shook his head. He made a soft whistling sound that he often made when contemplating a difficult problem. Tara misinterpreted the sound as a form of derision. She objected, "So what's the worst they can do? Cut off my other arm? Starve me to death?"

In weeks of furious activity, K'Rin installed a provisional government, which was little more than an augmented general staff. He centralized the few governmental functions necessary to prosecute the war, then delegated everything else to the regional governments—a stunning devolution of power. He assigned a junior officer to log all the nonmilitary requests, then issue the same answer: *Solve your own problem.*

K'Rin consolidated the Fleet. He withdrew the remnants of the Fleet from the frontiers. He left a few fast scouts to search for Chelle ships, but every fighting vessel returned to Jod to defend the home planet. K'Rin was convinced that the Chelle were working with the Cor, and therefore he was mystified that the Chelle had not pursued Cor's success above Heptar with an immediate assault. *They should be in hot pursuit of our Fleet trying to finish the job that the Cor started; instead, they're nibbling at the margins. On the other hand, the Chelle are hopelessly marginal—pusillanimous, although relentless.*

The outlying colonies howled in protest, but K'Rin curtly told them to rely on their own militias, which in most places did not exist. He recommissioned all the Rin and restored them to ships. However, he left T'Pan as captain of the *Kopshir*. He yanked an old general, under whom he'd served, Kren-Shew, out of retirement to command Jod's ground forces. With every decision came a backwash of requests, to which K'Rin's staff most often sent the reply: *Solve your own problem.*

K'Rin moved his skeletal government to the empty Tenebrea Academy on the tropical coast. The Tenebrea barracks now housed transient officials and couriers. K'Rin's office was a buzz of comings and goings. Every meal was a planning session or briefing. Every opportunity for light exercise involved a brainstorming session.

K'Rin rose before dawn and spent the first two hours alone, bathing, eating, all the while thinking. The quiet predawn hours gave him the time to sort his own thoughts. He valued the solitude as much as he had valued the comradeship on Klamdara. His desk was a polished slab of petrified wood. He had a small old-fashioned pad of cream-colored paper and three pens: red, green, and blue.

The quiet knock at his door almost startled him. "Come in." K'Rin set the green pen down and looked up.

The Chief of Staff, Bal'Don, entered. He carried a small teak box with a silver clasp. "Sir, the ambassador from the Artrix couriered this message from the Chelle. The Chelle were emphatic that the contents are for your eyes only."

K'Rin rolled his eyes to the ceiling. "Did you read it?"

"Of course." Bal'Don slid the box across the desk, then sat down in a comfortable chair. Inlaid on the box in ivory was the Chelle symbol, a möbius loop. "A present?" K'Rin opened the silver latch.

"No, sir. I think it's their declaration of war. The Chelle are making their move."

"Rather proper of them to get the paperwork in

on time." K'Rin opened the box. Inside the velvet-lined box was a parchment. He untied the crimson ribbon binding the parchment and rolled it open onto his desk, flattening the ends under the palms of his large hands. The parchment was a masterful job of calligraphy.

He started reading aloud, softly, *The Chelle have been champions of peaceful relations between species since time began.* . . . K'Rin looked at Bal'Don. The Chelle never could get to the point.

"It gets better." Bal'Don waved his hand, encouraging K'Rin to continue.

"I'll skip to the next paragraph." K'Rin searched the text. *It is with profound regret that we send this notice. However, we Chelle cannot in good conscience tolerate any longer Jod's crimes against species.* . . . K'Rin stopped reading. "I'll skip to the next paragraph." *In general you are cited for a pattern of arrogant disregard of Chelle rights, for failing to communicate, for being slow to apologize, and for showing a lack of deference. In particular* . . .

K'Rin looked across his desk at Bal'Don, who stifled a smile. "The next four pages of text is a litany of their complaints going back a hundred and fifty years."

"I know. Apparently, the final and unkindest cut was when you didn't invite them to oversee your transfer to power." Bal'Don reached past K'Rin's outstretched hand and pointed to the text. "Skip to the last paragraph."

Therefore, we Chelle are hereby forced to respond in kind. Henceforth, we withdraw our good graces and all further communication will cease . . . K'Rin muttered aside, "Thank the gods." . . . *and entirely owing to the Jod's fault, we now find ourselves in a state of war.* K'Rin let go of the parchment, which rolled itself into a loose cylinder.

K'Rin sat down in his chair, shaking his large head. "Bal'Don, I'll tell you something my father told me. The galaxy has but four types of species that we can describe in terms of their level of energy and level of competence. The galaxy needs species that are energetic and competent. The galaxy can tolerate the lazy competents as well as the lazy incompetents. However, the galaxy *cannot* tolerate energetic incompetents."

"Your father was speaking about the Chelle."

"He was." K'Rin tightened the parchment cylinder and put it back into the box. The silver latch clicked. "In the long run, the Chelle do more harm than a bona fide, energetic, and competent enemy. You said the Chelle are making their move. Where?"

Bal'Don held up a small data card. "Corondor. The Chelle are massing their *entire* fleet in the vicinity of Corondor."

"Are you sure?" K'Rin took the data card and scrolled through the screens. "Interesting." He got up and started walking to the door for the morning staff meeting. Bal'Don followed.

As he walked, Bal'Don provided some background not on the data card. "Sir, we import half of our food from Corondor." He lowered his voice. "Sir, the Jod have not experienced hunger in fifty generations. We can't let the Chelle take Corondor. The clans will object."

K'Rin stopped his walk down the corridor. Without taking his eyes from the data card, he said, "Do you propose I send what's left of our Fleet to Corondor? Last week the clans were just as adamant that we sacrifice the colonies to protect Jod."

"Perhaps we can send half of our Fleet to Corondor," Bal'Don suggested.

"Disastrous concept, Bal'Don." With one hand, K'Rin rubbed his tired eyes. "Stop worrying about the clans. They will be angry with us no matter what we do, so we might as well do our job as best we can. Don't add domestic politics to our problems." K'Rin rebuked his Chief of Staff without raising his voice.

He tilted the data card to catch the light. "A moment," he signaled Bal'Don to be quiet while he read. Data from deep-space buoys and long-range scanners painted a precise picture. The Chelle had an armada of landing craft ready to disgorge as many as one million ground troops onto Corondor—estimated time to commence hostilities, two hundred hours. K'Rin thought, *The prospect of losing the Jod's food supply is alarming. Also, if the Chelle manage to hold Corondor, they have the perfect base from which to attack Jod itself. However, if the Chelle falter at Corondor . . . .* He looked at Bal'Don, raised an eyebrow, and said, "Corondor presents an opportunity."

"How?"

"I recall that the Chelle make some ancient claim on Corondor—"

"They claim half the galaxy, for that matter," Bal'Don interjected.

"True, but at present they're concentrated on reclaiming Corondor. Now, the Chelle do not make decisions based on tactical considerations—everything is a matter of principle. They will fixate on Corondor, and we shall encourage them." K'Rin pulled a comm-disk from his pocket. "Kip."

A voice answered, "Here."

"Have you seen the reports about Chelle troop movement threatening Corondor?"

"Yes, sir. I am discussing some alternatives with T'Pan's staff."

K'Rin brusquely cut Kip off. "You can stop considering alternatives. Alert Captain T'Pan with a warning order—"

Kip said, "We already have a link to the *Kopshir*. I can patch him into this conversation."

"Do so."

After a pause of five seconds, T'Pan's voice answered. "Hal K'Rin, give me your orders."

K'Rin spoke in short, deliberate sentences. "The Chelle fleet will arrive in the vicinity of Corondor in two hundred hours. You will defend Corondor with ground and air assets—not with space assets."

"Sir?" T'Pan's tone indicated that he did not understand.

K'Rin repeated, "All the infantry, armor, and artillery—everything you can put on Corondor before the Chelle arrive. If possible, I want you to transfer the Jod home reserve to Corondor." K'Rin ignored the alarmed look on Bal'Don's face. He continued, "Inform General Kren-Shew that he has overall command of the Corondor ground campaign. Mark well my next order: keep the *Kopshir* and the rest of the Fleet out of range of Chelle gunnery."

T'Pan calmly tried to contradict the orders. "Sir, if we stay out of range, then the Chelle will be able to prep a landing zone with impunity. They can land their forces at will."

K'Rin answered calmly, "Let them. Tell General Kren-Shew to dig in deep. After the Chelle bombardment stops, the Chelle will pour all their troops onto Corondor. Kren-Shew must stay on defense. I do not want the Chelle invasion repulsed. Do you understand?"

T'Pan replied, "I hear what you say, sir. But I don't understand. You are ordering me to hold our biggest assets in reserve. Our doctrine has always been to repulse the enemy during the landing."

K'Rin cut him off. "Don't quote me the book, Captain. I want Kren-Shew to let the whole Chelle force land. I want Kren-Shew to offer just enough resistance to keep the Chelle committing more of their ground forces. I want a million Chelle ground troops stuck on Corondor, and I want their fleet stuck in a support role. If they're stuck on Corondor, they can't come after Jod. Kren-Shew has got to endure the beating for three, maybe four months."

T'Pan interrupted again, "Is that possible?"

K'Rin looked up from the comm-disk and smiled at Bal'Don. "You'd be surprised what determined infantry can survive. Meanwhile, Captain T'Pan, you keep your ships at the periphery. If you get a lucky shot, take it, but you stay out of range of their guns. Do you understand, Captain T'Pan?"

T'Pan's voice ached with reluctance. "Yes, sir."

"We cannot afford to let the Chelle hit the *Kopshir*. Now, Captain T'Pan, don't deviate from these orders. Don't look for a loophole. If you lose the *Kopshir* now, you will be the author of a blunder that'll make the Chelle look like martial geniuses. No, let the Chelle get themselves stuck on Corondor. Don't worry about Kren-Shew: He knows how to dig. And when the time is right, Kren-Shew's infantry will cut the Chelle to pieces. Keep me informed. Out."

K'Rin turned off his comm-disk and turned to Bal'Don. "It's true. The Chelle have squandered their best opportunity to finish us. I'm actually beginning to feel a bit optimistic."

Kip waited impatiently, ushered K'Rin into the briefing room. He handed K'Rin an agenda, and K'Rin handed the paper back to him without explanation.

The briefing room was peculiarly devoid of technology: no real-time screens, sophisticated sound, or lighting. Instead, the room walls were lined with white glass and a few scribblings from yesterday's meeting, protected by a green box and the word *save*. At the far end of the room, a flat five-foot screen hung from the wall. K'Rin had a long-standing bias: he did not want gadgetry to eclipse the content of any briefing. His stark room removed temptation.

As he entered the room, four Fleet officers stood around a thin conference table that bisected the room. Two were older than their rank indicated—recalled to active duty. Two were younger than their rank indicated—promoted into vacancies. Chairs surrounded the table. A pitcher of water and plain glasses sat on a tray in the middle of the table. Old-fashioned pens and pads of paper defined each participant's place. "Be seated," K'Rin said as he sat. "I won't be taking your prepared briefings today. I'm just going to ask you questions."

The younger participants sat up straight in their chairs, nervously scrolling through their data cards.

"Relax. You're making me nervous," K'Rin addressed the younger officers. Then he threw a question to all of them. "How fast can we get one of the mothballed dreadnoughts into operation?"

The elder of the four officers said, "Short answer, fourteen months."

K'Rin drummed his fingers on the wood table. "Fourteen months—might as well be fourteen years."

The elder officer rose and walked to the wall with a marker. "We surveyed the mothballed dreadnoughts. Their hulls are intact, but the propulsion systems and weapons systems must be completely overhauled. Best case—unlimited manpower and budget—we can deliver one of the mothballed dreadnoughts in fourteen months."

A second engineer, one of the younger officers, spoke. "Sir, if I may . . ."

"Please." K'Rin motioned him to stand.

"I surveyed the wreckage of the dreadnoughts above Heptar. The *Zat-Mar* hull is in the best shape—it can produce forward and starboard shields, and it has an operable inertia dampener. However, the *Zat-Mar*'s propulsion system and weapons' suite were vaporized. I think we can patch together a propulsion system from the *Lijstar* and the *Hal Stim*. We can cannibalize the torpedo section from the *Krol-Ty'E*."

"How long?"

"Ninety days for propulsion and weapons. However, I must tell you that the *Zat-Mar*'s environmental technologies are ruined. We'd need another ninety days to repair the environmentals, even to support a small tactical crew. Six months total."

K'Rin smiled. "No, you don't need six months."

The engineers around the table looked worried. "I guess I didn't make myself clear," the younger engineer said, "the environmentals are *completely* gone. . . ."

K'Rin stood and walked over to the wall. He took the marker from the older engineer. He drew a rough elliptical shape of a dreadnought on the wall. "Look, you've got the main bridge fore and an alternate bridge aft." He drew small circles indicating the relative positions. "They are tied together into the main computer—here." K'Rin drew a box behind the aft bridge. "Here's what you do. You take a small troop transport—company size. You might even take one of the captain's gigs if any survived the attack—"

"The *Lijstar*'s gig survived without a scratch," the younger engineer volunteered.

"Excellent. Take the *Lijstar*'s gig and bolt her into the landing bay of the *Zat-Mar*. Tie her bridge controls through the alternate bridge into the *Zat-Mar* main computer. You may have to forego the neural couch, but I think she'll have enough punch to make up for her lack of agility. You can run the ship and house the crew in the gig. Engineering will need to work in hardsuits, but what's a shift in a hardsuit?"

The younger engineer looked at the drawing. "I should have thought of that."

K'Rin handed him his marker. "I guess we old pilots are still good for something." K'Rin sat back down. "I want you four engineers to focus on two priorities. First, give me another dreadnought in three months or less. We've got a two-front war with the Chelle and Ordinate. The Artrix decided to sit this one out. The Terrans can send us materials. They're mobilizing an expeditionary force that will arrive too little, too late." He thumped the table with his fist. "Use your best crews and deliver the *Zat-Mar*. I want you to outsource the job of reclaiming the other old ships from mothballs."

Kip reminded K'Rin, "Sir, the second priority."

"Yes, thank you." K'Rin looked down the narrow table. "Also, I want you to increase the gunnery on every merchant marine we can press into service."

The elder engineer cautioned, "Sir, that's strictly forbidden in the Alliance Treaty."

K'Rin flashed an angry look down the table. "I'll pretend I didn't hear that comment." Returning to his point, he said, "For the first time in the history of the Jod, our Fleet is outgunned and outmanned. I am inviting the merchant marine to help. I can put their crews into uniforms, but you gentlemen are going to equip their ships with the right tools. You are going to make pirates of every merchant ship willing to take the risk. Questions?" K'Rin looked down the table. "Okay, gentlemen, let's get to work." K'Rin stood and watched the room empty.

Kip stayed behind for a brief interlude before the next scheduled meeting. "May I have a word?" He said, "We haven't heard from Commander H'Roo and that clone Eric for almost a month."

"I gave H'Roo the prerogative to operate without your supervision. Does that offend you?"

"Not at all," Kip bristled. "However, H'Roo should do you the courtesy of filing his flight plans. The *Tyker* is your ship, after all."

"What's your point?" K'Rin glanced sideways at his aide.

"Why give her weapons for her private army? We can't control her."

K'Rin held up his hand to silence Kip. "It was her

private army that freed us from Klamdara—or don't you remember? You let me worry about controlling Andrea Flores. I don't need you to cover my back."

Kip remonstrated, "Gratitude is one thing, but as a practical matter, we must manage a new government, a crippled Fleet in a two-front war, and a dysfunctional alliance. I simply suggest, sir, that as regards H'Roo and Andrea, we must keep our perspective. She did threaten to kill you, and we must be practical."

"Practical?" K'Rin shook his head. "Kip, you are doing a fine job organizing my days. I think you are an excellent staff officer. But Kip," K'Rin tried to find suitable words, "life isn't calculus." K'Rin remembered hearing those words just before he left home for the last time. His mother held a party to celebrate K'Rin's second ring—two decades of life, his initiation into the adult world. His mother and father were arguing about him. His father insisted K'Rin stay at home and apprentice for the Rin seat on the council. But K'Rin insisted on joining the Fleet as a pilot. His mother told the old Rin, *Life isn't calculus. Life is a dance.* His father raised his voice. *That ridiculous analogy won't work for our son any better than it worked for me.* His mother ended the argument, saying, *You never heard the music—*

"Sir?" Kip looked confused.

"Never mind." K'Rin dismissed his previous comment with an abbreviated wave of his hand. "Nevertheless, Kip, don't burden yourself with Andrea Flores or H'Roo Parh. They are my problem. Understood? Now let's see what's next." K'Rin dug his schedule from his pocket and read it. ". . . the captain of the *Kam-Gi*. I can handle this one alone, thank you."

A moment later a solitary figure entered the briefing room. He was overfed, wearing loose clothes and a small fortune in gold necklaces. He bowed awkwardly, twice, not sure of the protocol, but apparently sure of Hal K'Rin's awesome power.

K'Rin pointed to a chair. "Take a seat."

"Yes, sir. Of course—the seat." The captain of the *Kam-Gi* hurried to his chair as fast as a fat Jod could move.

"Bal'Don informs me that you delivered the supply of enzyme."

"Yes, sir. That we did."

"I commend you for waiting at the rendezvous for so many months."

The *Kam-Gi* captain relaxed. "Not an arduous duty, sir. We heard of your captivity, and naturally we were concerned, but prudence dictated our course of action. I told my crew: nobody moves this ship until we have confirmation of K'Rin's death." The captain choked on his own words. "I didn't mean it like that. What I meant was—"

"I understand. And I approve your reasoning."

"I thank you, sir." The captain squirmed in his chair.

K'Rin then leaned across the table and asked, "How would you like to make some real money?"

As the *Kam-Gi* captain leaned forward, his heavy jewelry jingled. "Real money has always had an allure for me—especially now. We can't get work on the civilian side. The damned Chelle are seizing cargoes and blockading all the ports. We spent all our earnings waiting for your release. So, if you've got work that needs doing, we need the work, sir."

"Good. I want to make you a proposition: well, actually, I'm going to give you a set of lawful orders, but I value your opinion."

"You're saying I don't have a choice?"

"Yes and no. I think you'll find my plan most profitable despite a few risks." K'Rin put his fingertips together like a little cage. "We'll upgrade the *Kam-Gi* with weapons and speed. Then I want you to fly into the Chelle system and burn Chelle merchant shipping."

The shock on the captain's face was irresistible. K'Rin smiled. "After they lose a few merchants, the Chelle will recall some of their warships to escort their merchant fleet."

"But, but—"

"We shall commission you as an auxiliary asset to the Jod Fleet, but you won't work for a wage. I'll pay you the price of each ship you destroy— prize money. We simply look up the insured value of the Chelle ship from the Intergalactic Ships Registry and pay you that amount. If you bag just one new fifty-tonner, and bring back images to verify the kill, you and your crew can retire as rich men. If you don't accept my offer, I'll seize the *Kam-Gi* and find a captain and crew that wants the work."

"I, uh . . ." The *Kam-Gi* captain tugged at the large gold earring, stretching the earlobe. "I don't have much of a choice."

"Theoretically, we all have a choice," K'Rin said with a pleasant smile. The smile was not returned.

K'Rin asked, "Do you know any other private carriers that might be interested in such an arrangement?"

"Why?"

"Think!" K'Rin tapped himself on the forehead. "Use your imagination. You can subcontract to as many privateers as you can find. I have great incentive to disrupt the Chelle's rear. Our Fleet is too thin to guard the frontiers. Until we get through this war, the Fleet can't protect you and the other private carriers. You'll need to arm yourselves just to survive out there. I'm offering you a chance to protect yourselves, your livelihood, and make huge profits."

"Dangerous work. We might get killed."

K'Rin grinned. "True. The trick is not to get greedy, right?" K'Rin knew that each success and each transfer of credit would prod the privateers to bolder enterprises. He trusted in the *Kam-Gi*'s initial success, and he hoped to attract hundreds of fortune seekers: Artrix, Terran, Jod; he didn't care who joined the armada of privateers or why. K'Rin simply wanted to throw a wad of unmanaged, unrehearsed, competitive chaos into Chelle's managed, rehearsed, and regulated economy. "But think of the money."

The captain of the *Kam-Gi* rose. "I accept your proposal. I have friends who will want a piece of this deal."

"Good. You and your privateers will live like kings."

The captain bowed awkwardly again, jangling his necklaces. He said, "It's not just the money. None of us want to live in a system controlled by the Chelle." Then the wily captain grinned. "However, the compensation is an excellent draw."

*　　　*　　　*

At the opposite end of the Tenebrea compound, Kip met in a small room with three associates. He carefully closed the door, avoiding any sound. The windowless room was dimly lit. Kip had carefully selected these three young troops—fiercely loyal to the Rin Clan and to K'Rin in particular. Kip pulled these younger officers into his confidence.

Kip put a hypothetical problem to them. "Suppose you are the safety officer for the *Tyker*. You know that the captain's gig engines have a loose drive coil that may cause a catastrophic explosion— let's say you rate the chances of a fatal explosion to be around five percent. You have the ability to pull the gig out of service until you fix the coil. You tell K'Rin about the problem, but he insists—indeed orders you—to prepare the gig for immediate departure. What is the loyal course of action?"

Each answered emphatically, "I pull the gig out of operation and endure K'Rin's short-term displeasure."

"I agree." Kip nodded somberly. "I have a similar problem. You were present at Klamdara when the Terran female, Andrea, threatened K'Rin's life—she is convinced K'Rin had an active part in the murder of her kin. Do you think her threat was empty or real?"

"Real," they answered.

"I agree." Kip lowered his voice. "What would we normally do to foreigners who threatened the life of our clan's headman?"

"We'd track them and kill them before they had the chance to carry out the threat."

"It has always been so. We took an oath to protect Hal K'Rin. By threatening K'Rin, Andrea also threatens the Jod government, and at this juncture in our history, she threatens the very existence of Jod. That Terran female is, in my layman's opinion, a psychopath. And she is a trained Tenebrea. She's quite capable of assassinating K'Rin. She may be crazy, but she is extremely capable."

Kip affected a concerned look. He wanted his confederates tied irrevocably to the decision. He said, "On the other hand, we took an oath to obey K'Rin. He ordered us not to interfere with Andrea. What is the loyal course of action? Help me, brothers, decide."

"We cannot allow the Terran female any opportunity to carry out her threat. We must kill her first."

Kip rested his hands on two of the confederates' shoulders. "You are loyal Tenebrea. Here is what I propose. For the present, we keep our concerns to ourselves. K'Rin wants the Terran female and the clones to go back to Cor to start an insurrection. Fine. If we are lucky, she will perish in the attempt. However, if she survives, then we must take matters into our own hands for the safety of K'Rin and the good of our people. We must swear to keep our work in strict secrecy—for K'Rin's sake and for ours."

The three put their fists over their hearts and swore. Kip bowed, "I will contact you three when the time is right."

Brigon ran onto the *Benwoi*'s bridge. He found Andrea leaning back in a comfortable chair, watching the black sky. He announced, "The miners just received a message from Earth requesting any information on the whereabouts of a ship with our description."

Andrea raised her chair to an upright position and turned her attention to Brigon. "Then H'Roo is looking for us."

"Oh, no. He's found us." Brigon crossed his arms over his chest. "I told the miners to give Earth our exact location."

chapter 11

Word about Tara's plans spread quickly throughout the cold mountain caves. Two thousand clones
opted to quit Tara's company. They hoped to find
more renegade clones in the vicinity of Qurush, then
migrate farther south toward a more temperate cli-
mate, far away from Sarhn and far away from the
fight that Tara planned to start. Tara allowed them to
take fifty old rifles, enough to hunt.

Three days later, the rest of the clones gathered
for Tara's exodus. The occasional whiff of putrefied
corpses stacked outside the mountains increased the
sense of urgency.

Standing precariously on a mound of old snow, Tara
stood with her cane tucked in the crook of her half arm.
She watched the changing weather with the interest of
survival. The precipitation was constant. Nighttime
sleet gave way to soft penetrating rain. The rain coated
everything with a crystal sheet, beautiful to see and
treacherous to walk upon. Smaller streams swelled and
spilled over their banks, creating large pools that froze
to a beguiling wafer-thin crust at night.

Dr. Carai stood at her side. He wore a wool cap to keep the constant drizzle off his face. Nevertheless, the tiny cold droplets collected on his fur. His mustache drooped. Carai spoke loudly to make himself heard above the din. "Everyone who's coming is ready."

Tara looked back into the gauzy fog and saw hundreds of shadows disappearing into a gray mass of clones. She hadn't counted the clones who chose to make the trek back to the precincts, but she guessed the number exceeded eighteen thousand. The wilderness clones had loosely organized themselves into groups of a hundred or more persons. Tara thought the groups were inevitable, organic, and beyond anyone's control. Fortunately, she had no desire to control this mass of starving clones, no more than a dam desires the labor of holding back a torrent of violent water. No, she was only going to help them get what they needed—food to survive. So she need only take them to where they wanted to go—back to Sarhn.

She watched the clones assemble for the journey. They carried packs or hauled sleds filled with weapons, clothes, but no food. Each clone carried a small pouch of wild oats gleaned from the thawing fields and hoarded for the three-day journey. Four sleds carried the two 20-millimeter guns they captured. One sled carried captured electronics, even an operating ground radar. They had no communications gear.

Tara grabbed her cane in her good hand and raised it and her stump over her head. The din quieted from front to back. Her voice carried. "Here's the plan. We march fifty miles per day for three days.

First, we march southwest out of the valley, until we hit the forest along the Sarhn River. Then we follow the river west until we reach the precincts. Two hundred of you have firearms. All of you have some kind of blade."

She pointed to the low clouds. "Despite the fog and clouds, the Ordinate will see us. However, they may guess that we're migrating south. When we turn at the river and head toward their city, they may attack. However, the forest gives us a tactical advantage until we reach the precincts. If the Ordinate security forces attack us, we use the heavy guns to knock down their hovercraft before they land. If they manage to land intact, we rush them. Remember, we outnumber them ten—maybe twenty or fifty to one."

Dr. Carai grabbed Tara by the hand and lowered her to the ground. He nimbly jumped after her, splashing the stiff slush as he landed. In a soft wheeze, he said, "None of us can stay dry."

They moved as a massive organism through the valley. They left a wide swath of mud-stained snow behind. They meandered along the mountain base to avoid the flooded valley floor. Sometimes the clouds hung over their heads by fifty feet. Mostly, the fog buried them. Soon Tara felt like she was walking on a treadmill with her eyes closed. She could only believe that each footstep did indeed fall ahead of the last. She kept the rising mountain slope to her left. A simple compass added some degree of assurance, but she could not shake the dread that she might lead her army in circles.

She knew that the Ordinate's overhead infrared sensors would quickly discover their migration. She hoped their numbers would discourage a confrontation.

The city of Sarhn was likewise buried in fog. However, the mood in Sarhn was bright. The Cor fleet had stunned the arrogant Jod. Cor success was assured. They had boundless confidence in their government and in Admiral Brulk, the hero of Heptar, who worked tirelessly to bring the Cor Ordinate into military dominance.

The citizens of Sarhn enjoyed themselves. The promise of spring, despite the dismal fog, chased away the memories of the bitter, confining cold. The city was far less crowded. After the destruction of the Clone Welfare Institute, many nervous citizens had left for more temperate climates, where there was no hint of clone unrest. In doing so, they forfeited everything for some marginal security.

The remaining citizens, who had endured shortages, now basked in plenty. They lived in the best apartments. They took the better jobs and received extra compensation to reward their fortitude. Now they congratulated themselves for their pluck. They had endured a host of cosmetic and hygienic problems caused by the sudden dearth of clone labor, when Brulk—as a precautionary step—banished the old-order clones from the city.

Now, with his plans coming to fruition, Brulk relaxed the prohibition to old-order clones inside Sarhn. Now, clone labor shoveled the heavy snow away and dumped it over the city walls. City sanitation improved as work gangs picked through mountains of garbage. Gardens were dressed, streets swept, plumbing repaired, facades painted.

Sarhn recovered her sheen, and Brulk received the credit.

Sidewalk cafés operated with the benefit of large outdoor heaters burning propane. Reminiscent of more comfortable times, clones waited tables and prepared meals. Their reward for their obedience was food and clothing. The remnant of old-order clones still in service understood that the *culling* process was finished. They could count on serving their standard time before retirement—all of them grateful to be spared early cancellation.

Seated at an outdoor table at one of the cafés was a pair of Cor Security Troops. They peeled off their heavy jackets to soak in the warmth from the catalytic heaters. They sat alone, away from the civilians, who did not need their afternoon spoiled by the particulars of Cor's plan to eradicate the clones who were presently serving them drinks.

The first lieutenant twirled a fork in a large bowl of herb pasta. Before lifting the fork to his mouth, he adjusted the large linen napkin to protect his clean gray uniform. "What do you make of the overhead reports of moving targets in the mountains?" He shoved the ball of pasta into his mouth and chewed.

His colleague set down a small glass of red wine. "Nothing new. We've known for months that runaways are hiding in the mountains."

Speaking while he chewed, the lieutenant asked, "But the numbers—I've never seen so many movers."

"A false signal. It's the cloud layers." He pointed skyward. "We're getting echoes. You know—if you stand between two mirrors, you see images of yourself blurring to infinity."

The lieutenant swallowed, and wiped some green

sauce from his lips. "The Moving Target Sensor doesn't work that way. I think we've got a migration of old-order clones heading south."

"How many?"

"I don't know. It's impossible to count. On the screen, the movement looks like one giant cluster about three hundred meters long and twenty meters wide."

"Don't believe it. You're getting a false signal."

The lieutenant shrugged. "I just read my Moving Target Sensor. It says another bunch of movers are heading due south toward Qurush. I think we should fly over and take a look."

"Bad idea. In this fog, you'd have to land in the middle of them and count noses, *if* they exist. Just write it in your report. Notify Qurush. Our standing orders are to monitor the clones—nothing more. You remember what happened to Lt. Botchi? If you lose a ship out there, you might as well dig your own grave. If Brulk tells you to monitor, you monitor. He tells you to do nothing else, think twice about breathing. "

The lieutenant laughed. "Right, sir. I'll prepare the message for your signature."

"Fine. However, don't exaggerate. You've got only one sensor working for you, telling you something nobody believes. If the clouds thin out a bit, you might get a confirmation with infrared. Then, I'd be happy to send a detailed report. Or, if your big cluster starts moving east toward Sarhn, then we have a better excuse for messing up the Admiral's itinerary. Admiral Brulk is on a factory tour with Dr. Sandrom. Then he flies to Lynx to commission another squadron of J-Class attack craft. We don't want him wasting time chasing echoes, do we?"

"I never exaggerate." The lieutenant was quietly obstinate. He slowly turned another forkful of pasta. He nodded soberly, "How 'bout this—the MTS makes another pass tomorrow morning. If the movers are still on-screen, I'll write the report, and I'll chose my words carefully so we won't get into trouble—*a significant number of movers were indicated in a southerly direction.* Does that work for you?"

"I can sign that." The officer finished a last mouthful of red wine, then commented, "Sometimes it's better to leave a little room in the language."

Andrea stood on the bridge waiting by the comm suite. She wore her black uniform, her hair pulled tightly into a utilitarian ponytail. Her jaw was tight as she anticipated H'Roo's hail. *I do not want to have this conversation.*

The *Tyker*'s call sign flashed on the forward screen, followed by H'Roo's image. Brigon got up from the navigator's chair and whispered a caution to Andrea. "Listen first. Whatever you do, don't lose your temper."

On-screen, H'Roo's face was somber from lack of sleep. He dispensed with the military courtesies and simply acknowledged the open comm link, saying, "Andrea."

"H'Roo Parh. You found us," Andrea answered coolly.

H'Roo dragged his finger across his chest. "The shallow wound you gave me is healed. I shall presume that you pulled your blade out of friendship."

"H'Roo, you should have minded your own business."

H'Roo allowed a thin smile. "You would be dead if I had."

Andrea clenched her fist at her side and said, "Brigon said you would find us, and so you did. I see you have inherited the *Tyker*: first K'Rin, then Tamor, now you."

Brigon came up behind Andrea and whispered, "Andrea, don't be a jerk."

H'Roo clucked his tongue at the obvious insult. "I'll just come to the point. K'Rin still owes Brigon two million rations of food and twenty thousand weapons. Hal K'Rin promised support, and you shall have it. He wants to open a ground campaign on Cor, hopefully to slow Cor's NewGen production and mobilization. He commissioned me to plan a raid into the Cor system, strike Lynx, knock down some of their satellites, and deliver you plus two supply barges to Cor. Thereafter, I shall be your liaison with the Jod."

Andrea crossed her arms over her chest. "Why should I believe anything you or Hal K'Rin say? H'Roo, you are so naive. Why should *you* believe anything Hal K'Rin tells you?"

At that point the clone Eric appeared next to H'Roo on the screen. A large bandage taped a bone knitter to his arm. His chin was black with stubble. "Andrea! This is our best—our *only* chance to get back to Cor and do any good."

Andrea pointed at the screen and said bitterly, "You, too. You knew that K'Rin sacrificed my Steve to save you. You lied to me as well."

Eric stepped toward the screen as if he wanted to

reach through space and throttle Andrea. "K'Rin didn't share his secret with me, and I didn't see the point in speculating. If you want to hate me, that's your business. But what are we going to do now? Tara and the rest of the clones are starving to death on Cor. The NewGen clones are coming on-line." Eric pressed closer to the screen. His image distorted as he pointed an accusing finger. "They're waiting for Brigon to come back with food. They're counting on both of you. You are their one hope."

Andrea and H'Roo looked at each other through the medium of short-range communications. H'Roo said, "Andrea, I'm going to deliver the food and weapons with or without your help. Eric can show me the way to Sarhn."

Andrea said nothing in reply.

H'Roo's neck flushed. "I'm wasting my time with you. May I speak with Brigon?"

Brigon stepped in front of the screen. "I'm here."

H'Roo continued. His eyes focused on Brigon. "As I said, I'm organizing a raid into the Cor system. It'll take a few weeks to assemble everything, but I have operational control of the *Tyker*, one destroyer, five escorts, a small deep-space fighter, and two supply barges. We lack the assets for a stand-up fight. However, we can carry enough munitions to obliterate the city of Sarhn and everything for five miles around."

Brigon contradicted H'Roo. "You mustn't destroy Sarhn."

"Why?" H'Roo asked incredulously. "The Cor Ordinate massacred our people at Heptar."

Brigon explained, "Thousands of clones still work at Sarhn. You'd kill as many clones as Ordinate."

"So?" H'Roo raised his hand to wave off his remark.

Brigon's cheeks turned red behind his tawny beard. "Your attitude toward my people does not inspire confidence."

"Then what do you suggest?"

Brigon answered, "The Ordinate's military assets cluster in the eastern quadrant of the Sarhn near the landing port. I can give you coordinates. If you take out those assets, we clones can take Sarhn intact. Then, with Jod support, we can defend Sarhn and ensure that you Jod have a safe port of call for future operations."

"So, you are inclined to go with me?" H'Roo scratched his ear and thought for a moment.

"I want to." Brigon turned and looked at Andrea, then at the screen. "I will go."

H'Roo said, "Very well, we will limit the strike to their military assets. The rest is up to you."

Andrea turned to walk off the bridge, muttering almost inaudibly, "You can set me down anywhere in the Terran system. I'll find my way."

Brigon reached out and grabbed her elbow. Turning to H'Roo's image, he said, "Excuse us for a moment. Screen off."

H'Roo's image froze. Brigon turned Andrea to face him. He said quietly, "You know that I must go back. I want you to go with me."

Andrea's face was a map of sadness. Little crow's-feet at the corners of her eyes turned down. The tension about her mouth vanished. Her simple black uniform lost its military edge and assumed the aspect of mourning.

Brigon repeated, "Andrea, I *need* you to come back with me."

Her voice became as small as a child's, keeping their conversation private. "I can go it alone. So can you."

Brigon put his lips close to Andrea's ear and whispered in kind, "I used to believe the same thing. But I was wrong. We can't do any good alone. We can do plenty of harm, but little good. I went with you to Klamdara because you asked me. Now I'm asking you to come with me back to Cor."

She nodded and muttered, "I'll go." Andrea turned her back and walked away, deflated by her own decision. Something deep in her soul told her that she'd never leave Cor again. K'Rin would get away with murder. Just thinking of K'Rin was like picking a scab crusted over her heart. She turned her face from Brigon to hide her disappointment. At the entrance to the bridge, she turned and said aloud, "You make the arrangements, Brigon. I'm going to my cabin."

She walked off the bridge.

The clones picked up the pace as they left the valley. They trudged through wet drifts of packed snow, then poured into the thick forest along the Sarhn River. Their relief was palpable. The valley offered little protection. There, the ubiquitous fog blinded them. Worse, in the clones' minds, the fog was like a one-way mirror, whereby the Cor watched them. They imagined the malicious grins on their unseen enemy. The unknowing and unseeing played cruel tricks on their ears. Every innocuous sound—a bird's call, a wolf's howl, a distant rumbling avalanche—became, in their collective imagination, the drone of gunships and hovercraft. The column trudged stoically through the valley, slump shouldered, fearing a sudden outbreak of gunfire, like lightning. They bunched together out of fear of separation. Now they spread out into a long, thin winding column in the trees.

The traveling was faster. At the head of the column, clones wearing snowshoes made a trail. The sleds followed, packing the snow littered with brown pine needles. The snow on the forest floor was drier and easier to walk on. The shade from the thick pines and firs also kept the many streams brick hard, easier to traverse. The forest's deadfall was no more frustrating than the valley's stones.

Dr. Carai stopped and bent over to rewrap his naked left leg, laid bare by a slime cat on Yuseat. All his leggings were wet from the snow, so this bit of maintenance was merely tucking in loose ends. His exposed toes hurt from the cold. A weary clone bumped him from behind, almost knocking Carai face first into the wet snow.

The trespasser stumbled, too. "Sorry," the anonymous voice said.

Carai felt the warm breath on the back of his ears. Carai forgave him with a wave of his furry hand. Then he shuffled ahead to catch up with Tara. He found her finishing a short conversation with two scouts. She seemed in good spirits. He asked, "Good news?"

"Yes." She waited for Carai to match her pace. "Our scouts reached the outskirts of the precincts. Everything was quiet. They saw no signs of Cor Security Troops—anywhere. However, they did see NewGen forces in the guard towers on the precinct fences. The scouts ran into a handful of clones, working the power and sanitation plants of the city.

Although far fewer in number, they were better fed. Otherwise, the precincts are practically deserted."

Carai pulled at his wet mustache. "Then the rumors about life improving for the precinct clones were true."

"Apparently, Sarhn couldn't function without a base of clone labor. Somebody's got to make the power and shovel the waste." Tara's scar along her right cheek bowed with her lopsided smile. She said with biting sarcasm, "Maybe they'll offer us our old jobs back." She laughed, and her hot breath billowed.

Carai thought out loud, "The Cor must know that we're on the move."

"If they didn't before, they know now. The scouts report that some of the precinct clones fled, raising the alarm." Tara shook her head. "Idiots. The Ordinate are making the transition to the NewGen technology. Pretty soon, NewGens will provide the civilian labor force, and those loyal old-order clones will become fertilizer for someone's garden."

"And you still think our numbers can overwhelm them?"

"In the near term, yes." Tara limped along quickly, stepping in the ruts cut by the sleds. "But we must run the Cor Ordinate out of Sarhn, before they run us out of the precincts."

Carai watched the small, disfigured woman with growing curiosity. He observed, "You really are spoiling for a fight, aren't you?"

She stopped, turned, and poked Carai with her stump. Her face hardened. Her lip, split, then sewn crudely together, curled with distaste for the Artrix's question. She replied, "I want resolution."

They resumed their march. Dr. Carai tugged at his

long mustache and emitted a low whistle. He had never seen combat before. From what he'd read on the subject, he was in no hurry to embrace that experience. No hurry. He said, "Tara. We are rushing headlong to Sarhn. I presume you intend to assault the city right away."

Tara stepped over a large piece of deadfall, struggling to keep her balance. "So far, patience hasn't served us well, has it?" Tara didn't wait for an answer. "When we take Sarhn, I can set you up in a laboratory. Sarhn has many advanced facilities. How long do you need to start a new crop of old-order clones, genetically repaired to restore fertility?"

"Depends on the facility," Carai hedged.

"Assume you have the biomaterials, the incubators, the nutrients—everything. I worked at the Clone Welfare Institute. I know where all the little off-site research labs are hidden. What I want to know from you is how soon can you undo their genetic engineering?"

Carai wanted to tell Tara to stop badgering him to speculate without data. But then he was intrigued that a sterile clone could be obsessed with progeny, especially since the progeny would never be her own. Tara had burned the institute to the ground. Perhaps she needed to stir the ashes.

For his part, Carai remained uncomfortable with the prospect of dabbling in clone technology—even to repair an obvious injustice. *After I help Tara make a fertile batch, what then? Do we risk repeating the old mistakes?* Dr. Carai whistled impatiently. "I can't say how soon. I need more data."

"Fine," Tara persisted. "Just tell me what you know."

Carai capitulated with a sigh. "My tests—actually autopsies—on a few clones that perished on the mountain gave me a few clues. The Ordinate created two barriers to fertility. They harvested the eggs from the female larvae—as you call them. As a second barrier to fertility, the Cor genetically altered the males, affecting either the pituitary or the hypothalamus. I can't tell which until I conduct some tests."

"But you *can* make a crop of fertile clones."

"Yes. Yes." An exasperated Dr. Carai stepped ahead of Tara to make eye contact. "The question isn't whether I can *make* them. The question is whether you can raise them to be adults."

"We'll manage."

Dr. Carai resumed his place at her side. He breathed heavily and amused himself with a thought: *I may see a whole generation of parents that can't say, "when I was your age. . . ."*

chapter 12

The four-Jod crew of the *Kam-Gi* nervously rehearsed their first attempt to bag a Chelle merchant ship. In almost every other word, they reminded each other of the money. Certainly larceny was in their blood, so it was the danger, not scruples against piracy, that put a slight tremor in their work.

The captain euphemistically referred to their new line of work as *ship's salvage*. True, their compensation had everything to do with the capital investment in ships. The crew winked: *Yeah, when we're through with a ship there won't be anything left to salvage*. Ironically, the captain's quip spawned their first idea.

They traveled to the Terran system, where they bought on credit a derelict drilling rig, presumably purchased for the scrap titanium and gold in the hull. The captain pledged his only asset, the *Kam-Gi*, as collateral and the crew had a good—although dark—chuckle: *like to see them collect*.

They hid a small atomic demolition munition in a locker near the drilling rig's docking hatch. They set a five-second trigger to an old-fashioned receiver, then spot-welded the panel shut. The *Kam-Gi* towed the nameless derelict rig behind them to the Orionis system, a major intersection of trade in the wide buffer between the Chelle and the Terran spheres of control.

They waited. Nervously. They played a montage of transmissions to indicate furtive—possibly illegal salvage work—chum on the waters for any Chelle in the area.

The first mate punctuated the silence: "If this works . . . ." His repetitious mutterings sounded like a prayer to ward off his own superstitions. The captain provided the now predictable antiphon: "It'll work."

The *Kam-Gi* captain dozed in his chair with a data card in his lap. A red light on his console started flashing, waking him with a start. He rubbed the sleep from his eyes and said, "We've got company." He looked at the sensor matrix. "They're still forty-five minutes away."

The first mate looked at the screen. "Chelle."

"Are they on an intercept course?"

"Not yet. But they slowed down for a closer look at us." The first mate smiled nervously. "They've initiated a level-three scan."

The captain slapped his knee. "Then we'd better set the hook." He pressed the transmission button and broadcast. In a theatrical voice, he panted, "We've been spotted! Get back aboard ship, quick! We've got to get out of here. Hurry!" He grinned at the first mate and the rest of his crew.

The first mate looked at the screen and soon

reported, "The Chelle have changed course and are accelerating toward our position."

For dramatic effect, the *Kam-Gi* raised its shields and increased power to the magnetic tow, both phenomena calculated to add to the Chelle's sense of urgency.

The *Kam-Gi*'s small communication screen flickered to life. The crew looked at each other with a mix of apprehension and glee. A trio of gray faces with large wet black eyes appeared. Their mouths formed small O's of surprise and disapproval. They wore simple beige smocks: mercantile—not military. The *Kam-Gi* captain exhaled deeply with relief.

The center figure shook a thin finger at the screen and with a high-pitched voice said, "Stand down. We demand to inspect your cargo."

"This is Terran space." The *Kam-Gi* captain blustered for show. "Do you wish to drag the Terrans into your war?"

"You started it," the center Chelle answered petulantly. "Besides, the Orionis system is *co-administered* by the Terrans and Chelle. You are the interloper here. Prepare to be boarded."

"And if we refuse?"

The humorless Chelle muted their sound transmission and quickly consulted each other. The three gray heads pressed together, nodded in unison, and the central figure said, "We hereby invoke the Alliance Uniform Code for Commerce, section four paragraph three, line . . ."

The captain interrupted, "Don't quote me gibberish. This space is neutral."

"Co-administered . . ."

"We're leaving."

"Inadvisable. We are armed. We will pursue you and board by force, if necessary. You cannot outrun us or outmaneuver us while towing your cargo."

The captain displayed a theatrical outburst of indignation. "You have no right. However, we have nothing to hide. You may board the drilling rig."

The sound muted again as the three Chelle put their heads together, nodding. Then with invincible confidence, the center figure announced, "Very well, we shall inspect your cargo according to our rights specified in the—" The *Kam-Gi* captain switched off the audio. The Chelle's thin lips moved, eyes blinked, and fingers wagged, but in blessed silence. The *Kam-Gi* captain turned a sideways glance to his engineer, who rolled his eyes.

The Chelle freighter loomed onto the scene, dwarfing the small *Kam-Gi*. The captain looked through one of the bow portholes and exclaimed, "She's two hundred tons empty." He whispered, "Gentlemen, we're rich."

"Or dead," added the first mate.

The *Kam-Gi* backed away from the old drilling rig to give the Chelle freighter room to dock. The Chelle navigated flawlessly, a fluid grace, not one wasted maneuver as they glided next to the rig's square crew compartment and the docking hatch. The *Kam-Gi* crew heard the *ka-chunk* of the locking bolts from microphones in the rig, then the hiss of the hatch, and a slight rush of air to equalize cabin pressures. The captain whispered aside, "Are you sure we're getting a visual and audio record?"

"I'm sure, Captain."

The captain's only fear was that the Chelle would find nothing of value on the derelict rig and might decide to let the *Kam-Gi* keep their worthless cargo. The captain laughed at his own anxiety. *The Chelle? Give back the rig?* He laughed again. No, they would find or invent some principle on which to stand. The Chelle would want the rig if only because the *Kam-Gi* had it. Worthless or not, the rig was as good as seized.

Just as the captain dismissed his one anxiety, the Chelle returned to the forward screen. The lips started moving again, and the captain quickly switched the audio back on. "—receipts for the cargo?"

"I'm sorry, I didn't hear everything. Please repeat."

The Chelle scowled as much as the sylph face could screw itself into a pained look. "I said, do you have the drilling rig's registration, and the proper salvage license—necessary receipts for the cargo?"

The captain raised his voice, shaking a fist at the Chelle. "Paperwork? I paid cash for that hunk of metal. I don't need any stinking receipts."

The three Chelle smiled together. Their thin lips twitched into bows, then re-formed into their disapproving O's. The one on the left literally washed his hands in the air. "If you cannot produce the proper documents, we shall be forced to confiscate the rig and take it to the proper authorities until such time as ownership can be proved."

The captain turned his back to the screen and held his head as if in anguish. He whispered to his first mate, "Now I'm going to gaff these fish, boat 'em, gut 'em, fillet 'em." He turned and lowered his eyes to the screen. He addressed the three Chelle with his hands folded politely at his belt buckle. "We, uh . . . we lost the paperwork. Listen, we're just merchants like you, trying to make a living. I know your people have a complaint with my government, but hey—I'm not political. I mean, you're probably right. Just let me go this time, okay?"

The three Chelle blinked their big wet eyes. "We can't."

"Well," the captain scratched his forehead, "maybe we can make a deal."

The Chelle perked up. "We're listening."

The captain faked a sudden burst of optimism. "We don't have any money. We used all our cash to buy the rig." He shrugged. "But we could share the proceeds. We could work together, you know. We could both strip the rig and share the proceeds—fifty, fifty. There's plenty of scrap to share."

Again, the Chelle muted the sound and the three heads turned to each other. This time they seemed to argue. They were not deciding whether to accept his offer. They would never accept a split when they might take all—especially with the regulations on their side, not to mention raw force. No, they were quibbling on the best rationale to reject his offer, that is, which rationale appeared more ennobling, as if in the vast expanse of space, some unseen audience would applaud or condemn the Chelle's actions. The *Kam-Gi*'s captain thought it all too funny, yet serious as death itself.

The sound returned. The Chelle in the center jabbed his bony finger at the screen. "We are incensed that you would try to bribe us from carrying out our sworn duties as merchant marines. You Jod have no honor. No wonder we are at war with you. I suggest you leave before we forget that we are civilians."

The *Kam-Gi*'s engineer immediately turned the *Kam-Gi* around and poured on the power. The Chelle made one last transmission. "Don't come back without the proper papers."

The *Kam-Gi* crew cut communications, put on dark goggles, and crowded the aft portholes. With a press of a button, the captain sent the detonation code to the drilling rig and suddenly a piercing blue light overwhelmed the black void. The *Kam-Gi*'s systems flickered from the electromagnetic pulse, and the crew ripped off their goggles, grinning. The captain exclaimed, "And my father said I would never amount to anything . . ."

Kren-Shew stood on a gentle slope, overlooking the frenetic preparations for war on Corondor. The air had the moist smell of dirt. The sound of straining machinery drowned out the birdsong he had noticed when he first set foot on Corondan soil.

Recalled from twenty years' retirement, Kren-Shew wore his old, faded beige uniform. His tunic was decked with rank and accommodations. He was middle height for a Jod, but powerfully built and athletically inclined, belying his age. In fact, he was a bit vain about keeping fit. He had soft hands and intellectual, steel-blue eyes set deep. His lips were thin, almost cruel, and he had a pugilistic jaw. He rarely smiled, but when he did, he brandished a broad row of yellow teeth, stained from a lifelong habit of drinking flannerberry tea spiked with rum.

Verdant Corondor seemed so vital, and he was turning it into a death trap. *Life and death always encroach upon each other.* Kren-Shew was old. His scalp was loose. He had seven rings beneath fleshy eyes. Few Jod ever lived long enough to add an eighth ring. Recently, he had given much thought to his long life and his inevitable death. He had made his peace with his own death. He looked at the young Jod laboring in the comfortable sun and sighed. *I will probably survive when so many of these young ones die.*

Kren-Shew studied the battlefield. Corondor was the most fructuous ball of dirt in the galaxy. Long days and warm soil encouraged germination of anything that touched the black soil. *A pity to upset so much fertility.*

One super-continent banded the planet. Two large oceans extended north and south, ending in small icecaps. The weather was perfect for vegetation. A robust greenhouse effect kept temperatures constant over all the landmass. Gentle breezes shoved ocean moisture inland. Eighty inches of rain fell on the flat land each year. Extensive canals managed the runoff and protected the rich loam from erosion. Grain-laden barges motored down the canals and along the coastal waterways to the one major port city: Erstewa.

Despite the vast agricultural enterprise on Corondor, the civilian population was sparse. Erstewa had fewer than fifty thousand citizens. This relatively new city was a whirling factory town: winnowing grain, preserving fish, sawing raw logs into usable lumber, then shipping the goods throughout the Jod system. The farmers—the name given to all Corondor citizens—were really scientists and engineers: botanists, ichthyologists, entomologists, mechanics, and roboticists.

The miracle of Corondor was ninety-eight percent gift and two percent labor. The rain, sun, and soil did the work with minimal prodding from the machines. The Jod merely had to stand with their hands open—intelligently open—to receive the gift and stay out of the way of the miracle.

Instead of manual labor, the Jod had for centuries relied on agrobots. They had no computer brain, rather a basic, insect intelligence made of analog circuitry. In fact, the machines looked like large metal insects or crabs with solar panels glistening from a thorax. They wandered in seeming randomness through the fields, aerating soil with jabs of their spikes that looked like long black fangs. The long-legged robots walked with quick jerky steps. They stopped to pluck weeds, test soil, and monitor plants for disease. Heavier machines wandered up and down the canals repairing levies, pruning vegetation, and measuring water flow. A different breed of delicate robots stepped gingerly through the hydroponic farms harvesting vegetables; a slithering snakelike model swam with the prawns and flatfish in the aquaculture ponds.

The Corondor farmers were horrified, then angered, by the prospect of the Chelle invasion. The Jod beat the Chelle thirty years before, but most of that fight took place in the heavens, unseen and antiseptic. Kren-Shew had warned the farmers that this struggle would get personal and dirty. Nevertheless, most farmers decided to stay on Corondor and trust the Jod military rather than flee their oasis of natural order. The farmers showed Kren-Shew's engineers how best to use the terrain. In return, Kren-Shew gave the farmers arms

and arranged to put them and their families far
behind Jod lines.

Wherever Kren-Shew looked, he saw the upheaval
of dirt. Jod combat engineers used large mechanical
awls to dig hasty positions, chewing large holes into
the perfect rectangles of dark green maize, red flan-
nerberries, yellow peppers, and mottled legumes. In
addition to the engineers, the hundred thousand Jod
soldiers seized every piece of dirt-moving equipment
on Corondor, anything with a blade or a bucket—
every shovel. They dug deep trenches. The pristine
fields suddenly looked like they were infested with
moles.

The infantry laid miles of electric wire, silver coils
to snag and hold attackers. They knew that the
Chelle would attack in waves with vicious solidarity
under the cover of blistering suppressing fire. But
the Jod also knew that the Chelle tended to fold
with even greater solidarity whenever their attack
was frustrated. So the Jod dug triangular trenches
four feet deep, just beyond the reach of the typical
Chelle soldier to climb over. They sited their mortars
to explode and rain death down on the Chelle
bunched together in the trenches.

The agrobots worked around the disruption,
learning slowly to sidestep the holes. The farmers
turned off the canal robots that stubbornly tried to
smooth the berms and trenches that the infantry
dug.

Wherever possible, the engineers used natural
barriers and cultivation to augment their barriers.
Where a field of aquaculture ponds restricted foot
movement to the levies, the Jod sighted their
unmanned laser cannon along the narrow footpaths

atop the levies. The Chelle would pay in blood for every inch of Corondor soil.

The Jod built their heaviest defenses around Erstewa. They tapped into the fusion plants to power a land-based deep-space cannon. Again, they dug deep. They poured tons of quick-setting cement to build a hasty bunker, knowing full well that the cement would not have time to cure before being put to the test.

In five days, the Jod dug deep enough to put twenty feet of soil between every soldier and the Chelle bombardment. Not as elegant as an energy shield, but every bit as effective: "Never," said General Kren-Shew, "underestimate the attenuating power of dirt." He even ordered all commands to bury their antennae and set their communications to very low frequency. He was proud of the Jod infantry, of their backbreaking work—especially because the common soldier was skeptical of the concept of operations. Never had the Jod allowed the enemy to land unopposed. Doctrine had always taught them to repel an invasion *before* they touched down. Kill them in their ships.

Kren-Shew wandered to the awning where his staff and commanders worked over maps. The group snapped to attention as he entered.

"As you were," Kren-Shew said. His voice was still steady, although not as loud as it was in his younger days.

He approached a group of his regimental commanders and asked them, "How are the troops?"

One of them volunteered, "Sir, I'm having a hard time explaining the concept of operations to the troops. Now, I understand that we need to buy three

months to bring another dreadnought into service.
We will all do our duty. It's just that . . . that . . .
well, sir, we are trained to counterattack."

Kren-Shew scratched his upper lip with his finger
as he listened. He replied, "When you were digging
in the fields, you probably ran into one of the native
plants, the Corondoran Jaw. It's an odd pale-green
plant with stringy leaves and five stalks. At the end
of each stalk is a little star-shaped, pinkish flower.
Have you seen them?"

"Yes," the regimental commanders all replied warily.

Kren-Shew said, "Good. The Corondoran Jaw flower
looks harmless enough, smells like spiced honey,
and attracts flying insects."

The general held out his two hands like two
halves of a clamshell. "An insect lands on the soft
pad in the middle of the flower to feed. Its feet stick
to the sweet gummy sap on the lower petal. The
insect makes itself busy feeding on the nectar.
Meanwhile, small spikes at the edge of the flower
rise like teeth to keep the insect in place. Then," said
the general as he closed his hands slowly, "the flower
closes on itself to devour the fly. All of this takes
time, an eternity for the doomed insect. Three
months, gentlemen. We keep the Chelle stuck here
for three months. Then we devour them."

He could see that the regimental commanders
still were not convinced. Kren-Shew added,
"Personally, I think the strategy is brilliant. At present, we are at a serious disadvantage for a fleet
engagement in open space. On the other hand, we
have the advantage fighting on the ground. Our
troops are better than theirs. Terrain favors the

defender. We can get them in a clinch and hold them until K'Rin restores the Fleet with a second dreadnought. Then we'll have the advantage in both space and on the ground, and we will counterattack. I promise you, we will wade through the Chelle and spill their blood."

Kren-Shew paused and looked each of his commanders in the eye. He knew that none of these men had ever led troops in combat; therefore, letting go of doctrine was doubly hard. "Tell your soldiers this: for a thousand years, we infantry have relied heavily on the Fleet. Now the Fleet must rely heavily on us. For the rest of their long lives, wherever your soldiers go, every Jod will know that they saved the Fleet, they saved Jod from the Chelle." Kren-Shew finished by closing his hands into a double fist.

Hal K'Rin cleared his schedule in order to meet the *Tyker*'s shuttle. He canceled three appointments and left Kip in the office to make the necessary apologies. Kip asked pointedly, "Why don't you keep your appointments, and I'll debrief Commander H'Roo?"

"No, Kip." K'Rin insisted on debriefing H'Roo alone, a decision that annoyed Kip.

Kip complained, "No disrespect intended, sir, but you used to be more levelheaded as regards the Terran female. Now, you seem far too invested in this Terran female, who only wishes you ill."

K'Rin frowned, replying, "I wish her well, and as far as you're concerned, my wishes take precedence over hers."

K'Rin left the building and stepped into a

bright patch of sunlight. A sudden storm had splashed the walkways and left puddles on the tarmac. Steam rose, adding to the humidity and the bitter smell of wild herbs. K'Rin used this short moment of solitude to collect his thoughts. *Of course she wishes me ill: she has the claim of blood debt against me.*

K'Rin walked to the nose of the shuttle. Ground crew performed their drill unaware of K'Rin's presence. H'Roo Parh stepped down the ramp, tired. He paused to take a deep breath, which faded into a sigh, then a yawn.

"Commander H'Roo," K'Rin spoke up. "Do you need to rest first?"

H'Roo turned, embarrassed by his natural weakness. He covered his mouth, fought a second yawn and replied, "No, sir. We can speak now."

"Good." K'Rin stepped closer. "How did it go?"

"I found her."

"The Terran system?"

H'Roo didn't answer directly. "Brigon agreed to take the supplies and go back to Cor. Andrea—reluctantly, I think—agreed to go with him. As soon as you can detail a squadron for the raid, we can collect the supplies and go. I presume you want us to move with haste."

K'Rin's thoughts settled on Andrea. *She went for the sake of Brigon?* He answered casually, "Of course." Then he asked the real question: "How is she?"

H'Roo responded in a tone that in other circumstances would have been insolent. But H'Roo's fatigue and nascent anger overwhelmed his impeccable manners. "How do you think? She's in a lot of pain—pain that you—" H'Roo caught himself. He clipped the end of his thought but did not retract the accusation that he refused to finish.

K'Rin pointed up the walkway to a garden hedged in jasmine. "Walk with me." The tone of his voice warned H'Roo to guard his speech around the enlisted ground crew. H'Roo matched his longer stride to K'Rin's and they stepped away from the shuttle.

"I know more about pain than you do," K'Rin said. "I thought a lot about pain while we were imprisoned on Klamdara. I felt it; I saw it. I even thought about Andrea and her pain. I figured out what causes pain."

H'Roo kept his eyes forward. "What causes pain?" he asked tersely, almost rudely.

"Pain is the result of struggle. We struggle with ourselves, among ourselves, with the vagaries of nature, and the one certainty of nature: death. The only way to avoid pain is to avoid the struggle. Some kill the mind; others kill the body. Either way, they give up the struggle."

"Andrea will never give up." H'Roo anticipated the direction of K'Rin's argument. His voice betrayed a note of sarcasm. "You realize, of course, that her definition of the struggle is to kill you."

K'Rin pressed his lips together and shook his head. He exhaled and said, "Perhaps you can help her find another definition. What's done is in the past. I can only do so much now." K'Rin reached into his pocket and produced an injector. "Just in case Dr. Carai can't provide. . . ." He handed the injector to H'Roo and said, "Andrea will need the enzyme soon. Make sure she gets her dose on time.

If anything happens to me, I charge you to ensure that she never lacks for enzyme."

The Chelle flagship looked down on the green and blue planet of Corondor. The three marshals in charge of the invasion stood on the bridge wearing uniforms with their gold rank prominently displayed on large shoulder boards. They wore small pillbox hats braided by gold filigree. Two marshals wore scarlet sashes, an additional reminder of rank. The third wore a gold sash.

One scarlet-sashed marshal ordered, "Long-range sensors: report."

Three Chelle turned from their console. One spoke, "The Jod dreadnought and support ships have withdrawn out of range. The planet surface is quiet, although we detect evidence of defensive preparations around Erstewa."

All three marshals nodded. They stood like a small wall of invincibility in front of the forward screen. The screen displayed their armada, arrayed in Corondor's night shadow: ships bristling with cannon and antennae, illuminated by their own bright signal lights. The two red-sashed marshals commanded two hundred ships and a thousand landing craft filled with hardware and a quarter million soldiers: the largest invasion force ever assembled by the Chelle. The marshal with the gold sash—the political officer—asked, "Did you send the hail?"

A technician answered, "Yes, Marshal Pock."

"And their reply?"

"They did not reply."

"What?" Pock scowled at the technician. "Open all frequencies and retransmit our terms." He straightened his gold sash and stepped forward to cast the best image. He stood at his full height of four foot five inches—tall for a Chelle. He thrust his small chin forward, a sign of aggression. The small nostrils flared and his large black eyes narrowed slightly.

He waited. Without turning his head, Pock glanced toward the communications technician who leaned over the console. Without moving his lips, he whispered under his breath, "Response?"

The technician shook his head.

Again, under his breath, he asked, "Nothing? Are you quite sure?"

An affirmative nod.

Then louder, Pock asked, "Did they get our transmission?"

The technician retreated behind his high-back chair and replied meekly, "We won't know unless they answer."

Pock scowled at the screen. His high-pitched voice lowered a semitone to inflect his displeasure. "Inhabitants of Corondor. This is Chelle Marshal Pock, spokesperson for high command of the Chelle Fleet. We are here to restore to Chelle our property, Corondor. Our records clearly show that Chelle astronomers discovered Corondor first. You have one hour to surrender Corondor or face the might of our combined arms."

One marshal with a scarlet sash whispered, "You just extended your first deadline."

Marshal Pock quickly corrected himself. "Fifty-eight minutes. You have only fifty-eight minutes left."

Silence ensued. After a long silence, the two marshals looked at each other in disbelief. Pock screwed his small face into the picture of suspicion. "Is it some kind of trick?"

"How?" the others asked.

Pock whispered, "Do you think they're planning a counterattack?"

"With what?" The other marshals almost shrieked in their high voices. "Their fleet retired from the area of operations. They have nothing."

Pock ground his teeth in frustration. "Why don't they answer?" He spoke louder to his staff assembled on the bridge. "Anyone? Can you tell me why the Jod don't answer?"

Nobody on the bridge offered an opinion; rather, they turned to their stations to avoid the marshal's swelling anger. Pock drew his finger over his throat signaling the technician to cut the transmission. He paced the bridge. His heavy gold sash shook as he walked, mimicking his agitation. He jabbed his long finger in the air. "I know." He turned to lecture the rest of the bridge. "They're too proud to admit defeat. Fools! Those arrogant Jod . . . don't they realize who we are up here? Do they think we will just go away if they ignore us?"

Both marshals with the scarlet sashes turned a darker shade of gray to match their anger. Both clenched their delicate hands into small fists. One said, "Let it be recorded that we made the civil gesture of inviting Corondor's surrender." The other added, "Also, let it be recorded that we interpret their silence as refusal." He turned to Pock. "Shall I commence the bombardment?"

"Yes. Flatten Erstewa." Pock sat down in his chair. A moment later, he saw the fire pour down.

Crimson and yellow lights converged on a pinpoint of land next to the southern ocean. "Magnify." Pock wanted a better look at the destruction, but a cloud of dust, smoke, and steam rose slowly, obscuring his view. He beat his small gray fist on the cushioned arm of his chair.

chapter 13

Nighttime collapsed around the last faint light of day. Tara halted the column at the edge of the forest, where she stood like a wary deer looking over the field that extended toward the clone precincts. She held her cane in the crook of her bad arm, and held binoculars to her eyes. The cane was more habit than crutch, now. *Where are the Ordinate Security Troops? What are they waiting for?*

"Spread out. Sweep the precincts," she ordered. Two hundred armed clones wearing snowshoes shuffled their way along the edge of the forest, a thin line of eyes and ears stretching for five hundred meters.

Drifts of snow scalloped the field. She saw corn stubble poking through the crusty snow in the troughs of the huge white waves that disappeared into the unrelenting fog. No moon, no stars, only the cold black of night. The air was as still as death. In the distance, through the gauzy fog, she saw dissipated lights coming from the clone precincts, the yellowish light of the street lamps.

Tara could see only the first four armed clones to her right and left. "Move out." Tara dropped the binoculars that hung from a strap about her neck and used her good hand to retrieve a cold pistol from her belt.

With each tentative step, she expected to hear gunfire, expected the dim lights on the horizon to explode into blinding xenon search lamps. She walked up and down the snowdrifts, pausing at the crests to look and listen. The distant lights began to coalesce into brighter points. She thought she saw a distant pattern of lighted windows in a high-rise, a red blinking light marking the roof. Tara didn't hear anything but the shuffling of snow and the occasional crack of dried corn stalks. In the rear, she heard the muffled sound of thousands of feet trudging after her, and the crunch of snow beneath the sled runners.

The black buildings grew as they approached. The fog thinned, and Tara saw her comrades spread out in an irregular line with kinks and knots. They stepped out of the fields and over large heaps of dirty snow, shoved to the edge of the precincts.

Carefully, Tara stepped over a ridge of snowdrift. She saw the fifteen-foot perimeter fence and guard towers and her gut tightened. The lights along the fence cast cone-shaped specters. A continuous spiral of silver ribbon, sharp as razors, ran along the top of the fence. Every hundred meters, short towers built of cement pipes held hexagonal pillboxes aloft. Gun ports faced each direction. The towers were empty. No clones, no security—the precincts were deserted.

Pointing her cane, Tara directed her people toward the tire tracks and a gate. They broke the simple lock and let themselves in. Immediately inside the fence, they found the animal sheds. Lying on the snow near bales of alfalfa were piles of entrails, heads, and skins of several dozen bovine and sheep. Each head had a neat bullet hole in the skull.

Tara bent down over a frozen pile and felt the large head of a cow. "How long have these animals been dead?" She thought the bluish-white tongues might indicate some degree of putrefaction.

A large wilderness clone bent down and looked at the milky white eyes of the cow. "One, two days at the most." Looking up at Tara with a grin, he said, "We can eat the rest of these animals."

"Find Hart and tell him. Then check the granary," she ordered. "You," she summoned another clone squatting next to the cow's severed head. "You know this precinct?"

"I worked around here." The tall clone stood. He wore a ratty shawl tied over his head. With a thin hand, he made a circle in the air. "I know these parts."

"Come with me. We'll check the greenhouses."

Tara shuffled through the animal pens past frozen dung and bloody entrails, toward acres of glass sheds. The sheds were completely black. Tara found the doors wide open, where she removed her snowshoes and entered. The lanky clone followed. He found a large knife switch and turned on the lights. Fans began to hum to life.

For the length of the building, hydroponic baths and dirt tables held plants that appeared limp as seaweed but felt as brittle as straw, delicate black and brown ice. *Perhaps some of the roots survived.* Tara ordered, "Get a work party in here. See what you can save."

Tara found a small wooden stool beneath one of the ultraviolet lights. She sat down to reflect. *They left in a hurry. Did they know we were coming? They cleared out the food and left. But where to?* The precincts were large enough to house a million clones that in turn supported an Ordinate population of less than one hundred thousand. The Ordinate had methodically starved and otherwise killed the precinct clones—she guessed that they had culled the population down to the thirty or fifty thousand essential laborers needed for Sarhn to function. She had a chilling thought: *Did the Ordinate come in and massacre the rest?*

Tara shook her head. She'd seen no sign of a final struggle. *The Ordinate would just as soon bury the slaughtered cow remains as bury a clone. The Ordinate didn't massacre the precinct clones. The remaining precinct clones could have gone to only one place. The Ordinate must have corralled them into Sarhn proper because they still need old-order clones for labor.*

Tara recalled reports from the refugees. The Ordinate population had also shrunk: some left for fear of the clones; some left the discomfort of winter and shortages. Tara smiled at the thought of Sarhn's new demographics; half the population were indispensable clone laborers and half were Ordinate. *Nevertheless, the Ordinate must be confident that they can eliminate us all soon. I wonder how the remaining clones will react when we attack the city?*

The overhead lamp began to feel warm against her skin, already used to the freezing cold. She left the greenhouse and continued walking to the large buildings. She saw scores of her people skulking through the streets. The main body had arrived.

They looked like shadows invading a familiar burial ground. But the somber shadows quickened their pace as they progressed into the precincts.

Some of the large dormitories were completely black: doors boarded shut, long empty. In other dormitories, lights shone randomly. Tara stopped and smelled the dank air. She expected the pungent cooking odors of cabbage or lentils. *Nothing—everyone gone.*

A dilapidated street tram stood still at the end of the tracks. Tara bent down to inspect the metal rails. *No rust.* She followed the tracks toward Sarhn.

As she walked up the main thoroughfare straddled by light rail, she received reports from the patrols in other precincts. Empty: granaries, food lockers empty, kitchens empty, except for the beans and rice spilled on the floor. The dormitory rooms yielded small caches of food hoarded by the occupants. Every scrap of food was greeted with enthusiasm.

The power plant ran at one-tenth capacity. The buildings received just enough heat to keep pipes from bursting. *The Ordinate want to protect their capital investment in the precinct. They must plan to settle the NewGens here.*

Tara saw Dr. Carai walking with a gray-haired woman, whom Tara recognized as the PTR model nurse. The old woman had served her clones when they lived underground at Precinct 15. The woman found her way to the mountains with Brigon and practiced her minimal healing art there. Tara remembered opening her eyes and seeing a woman with gray hair tied in a tight bun. *Remember me? I'm Patrite*, the woman had introduced herself as she carefully sewed

Tara's face back together. While she sewed, she talked in the most soothing tones. Through the confusion and pain, Tara heard her say, *You will live if you want to.* Everyone else called her *Doc.*

"Patrite," Tara called. "Dr. Carai. Come with me."

The Artrix turned at his name. The old woman almost seemed startled.

Carai said, "I can't." He held the old nurse steady.

Patrite was blue with cold and she had a deep rattling cough. Tara approached. The old woman seemed too frail to move; yet she did. She coughed a shallow puff of air, then sucked in a tight gasp.

"The Doc got sick in the forest," Carai said softly. "I need to stay here with her and help her get well."

A faint whisper contradicted him. "I'm dying. Pneumonia—bacterial," Patrite gasped. "No antibiotics. I told him," she pointed a twig of a finger at Carai, "to leave me. He thinks he can—" She coughed, wincing from the pain in her chest. "He thinks he can cure me. Pure vanity." She looked at the taller Artrix with affection. "But, I'm dying. I ought to know." She ran out of breath. Her thin chest spasmed.

Tara looked at Dr. Carai for confirmation and he nodded grimly. The pale fur on his face made his dark eyes distant. Tara turned to the woman. "Can we get you anything?"

"I'm cold," Patrite admitted. "And tired. I just need to lie down."

Tara summoned one of the larger wilderness clones wandering up the street. He was gaunt but large and muscular. She asked him, "Carry the Doc back to the greenhouse in Precinct 32. Do you know where that is?"

"Yes." The clone accepted his assignment without complaint.

"Put her under the lamps. Warm her up. And stay with her as long as . . . keep her company."

Tara reached forward and took the old nurse's hand, all bone, knuckles, and sinew.

"Up you go, Doc." The large clone picked her up, cradling her in his arms as if she were a small child. He walked against the tide of humanity pouring into the precincts.

The bombardment of Erstewa lasted exactly three hundred and sixty minutes. The ground shook from the temblors of war. Then it stopped as suddenly as it had begun.

A young Jod soldier crawled out of his fortification. Still dizzy from the pounding, he crawled on hands and knees up the side of a new crater, dragging a powerful telescope in a stiff case. He had a comm-disk taped to the inside of his helmet.

He looked around and saw other Jod crawling out into the daylight, wobbly but functioning. Judging direction by the late-morning sun, he set up his telescope facing the direction of Erstewa. He screwed the base together and squinted, trying to find Erstewa with his naked eye. He couldn't. Confused, he looked at the flat horizon and checked his topocard. Erstewa was in the direction of the ocean. He blamed the ringing in his ears and a slightly blurred vision.

The comm-disk chattered at him, "What's taking so long?"

"I'm working, I'm working," the soldier snapped back. He dropped a wing nut that fastened the optics to the base. "Damn."

"What?" the comm-disk chattered back.

"Nothing." He found the wing nut in the dirt, cleaned the threads, and finished building the telescope. He plugged in the transceiver so the men below could see the digital images. He looked in the eyepiece and carefully turned the small worm gear to survey the horizon.

The comm-disk asked impatiently, "Where's the city?"

He raised his head from the eyepiece. "It's gone."

"What do you mean: it's gone?"

The soldier looked over the pocked terrain. He could not distinguish between the masticated fields and the rubbled city. All lay flat and black. The sole difference was the lingering smoke around the former city. Farther out in the harbor, the long hulls of ocean barges lay belly-up in the shallow water. He zoomed the telescope to maximum power. He saw concrete piling snapped at the ground and twisted nubs of reinforcing bar. "There." He spoke into the comm-disk. He slowly backed the zoom to show the complete devastation of the city.

Moments later, the blue sky filled with silvery ships. They flew in formations like migrating birds, descending on the flat land. Thousands of ships grew from faraway specks into large transports. They settled like fat flies on a carcass, then disgorged countless landrovers and armored vehicles. The Jod soldier watched in awe as a million Chelle covered the ruins of Erstewa with their sleek armored vehicles. He zoomed in to see one of the flat landrovers. The squat hull lay nearly flat on the ground on two dozen dark-green wheels. The back of the hull was hinged front to back, so that the landrover moved with liquid grace across the uneven ground. Near the front of each landrover was a small crystal cupola. The bend in the crystal distorted the face of the Chelle vehicle commander, exaggerating black eyes. Each landrover was large enough to carry fifty Chelle infantry.

Interspersed among the landrovers were armored vehicles bristling with weapons: both energy and kinetic.

The ground was infested with the Chelle craft. They formed a series of rings around the ruins of Erstewa, advancing like the concentric circles caused by a stone tossed into a still pond. Looking at the mass of infantry and armor arrayed before him, the soldier felt his legs ache with an urgent desire to flee. Yet he knelt by the telescope, watched, and controlled the rising anxiety in his voice. "Thousands of them. Tens of thousands—I can't count them all."

The regularity of the formation fascinated the Jod soldier. Their front line was as precise as if they were on parade. The columns and rows stayed equally precise despite the havoc inflicted on the ground by their bombardment. He spoke into the comm-disk. "Pass the word to all gunners. The Chelle vehicles appear to stay equidistant—about twenty meters apart."

"Confirmed," the comm-disk answered. "Tell us when they have completed their landing."

The soldier shifted his weight to sit on the ground. The aching in his legs began to subside as the situation assumed surreal proportions. He sat alone on his small hillock looking across a plain of a million soldiers who were as yet unaware of his presence. He began to feel like a spectator on the safe side of a one-way mirror.

He calmly unpacked his rations, ate a light meal, and drank water as he watched the landing progress throughout the afternoon. Finally he saw the last wave of landing craft settle onto the ground. The blue sky was clear, except for whiskery contrails slowly dissipating. He spoke, "They're all down."

The comm-disk answered, "You'd better get back down here."

The soldier reconfigured the telescope to operate with remote signals. As he did, he saw two large clamshell doors open to his left. Loose dirt fell from the doors, revealing a gaping hole and the three thick barrels of the deep-space particle-beam cannon. A loud buzz and thunderclap shattered the silence as an opaque beam instantly arched into the dark blue sky.

Then a brilliant flash of orange sparkled above. They had hammered one of the Chelle's capital ships. The Jod soldier scampered back to his underground lair, knowing that the Chelle must soon return fire.

In an orbit above the desolate planet Vintell, the *Tyker* parked with a small battle squadron and a deep-space tug towing two cylindrical, unmanned barges. The smaller *Benwoi* lay back to back with the *Tyker* like a small growth connected by the docking hatch.

Andrea stood at the hatch. H'Roo's voice came across the intercom, warning her, "Hold fast to the metal rungs by the hatch."

"I know." Andrea braced herself. The hatch

opened and the *Tyker*'s artificial gravity overwhelmed the *Benwoi*'s. She slipped headfirst through the hatch, spinning to land feetfirst with a loud *clang* on the metal platform below.

H'Roo Parh stood with his hands behind his back, watching. Eric stood beside H'Roo. His arm was still in a boneknitter.

Andrea ignored H'Roo. Instead, she looked up through the hatch and saw the upside-down *Benwoi* and the clone Chana preparing to drop through the *Tyker*'s ceiling. Chana turned and flailed with her feet to find the ladder rungs—less artful but just as effective as Andrea's entrance. Brigon followed.

H'Roo said, "Please follow me. We're going to the conference room."

From behind, Andrea noticed H'Roo's new rank sewn onto his sleeves. She taunted him, "I see K'Rin has rewarded you with a promotion. He must be able to count on you to keep his secrets and use people."

H'Roo stopped in his tracks. His neck flushed a slight burnt orange; then he resumed without comment.

Andrea looked around the *Tyker*. She recognized—or thought she recognized—the corridors, the rooms. *I was here. K'Rin brought me here after he killed Steve. His surgeon dressed my wounds. I chose to keep the scar on my shoulder.* Andrea felt her shoulder through the simple jumpsuit. The slight rise in her flesh barely affected the smooth lay of cloth against her skin. *He should have left me on Earth. He should have left me to die.* Her mind was unable to imagine life on Earth without Steve. She refocused her eyes: the *Tyker*, H'Roo, Eric, Brigon, the clones, and K'Rin. For good or ill, this was her reality now.

Eric walked behind her, preferring the company of Chana. Andrea turned and said, "You were aboard this ship during the Harbor Massacre, weren't you?"

Eric replied, "Yes. K'Rin held me for questioning."

Andrea stiff-armed Eric, stopping him in the corridor. She glanced at Chana and Brigon, warning them to stay out of her argument. She asked coldly, "When did K'Rin tell you about Steve?"

Eric looked down at Andrea's palm pressed against his sternum. "As soon as you arrived, K'Rin restricted me to the upper decks, right around here, if I'm not mistaken. I knew he wanted to keep us separated. He didn't tell me the particulars about your husband till later. He did tell me to hide my mark from you." Eric held up his left wrist with the blue disk and yellow halo.

Andrea mumbled, "If ever I find out that you're lying to me, I'll kill you, too."

Eric didn't back away from the threat but threw it back at her. "After you kill me and K'Rin, you'll need to kill all the Jod whom K'Rin sought to protect at your expense."

"That's enough," Brigon cautioned.

Eric continued without pause, "Then you need to kill the Cor—all of them—to make sure you get the bastards who sent the Hunters to Baltimore. You need to kill the Chelle who kidnapped Terrans almost a thousand years ago to start the Cor Ordinate—"

"I said, that's enough!" Brigon grabbed Eric's good arm, but Eric jerked himself free.

"Keep your hands off me." Turning back to Andrea, Eric said, "While you're at it, you might as well kill all the Terrans, whose spawn became the

Cor. Hell, kill all the Artrix for good measure. They might have had something to do with your misery. Then you can really get to the root of your problem: you can kill yourself."

By this time, H'Roo stepped back to diffuse the escalating argument. Chana and Brigon braced themselves to intervene. Brigon pushed Eric back as Eric pointed to Andrea with his free hand, accusing, "Truth is, Andrea, you and K'Rin are more alike than either of you care to admit."

Eric's last verbal salvo jarred her senses: *Me and K'Rin, alike?* Andrea tried to summon the old rage that had served her so well in the past. She couldn't find it in herself. Instead, she dismissed Eric, saying, "You don't know what you're talking about." Yet, as she said the words, she wondered if he did. She told herself, *My quarrel is not with Eric. Nor with H'Roo. My quarrel is with K'Rin.*

H'Roo stepped between Eric and Andrea. "My mission is to get all of you to Cor—alive. Then you can indulge yourselves."

Andrea put up her hands in frustration. "I'm okay." She stepped past Eric and said, "Let's get this over with and get me off K'Rin's ship." She turned and glared at Eric. "Just a lot of bad memories here."

Eric shrugged Brigon's grasp from his good arm. "I came into this world with bad memories."

In the conference room, they found other Jod Fleet officers seated around the table. Andrea followed the briefing with only passing interest. Her thoughts followed K'Rin. She imagined him seated at the head of the table, where H'Roo sat. *I should have stayed aboard the* Benwoi.

H'Roo summarized the concept of the operation. "After we come out of FTL speed, we dive straight for the planet Cor. Our total time in the system will be one hour and twenty minutes. The destroyer peels off for a programmed bombing run at Lynx. The deep interceptor takes down as many Cor Ordinate satellites as possible on one pass."

H'Roo flashed an aerial picture of Sarhn on the screen. Andrea realized the image was old, because it still showed the most prominent feature, a huge ziggurat that had been the Clone Welfare Institute. To the right of the ziggurat, outlined in red, was the target zone: the Sarhn spaceport and barracks.

H'Roo pointed to the targets outlined in red. "The rest of us fire our ordnance at Sarhn—primary targets, their military assets and landing facility. The bombardment will create confusion. The tug transfers operational control of the supply barges to the *Benwoi*. Then, the *Benwoi* dives in after our short prep and goes to ground. The unmanned barges follow and auto-land within a kilometer of the *Benwoi*. Then the rest of us get out of the Cor system as fast as we can, because let me assure you," H'Roo looked around the table, "we will have kicked the anthill."

Addressing the Jod commanders, H'Roo said, "You have your detailed routes, schedules, and target list. Any questions?" H'Roo looked around the table. "We depart in two hours. Good hunting."

The other Jod officers filed out of the room. Eric and the contingent from the *Benwoi* stayed behind. H'Roo addressed Brigon, saying, "Eric needs a transport to Cor, and he can't go in a barge."

Quickly Brigon replied, "That's up to Andrea, not me."

Eric also turned toward Andrea, and asked, "May I have permission to come aboard the *Benwoi*? If I don't travel with you, I have no way to get to Tara."

Andrea looked hard at Eric trying to discern his motives. She studied Eric's eyes—Steve's eyes. Andrea blinked away her personal pain, clearing her mind. Eric had dismissed the wounded Tara as damaged goods—perhaps a forgivable reflex burned into his clone programming, his bad memories. Yet he seemed to have strong regrets about leaving Tara behind, even an urgency to return with the promised help. Now, they were late—not their fault, but how might Tara know? *He's worried that Tara will feel abandoned again. I can see it in his eyes—the worry.*

Brigon interpreted Andrea's pause as rejection. He answered for her: "No, Eric. Fifteen minutes ago you two were at each other's throats. I don't think—"

Andrea interrupted, "That was my fault." She crossed her arms across her chest. "Eric can travel with us to Cor."

H'Roo offered her a polite bow. "I'm glad to hear you say it."

He handed Brigon a small black case and said, "Electronics don't travel well on barges, so here are the tactical comm-disks you requested." H'Roo produced a thinner green box and slid it across the table to Andrea. "This is a deep-space burst transmitter. You can send secure messages to couriers that we shall have at the Cor frontier. We ask that you send us updates as well as your supply requests. You can't receive messages."

"I remember how to use the transmitter." Andrea took the green case by the handle and pulled it toward her.

H'Roo stood and the others imitated him. He said, "I need two minutes alone with Mat Andrea—Tenebrea business."

Brigon took Andrea's green case and led Chana and Eric out of the room. "We shall prepare the *Benwoi* to depart."

H'Roo turned and pulled open a drawer from the long credenza built into the wall. He pulled out a box made of honey-colored wood and a stainless-steel auto-injector. "Andrea," he laid the two objects on the table. He stepped back. "Hal K'Rin told me to give these to you." He pointed to the box and the silver injector.

Andrea looked at the two objects, but kept her hands by her sides.

H'Roo opened the box to show her a set of gold braid. "K'Rin promoted you to the rank of commander. Also, he's worried that if anything has happened to Dr. Carai, you might need a dose of enzyme. By my calculation, you are already well into your grace period." He pushed the auto-injector across the table. The small cylinder spun to a stop, inches from Andrea.

"How do I know this injector isn't filled with poison?"

H'Roo arched his brow. Parallel furrows formed on his forehead—surprise, then bemusement. "What an interesting predicament."

Andrea grabbed the injector and self-administered the dose into her left arm. Then she walked from the table leaving the ornamental box and gold braid behind.

Tara didn't stop to sleep or eat. She walked alone through the precincts and through the forest.

Outside the Sarhn wall, the world was serene. Tara expected more activity, especially at daybreak—machines perhaps. But Sarhn's populace was slow to rise.

She stood at the tree line behind a thicket of holly. A thick hoarfrost covered the pine needles of the trees. The morning sun tried in vain to burn its way through the fog. However, the natural light, even in its weakened state, overpowered the haze of Sarhn's artificial lights. A swarm of midges danced like a curl of smoke. Despite the cold, she smelled the tannin rot of pine needles. In the immediate fore-ground, a magpie with white chevrons pecked at a large pinecone.

She leaned against a thick pine with her binoculars pressed against her face. From her blind, she studied the Sarhn defenses. A series of small trucks, driven by clone labor, dumped loads of dirty, wet snow over the wall onto the pile that had already grown to half the wall's height. An entire season of heavy snow lay compacted at the base of the stone wall.

Outside the wall, the sonic barriers hummed. The invisible deadly barrier, designed to disrupt tissue, boiled away the snow, carving a parabolic curve into the artificial slope of snow dumped over the wall. The water that ran from the sonic barrier collected into great pools of ice, adding yet another physical barrier. The Sarhn defense was a bad dream: ice, then squealing steam, an invisible barrier of sound, an inverted wall of snow, then twelve feet of slippery stone wall. *We'll need to get past these barriers without destroying them. We'll need these barriers intact when it's our turn to defend the walls—especially the sonic barrier.*

She increased the magnification of her binoculars and turned slowly, studying the crest of the wall. Her eyes fixed on a solitary figure standing on the wall, looking back at her through a similar pair of binoculars. She knew the face: a NewGen. It wore a simple battle uniform and carried a heavy automatic rifle slung by a heavy strap, hanging loosely at the waist. The NewGen lowered the binoculars and looked in her direction with the same cold eyes she remembered from the South Mountain assault. Tara felt her blood chill.

She wasn't mistaken. The figure on the wall was looking directly at her. *He won't even waste a bullet trying to hit me at this distance. They know we're here. They're waiting.*

A pair of low-flying troop transports hovered in from the south. They gave wide berth to the precincts as they dipped in and out of the low clouds. The transports strained from the load. The whine of the turbines made Tara's back teeth hurt. She shifted her binoculars to study the two ships. The side doors were open for ventilation. Inside one ship, she saw large men huddled together, pressed as thick as possible, even causing a bulge in the webbing that kept the cargo from spilling out the side doors. The cargo was NewGens, perhaps a hundred of them. The second ship carried pallets of supplies.

Looking up at the burdened hovercraft, Tara realized, *The Ordinate must have ordered the airlift, anticipating a siege. They let us come into the precincts unchallenged. They've locked themselves inside the Sarhn walls. I wonder what they are planning for us now.*

The low clouds began to lift as Tara walked back into the precinct. She did not welcome the few patches of blue and intermittent sunbeams. She wanted the cloud cover, but she realized that the afternoon would become increasingly bright. The Ordinate could use their air assets to harass them.

She found a group of her armed clones waiting for her near the perimeter fence. They were practically asleep on their feet. She approached a clone she recognized. "Ogorm, set up an observation position outside the Sarhn wall. Run a landline to our command post. I'll bet you can find miles of fiber and gear in the perimeter towers." With a sweeping gesture, she pointed to the metal fence hung between concrete posts and the squat towers. "Understood?"

"Yes." Ogorm blinked away the sleep. "We could use some rest first."

Tara nodded. "The Cor know we're here. Do you want them to kill you while you sleep? Set up your observation position, then rotate your people to the dormitories for rest and food. I want all our weapons above ground in point defenses. Who knows when the Ordinate will attack?"

"I don't know where everybody is," Ogorm complained.

"Then, you'd better find them and get organized." Tara frowned, then sighed. "I want every rifle in the hands of an alert person all the time. Put the two 20-mm guns at opposite ends of the precinct. Do not fire at their reconnaissance or supply ships. Fire only if the Ordinate attack the precinct."

Ogorm scratched his ear under his wool cap. "I'll

keep the first watch." He wandered off to assemble his people.

A few pedestrians on their way to work idled across the street in front of the Sarhn ministries. In the courtyard, a work gang of old-order clones planted blue and purple pansies in formal beds. They worked under the watchful eye of two armed NewGens.

Scaffolding embraced the facade of the great hall, and along the narrow planks more old-order clones carefully repaired old mortar and restored the finish to the white marble. More NewGens patrolled the base of the scaffolding.

Madame Prefect watched the progress from a balcony. She stood in the fresh air and inhaled deeply. She wrapped a green shawl around her shoulders and admired the carefully manicured lawn cleared of the killing snow and rejuvenated by heat rising from underground apartments. She said, "Sarhn is most beautiful after a hard winter, don't you agree, Admiral Brulk? Come and take a look."

Brulk stepped onto the balcony. He forced himself to lean over to look down into the garden. He gripped the balcony railing tightly. Ironically, Brulk suffered a twinge of vertigo. "Very nice." He backed away.

"These last old-order clones seem to be operating efficiently. I'll almost miss them," Madame Prefect said casually. "But I must admit, we all feel more secure with the NewGens."

"Secure. Yes, secure." Brulk repeated her word with confidence. He rubbed his hand through his short salt-and-pepper hair. "Dr. Sandrom sends us a hundred copies of NewGens per day now. In three weeks, we will double the order. Three weeks after that, we'll have ten thousand NewGens at our disposal. Then, we cancel the last old-order clones inside the city. The renegades have done us the favor of coming out of their mountains and congregating outside the walls. Now we can rid ourselves of the lot without digging them out of their caves."

"You trust Dr. Sandrom completely, don't you?" Madame Prefect stepped past him into the room and shed her green shawl onto an overstuffed chair.

Brulk followed. "At present he is essential to our success."

"But?" she raised her pitch, anticipating a second half to Brulk's answer.

Brulk obliged her by finishing his thought. "I would trust him better if he were more expendable. I don't trust anyone who is not expendable." Brulk looked at the brass wall clock to break eye contact with the Madame Prefect. He expanded his thought in the privacy of his mind. *That is why I prefer NewGens. They are by design utilitarian and expendable.*

"Even me?" The Prefect feigned a bruised ego.

I have real work to do. Enough banter. Brulk smiled through tight lips, still gazing at the time. "Oh, Madame, I trust you completely," he lied. "And don't worry about Dr. Sandrom. It's just that we can trust him more after he finishes automating NewGen production. If you will excuse me, Madame, I really must go."

"I understand." Madame Prefect began walking Brulk across the parquet floor to the double doors. "The Cabinet approves your plan. You have them wrapped around your finger now."

Brulk raised an eyebrow. He cared very little what the Cabinet thought.

The Prefect continued her flattery. "You showed some real diplomacy this week."

"How?" They reached the door. An old-order clone wearing simple livery opened the door.

"You did, after all, compromise to permit a modicum of normalcy."

"Compromise?" Brulk raised an eyebrow.

"You let us keep sufficient clone labor inside Sarhn. Now that the council believes they can influence you, they are happier to follow your lead. It never hurts to show some political sensitivity."

Brulk bristled at the suggestion that those overfed, soft, insipid creatures believed they could influence him, but he minded his temper. "Your ministers managed to convince me that the civilians would not do servile labor."

"Citizens," she corrected his choice of words.

"An old habit, pardon me."

Before he stepped into the hall, the Prefect reached out and grabbed Brulk's hand. Brulk was slightly repulsed, but the Prefect's words diffused any hint of affection. "Admiral Brulk—"

"Yes, Madame," he answered with precise, cool etiquette.

"I know you are ambitious. I will retire soon—perhaps by autumn. You will take my place. I know it."

"Why are you telling me this?" Brulk was genuinely curious. For the first time this afternoon, he preferred to stay and listen to her.

Her cheeks blushed slightly, giving accent to her winter pallor. "I believe that you will destroy anybody who gets in your way. I just want you to know that I won't be in your way. I plan to retire to the southern archipelago and live my last decade or so in comfort. And perhaps, from time to time, I can give you advice."

Brulk tried to match her candor with his own. He asked, "Advice on what, for instance?"

She let go of his hand, leaned forward, and whispered, "For instance, when to get out of the game."

With the perimeter guard and the Gatling guns in position, Tara allowed her migration to rest one day. Eighteen thousand clones tended their cold injuries. They swapped their rags for dry clothes left hanging in abandoned cubicles. They ate the few scraps of food they found, and slept in the relative comfort of dormitory cots. Then everyone returned to work.

The majority of the returning clones worked in small parties to gather anything edible. Ten thousand clones worked with one purpose: to collect enough food to survive a few weeks. They filled a large freezer locker with the frozen animal entrails and heads. They searched the dormitories, room by room, gathering small sacks of bread crusts. They swept the pantry floors in the communal dining rooms, collecting loose grain, lentils, and other food particles. They picked through garbage.

The steward, Hart, sent parties to the river to cut holes in the ice and catch fish. Others scavenged in the forest, digging through the wet snow and thawing dirt to gather the tightly bound fronds of ferns waiting for the warm sun. Thousands of workers brought their small treasures to the steward who gathered the food into Precinct 15.

The underground quarries beneath Precinct 15 were just as Tara had left them. Most of the light bulbs had burned out, but Tara navigated flawlessly in the pitch black. Her feet remembered the uneven floors. She unconsciously avoided crevices that tripped many of her subordinates following behind. They held torches overhead.

Despite his excellent night eyes, Dr. Carai walked closely behind Tara, periodically reaching out, touching her shoulder to reassure himself. Tara didn't mind the gentle pokes as she was more intent on navigating the twists and turns in the monochrome blur of rock. She commented, "Long ago, clones like us quarried this granite to build the Sarhn walls." She tapped the wet stone walls with her cane.

"Turn right," she said. And she led them down a long narrowing corridor. The floor became slick with damp mud mixed with chips of granite sloughed off the ceiling and walls. Suddenly the corridor stopped where the granite ended, and a wall of dusky gray clay and dirt began. The group bunched together like an uncomfortable plug. The smoke from the torches filled the confined spaces. Tara squatted down on her haunches to keep her face out of the oily smoke.

"We are at the farthest end of the quarry. As you see, they ran out of rock. We are about thirty-five feet below the surface. Straight up is the forest that serves as a buffer between the precincts and Sarhn."

Tara pointed at the dirt with her stick. "If we dig straight for seven hundred meters, we'll go beneath the sonic barrier and probably hit the foundation of the wall. Then, we dig straight up until we reach the pile of snow that they've dumped over the wall." She turned to a small man with intense blue eyes. "Stuart, you used to lay pipe, right?"

"Yes, but. . . ." Stuart held his torch closer to look at the clay.

"I want you to lay a big pipe, seven hundred meters—that way." She poked her cane into the sticky dirt. "You can have anything you need."

The clone, Stuart, sat down with his legs spread apart. He handed his torch to a neighbor and started calculating on his fingers. He muttered, "Fortunately, the permafrost didn't get this deep. Let's see: ten days, seven hundred meters, seventy meters per day, three meters per hour." He looked back at Tara and the small crowd leaning over his shoulder. "I can rig a couple ditch awls and cut the dirt. If we work around the clock we can cut the dirt. The trick is going to be hauling twelve yards of dirt—I'm guessing eight to ten tons of clay—out of here each hour. Plus, we need electric light, not these things." He pointed at the torches. "We need timber to hold up the ceiling. But the big trick is hauling the dirt."

Stuart closed his eyes as he calculated the rough numbers. "We need about five hundred strong backs per shift, four shifts. We need wheelbarrows, carts, and fifty-pound sacks. Plus we need a place to dump the dirt."

"Sort it out." Tara sat on the ground with her legs crossed. Her auburn hair fell in her face. "After we dig our way into Sarhn, I can drop the sonic barrier. We may be able to open the main gate. Then, we can storm the wall with all eighteen thousand of our people."

A voice in the shadows said, "We don't have nearly enough weapons."

The dearth of weapons was not news. Tara answered, "We have our hands, if nothing else." She looked up. "The Ordinate are importing about a hundred NewGen warriors each day. I've seen these creatures up close." She pointed to her face with the purplish stump below her elbow. "They are genetically engineered for combat. They are difficult but not impossible to kill. They are neurally programmed to operate without a sense of self-preservation, so our overwhelming numbers won't intimidate them. We have only two 20-mm guns. Our large-bore rifles will knock them down. Truth is, we've got to kill most of them in hand-to-hand fighting. I figure four of us can hold one NewGen."

An older female opined, "We could stop them if we had curare."

Tara turned and faced the woman. She had dark brown hair with gray at the temples. The thin face had downturned lips. Tara asked, "What is curare?"

The woman reached into her woolen blouse and pulled out a leather sheath tied to a leather cord around her neck. She extracted a small steel spike, no bigger than a large thorn. She said, "Brigon's mother, Plova, taught me this defense. In summertime, we caught small grass serpents—green and gold banded. We milked their venom, curare, and we doped our blades or small spikes with the poison—very dangerous to handle. If you scratch yourself, the tiniest scratch, you're paralyzed. Mostly likely, you stop breathing and die. They say you see dimly but hear clearly everything around you as you lie still, unable to lift a finger or close an eyelid. I killed a

Cor Security Trooper—a big man—with one small jab of this spike."

The woman held it up for everyone to see. "Don't worry, the point is clean."

"What happened to the Cor Trooper?" a third man asked.

"He froze. The pupils of his eyes dilated. I could see his heart pumping beneath his ribs and his pulse in the neck arteries. But he couldn't move to defend himself."

Tara addressed the group: "Where can we get some of this curare?"

"We can't—not in winter," the old woman answered. "The grass snake is rare enough in the summer and nonexistent after the first frost."

Dr. Carai raised his thin furry hand in the flickering torchlight. "I can make a synthetic."

Everyone turned to face the Artrix. Carai sat on his haunches with his bony knees near his thin chest. He pressed his long fingers together and put them to his lips. Tara asked for all of the clones, "How?"

"The nervous system has an enzyme that—" Carai interrupted himself. "Never mind that. I need to extract the acetylcholine from all the frozen cow and sheep brains that we found in the animal yards. I might extract one or two milligrams per brain. Using some common chemicals—sulfur compounds, and other agents—I can change the acetylcholine into succinylcholine which you can use just like curare." He turned to the old woman. "You got curare from snakes? Fascinating," Carai wheezed.

"How much can you make?" Tara asked.

"Depends on the number of brains. Maybe enough for a thousand doses."

Tara stood up, pointed down the corridor, and said to the nearest clone, "Quick. Go. Find Hart. Tell him Dr. Carai needs all the cow and sheep brains found in the animal yards. Run."

chapter 14

Tara carefully paced the length of the tunnel, counting her measured steps. *Five hundred fifteen . . . five hundred sixteen . . . We're more than three-quarters finished.* Her shoulder brushed against the dirt and timber wall of the tunnel as she sidestepped the continuous flow of laborers. They worked silently with heads bowed to gulp the fresh air pumped in through a long and ever-growing black airhose.

The tunnel was hot from body heat. Male and female laborers were covered with a thin slick of mud, the mixture of dust and their own sweat. They wore simple bandanas covering nose and mouth. Their hair was matted with the grime: they themselves looked like animated dust returning to their source. But their eyes reflected in the artificial light, tearing from the irritation of the dust.

An electrician passed her carrying a short string of lights. Every tenth clone carried a beam of fresh pine or hornbeam into the hole to brace the dirt ceiling.

The shrill sounds of the ditch awls quashed any conversation. The constant vibration shook particles of loose dirt from the ceiling. Tara saw Stuart directing with hand signals. He stood behind a slender tripod, on which he mounted a spotting laser to guide their work. The ruby-red dot reflected from the shadows. The ditch awls cut a monotonous pattern, chewing the forward wall and spitting the loose dirt behind. Shovelers attacked the loose dirt, filling sacks and wheelbarrows. An endless stream of bodies carried the dirt away.

Two large clones with sledgehammers beat vertical beams into the wall bracing up a thick ceiling timber. A third clone with a smaller hammer tapped in shims to anchor the ceiling support.

Stuart pointed to the newest set of beams, directing the electrician to add another light. Each light represented another five meters of progress. Tara tapped Stuart on the shoulder and they retreated from the loud noise to exchange a couple of words.

Tara reached into her pocket and produced a bottle of water. Stuart thanked her. He removed the bandana covering his mouth. His face was two-toned: pale from the nose down, grimy from the nose up. His back hair was covered by a small skullcap of loose dirt. He took a short drink and passed the bottle to the men working the mechanical awls. Stuart had large bags under his eyes. He spoke loudly above the noise of the awls, "We're on schedule." He ignored the loose dirt that fell on his head and shoulders.

"Can I get you anything?" Tara shouted back to him.

He pointed at the stream of clones carrying dirt away. He shouted, "They're hungry."

"I know." She brushed some dirt from her auburn hair. "We swept the kitchens, the dormitories. The greenhouses are putting out shoots, but nothing edible. We've sent hunting and fishing parties out." She smiled wanly. "That Artrix is starting a mushroom farm with the dirt they're hauling into the caverns. We can't do more. Stuart, the food is on the other side of this tunnel. Keep telling everybody—*the food is on the other side.*"

Stuart looked up suddenly at the ceiling. He reeled.

"What?" Tara asked. He had reacted suddenly to some sound or vibration that escaped her.

"Stop the awls!" he shouted above the noise. "Stop the awls!" he screamed. But the clones on the machines were deaf to his cries. He stepped into the line of dirt movers. "Back!" He shoved the unaware workers and Tara away from the machines that continued to whine.

Then for an instant, the crack of timber eclipsed the sound of the awls. The ceiling fell in and the awls abruptly died. Everybody on Tara's side of the cave-in froze in terror. A couple of the clones dropped their loads and ran.

"Oh, no!" Stuart broke the silence. He looked around. "Get shovels up here. Anything. Dig with your hands." He grabbed Tara's cane and started prying the dirt away. Twenty clones fell onto the loose dirt, viciously clawing their way through with their hands.

Tara felt inadequate with her missing hand. She watched from a short distance. Her chest was tight. She knew she must not take up the space in the line of diggers as much as she wanted to help. In her mind, she knew that the two dozen men and women on the other side were trapped.

Tara backed away to give room to the rescuers. They fell to their knees and dug until their hands were raw and bloody. Time meant nothing—and everything.

In moments, shovels arrived and the stronger clones flayed the dirt till they were exhausted, each handing his shovel to the next digger. Others, using their hands, filled wheelbarrows to haul the dirt farther back into the tunnel.

The air became dank, as the ventilating hose had been buried. One of the stronger diggers fainted from lack of oxygen. As other clones hauled the limp clone from the action, Stuart grabbed a shovel and held it over the ventilation hose where it entered the wall of dirt. He hesitated, and all eyes turned to watch his next move. Stuart drove the edge of the shovel down, slicing the black hose—the windpipe to the tunnel.

The cool breeze of relatively fresh air resumed in a gush that stunned the diggers. By cutting the black hose, Stuart had cut the air to their comrades buried on the other side of the cave-in. The diggers stopped and looked at the severed hose. "Dig!" Stuart hollered and he started moving dirt with his shovel. "They may have a pocket of air."

The wall of diggers threw themselves into the work again.

"I found something!" one of the diggers yelled. Two boots turned sideways. The soles were worn through, revealing the dirty pale feet. Tara pressed forward to see. They grabbed the boots and pulled with all their might, dragging the body from the soil.

"He's dead." A digger placed his ear to the body's mouth. The lips were blue, the eyes shut peacefully.

"Get him out of here," Stuart ordered.

Several of the diggers lifted the lifeless body with their bleeding hands and unceremoniously laid him in a wheelbarrow. An empty wheelbarrow arrived at the front anticipating more bad news.

The second victim lay in a fetal position. His head lay on his half-filled burlap sack like a pillow. He held his hands over his face as if hiding. The heavy dirt had pressed the life out of him. One after another, the diggers exhumed the dead from the loose dirt. With each case, they put their ear to the chest; they opened the eyelids in hope of some flicker of life. Always, they got the same sad result. The electrician lay facedown with the wire and broken bulb in his hand.

As they dug deeper, the danger of another collapse increased. They rushed in timber to brace the ceiling. Finally Stuart's men reached the ditch awls. The mechanical beasts lay on their sides next to their operators.

"We've got a live one." A digger cradled one of the awl operators in his arms. The man was barely alive with shallow, unsteady breathing. But the bluish tinge in his lips faded and he opened his glazed eyes and began sputtering dirt and phlegm.

Tara stepped into the midst of the diggers whose eyes followed the sole survivor being wheeled away. "We must resume digging."

The exhausted men looked at her in disbelief. They leaned against their shovels, perspiration dripping from their faces. The simple, dogged purpose they brought into the tunnels had left with the dead who were carted away. Now they mumbled in confusion. She said, "Stuart, get the next shift in here early. These diggers are done for the day."

Stuart stepped through the small crowd. He shook off his fatigue, set a ditch awl upright, and started the motor. As it idled, he hollered, "Either dig, or get out of the way."

H'Roo disliked traveling faster than light. The forward portholes swam in churning, unintelligible light; the aft portholes were black, a void. The screens showed a virtual star map—identical pinpricks of artificial light moving in little jerks as the *Tyker*'s computer updated the plots.

But this time, he wondered if he might prefer to stay in the safety of FTL travel. Because this time, when the *Tyker* returned to kinetic speed, the screens would focus on the Cor system. He paced the bridge, consciously trying to hide his nervousness from the others. *What is worse: seeing that the commander is nervous, or seeing that the commander is artificially calm?*

The pilot-navigator lay on the neural couch. The two weapons specialists readied themselves at their tactical screen, checking and rechecking their systems and rehearsing dry fire drills. The chief engineer, and other Tenebrea, watched the analog displays of the engines, dampener, and shields—an array of waves and colors dancing on the same screen. Although the *Tyker*'s bridge was filled with competent staff, H'Roo felt isolated, wound tight.

He wasn't afraid for his safety. He had been wounded, after all, on Earth when he and Andrea ran into the Hunter Team at the Dewinters' house. He had flown the *Benwoi* to Cor in worse circumstances. He had fought, greatly outnumbered, on Klamdara.

H'Roo knew, or he accepted as his fate, that he would not be harmed on this mission. So his fear was not what one normally associates with physical weakness or lack of resolve. H'Roo took immediate consolation in knowing that his fear was not venal. Perhaps his fear was appropriate: he feared failure. After all, the burden of success or failure was his alone.

He looked at his data card in his right hand, reviewing his decisions. He noted with clinical curiosity that his hand trembled slightly. He glanced around the bridge to see if anyone else detected his onset of nerves. They didn't; they were busy tending to their own challenges.

The data card displayed his plan—carefully synchronized maneuvers that must happen precisely. *Am I relying on false precision?* H'Roo wondered. *I can't second-guess myself now. A good plan in time is better than a perfect plan too late.* He would have the uncomfortable job of watching his plan unfold with few ways to influence the outcome. When they decelerated to kinetic speed, they must first regroup. The time needed to regroup depended on the spread of their entry into the Cor system. The spread depended on the infinitesimal variation in the atomic clocks aboard each vessel. *Three minutes? Perhaps thirty minutes?* H'Roo had not heretofore considered the variance between the *Tyker* and the *Benwoi*'s clocks. The plan required that the *Tyker* pass control of the unmanned barges to the *Benwoi*.

H'Roo looked up at the chronometer. He said aloud, "Everybody, look sharp. Be quick."

One minute left in FTL drive. There are so few absolutes. Light is absolute. Time muddles everything. He rehearsed the operation a last time in his mind.

Regroup. Pass the barges. Then the destroyer and two escorts—Beta group—turn abruptly to attack Lynx. The *Tyker*, *Benwoi*, and three escorts—Alpha group—dive toward Cor, release ordnance, and flee—all except the *Benwoi* and the barges. They run to ground. The small fighter circumnavigates Cor, knocking out satellites.

In some ways, H'Roo preferred a stand-up fight than this quick sucker-punch-and-run strategy. But he had no idea how many combatants the Cor could muster. He knew the Cor had mustered enough resources to decimate the Jod Fleet—a discomforting thought.

The lights on the bridge dimmed as the *Tyker* decelerated. H'Roo braced himself against the navigator's couch for the minor shift in the dampener. "Locate other ships."

The tactical officer paused at his screen, then said, "Got 'em."

"Time to rendezvous?"

"For the Jod ships—six minutes, eight seconds. Our satellite killer has already gone ahead."

"The *Benwoi*?" H'Roo asked, allowing his agitation to sound in his voice.

"Sir, the *Benwoi* is way ahead of us."

"Time? Distance?" H'Roo demanded loudly, annoyed at the vague report. He had worried that the *Benwoi*, not of Jod construction, might add more variance in the plan. He was unfortunately correct.

"Two hundred and ninety thousand miles or seventy-one minutes if the *Benwoi* comes to a full stop, less if she reverses course."

H'Roo commanded, "Open tactical channel." He saw the green light flash on the screen. "Beta group. You're on your own. *Benwoi*, report."

"We read you," Andrea's voice came back three seconds later.

"Slow to half speed until we catch up." Then H'Roo addressed his three escorts. "Alpha group, converge on the *Benwoi*."

One of the weapons specialists interrupted, "Sir! Sixteen attack craft, vicinity Lynx, on our bearing: estimated time to weapons range—twenty-one minutes. Eight similar craft, vicinity Cor, also accelerating toward us—estimated closure to the *Benwoi* fifty minutes."

H'Roo spoke again, "Remember, the Cor attack ships will try to ram through your shields. They have quark torpedoes. You must kill them at long range or evade. Complete your missions and get out. I'll see you back at Vintell."

H'Roo turned to his communications tech. "You monitor Beta group. Keep Alpha group's channel live to the bridge."

"Yes, sir."

"Navigator, prepare to jink the course to evade incoming torpedoes."

The otherwise silent, almost catatonic, navigator breathed a quiet affirmation. H'Roo walked from the neural couch to the weapons console and watched the converging points of light. The *Benwoi* was in the middle, beginning to carve a broad arch to evade the incoming Cor J-Class attack craft.

The long minutes were grinding. Everyone's hands lay nervously on consoles. The navigator on the neural couch began to breathe heavily. H'Roo saw the *Benwoi* growing on the forward screen. "*Benwoi*, accelerate on my mark. Stay on our starboard side."

"Affirm," Andrea's cool voice answered. "Sarhn is on the opposite side of Cor."

"Alpha group: prepare to fire a barrage at the incoming Cor attack craft on my mark. Time detonation for two thousand miles. We'll break up their formation, then use Cor's gravity to accelerate past them. They'll turn and chase, so prepare to put all your shields aft."

The weapons officer reported, "Enemy weapons powered up. They've ranged us."

On the screen, H'Roo saw the closing Cor ships. "On my mark, all port tubes. *Fire*." The *Tyker* shuddered slightly as a set of three torpedoes fired to port. H'Roo saw the escort's missiles accompany his into the distance.

A minute later, the black void burst into light as the spread of torpedoes detonated. H'Roo knew that at such long range, the chances of hitting the craft were slim, but the Cor would have to change course to avoid the wall of fire that he'd push in front of them. They'd have to momentarily power down their electronics to avoid electromagnetic pulse damage. But the enemy ships accelerated past the ball of light, maintaining their intercept course with the *Benwoi*.

The tactical officer raised his voice. "Negative hits, sir. They just returned fire."

"Begin evasion," H'Roo spoke calmly. Now that the fight had begun, the simplicity of kill-or-be-killed bridled the wandering of his active mind.

"Sir, enemy torpedoes closing in nine seconds, eight . . ."

H'Roo ordered, "Drop decoys. Stand by with lasers to detonate any torpedoes that get through. Put shields aft."

From the aft tubes, the Jod ships spit small packets that inflated instantly in the vacuum of space. Five of the decoys drew torpedoes harmlessly away. The explosion caused the *Tyker*'s sensors to momentarily dim. Lasers caught the last three incoming torpedoes barely four hundred miles to the rear.

"Damage report."

"Escort two: shields damage, twenty percent."

H'Roo looked at the status board. All other ships remained one hundred percent. "Target the enemy ships. Put another barrage in their path . . . on my mark. *Fire*."

Another burst of light—this one with a blue halo.

The tactical officer announced, "One Cor ship destroyed. Others off course, but regrouping."

A pair of Cor torpedoes sailed harmlessly to the port arching down toward the planet and exploding in the atmosphere.

"At last, some luck." H'Roo took his eyes from the aft screen to the forward screen. They began their turn as Cor's gravity bent their path into an orbit. They passed through Cor's night. In minutes, they would wake the citizens of Sarhn with a dozen thunderbolts.

The thin shell of atmosphere offered them scant protection from the pursuing Cor. Again the tactical officer spoke, while keeping his eyes glued to his console. "We passed control of the barges to the *Benwoi*."

Brigon's voice answered, "We have both barges in tow."

H'Roo cautioned him, "Watch your speed. You mustn't outrun them: barges can't maneuver like a ship."

The Jod force continued around the planet at maximum speed. As the Cor sun peered over the horizon, the weapons technician said, "Sarhn is cloud covered, but I have infrared confirmation."

"Damn," H'Roo muttered. *Infrared increases circle probability of error.* "Can you make out their landing facility and barracks?"

"As best I can, sir. I have the image and coordinates locked into our ordnance."

H'Roo looked at the status board again. The escorts' surface weapons were likewise locked on target. "Drop ordnance."

The forward screen magnified to follow the two dozen warheads entering the atmosphere. Small shock-rider spikes protruded from the nose of each warhead to split the thin air, reducing air friction, increasing speed and accuracy of the falling munitions. The clouds below looked like a large spill of milk over the land and ocean. The warhead, now black specks, disappeared leaving contrails behind. "Time to impact, three minutes," the weapons technician volunteered.

Three long minutes. We won't be here to see it, H'Roo thought. "Calculate our jump out of here."

Suddenly, a surface cannon from Sarhn opened fire at the Jod. A bright yellow bolt cut through the black. Sensors reported a splash of matter against the *Tyker*'s shields, and the number two escort disappeared from the status board. H'Roo snapped, "Let's get out of here." To Andrea he simply said, "Good-bye, Andrea. Good luck."

Another blast of light blurred the *Tyker*'s screens. The floor ripped out from under H'Roo and he fell to his knees. The screens flickered, then dimmed to black. The navigator arched his back painfully, straining against the cords lashing him into the neural net.

"We're hit," the tactical officer reported the obvious.

"Get us out of here," H'Roo ordered without raising his voice. "Now!"

"Good-bye, Andrea. Goo—" Ear-splitting static followed. Andrea winced at the shrill noise. The *Benwoi*'s screens wavered, and she saw the energy bolt slam the *Tyker*. The *Tyker*'s shields turned cobalt blue, then buckled beneath the heavy bolt, but the ship remained intact. Andrea leaned against her shoulder straps to get a closer look.

"H'Roo!" she yelled, knowing he couldn't hear. She turned the nose of her ship down and accelerated toward the planet, rocking erratically to frustrate the Cor's aim. She kept one eye on the screen to watch the *Tyker* correct pitch and yaw. *H'Roo still has helm control.* Andrea was relieved for a short moment.

A torpedo flew past, exploding into a fireball that Andrea flew through. "How far back are those Cor ships?"

Brigon reported, "They're closing in. Wait. Our two escorts have turned to engage the Cor at close range. Look, they just blasted a pair of the Cor attack ships to pieces."

Andrea couldn't look. She was about to hit the atmosphere and she needed to hit the angle precisely to keep the barges in tow.

Brigon slapped the console. "Good shot! We got another one." Looking at the screen, he saw a bolt of light flash by. The sensors registered the surge of energy. "Damn. That ground cannon is still firing into the middle of the ship to ship fight."

Eric, who sat in the navigator's seat, commented with authority, "The Cor don't much care if they kill their NewGen pilots, as long as they get us."

Andrea glanced at the rear screen. She saw the Cor ships fading quickly in the distance as the *Benwoi* pulled away from the center of the conflict. Quickly, she focused on her piloting. The two barges responded less quickly to her evasive swings and she feared she might collide with her own cargo.

Brigon related the drama on his screen. The two Jod escort ships fought furiously, protecting the *Tyker*. Another ground bolt surged past, disappearing into black space—a miss.

The chaos of the fight was stunning. Andrea wanted to watch, but she had to pilot the *Benwoi*. She had to control her speed. If she lost the barges, the mission was a failure.

Another blast from the ground cannon missed the *Tyker* and blasted one of the Cor attack ships into a shower of sparks. Brigon approved, "Only three Cor ships left."

A second later, the surface of the planet glowed white where the Jod bombs hit. The searing heat burned a hole in the milky clouds exposing blackened ground and rising flame. The clouds rippled, peeled back, then slowly spilled in to fill the hole. The surface cannon was no more.

Andrea fired braking engines as she entered the outer atmosphere. She felt the pressure against her straps.

Without taking his eyes from his console, Eric announced, "The *Tyker* is about to jump."

Andrea allowed one eye to watch the rear screen.

She saw the *Tyker*'s engines glow white, a preparation to jump to FTL speed. "Go, H'Roo," Andrea talked to herself. "Go, go, go. . . ." As she spoke, the *Tyker* disappeared, not in a fiery ball of destruction but in a pinpoint of light. *He made it.* The two escorts that had fought so brilliantly, immediately turned to run. They, too, made the jump.

"We're not through yet." Brigon looked over from his console. "The remaining three J-Class ships are accelerating toward us."

"They'll burn in the atmosphere at that speed." No sooner had she said the words than she realized that self-preservation was low on the NewGen scale of needs—at this time, much lower than destroying the *Benwoi*.

Andrea gritted her teeth. *Self-preservation is higher on my scale. If I continue to accelerate with the gravity, the* Benwoi *and the dumb barges will burn up like a trio of meteors.*

Not waiting for orders, Eric fired the *Benwoi*'s small laser cannon aft, predictably without effect. Andrea noticed, annoyed at the futility of small laser. However, she refrained from commenting. *Let him think he's helping. He can't do anything else.*

Encumbered by thickening atmosphere, Andrea had to abandon the zigzagging of evasion for fear of losing the barges. She simply flew with an eye to the rear screen, watching the three attack ships hurl themselves down, closing the gap.

Brigon's voice was edged with anxiety as he reported, "The Cor ships are in range to fire their torpedoes." Brigon watched the rear screen and the tight formation of the attack craft. The noses on the Cor ships were glowing pale yellow. He asked,

"What happens if they fire torpedoes through that kind of heat?"

Andrea answered hopefully, "The torpedoes might blow up in their face."

Brigon looked up from his screen toward Andrea. "That's why they're not firing. They know."

Eric asked, "Then what are they trying to do?"

"Ram us." Brigon watched the three balls of fire converge as they came closer. "Can't we go a little faster?"

Andrea remembered the *Benwoi*'s last near-fatal landing on Cor. "We can't go any faster. In fact, we need to slow down. Our own hull temperature is in the red. If I lose control, we lose the barges." *The mission.* Andrea tried to forget the man-made meteors chasing her as she watched her heading and speed.

Eric stubbornly continued firing the aft laser at the closest of the fireballs. The thin crimson light disappeared in the white heat and trailing flame.

The Cor ships continued to close the gap. Brigon no longer needed to magnify the image on his screen. His voice was more tense and unconsciously louder as he related the scene. "They look like three fireballs chasing us. A white light and a mile of flame behind. They're closing, *closing . . .*" His voice grew louder. *"Closing."*

Andrea snapped, "Tell me something I can use."

Brigon answered back, "We've got to go faster." He braced for the impact.

"We can't," she snapped back.

Eric interrupted, "I think our laser is cutting. I see a hole." Eric was right. The laser punched through the attack ship's hull—creating a slight imperfection with catastrophic results.

The ensuing explosion engulfed all three Cor attack ships. Their power plants exploded in one spasm of energy that rattled the *Benwoi*'s sensors. Half the molten hull of the Cor's lead ship bashed the *Benwoi*.

Andrea felt the *Benwoi* lurch forward. She struggled with the controls. "Numbers two and four engines down. Port steerage nonresponsive."

Eric asked, "Can we land?"

"We're going down, if that's what you mean." Andrea steadied the ship on their course, putting the remaining three engines in full reverse to fight the pull of Cor's gravity. She ran a series of calculations. Without taking her eyes from the console, she reported, "We'll hit the ground going about two hundred and eighty miles per hour."

Eric looked up. "So that's all there is."

"We're not dead, yet." Andrea remembered a September day on the Chesapeake Bay. A black squall line approached from the south. Steve sent her to the cockpit to take the wheel while he secured the gear and dropped the jib. Steve said, *Keep the engine at two thousand RPM, and keep her pointed into the wind!* She remembered trembling as she watched the black wall of rain and wind coming at her small boat. Instead of running away, they sailed directly into the fury. She exclaimed, *I can't!* Steve was reefing the mainsail as fast as he could, yelling at her in the harshest voice she'd ever heard from him. *Don't you dare lose my boat for lack of nerve.*

She didn't remember the white-knuckle details of the next sixty minutes as the squall beat them with wind, rain, and eight-foot waves. But she remembered that Steve left her at the wheel and watched.

He defended this seeming lack of gallantry saying, *Someday, I won't be aboard, and you'll have to handle the weather by yourself.*

Andrea commanded, "Eric, go back and tell the others to get into an empty bay and strap themselves in. Get everything in the lockers or tied down. We've got four minutes before impact. Any loose equipment or debris will kill. Brigon—"

"Yes."

"We aren't going to land in the mountains—that's for sure. Find me some water. We'll ditch her in there. I can pull up the nose a bit and skip her like a stone on the water. "

Brigon saw the ocean peering from beneath the cloud cover, but the edge of the ocean was perhaps eighty miles away from the shrinking hole in the cloud cover left by the heat from the *Tyker*'s bombs. "The ocean?" he asked.

"Wherever we set down, the barges set down near us. Can we do better than the ocean? Any lakes? Pull up the virtual maps of Cor."

Brigon complied. The clouds disappeared as if by magic. The artificial image showed Sarhn without the blackened scars of the bombs. The precincts spread out in a great semicircle toward the south and east. The virtual image did not show the ice or snow. The forward screen showed contour lines depicting terrain. "The river. Aim for the Sarhn River."

Andrea looked at the virtual image on the forward screen. "Can you find anything a little farther from Sarhn? They'll be all over us before we can crawl out."

"Nothing big enough to ditch in."

Andrea shook her head and muttered, "One problem at a time." She took a deep breath and began a long arc. She had only her starboard steerage so she had to make a giant sweep around Sarhn, over the mountains, and hit the river somewhere between the precincts and the mountains. The chances were high that they'd flip and roll like an egg, scrambling the contents within the shell. *We are most likely going to die, but the barges will land intact using their braking rockets. Then it's a race whether the Ordinate or the clones get to the barges first.*

Fifty feet beneath dirt and granite, Tara felt a sudden tremor. She looked up at the dirt ceiling, cringing at the prospect of another cave-in. Then she felt an aftershock followed by a boom and rumble. Clods of dirt fell onto her head. *A quake?* She tucked her cane under her arm and walked briskly up a set of stairs to topside. A runner stopped her. "They're bombing!"

"Get everybody inside! Which precinct are they hitting?" Tara assumed that Cor gunships were bombing the precincts.

"You don't understand. Somebody just bombed *Sarhn.*"

"What?" Tara ran with a limp to the entrance and out into the open air. A crowd of clones stood in the middle of the small plaza gaping at the horizon. A pillar of smoke and fire rose over the eastern end of Sarhn, the barracks and spaceport. The heat rose like a fist through the clouds. In the distance, sirens wailed.

"Eric?" she wondered out loud. *He and Andrea brought back the Jod. Who else would drop explosives on Sarhn?* She prodded one of the clones with her cane. "Everybody!" she yelled to grab their attention from the fire and speculation. "Be alert! Remember what the Jod look like. They have no hair. Broad shoulders. They have colored rings beneath their eyes."

She grabbed another clone by the jacket. "Find Ogorm. Tell him to bring fifty men with rifles. Meet me at the rear perimeter fence near the 20-mm gun. Eric will assume that we're still in the mountains." The runner left and Tara began trotting down the middle of the rusty rails toward Precinct 32.

As she ran, she saw a gray streak and trail of smoke break through the clouds at a shallow angle to the ground. The ship, or whatever it was, was like a black seed with a long feathery thread trailing. In two short seconds, the ship disappeared over the rolling hills that led to the river. *Something is terribly wrong.* Tara's heart sank.

Two large cylinders followed the gray streak, but in a graceful arc. Stubby legs appeared from the base of each cylinder. They settled down slowly over short but bright plumes of white fire. Tara bit her lip and trudged up the train tracks.

Ogorm caught up with her. "Tara Gullwing!"

She felt her heart pounding in her rib cage. "Did you see the three objects land?" She pointed over the horizon with her stick. Her limp became more pronounced as she tried to keep up her pace and pointing with her cane. The stump at the end of her elbow began to ache and burn, a pain that bothered her only when she worked herself into a hard sweat, the same searing pain she felt when the NewGen cut her arm off.

Ogorm answered, "I did. What are they?"

Tara stopped: she was out of breath from the running and the pain. "I don't know. My guess is that they're supply ships. One of them came down hard." She tried not to show the pain as she clutched her throbbing arm to her chest. "We've got to get to them before the Ordinate does." She grabbed another clone. "You, run back to the precinct. Tell Hart what's happened. Tell him to send bearers and sleds. Hurry."

The lone runner sprinted back to the precinct while the fifty armed clones slogged toward the river through the snow. They formed two columns. Tara followed their tracks in the snow and watched them disappear over a low hill. Her normal breathing returned. The throbbing abated.

Behind, she heard the whine of turbines. *Hovercraft!* Instinctively, Tara squatted on the snow-covered ground. She looked up to see the diffused searchlights of the hovercraft crisscrossing the ground. Two hovercraft flew just below the cloud level in a straight line toward the river. *No gunship?* Tara realized that these two craft were probably the only surviving air assets left after Sarhn's bombardment. She watched the two craft approach quickly.

Suddenly, Tara heard the loud clatter of her own 20-mm Gatling gun. The nearest hovercraft rolled, then abruptly augured into a hillside with a violent crash, kicking up a spray of snow—no fire. The second hovercraft turned and fled back to the city.

The distant spray of snow filtered down. Two NewGens crawled out of the wreckage, dragging themselves slowly in the direction of the river. One

stood and quickly crumpled into the snow. *Their legs
are broken. How could anything survive that impact?
Amazing*, Tara thought. *Perhaps we can capture one
and test Dr. Carai's synthetic curare.*

Tara trudged to the crest of a long slope overlooking the Sarhn River. The thin set of tracks in the
snow pointed the way. She saw fifty dark figures
bobbing as they jogged in the knee-deep snow. Two
large black cylinders lay on their sides on the near
shore. The Sarhn River was smooth white ice except
for a large jagged tear that cut like a giant fishhook
from the center channel to the far shore. Tara
squinted, wishing she had brought her binoculars.

At the end of the tear in the ice, she saw a short
and ephemeral rise of steam. The *Benwoi*. Tara recognized the damaged hull of the ship. It lay on its
side with the nose down, wedged on the thick side
near the riverbank. Black water skirted the starboard
side of the ship. She was sinking slowly. The ship
was buoyed partly on frozen water, partly on frozen
land. Tara could not see the forward hatch, nor
could she see any signs of life. She quickened her
pace.

Andrea woke with a start as she felt another's
hands on her chest. She was hanging over the side
of her chair in her straps. It hurt to breathe. She
started to sit up, but a pain in her shoulder stopped
her. So she slumped against her straps. Her head
spun and she felt nauseous, but she forced her eyes
to focus. Everything seemed dark. She smelled the
ozone and heard the spitting of broken wires.

Large hands carefully but quickly unfastened her
shoulder harness. One beefy hand pressed her

against the back of the chair. Cold fingers pulled back her shirt at the neck. She felt eyes peering, the hot breath, and beard of a smelly man. She heard the baritone voice next to her ear. "This one's cut from her straps, but no broken bones."

"Get her out." Andrea recognized Tara's voice in the background. "Get *everyone* out of the ship before it sinks."

Tara's alive, Andrea thought. Her head ached. Her neck felt sore. She tried to turn her eyes toward Tara's voice. She looked around to see the hulk leaning over her, ministering to her.

Only the amber emergency lights worked. The people on the bridge were a confusion of shadows. Andrea looked across the bridge. Brigon was gone. *Dead? Can't be.* She saw Brigon's straps dangling from his empty seat. *They wouldn't move a dead man.*

Tara's voice directed two shadows, climbing an awkward incline, almost on hands and knees, to drag Eric's limp body out.

"Can you walk?" The baritone voice spoke directly in her face.

"Yes." She answered without considering for an instant that she might be unable.

The large clone grabbed a handful of Andrea's shirt and lowered her to the slanting deck. The floor was unsteady, rocking like a boat. She crawled out from the bridge and toward daylight, entering the hull through a crack wide enough to climb through. Her right hand was numb.

Ahead, she saw Chana squeeze through the opening into the daylight. Other clones lay in the yoke where the floor met the wall. Some fidgeted. Others lay deathly still. Tara's people quickly stuffed the unconscious ones through the hatch to safety. *"Go! Go!"* Urgent commands echoed around the ship. "We're taking on too much water."

With her good arm, Andrea pulled herself into the light. The *Benwoi* shuddered from the river's strong current, large chunks of ice banging against her half-submerged hull. Ice water sloshed into the hatch, splashing her from the waist down.

Andrea cleared the hatch and slid down the pocked skin of the *Benwoi* toward the ship's bow, over the forward porthole to the ice. She waded through ankle-deep water to the riverbank—solid ground.

She paused to study the cadre of wilderness clones that worked around the crash site. She thought: *They are just gristle and bone.* They carried armloads of gear from the *Benwoi*: food, clothing, electronics hastily ripped from sockets, their cables dangling behind. She saw the dark green box that held the deep-space transmitter. *Good, I can send H'Roo the message.* Andrea composed it in her head: *Your landing was better than mine. I totaled the* Benwoi.

" 'Scuse me." The clone Ariko, soaked from head to foot, brushed past her carrying four of his long rifles.

Andrea stepped out of the way. She felt her own bruises crossing her shoulders. The cold numbed her hands and feet, but only added to the sharp pain across her chest. She trudged up the slope away from the ship. She heard voices behind yelling, "Everybody out! Now!"

Andrea looked skyward and saw the low clouds

moving rapidly west to east. The white landscape blurred at the horizon where the gray flannel blanket of clouds engulfed the white sheets of snow and ice. She couldn't make up her mind whether the sight was beautiful or depressing. Along the riverbank, she saw a small cluster of people—some working, some waiting.

Chana wandered up the bank to ice-covered rocks and a line of thick willows leaning out to drape their budding branches toward the frozen river. *No, Chana was not wandering; she made a straight path to Brigon.* He lay between two large tree trunks on a snarl of roots at the crest of the riverbank. A thin woman pressed a bloody towel to his forehead, covering his eyes. His bloodstained shirt was torn in a precise *X* where the shoulder straps cut him. He appeared to drift in and out of consciousness. Andrea felt a sudden calm, seeing Brigon alive.

Chana knelt next to Brigon and tried to minister to him. Andrea heard the anxiety in Chana's voice, but not the words. Brigon raised a hand and weakly pointed back to the sinking *Benwoi*.

Immediately Chana rose and bounded down the slippery bank, hobbled by a bad ankle. She almost ran into Andrea. Andrea sidestepped and called after her. "What's the matter?"

"The wilderness cloaks!" Chana slipped on the ice as she waded through the water. A large male pulled her to her feet and restrained her. "The ship is flooded. You can't go in."

"*I've got to,*" Chana insisted, but the clone stood between her and the ship.

Another tall thin male, wearing a thick parka soaked to the waist, stood on the hull as the last clones crawled out of the hatch. He cursed the freezing water, then called into the ship through chattering teeth, "Cloey! Get out now."

A woman pushed a last limp passenger from the hatch into the thin man's blue hands. He pulled her out against the water pouring inside the ship. She climbed onto the unsteady hull, pale and shivering. "The rest are dead." Cloey, blue from the cold, and her friend carried the injured clone across the unsteady ice just as the *Benwoi* slipped under the black water. Andrea watched it sink.

Chana bowed her head as the *Benwoi* disappeared. She had failed to get the cloaks.

A steady roil of bubbles marked the spot where the *Benwoi* sank. Andrea thought, *We lost so much. But we could have lost so much more.* She looked back at Brigon. Nearby, other *Benwoi* passengers lay broken on the snow, but alive.

Farther upstream on the bank, two clones held a cup of water to Eric's lips. Tara crouched to prop Eric's head up with her good hand. Her auburn hair clung to her sweaty face. Andrea especially noted Tara's pallor and the bluish skin of her eyelids. She saw Tara's soft eyes behind the scar, and she recoiled slightly upon seeing her raise her purple stump of an arm to pet Eric's cheek. Tara's lips moved, but the whispered words were for Eric's ears alone. She stroked his hair and looked over at Andrea, her hazel eyes wet with emotion. Andrea read her disfigured lips: *Thank you.*

Andrea thought it was fitting for Tara to have Eric back—to meet them as they landed. Then the incongruity struck her. *How*, she wondered, *did Tara get here so fast?* Andrea turned a full circle and looked

around the flat terrain on either side of the wide
Sarhn River. *We can't be near the mountains.*

Across the river, she saw the two black cylinders.
One leaned precariously, its stubby feet sinking into
the thawing ground. Already the clones had cracked
the seals and opened the wide hatches to inspect the
cargo. She saw them raise the Jod weapons to their
shoulders, looking down the barrels. They inspected
the other military hardware: the silvery shields.
They're more interested in the weapons than the food.
In the distance, through the intermittent fog, she
saw a swarm of clones descend on the barges like
ants on sugar.

Andrea looked back at Tara with admiration as
she realized, *She moved them all back into the
precincts.*

chapter 15

Admiral Brulk walked through the smoldering stone and timber that had been the west wing of the Sarhn barracks. Other officers walked behind him awaiting orders, taking notes. Brulk's face was stiff with anger and concern. The Madame Prefect walked beside him with her small entourage. She wore an ankle-length white fur coat. Her dark lipstick made her face look pale.

They walked through the rubbled barracks. All the roofs were gone. Only a few isolated walls stood precariously. She lamented, "These were the finest old terra cotta buildings on Cor. I doubt we can replace them."

Brulk gave her a dismissive look. Then he looked past the half-standing walls' rubble and saw the damaged spaceport. All four gunships were damaged beyond repair. Six of the eight hovercraft were burned husks. Of the surviving two, one had been shot down just outside the precincts. An orange crane pulled a large merchant vessel away from a collapsed hangar. Work crews with earthmoving equipment filled a twenty-foot crater in the middle of the tarmac. *A setback, but it could've been much worse.* Brulk kneaded his left hand in his right. *Half my NewGens wasted. Two weeks lost.*

Madame Prefect stood next to him and surveyed the destruction. "I suppose we are fortunate that the Jod missed the heart of our city."

Brulk took a controlled breath, then fixed her with his steely eyes. "They didn't miss. They struck our military assets on purpose." Brulk turned abruptly and asked an attending officer, "Did they hit Qurush?"

"No, sir." The officer consulted a data card. "As best we can tell, no other cities were hit. The Jod attack against the Lynx ship building factory was ineffective. But they took out seven of our nine multitask satellites. We lost communications with two-thirds of the planet. We don't have satellite surveillance left."

Brulk looked up from the screen. "We need to replace those satellites as soon as possible."

"Sir, we've already placed the order through the Chelle emissary, Firbin."

"And what did he say?"

"Sixty days."

Brulk handed the screen back. "I'll speak with Firbin." Brulk folded his hands and pressed them to his lips as he surveyed the twisted metal of the spaceport hangars. "And what damage did we inflict on the Jod?"

The officer offered some good news. "By our count, we destroyed three Jod escorts. We rammed an armed merchant with towed cargo and sent it crashing south of Sarhn. We damaged the Jod destroyer and light cruiser, but they both escaped. We lost seven J-Class attack ships. If you compare tonnage lost, the Jod got the worst of the fight. If that's the best the Jod can do . . ."

Brulk cut him off. "Let's not fool ourselves."

The Prefect hiked her fur higher as she stepped over a charred piece of timber. "What do you think was the purpose of their attack?"

Brulk turned and looked at the beautiful buildings in the civilian sector of Sarhn, then back at the ruined barracks. *Not retribution for Heptar—that's certain. They sent supply barges and a merchant ship.* He answered, "My guess is that the Jod want to supply the old-order clones with weapons."

The Prefect stiffened. "Admiral Brulk, I suggest that you tell Dr. Sandrom and have him divert all the New-Gens at his disposal to Sarhn—*immediately*. We will not take any chance that a rabble of armed clones might get inside these walls. I shudder to think . . ."

Brulk countermanded her instantly. "No. Qurush shall continue to get first priority for NewGens. We will not alter the schedule now. If anything un-toward happens to our facilities at Qurush, we are ruined."

The Prefect got red in the face. "You would hand all of this," she expanded her arms to embrace the beautiful city with its ornate buildings and gardens, "to the old-order clones just to protect a factory town like Qurush?"

"In the blink of an eye." Brulk stepped closer to the Prefect so he might speak in a low voice. "If you begin to lecture me on Cor Ordinate culture, I swear, I'll—"

The animus in his voice was clear. Madame

Prefect backed away. She, too, was angry but impotent. She gathered her small entourage and left.

Brulk returned to his officers who watched in awe as the head of the Cor Ordinate government retreated from his icy words. He abruptly addressed them, "Do we have confirmation of the crash site by the river?"

"Not yet. If we fly below the clouds so we can see, the clones in the precinct can use their 20-mm guns against us."

"Damn this weather." Brulk looked up at the low clouds.

"The clouds are supposed to clear tomorrow. We'll be able to see the river and stay out of range of their guns."

"Do so. Report your findings as soon as you can." Brulk picked a dry scale of skin at the side of his lower lip. "In the meantime, double the NewGens on the wall. Instruct them to shoot anything that moves in the forest. I don't want those precinct clones to get any ideas just yet. And send a message to Dr. Sandrom. I need every NewGen he can spare, but not at the expense of the Qurush operation. Now, go." He shooed them away with a swipe of his hand.

His staff left him alone.

Brulk shut his eyes and rubbed them with the thumb and forefinger of his right hand. Brulk didn't care for others' opinions anymore—nor their company. As soon as he was alone, he felt his inner calm returning.

He walked deeper into the smoldering ruins of the spaceport. All around, the NewGen worked with minimal supervision. *Interesting. Dr. Sandrom must have programmed them with some automatic recov-*

ery instructions. He watched undamaged NewGen haul the dead from a collapsed hangar and stack them unceremoniously on the cracked tarmac.

From a pile of rubble, a NewGen carefully lifted a timber off another's legs. Both NewGens were identical in every feature except for the facial bruises on the trapped NewGen. The trapped and injured NewGen sat up slowly and helped push the timber, a beam weighing five hundred pounds or more—no grimace, no complaint, not even a show of stoic endurance, just results. Beads of perspiration collected on the injured NewGen's brow. The cooperating NewGen pushed the timber aside, and it fell with a loud resonance against a broken concrete slab.

Brulk was fascinated by the fact that the two NewGens did not exchange words. Both knew what had to be done. The rescuer copy bent over to inspect the other's wounds. Both femurs were snapped. Jagged bones protruded through the blood-soaked trousers above the knee. The left boot was mangled as was the foot inside. The injured NewGen also looked and seemed only mildly perturbed by the extent of the wounds. Brulk edged closer to see what would happen next.

Then the rescuer unsnapped his holster and removed a heavy pistol. Still, the two clones exchanged no words. Although the injured NewGen's eyes widened slightly as the barrel approached his forehead, he lay back down, and turned his head. Brulk found himself looking into the crisp blue eyes of the wounded NewGen.

The loud crack of the pistol shot followed. The NewGen's head bounced roughly against the hard ground. The back of the skull split away, but the crisp blue eyes continued to look back at Brulk. "Magnificent," Brulk uttered. "Simply magnificent."

The steward, Hart, grinned with satisfaction. The clones emptied the cylindrical barges and dragged away pallets of dehydrated food. They carried plastic cases of weapons of design and power beyond their simple imaginations. Then Tara directed the clones to topple the cylinders and roll them down the gentle hill onto the ice. And there, they used axes to break the ice and sink the cylinders. They hauled all the supplies into the quarries beneath Precinct 15. A light snow blew in from the west covering their tracks.

That evening, Precinct 15 came alive with anticipation and optimism. The clones ate their fill of hot rations. Each received a Jod weapon: a laser rifle or energy lance. They opened cases of grenades. They began to speak in terms of *when* they conquered Sarhn, not *if*. They bolstered their expectations and courage with hypotheticals: eighteen thousand clones armed to the teeth could sweep the city in a day—hell, in an hour. The few veterans in the group listened quietly without comment.

Tara finished a hectic meeting with Hart. Then she and a squad of attendants carried plates of food to the makeshift infirmary to feed the *Benwoi* crew—what was left of them. She carried a plate of hot food in her good hand, her cane trapped under her arm.

She found Andrea and Brigon sitting side by side on a simple wooden bench. Andrea leaned stiffly with her back against the stone wall with her chin up and her eyes shut. Her ribs were taped with tight linen bandages, tied with an odd little bow beneath her breasts. Brigon sat with his bandaged head in his hands, unaware of Tara's entrance. A bloody bandage wrapped around his head caused his hair to stand up in a comical tuft. His hand was bandaged for a sprained thumb.

"Andrea," Tara whispered.

Andrea opened her eyes, alert. She recognized the hazel eyes peering through thick bangs of auburn hair.

Tara raised her arms to greet Andrea, and her wooden cane fell clattering to the floor. Brigon winced at the noise. He raised his head. His eyes were still glazed from his concussion.

Tara said, "Thank you both for coming back." She handed Andrea a plate of food. Another attendant carefully put a plate into Brigon's hands and handed each a spoon.

"I'm sorry I couldn't talk to you before. So much going on, and . . ." Tara's disfigured smile exuded the warmth Andrea remembered.

Andrea stopped her. "That's all right." Andrea looked at other attendants carrying food to Chana and Ariko, who alone managed to walk away from the crash without a mark. A small woman patiently sewed shut a gash in a crewman's forehead. Seeing the clones without their heavy clothing, Andrea realized how desperate they had become. They were cadaverous: thin from months of starvation, sunken cheeks. She could count the vertebrae in their necks. "How did you survive?"

Tara looked down and shook her head. "The fact is,

we were dying quickly—only eighteen thousand of us left. I gave up on you two and brought most of them here. A couple thousand others quit the mountains and headed south. I didn't know what else to do."

Andrea looked back with unspoken admiration. *We leave you half dead, your arm cut off—canceled as Eric might say—and still you manage.*

Brigon blinked and smiled through a twinge of pain and said, "So, you took over my operation, didn't you?"

Andrea said sharply, "If she hadn't, we'd be twenty feet under ice water right now."

"Yeah, with half my crew, my cloaks, and the comm-disks." Brigon put his aching head back into his hands as he juggled his plate of food on his knees. "Damn, the room spins with my eyes open or shut." He reopened his eyes and spoke to Tara. "You did the right thing. However, let's settle one matter right now: who is going to lead the clones after today—you or me?"

Tara eyebrows turned down. She said bluntly, "We've made plans."

"*We?*" Brigon winced. "I see. And to think that I was worried about leaving Eric behind—worried that he'd do something rash." Brigon took his spoon and idly shoved a lump of hash around the plate. He smiled despite himself and said, "Well, I guess I can relax now. What are your plans, Tara?"

Tara squatted to pick up her cane. Looking up at Brigon, she answered, "We are going to storm the city in four days."

Brigon brushed a particle of food from his tawny beard. He raised an eyebrow and looked at Andrea for confirmation. "This, I've got to see."

Tara stood and tapped Brigon on the knee with her cane. "Finish your hash. I'm going to check on Eric." She motioned to a line of cots in the infirmary. "When I come back I want to show you something." She turned and walked away.

When Tara was out of earshot, Andrea chided Brigon, "Last year, you criticized her for being too cautious."

Brigon set his plate of food on the floor. He winced at the pain between his eyes. "I'll be more careful when I criticize."

Andrea said, "Do you think she's making a mistake?"

Brigon leaned forward to face Andrea more squarely. He whispered, "She has no choice. Perhaps I'd do the same. Out here, they're like lambs waiting for the wolves."

"You like being the headman; you can admit it." Andrea set her plate of food beside her on the bench.

"I took the job of leading this mob only because *you* asked me to." Brigon's cheeks turned ruddy behind his tawny beard.

"Maybe in the beginning . . ." Andrea tried to diminish her responsibility.

"Maybe. However, I started thinking about the long term." Brigon's eyes fixed on Andrea's face. "I started thinking about *us*. I figured maybe we could beat the Cor Ordinate with K'Rin's help. Then we might make a new life for us here."

"I don't want K'Rin's help." Andrea raised her arms slightly. Her tight chest bandages constricted her movement.

"We need his help," Brigon insisted.

"I don't want to owe him a thing." Andrea looked away.

Brigon spoke through clenched teeth. "Indebtedness and gratitude do complicate things. You might have to stop hating K'Rin and get on with your life."

"I can't." Andrea got up to leave.

"Can't or *won't?*" Brigon pointed at her with his bandaged hand. "Steve would want you to get on with life."

"How dare you presume to speak for Steve?"

"Fine. I'll speak for myself. I would want you to get on with your life. I presume that Steve loved you, and therefore, he would want the same."

Andrea started to leave, but her exit was interrupted. Tara arrived from down the hall; the *tap tap tap* of her cane preceding her.

Turning the corner, Tara glanced disapprovingly at the uneaten hash, then said, "Come with me. I want you to see something that your friend, Dr. Carai, has been working on—a way to stop the NewGens."

"With what?" Andrea asked.

"He's made a synthetic curare called succinylcholine—he calls it *snap*. We've got a little demonstration planned. We captured a NewGen from a downed hovercraft."

Brigon slowly rose to his feet, with his good hand pressed against his throbbing head. "I want to see this."

Tara took Andrea by the arm and the two walked down a quarter mile of granite tunnels. The damp granite walls absorbed the limited light of pale green lamps. Brigon followed them through the gloomy corridor that led to a well-lit chamber.

Waiting for them was an assembly of Tara's cell leaders. At the far side of the room stood the Artrix,

Dr. Carai. In the heavy wooden chair next to him, a bare-chested NewGen struggled against the heavy cords that bound him tightly. Already the cords cut the NewGen's wrists and ankles, but the NewGen jerked violently trying to snap the cords or break the chair. Tara left Andrea and Brigon standing at the back of the chamber and joined Dr. Carai.

The NewGen wore only a pair of pants cut off at the knees. The left side of his rib cage was black and purple—an injury caused by the hovercraft crash. Although the abdomen muscles were chiseled definition, the gut distended slightly from internal bleeding. The NewGen's scalp was torn behind the left ear.

Nevertheless, Dr. Carai backed away, unwilling to trust his safety to the strength of the redundant cords and the chair. Tara stepped in front of the group. She raised her cane in a gesture to stifle the murmuring. "Most of you fought at the South Mountain ambush. Some of us—" she referred specifically to herself, "engaged in hand fighting with NewGens. They are stronger than any two of us: taller, heavier. They are exceedingly hard to kill. They do not falter from pain. And they fight until they are dead."

The group bunched around to look at the NewGen struggling in the chair. The large biceps quivered. Blue veins beneath the skin protruded. Thigh muscles bulged. The chair scraped against the floor. Tara pointed at the large NewGen. "In the eight days since we returned to the precincts, our observers have counted more than fifteen hundred NewGens shipped into Sarhn. The Jod bombardment of the Sarhn barracks probably killed a fair number of them. However, we must prepare to fight many of these creatures waiting for us on the other side of the wall."

The captive NewGen increased the struggle. Tara fought her instincts. She stepped closer to the chair to show that the NewGens were not super beings. She rested her small left hand on the NewGen's shoulder. "Carai has developed something that can stop these creatures." She motioned with a nod of her head for Carai to step forward. "Demonstrate, please."

Dr. Carai cleared his throat. He approached Tara, handed her a small silver pin coated with succinylcholine. He whispered, "I . . . I, uh . . . I can't kill it."

"Okay." Tara let Dr. Carai fold into the small crowd. She held up the tiny pin in the light. "The drug on this pin is supposed to paralyze the NewGen. Is that right, Doctor?"

"In laymen's terms, yes." Carai's voice ended in a nervous wheeze.

"At least, explain the symptoms, so we know what we're looking at."

Carai tugged uncomfortably at his mustache. "The place where you stick him immediately goes numb— the muscles no longer respond. Paralysis soon grips the entire body—ten seconds maybe. You might detect a minor reflex, but the skeletal muscles are completely useless. Soon, the breathing fails. Without intervention to get oxygen to the lungs, the patient—I mean, the NewGen—usually loses consciousness and dies."

"*Usually?*" Andrea asked from the back of the chamber.

Brigon elbowed her gently. "Always."

Carai answered, "Not always. Depending on the

dose, the drug wears off in three to five minutes. If you accidentally dosed yourself, I could blow air into your lungs—breathe for you, and in a few minutes you'd start breathing for yourself."

Brigon muttered sarcastically, "I stand corrected. Make a note: do not blow air into the lungs of a drugged NewGen."

Tara scowled at Brigon's interruption. Then she drew the tactical lesson from Carai's medical observation, buttressed by Brigon's sarcasm. She turned to her cell members and instructed them, "We do not wait three to five minutes to see if the drug kills. We do not give them an opportunity to revive. After we paralyze the NewGen, we immediately finish the job."

Tara stepped away from the chair. She held the tiny pin aloft. "In this test, you can observe the effects firsthand." Tara walked in front of the crowd so each might see the insignificance of the pin, so each might appreciate the magnitude of the drug. She stopped in front of Andrea who glanced at the deadly weapon held between Tara's forefinger and thumb. Andrea saw that this show was in part to build confidence in the clones who must soon face the daunting challenge of close combat with NewGens. She approved of Tara's showmanship.

Tara calmly took her new weapon to the NewGen, still struggling in the chair. She stuck the pin in the NewGen's right shoulder. Instantly all the straining in that arm stopped. After a few weaker twitches, the legs relaxed. The NewGen's face froze, eyes open. Andrea saw the carotid artery pulsate.

The absence of struggle brought a hush to the chamber. Tara leaned closer. She said softly with clinical amazement, "His eyes are dilated. Come look."

Although tentative at first, the others crowded closer to see. Tara cautioned them, "Don't touch the pin: it still has enough snap to put you down." Then she stepped back to watch the others become familiar with NewGen mortality. They poked the New-Gen's supple flesh. One clone gently touched the NewGen's right eyeball. The eyelid twitched slightly, sending a gasp through the crowd. Turning, the clone looked up at Tara. "He felt that, didn't he?"

Tara replied, "His sense of touch is unimpaired."

"And he can hear everything we say, can't he?"

"Oh, yes," Tara assured the woman. "He knows exactly what's going on around him. However, he can't do anything about it."

The NewGen didn't breathe. Lips and fingernails turned blue. A middle-aged female clone wiped the sweat from the NewGen's almost hairless chest with her sleeve. Then she pressed her ear against the sternum. "I can hear his heart pounding faster. No, it's slowing down now."

"Let me hear." Another clone pressed his head against the chest and listened.

Andrea watched the clones jockey for position. Several pressed their ears against the chest. Finally, one of the voices in the huddle exclaimed, "It stopped."

Tara raised her voice to get their attention. "Now, everybody, listen to me. Never assume that a NewGen is dead. You kill them, and kill them again. Do you understand?" She held up the stump of her arm to emphasize her point. "They don't die like normal people. You must dash their brains in, cut their hearts out. If you think you've killed them a second time, you kill them a third time." With that she pulled out a large caliber pistol and put the barrel at the NewGen's forehead. The NewGen's chin rested against his chest as he slumped in the chair, held only by the cords cutting into the purpling skin. "Stand back."

The small crowd quickly stepped away behind Tara and her pistol. She fired a round point-blank into the NewGen's skull, blowing the back of the head clean off, splattering brains across the floor. Tara said with a note of satisfaction, "Now he's dead." She looked at Brigon and Andrea. "Any questions?"

Andrea looked at Tara disapprovingly but said nothing. Tara lowered the pistol to her side. She read Andrea's eyes and challenged the unspoken criticism, "What?"

What can I say? Andrea looked back into the hazel eyes beneath the auburn bangs, a disfigured face silhouetted against the dark wet splatter on the wall. *Do I say that I liked you better before I taught you to kill? That I liked you better before you became more like me?* Andrea forced a thin smile and replied, "I'm glad I don't have to clean up that mess."

Admiral Brulk found the Chelle emissary waiting in his office. The diminutive emissary, Firbin, sat in a chair with his feet dangling above the polished marble floor. His long, delicate, and precise fingers gently massaged his thin knees.

"Firbin," Brulk spoke brusquely.

The emissary slid off the chair and extended a

hand, imitating the Ordinate custom of clasping hands at greetings and departures. Brulk looked at the long fingers without reaching out. He disliked Chelle hands, especially the exaggerated fingers. *Seems like they belong to the hand of a vivisectionist. That's it.* Brulk was amused by his own insight. *The Chelle are a species of vivisectionists.* "Sit down," Brulk commanded.

Firbin's thin lips turned to a pout as he climbed back into his seat. With fastidious protocol, he asked, "What does the Cor Ordinate require of the Chelle?"

Brulk sat at his desk and pasted a false grin on his face. "I ought to throw you out that window, and see how high you bounce off the pavement."

Firbin's large black eyes grew larger with indignation. "Admiral Brulk!"

"You were supposed to patrol our frontier. Yet the Jod manage a raid against us. How can that be?"

Firbin crossed his legs defensively. "I admit that our patrols along your frontier are thin . . . ."

"Nonexistent," Brulk snapped.

Firbin licked his lips. "Our home guard must patrol our space to protect against increasing threats to our mercantile ships. Our entire fleet, except the home guard, has laid siege to the planet of Corondor—illegally subsumed from Chelle only fourteen generations ago. We have landed more than a million of our crack troops on the planet and surrounded the bulk of Jod's army."

"Why don't you just capture Jod?" Brulk demanded.

"Our strategy is more elegant. Corondor is the Jod's main source of food. If we capture their food supply, the Jod can't last a year without coming to terms."

"I want the Jod neutralized. I don't give a damn about coming to terms. I swear, you Chelle would rather argue than win."

Firbin straightened his spine. His large black eyes looked at Brulk with disdain. "Terms are important."

Exasperated, Brulk asked, "What about Earth? Can't the Jod get food from Earth?"

"Oh, the Terrans? We blockaded their system." Firbin waved his thin hand. "The Terrans can't help the Jod."

Brulk shook his head but kept his thoughts to himself: *You Chelle couldn't intimidate anyone.*

Firbin continued, "The Jod have their entire Fleet—what's left of it—stationed just outside our reach, while we grind their land forces into the dust." He rubbed the narrow palms of his hands like millstones. "If they move their Fleet to threaten Cor, we have a straight run at their homeworld. The Jod will not send any significant force against Cor. This insignificant raid was a desperate act perpetrated by a desperate foe."

Brulk had heard the same assessment from his staff. *A desperate act. Nonsense.*

"Besides," Firbin chirped, "I hear that the Jod suffered more from their attempt than did the Cor."

Brulk got to his point. "The Jod managed to knock out all our surveillance satellites. We still have about two million old-order clones spread over the planet and no way to track them. About twenty thousand or more are right outside the Sarhn walls. Moreover, the Jod dropped supplies—my guess: arms. We need you to get us a new set of surveillance satellites immediately."

Firbin counted on his fingers. "First, we need to build them; then, test them; then, ship them to Cor; then, install them in orbit; then, test them again . . . three months, minimum."

Brulk stood up and approached the seated Chelle. "No. You don't understand. You simply take some of your existing birds on station in the Chelle system, haul them here, and set them in orbit. Three weeks, maximum."

"Impossible. We would never give up our own early-warning capability."

Brulk walked over to the Chelle emissary's chair and put his hand around the back of Firbin's little neck, just above the collar of the short cape. His middle finger and thumb almost made the full circumference of the small gray neck. Brulk squeezed slightly. Firbin's neck became rigid in his grasp.

"Stop that. Take your hands off me!" Firbin protested in a loud sibilant whisper. "You're hurting me."

Brulk relaxed his grip slightly, moderating the pain. "Firbin, get me the satellites in three weeks. It's a matter of life or death—your life or death. Do you comprehend?" Brulk let go.

Firbin slid off the chair and backed toward the door, rubbing the back of his neck with one hand and making a small fist with the other. "Don't threaten me unless you want to take on all of Chelle."

Brulk gave a truncated laugh and said, "Three weeks. Or I'll wring your neck like a chicken's." He held his hands up to demonstrate.

Tara sat on a wooden stool by Eric's bedside. Eric slept soundly, his head wedged between two rolls of wool cloth. His eyelids were purple and swollen. A clean bandage covered a large lump on his forehead. Leaning over a small wooden table, Tara penned cryptic notes on a mildewed pad of paper, just trying to improve the dexterity of her left hand. A tray crammed with empty plates lay on the floor.

Andrea stepped into the infirmary and asked, "How is he, today?" She carried a section of white plastic pipe in her hand.

Tara looked up and whispered, "Dr. Carai says he'll be up tomorrow."

"Eric was very anxious to get back to you."

Tara smiled and commented, "He would never admit that to me."

"He might. He's learning." Andrea placed a four-foot section of white plastic pipe in the middle of the wobbly table and said, "I brought you something." Andrea dragged a nearby chair to the table and sat opposite Tara.

Tara set her pen down, picked up the long pipe. She held the thin plastic pipe between her thumb and forefinger. "Plumbing?"

"A blowgun."

"A *what?*" Tara held one end of the pipe in her hand like a rapier. Andrea reached over and took the pipe back.

"Don't bend the pipe; it's got to be perfectly straight." Andrea reached into her pocket and retrieved a six-inch dart fabricated from a hypodermic needle. "I found a stash of veterinary supplies."

Andrea handed the dart to Tara, who inspected the simple craftsmanship. Near the base of the needle was a thin plastic sheath, the same diameter as the pipe. Below the sheath along the last inch of needle, Andrea had glued three paper fins or fletches. Tara said, "Show me how it works," and she handed the dart back.

Andrea tucked the dart into one end of the pipe. "This technology is over forty thousand years old. My father used to laugh and say that the Mayan branch of our family used these weapons. They would coat the end of the dart with curare—that's how I got the idea—and they'd shoot their prey." She raised the pipe to her lips. "This is only the third time I've shot this dart, so make allowances. I'll aim for the middle of the cabinet at the far end of the infirmary."

"That's fifty feet away."

Andrea nodded. She took a deep breath and blew with a sudden puff. *Smack!*

Tara stood up and walked to the cabinet to retrieve the dart. "It's stuck."

"I brought some pliers." Andrea followed.

"How fast was that dart traveling?"

"About two hundred, maybe two hundred and fifty feet per second. If I use a five-foot pipe, I can add another fifty feet per second and increase my maximum range by another fifty feet." Andrea looked at Tara's quizzical face. "I used to play with these things when I was a kid. My father never knew." Andrea smiled at her secret. "I can teach your people to hit a three-inch target at fifty feet—one day's practice."

Tara took the pipe in her hand. "How long would it take you to make a half dozen pipes with sixty darts?"

"Give me one helper, and we can finish by sundown. I can train your people the next day." Andrea pulled a small pair of pliers from her pants pocket and plucked the dart from the door.

"I'm going to send you a fellow named Ogorm. Meantime, can you spare thirty minutes for a walk below? I want to show you something."

Tara led Andrea through the underground maze. At first, Andrea thought some of the sights were familiar until she realized that all of the twists and turns looked familiar. Along the way, Tara explained her simple plan: dig their way into Sarhn, disable the sonic barrier, then rush the walls with eighteen thousand clones—"armed, thanks to you and your friend, K'Rin."

Andrea stopped. The corners of her mouth turned down as she told Tara, "K'Rin is not my friend. He is my enemy, now."

"I don't understand."

"He set Steve up. He gave my Steve to the Cor Hunters so that he could keep Eric safe. He used me to get at the Cor Ordinate. Tara, he's armed you because you are more useful to him armed. He's using you."

Tara paused in thought for a moment. "I'll take the help anywhere I can find it. He has his agenda. I have mine. We'll know whether he's cynical if he tries to take the weapons back." Tara winked, closing the gap in the scar. "Besides, I've been used worse."

Tara turned up a shadowy corridor. A wheelbarrow crowned with dirt passed on their left. A female clone leaned against her load pushing it slightly uphill. They passed a gathering of dirty laborers queued to enter the tunnel. A twelve-inch tube of black plastic ribbed with tough wire snaked into the tunnel. "Follow me."

Andrea stood at the entrance. The straight, narrow tunnel looked like a study in perspective or an optical illusion; each uniform cross beam appeared slightly smaller than the one before. Andrea felt like she was standing between two perfectly matched mirrors. The tunnel ran uncannily straight. The measured cross beams, the lights, and the black tube converged to a point of light—or darkness. She couldn't be sure. A parade of figures blinked in and out of the lights pushing or carrying loads, each figure larger than the next. Andrea blinked. "How far does the tunnel go?"

"You can't begin to see the end: seven hundred meters."

"You have been busy."

They marched through the low tunnel and the dank air for a full fifteen minutes. Then they heard a high-pitched rumbling. The wooden braces and cross beams condensed to form a narrow wooden trough. Andrea asked, "What's going on here?"

Tara pointed to the wooden ceiling. She leaned closer to Andrea and spoke loudly above the din. "We're directly below Sarhn's sonic barrier."

Andrea nodded and followed Tara the last thirty feet. The shrill din of the sonic barrier faded quickly, replaced with a cacophony of voices. Stuart supervised from below. He had rags wrapped around his blistered hands.

"Look out!" A small avalanche of dirt rained down.

The tunnel turned abruptly up. Two clones worked on shaky ladders jabbing the ceiling with their shovels, causing loose dirt and rock to rain down on themselves. Clones with flat shovels collected the clods, tossing them into a waiting wheel-barrow.

Another spill of wet, frozen clods thundered down the shaft. "Look out!" The warning sounded too late.

"Ow! Give a little warning next time." The shovel-ers below backed away from the last remnants of debris tumbling down.

"Sorry," a voice from above cackled.

"Sorry, my ass," the ground shoveler yelled up the shaft. He showed Stuart his shoulders and arms. "Look at these bruises." He wanted intervention or sympathy and got neither.

"Take the wheelbarrow out." Stuart took his flat shovel and gave it to the laborer next in line. He sounded weary and distracted.

Tara tapped him on the shoulder.

"*What?*" He reeled around angrily to address the interruption. "Oh, it's you."

Tara asked, "When's the last time you had any sleep?"

"I don't know." Stuart changed the subject abruptly. "We're almost through."

As if on cue, a chunk of white ice rattled down the shaft and rolled out to Stuart's feet. The assembled workers watched as the chunk of ice spun to a stop. Tara grabbed Stuart by the shoulder and pulled herself up to the taller man, planting a kiss on his grungy, salty cheek. "You made it happen, Stuart."

Stuart poked his head into the shaft. "Stop dig-ging."

A pair of tired voices from above replied in uni-son, "About time . . ."

Tara shook her fist as a sign of solidarity. "Now

we can put away our shovels and pick up our rifles. We'll spend the rest of today and tomorrow preparing. Then, two days from now, at daybreak, we storm the walls and take the city." She raised her voice. "Are you with me?"

The small crowd boomed, "We're with you!"

"We built Sarhn," Tara hollered down the tunnel. "Let's take our city back."

The workers cheered boisterously as they walked out of the tunnel, fatigue suddenly a distant memory.

chapter 16

Brigon sat with his back against a massive cedar. He felt naked without his wilderness cloak. He looked up through the leafless branches past a spruce that jutted skyward like a bristling spire. The night sky was cloudless. Agitated stars filled the black dome, and a quarter moon cast a pale glow on the Sarhn fortifications. Unable to use his swollen hand, he used his teeth to unwrap a food bar, then took a bite of the cereal pressed in a malt syrup. He looked at a chronometer strapped to his forearm. *Not long now.* He patted the flare that lay across his lap.

The faint light that permeated the forest cast a thousand shadows. Brigon saw in each shadow the soft edges of a shoulder, a head wrapped in rags, an occasional puff of steamy breath. Hidden in the trees along the entire length of the southern wall, eighteen thousand clones waited as he did. Their ragged clothes blended with the bark. Brigon wondered what they were all thinking as they waited for the red flare that he cradled in his lap, a burst of light that would launch the assault up the snow embankment and over the wall.

Brigon heard the deadly hum of the sonic barrier. Perhaps only the power of suggestion, he felt an annoying vibration in his teeth. He recalled his last instructions from Tara: *When the hum stops, the sonic barrier is down. Send up the red flare.* Concentrating on the hum gave him a slight headache.

He peeked over his shoulder at the wall. The Ordinate in Sarhn had conveniently dumped the snow from their streets over the wall, reducing its height from a formidable forty feet to a paltry ten or twelve.

However, all along the wall, interspersed every fifty feet, the NewGens manned large lasers and large-caliber Gatling guns. Sentries, wearing black helmets and body armor, walked the wall between gun emplacements. Through the clear plastic face shields, the pallor of their faces made them look half dead. Brigon smirked because the red flare would trigger Ariko's snipers and a burst of small arms fire to pulverize the NewGen gun emplacements. He mused, *The thousands of bullets that don't puncture their body armor will simply beat them to death. Dead is dead.* Brigon looked at his chronometer again—little time had passed.

Brigon held up his swollen right hand and tried to make a fist. He couldn't. *Can't even hold a gun in my right hand—I'm reduced to supervising.*

Brigon finished his food bar and tried to occupy his mind by rehearsing the plan. *Minimal plan,* he thought. *Overrun the city, corner the NewGens in their barracks, and kill them all. Kill anything that wears a uniform—simple enough. How else do you organize eighteen thousand untrained clones? You don't. So, you just point them in the right direction and hope everybody starts at the same time.* He felt the crude flare in his lap. *What happens if Tara and Andrea can't shut down the sonic barrier? We have no backup plan. We don't even have two working comm-disks.*

Brigon corrected his own errant thought: *Andrea won't fail.* He saw her in his mind's eye. He felt his stomach tighten as he recited short speeches that he would make to her if the time were right. But the time was never right—never seemed to be right enough. Now they were running out of time, or he was running out of patience. He would look sympathetic—no, he'd take her by the shoulders and say, *Don't you see that we belong together? I want you. I love you. I used to think that my life was just going to be one long pointless joke—the clone child hiding in the wilderness, bushwhacking Cor Security Troops for amusement, and stealing from the clones for necessity. I could stay hidden in my mountains and mock the Cor. I wouldn't have to care about anybody or anything—just live for the moment. My life was only going to last until my first mistake.*

But you came along and with you a whole new set of possibilities. If we became mates, you would bear children. If we had children, I'd need to care about everything. My mother cared about everything. Now, I understand why. She cared about everything for my sake. But she was happy. I want to be happy like she was. I want to see you as happy as she was—despite everything. For the first time in my life I see the possibilities: the end of the Cor Ordinate, the end of cloning. We have a new world just waiting for us. I want us to get married in the way the Ordinate do, set up a household, and raise a family. In his imagination he saw Andrea's face melt into a warm smile, but the smile collapsed into angry determination.

He muttered under his breath. "I would do anything for her—except, I won't help her hunt down K'Rin."

Pssst! Brigon heard a voice in the tree. He looked up and saw one of Ariko's snipers in a heavy bough pointing furiously at the wall. Brigon turned back and held a pair of whitewashed binoculars to his face and surveyed the wall. Bright intersecting floodlights illuminated the ground between the forest and the sonic barrier. The pile of snow abutting the wall remained in shadow. Brigon saw the black tip of Tara's walking stick poking through the white crust of snow. *They're ready to come up.*

Brigon watched the NewGen sentry on the wall turn his back and walk slowly away from Tara's spot. He keyed the comm-disk and whispered, "You've got two minutes to get over the wall—a twelve-foot free climb. Sentry is twenty feet to your right and walking away. A gun emplacement is thirty feet to your left."

As he finished his report, he saw a small cave-in. Figures dressed in mottled white coveralls and round hoods scrambled to the base of the stone wall. Brigon recognized Andrea by her shape, long arms and legs, and Tara by her missing forearm. Ten others poured out of the tunnel and huddled at the base of the wall. Andrea and five others had long white pipes strapped to their backs—the blowguns.

One of the figures in white passed out steel claws with grips. Brigon watched them probe the wall crevices and deftly pull themselves up the wall and over. A pair of the larger men in white helped Tara, one below offering a shoulder for her foot, another above hauling her over by her good hand. They hid below the rim of the wall. The ubiquitous hum of the sonic barrier covered any noise they might have made climbing the wall.

The sentry continued his slow walk away. The two gunners fixed their gaze beyond the sonic barrier into the dark forest. *So far, so good.* Brigon keyed the comm-disk. "They didn't see you."

Brigon saw a threesome of heads with hoods off, rise above the wall rim; each held a blowgun to the lips. The sentry walking away stumbled and fell. The two gunners slumped out of sight. Then, the blowgunners ducked below the wall rim. Looking back into the trees, Brigon saw faces peering, inquiring with their looks. Brigon held a thumbs-up to indicate that Tara and company were in. He saw a thousand shadows sift among the trees, and he could almost feel the electricity of anticipation. He knew that the news would trickle through the forest to Eric's position opposite the main gate.

Tara bounded down the last five steps from the wall. At the bottom she, Andrea, and the others stripped away their whitewashed coveralls. Underneath, they wore the simple smocks and jumpsuits of clone laborers. Tara whispered out of breath, "All right. We're going to walk into the power station just like any other work party, about ten blocks away. Don't speak unless spoken to." She let her long sleeve fall to hide her deformity. She couldn't hide the scar on her face. "Andrea, you take the blow-guns."

Andrea collected the six blowguns, each loaded with a dart dripping with fresh succinylcholine—*snap*. She held them fisted together like simple plumbing materials. She and Tara walked in the middle of the languorous pack as it shuffled with deliberate reluctance down the deserted predawn streets.

She saw an occasional clone street sweeper picking garbage from the sidewalks. A few office buildings' lights switched on. A cat mewed at a door stoop, complaining about the cold. A fat café owner burst from a side door wrestling with an apron. He crashed into their small phalanx, cursing them, "Get out of my way! You stupid clones!" He shoved Tara, who fell backward over a catalytic heater. Andrea caught her as Tara's head hit the propane tank.

"I'm all right." Tara quickly got back on her feet.

The other clones turned their faces and shuffled on, although they were well equipped for a lethal rebuttal to the café owner.

Across a plaza, Andrea saw a young woman, about her age, walking toward them. The woman had dark hair and straight eyebrows. A bright streetlight sparked the woman's cornflower-blue eyes. She carried a satchel of books and art supplies. *A teacher*, Andrea thought, *for small children*. She watched the woman pass on the opposite sidewalk and she wanted to tell her, *Take the children away today. Take them anywhere.*

They walked several more blocks through the center of Sarhn, until they arrived at a drab cement building surrounded by a tall fence. Signs warned that the fence was electrified at the top. A wide-mouth cylindrical vent crowned the building, issuing steady billowing steam into the crisp air. Tara whispered, "We're here."

They saw a young Cor Security guard sitting in a well-lit booth near a thick metal gate that rolled across the roadway. The building had no lighted windows, ironic because all the light, all the power in the city, emanated from this auxiliary plant.

Tara spoke. "I had a friend who worked here. The control room is upstairs. From the control room, they route power throughout the grid. We should be able to open the main gate, then shut down everything else. Let's go. Andrea, you talk to the guard. He mustn't see my face."

Andrea nodded, then led the work party to the booth. She tapped on the glass, startling the young man. "Jeez!" He hopped up spilling a cup of hot liquid to the floor. An ephemeral cloud of steam briefly fogged the glass. Now angry, he stepped out of the booth. "Get out of here. No clones allowed in the power plant."

Andrea affected a look of bewilderment. "But we have orders."

"Impossible. You're in the wrong place." He brushed some of the hot water from his tunic. "Go away."

Andrea stepped closer. "May I show you my orders?" She unfastened the two top buttons on her jumpsuit.

The young man paused. *"Orders?"*

Andrea slipped her hand inside her drab jumpsuit and felt the handle of her titanium knife in its sheath and all the heavy tape on her ribs. She stepped close enough to put her left hand on the young man's shoulder, and to fix his eyes with hers. Then with a swift thrust she shoved the knife through the guard's third and fourth ribs. She put her hand over the stunned man's mouth to stifle his cry, then laid him backward on the pavement as if putting a child to bed. He grabbed hold of her loose jumpsuit, not to grapple, but more in a doleful *why?*

Andrea whispered a reply, "We need to get inside. You would try to stop us—"

A voice behind her asked, "Who are you talking to?"

Andrea turned and saw Ogorm's perplexed face. She replied quickly, "No one. Talking to myself."

The guard's hand let go, and Andrea pulled her knife free. She wiped the wet blade on the dying man's coat, then followed the others inside the gate and into the building through a loading dock door.

Eric glanced over his shoulder waiting for the red flare. Pink wisps of clouds appeared as the stars lost themselves in the approaching dawn. It promised to be a warm day. Thousands of armed clones, male and female, filled the woods. The combination of the artificial glare from the floodlights along the wall and the forest shadows hid them well enough.

His section of wall included Sarhn's main gate. The light rail connecting the clone precincts to Sarhn terminated here. Past the train platform metal turnstiles stood silent and empty. The chrome sign above the gate stood in shadow in front of the walls' floodlights. He read the reversed text: **WE LIVE TO SERVE!** NewGens patrolled the wall with quiet discipline. So far, surprise was intact.

Three hundred meters of naked ground—his people had the farthest unsheltered run at the wall. *If Tara manages to open the gate, we rush through. If not, we run up the snow embankments and climb over the walls.* He hoped the thousands of combatants behind him remembered this simple if-then-else statement. *If not the gate, then the wall, or else we die in the snow.*

Then he heard a loud *clunk* and the grinding of old gears. *She made it!* Eric leaned forward from his position to see better. Bits of snow and ice fell from the lintel of the gate. The guards atop the wall ran about looking down the sides. Even without binoculars, Eric could see the confusion in their faces as the gate doors slowly opened. He heard shouting from the wall. A dozen NewGens ran to their gun emplacements. Then the low hum of the sonic barrier fell silent.

Far to the right, Eric heard a dull pop; looking up, he saw the red flare. A deafening roar of weapons crashed like a tidal wave against the wall from right to left. In an instant the Security Troops and NewGen guards were dead. The forest smelled of cordite and ozone.

All along the forest, eighteen thousand voices rose and fell like a thunderclap. Eric stood and added his voice. "To the gate!"

From the forest, a swarm of fighters ran toward the wall to begin an orgy of violence. They fired blistering volleys of lead. The rim of the old stone wall became a blurred splash of rock chips and lead. Sporadic fire returned. Eric saw one of the NewGens slumped over the wall, pockmarked. Although mangled by small-arms fire, the NewGen managed to fire a weapon into the crowd. "To the gate!" Eric yelled again. He knew they must get inside Sarhn before the Ordinate sent reinforcements.

Shabby clones poured through the streets like floodwaters. The mass of human forms blurred into a single organism of fury, a single organism with a single will. The clones rushed toward the barracks, chasing the few hapless Ordinate Security Troops that survived the initial onslaught.

Brigon no longer worried about command and control: he was subsumed into the mass racing toward the barracks. The clones acted on their last instruction: *Envelop the barracks, kill every NewGen and Security Troop.* Now just another foot soldier, Brigon ran in the middle of his horde, frustrated as he fell farther behind. He ran off balance; his right arm was strapped to his side. He held his heavy pistol in his left, wondering if he'd even fire another round now that they were inside Sarhn.

Brigon had to wend his way around a cluster of clones who had caught one of the fleeing Ordinate Troops. "Leave him—he's dead," he ordered.

But the clones ignored him. Instead, they bludgeoned and hacked the Ordinate's body as if they wanted to scatter his atoms. Brigon smiled nervously at the brutality as he ran past, an odd bout of gallows humor—a new sensation. *Today is going to be a reckoning for the Ordinate.* The crowd pressed him forward.

The cacophony of footfall, voices, and weapons added to the mayhem. Brigon sensed the collective motivation of the horde—*get it over with*. He resolved not to waste time trying to manage today's wildfire of violence—it would have to burn itself out. Soon they would smash into NewGens.

They ran across the rubbled field that was once the Clone Welfare Institute. Brigon climbed a heap of twisted metal to get a better look. He saw the other arm of the invasion crash through the streets—Eric's column came sluicing into the open space. The horde instantly doubled in size. The noise—voices, gunshots, and whining lasers—was deafening. Brigon watched in awe as the horde poured through the street toward the barracks. He no longer recognized individual faces. Surreal. All his life, Brigon staked his survival on fighting intelligently, using small numbers with great efficiency. *Now this—a swarm.* Not a particularly intelligent style of warfare, but stunning. Brigon climbed down from his perch and resumed his place in the moving throng, thinking, *Let's get this over with.*

Admiral Brulk stood in front of his window looking down into the street. He focused his eyes on his own reflection as he buttoned his tunic. The thick glass muffled the gunfire that sounded like a heavy downpour on a tin roof. He had the first reports: ten to twenty thousand clones had stormed the walls and begun a disciplined turning movement to surround the barracks. *How could that many clones have survived out there? In a frozen wasteland, without food?* He wanted to doubt the reports, but he saw through the window the twinkling flashes of gunfire. He heard the constant racket, punctuated by an occasional explosion that rattled the window.

The panicked civilian population was fleeing toward the East Gate, leaving the city. He saw them running down the streets, many in their nightclothes.

To his amusement he saw some of the household clones scampering away with the other civilians. How he despised the old-order clones—but not nearly as much as he now despised the insipid civilians that fled their own homes.

Even the civilians on his administrative staff had fled. He had sent his uniformed staff into the conflict to die. He felt no affection for them: they had failed him. How could they fail to know the presence of so many clones? *Worthless.* He suspected that most of them would flee the city with the rest of the civilians. He saw one of his Security Troops stripping away his tunic, trying to blend into the civilian refugees—it made him sick to witness such cowardice.

He buttoned his collar button and felt the stubble of his beard. *Pity that I don't have time to shave.* Brulk picked up his belt and holster from his desk and carefully buckled it around his waist, aligning the center of the buckle with the lowest button on his tunic. He felt the smooth handle of his small pistol in the palm of his hand.

He heard his door open suddenly. Brulk turned around to see the Madame Prefect rushing in. Her gray hair was wild, her face ghostly white and her lips thin—lacking the false robustness of her cosmetics. She wore a simple gown and a leather coat that hung from her shoulders to the ground.

She reported loudly, "Armed clones are sweeping through the streets!"

"You don't say?" Brulk answered sarcastically, as he bit his lower lip. The old woman was comical in her disheveled appearance. The leader of the entire Ordinate world stood before him, telling him old news with an exaggerated sense of urgency. Brulk sat down in his chair and folded his hands on the polished wood.

The Prefect said, "We need to evacuate the government—temporarily. Notify Qurush to send armed transports."

Her attempt at command brought a wry smile to Brulk's face. "Call them yourself. I'm busy." He motioned with his thumb to the dark window behind him. "I won't be evacuating. This battle will be won or lost by my NewGens at the barracks long before Qurush can respond. If you want to go, you'll have to take your chances walking out of Sarhn."

"Well, what else can we do?" the Prefect shrieked. She shed the last of her regal demeanor.

To Brulk the conclusion was foregone. *What shall we do? Don't you know, you old cow?* Her presence annoyed him and at the same time amused him. He said with mock concern, with almost paternal tenderness, "Maybe you could hide under your desk." Then he burst into uncontrollable laughter.

The Prefect's face blushed crimson as the assault on her pride quickly eclipsed her fear. She turned and fled the office.

Brulk's laughter ebbed quickly after the object of his scorn left the room. Then he pulled his pistol from its holder and laid it on the empty desk. He carefully aligned the short barrel with the grain in the wood. He knew his only hope was that his NewGens would prevail. If not, his last friend in the world was lying on his desk.

Tara and Andrea led their small party away from the auxiliary power station. They ducked in and out of the stream of refugees scrambling toward the East

Gate, trampling each other as they fled the noise
and rumors of mayhem. Men and women ran helter-
skelter holding small children or bundles of clothing.

The crowd recognized Tara's small band as being
clones—the rumpled lime-green jumpsuits. Plus,
Tara's party was headed toward the fight. When
Andrea made eye contact with the fleeing Ordinate,
they averted their eyes. *Raw fear.* Occasionally the
press of the crowd jammed the clones and the fleeing Ordinate together and the Ordinate spilled
around, shaking with fear. Andrea thought, *In this
alley, the Ordinate outnumber us a thousand to one,
and they fear us. Fear is blind.*

She knew instantly that the eighteen thousand
clones sweeping through the city to envelop the barracks would prevail. The battle would be over soon.
She was anxious to get to the fight. Only the
NewGen would stand and fight, and they would
lose completely. The old-order clones had always
had the sheer numbers, the *Mass.* A combination of
Brigon's instruction and the Jod weapons gave the
clones the *Knowledge* they required to make war.
Suffering in the wilderness filled them with the
Spirit for combat. She recalled the fundamental
algorithm of war from her own military training: *The
army with the greater Mass, Knowledge, and Spirit is
invincible.*

Tara turned out of the main stream of refugees
into an alley. Andrea objected, "The fighting is that
way." She pointed.

Tara ignored Andrea's protest. "Follow me. I
know the city better than you." Tara indeed knew the
alleys and kept the clones out of the worst torrents

of panicked humanity. Andrea watched the crowd for any signs of NewGens. She saw none.

Tara directed them into a broad courtyard with a formal garden. Large poplars, ready to burst into pastel green, loomed at the corners of the garden. Ornamental gas lamps provided some cheerful light to deserted paths. The howls of battle echoed against the courtyard wall, contradicting the serene setting.

Tara paused at a large stone gateway.

Andrea asked, "You see something?" She instinctively pressed herself into the shadows.

"I have an idea." Tara pointed with her stick. "The buildings around this courtyard—this is the main government complex. The Ordinate have their operations center in one of these buildings. If we can take their ops center, we can find out how the rest of Cor plans to react."

Andrea thought for a moment, then concurred. "You're right. We can do more good here. So what do we do?" Andrea asked.

Tara motioned to a side entrance near a set of garbage bins. "We go in the back, up to the top floor, then work our way down."

Eric ran near the front of his loose formation. He saw the rubbled barracks ahead and ordered, "Keep those shields front! Bring the twenty millimeters forward."

The mass slowed. Large men carried rectangular shields to the front where they stood shoulder to shoulder, creating a wall of mirrors. The shields, old Jod surplus, could attenuate lasers but not kinetic munitions. Two teams of clones manhandled the twenty-millimeter Gatling guns forward. Makeshift tripods dangled from the forward casing. Another squad of clones strained under the weight of belted ammunition.

Eric ran to the top of a heap of bricks, rubble from the barracks' outer wall. The barracks—the few left standing—were empty. His heart felt light: perhaps the Jod bombardment had killed most of the NewGen. Climbing higher, he looked past the barracks toward the broad spaceport apron pocked with bomb craters and littered with debris from husks of burned ships and damaged hangars. In the open area stood formations of NewGen wearing heavy infantry armor and bristling with weapons. They stood behind berms of wreckage and dirt hastily shoved together in the past ten minutes. A handful of Ordinate officers ran between the dense formations trying to coordinate fields of fire.

Eric counted ten phalanxes, each with fifty large NewGen soldiers. Each phalanx anchored itself on an armored vehicle placed at the center of each berm. The turret-mounted laser cannon scanned the killing ground to their front.

What is their plan? Eric wondered. *They have no plan, except to die and take as many of us with them as they can.* He looked down at the seething mass pressing through the barracks yard toward the broken buildings. The first ranks caught sight of the NewGen formations and they paused behind their silver shields. Teams hastily set up the two Gatling guns on separate piles of rubble. The clamor subsided into a momentary hush, like some perverse benediction that rippled from front to back. The NewGen lowered their weapons. Eric held his breath as he watched the scene below him. He lowered his head behind a fragment of wall, anticipating the shock.

Then, a thousand counterpoised weapons fired in a brilliant spasm of violence. The energy bolts and lasers lit the gap between the combatants like heat lightning spidering through the ether. Muzzle flashes presaged a hail of bullets. The Gatling guns roared. Gunfire echoed like thunder. The angry cries of the old-order combatants sounded like a gale.

Both sides staggered from the blows. The NewGen pulled their dead and wounded back, using the dead to plug gaps in the berms. They worked in efficient silence. In contrast, the old-order clones let loose a loud cry and swarmed through the breach in the barracks walls, racing across the hundred meters of withering fire. The Gatling guns replied in kind, sawing the NewGen in half.

Eric jumped down from the pile and ran into the melee. He saw five hundred of his own people collapse clumsily as if tripped by their own feet. But hundreds more raced by.

The silver shields bought fifty precious meters in the face of the laser cannon, but soon the crimson lasers raked the clones, who ran recklessly over their own dead to reach the NewGen berms.

The first wave to reach the NewGen were half dead upon reaching the berms. They slipped and fell in their own guts, all the while discharging their weapons at the NewGens. With their rapid volleys, they pummeled the NewGen, breaking down their body armor, slowing their return fire, allowing the second and third waves to crash through. The old-order clones smashed the NewGen formation, firing point-blank. Three or more clones grappled with each NewGen, each jabbing with their small ice pick weapons doped with the snap. The NewGens fell limp, whereupon the clones attacked them mercilessly, hacking with knives and hatchets. The ground was slippery with gore. In a moment the laser cannons fell silent. Eric saw his swarm drag the gunners from their metal shells and beat their soft skulls against the stiff iron hulls.

Eric arrived in the middle of the third wave. He climbed over the husk of a bombed hovercraft. He emptied his pistol into the back of a NewGen locked in a death grip with a pair of clones. They crawled away, wounded. Eric climbed over the NewGen body. He ripped the faceplate off. The steel blue eyes flashed back and a strong hand reached out, grabbing Eric's arm. Eric quickly put a bullet between the NewGen's wide eyes and felt the strong grip slacken.

The fight was now all around him. Eric rushed toward the front. He ran up to brawl, where a NewGen successfully fended off a pack of old-order clones. It was a grizzly standoff. The clones fired point-blank. The NewGen's body armor absorbed most but not all of the shock of the bullets. Blood oozed from holes in the torso. Using a short carbine, the NewGen returned fire with more deadly effect. The pack of clones, wounded and healthy alike, rushed the NewGen, tackling him. But, the NewGen tossed the smaller attackers aside, thrashing wildly with a thick blade in one hand and firing the carbine with the other. The NewGen regained his feet, and with cool discipline, began to dispatch the clones who had attacked him.

Eric pulled a small skinning knife from his sheath. The blade, wet with snap, glistened. He held the knife blade out for a thrust. His neck was still stiff, but he shirked the pain and charged. The NewGen swung around with his carbine. Eric stepped inside the sweep of the barrel as the NewGen fired. Eric felt the burn of the hot gasses on his hip but no bullet wound. Unable to use the carbine at such close quarters, the NewGen slashed with his large blade— a blow aimed at Eric's head. Eric caught the NewGen's forearm, but not without suffering a gash in his hand. The NewGen knocked Eric down and fell on him for a lopsided test of strength. The NewGen used weight and strength to force his blade against Eric's throat.

Eric struggled. He knew he lacked the raw strength. He could hold the NewGen for the moment, but not for long. Blood from the cut on his hand dripped onto his face. Yet Eric felt exuberant. For this kind of fighting he was made. Some dark notion in the back of his brain told him: *this struggle is good!* Eric knew the sensation of self-assuredness must be artificial—part of his neural mapping.

The pain was real. He felt as if the bones in his forearm would snap from the strain. Yet his memory told him that the cut on his hand, the pain meant nothing. His own blood dripping in his face meant nothing. Killing the opponent was everything. *I'll use any help, real or not.* But he lacked the strength, and his small skinning knife doped with the lethal dose of snap was pinned between his chest and the NewGen's armor. He pressed the skinning knife against the armor and pressed with all his strength. He felt the point of his blade break, and his heart sank. *I'm just as likely to para-lyze myself.*

Eric felt the first sensation of panic that he'd ever known: *He's much stronger than I am.* But he fought stubbornly against the slow descent of the New-Gen's blade. Then Eric noticed that his chest was wet, not from his own blood or sweat, but from the blood of the NewGen. Some bullets had punctured the armor.

He felt the slick armor with his fingertips until he found a hole. He probed the hole with his finger, then carefully inserted the broken blade into the wound, and gently slipped it two inches deep into the shallow bullet wound.

In five long seconds, the NewGen's grip relaxed. The struggle ceased, and Eric shoved the heavy burden aside. He stood straddling the NewGen, ripped away the chest armor and fired the fatal shot into his opponent's heart.

Eric was exhausted. He straggled after the other combatants, pausing to take careful shots. At every stop, he saw a pack of clones beating a dead NewGen, killing the creature for the third or fourth time. The stunned NewGen lay pinned to the ground by three men and the drug, while a scrawny female raised a thirty-pound chunk of cement in the air, the jagged part pointed downward. With all her might she smashed the weight into the NewGen's faceplate, flattening the head, splattering blood on herself and her accomplices. They whooped and got up to find another.

The Ministry of Security was deserted. The long halls gleamed from polished stone floors and mirrored walls. The halls were empty except for large planters that held stout palm trees. Andrea took the point and moved up the hall using the planters as cover. The other clones followed, mimicking her. The building was silent except for the rustle of their own equipment and the faraway din of battle.

Andrea raised her hand, signaling them to halt. She backtracked to Tara. "I heard a voice." Ogorm scrambled forward to hear the news. Andrea pointed down the hall. "Second door."

Ogorm pulled a pistol from his jacket. Andrea shook her head and drew her knife. She cautioned in a hushed voice, "Better if we don't make any loud noise."

"Understood." Ogorm scurried back to his group and crouched by a terra-cotta planter.

Andrea slid along the wall to the first door. It was wide open. She quickly stole a look inside. *Three empty desks. One lamp turned on.* Turning to Tara, she reported in a faint whisper and a shake of her head, "Empty."

The lone voice she heard was near, yet muffled through doors and walls. Andrea ran to the second door. It was ajar. She took a more leisurely look through the crack in the door. *An anteroom, brightly lit. Papers lay strewn on the floor.* She saw another ornate door swung open to a dark room and the voice. She heard more clearly. The voice, a strong, determined baritone spoke calmly; however, it berated unseen, silent subordinates with blistering language. *What galls me the most, gentlemen, is the missed opportunity. The failure in intelligence is staggering— you told me the wilderness clones numbered a thousand or fewer. Your intellects are wanting. Do you see how many came over the walls? How can it be that you were so badly surprised by clones? And to see our own Ordinate Troops flee in a panic . . . truly a gutless bunch you are . . .*

Andrea beckoned Tara forward. Tara asked, "How many?"

Andrea shook her head. "Don't know. Some military brass is in there ripping his staff." She smirked.

"Why aren't they outside fighting?" Tara asked, nodding toward the outside and the distant roar.

"Don't know." Andrea beckoned the others to follow. She slipped into the anteroom under cover of the diatribe: *And you cabinet members . . . I told you to keep the clones out of Sarhn proper, but did you listen to me? I told you that we needed to mobilize the civilians into a paramilitary force . . . I told you . . . I've had it with the lot of you. You're too soft. You lack the will to succeed. Now you're going to get what you deserve for your . . .*

Andrea shimmied around a desk, creeping toward the door. She held her knife in her right hand. She glanced quickly through the door in the direction of the voice, then returned with her back resting against the ornate door frame. She didn't believe what she'd just seen. She snatched a second look—a long look, for she was certain the man was so preoccupied with himself that he'd not notice her if she walked in the room and stood at his side. She saw a middle-aged man in uniform talking to his own reflection in a floor-to-ceiling plate-glass window. He gesticulated with a short pistol, pointing it at his own reflection, then waving it about. His tunic was buttoned to the neck, but otherwise he looked like he'd just got out of bed: unshaved, disoriented from a bad dream perhaps. The voice boomed, "You don't deserve victory. Well, I'm not going to share in your fate. If the clones don't kill you, you can go explain this mess to the rest of the Ordinate and see if they accept your excuses . . ."

Andrea felt a tap on her leg, and she pulled herself back into the anteroom to answer. She reported. "Just one man. He's got a gun. He's insane."

Tara looked around the doorjamb and returned with a knowing smile that exaggerated the scar that ripped through her upper lip. She whispered, "It's Brulk."

Andrea knew the name: Brigon's father. She didn't know what to do with that information. The voice in the other room, Brigon's father's voice, fell silent. Andrea and Tara both stole a look. Brulk had taken his seat. He still faced his own reflection in the dark glass. He leaned closer to the glass, then raised the pistol, and placed the short barrel against his temple.

"If he fires that pistol we'll have company soon enough," Andrea whispered.

Tara beckoned Ogorm forward and pointed her forefinger at Brulk. Ogorm quickly loaded a dart glistening with a dose of snap into his blowgun.

With his left hand, Brulk rubbed the stubble on his chin while he pressed the barrel of the pistol against his head. It pleased him that he did not see any fear in his own eyes. "I am probably the only person in Sarhn who isn't afraid," he said aloud.

He felt the comfortable trigger against his forefinger. The slender crescent of brushed steel felt cold and wet in the crease of his finger. His pistol had the standard two-pound pull. He decided to apply the pressure ever so slowly. He wanted to feel the mechanism give. By concentrating all his senses on the inanimate trigger, he would not feel the bullet crashing through his skull and ripping through his brain.

He squeezed the trigger ever so slowly. *One ought to savor the moment before oblivion. Why?* The thought amused him and he relaxed his finger slightly. He didn't want to accidentally shoot himself in a spasm of humor. This last bit of irony washed over him and left him suddenly depressed. *At least I played for high stakes . . .*

Brulk felt a slight sting in the back of his neck. *Nervousness?* Oh, well, one less discomfort to worry me now. He squeezed the trigger. But nothing happened. He tried to close his eyes and squeeze the trigger harder, but he could neither shut his eyes nor make his hand obey. *Numbness.* The room grew dim, but he could still comprehend images.

Brulk looked into the plate glass at his reflection. He saw his hand slump and the pistol fall from his fingers. *Am I dead?* he tried to speak but the thought was stillborn. *I can't speak.* He tried to turn his head. He couldn't. *I am dead,* he mused. *This is awful. I'm frozen here at this moment with nothing but my thoughts—what a bad moment to be frozen in. What if death is not oblivion?*

Then a movement reflected in the plate glass caught his eye. He saw a face—not his own. The female face bore a thick scar from hairline to chin. The bifurcated lips turned into a satisfied smile. *A devil?*

The sight startled him, but Brulk felt nothing but a quickening of his own heart and a shortness of breath. He heard the soft sound of feet on his carpet and the rustle of clothes. Then he felt a hand on his shoulder—a small, strong hand holding him steady in his chair. He felt the fingernails digging into his shoulder. *Oh, no!* Brulk groaned inside. *I can hear; I can feel everything. But,* he corrected himself, *I don't feel the wound in my head.* He tried to control the terror welling up inside his mind, but he knew that he had no control of his body and therefore lacked the options of fight or flight. He fixed his eyes on the female face.

The deformed lips moved and he heard a sweet voice mocking him. "Admiral Brulk."

Am I dead? Brulk wanted to ask but the only sound he emitted was a weak unintelligible grunt.

A shock of auburn hair fell over the face. Hazel eyes tried to engage his. The lips in front of his face moved again. "We heard you talking to an empty room. That's not healthy."

Brulk saw a second face before him. The second face, also a woman, was dark, beautiful but unforgiving. Her dark brown eyes shifted from him to the woman with the scar. The darker woman said with disdain, "Tara, just finish him. Let's get out of here."

"No," the pale woman with the scar spoke to her dusky comrade with clinical curiosity, "I want to watch this."

The dark woman backed away, shaking her head, looking directly into Brulk's dimming eyes.

Then, I'm not dead. Again, Brulk's words failed. He could feel that his mouth hung open. He could feel the dry air at the back of his throat. He felt the strong urge to inhale but he couldn't. A new panic set in, as he knew the shallow puffs of air in his throat would not sustain him. Suddenly, he wanted to live.

The face with the scar filled his view. He felt her warm breath against his face. He desperately wanted to suck some of that breath but he couldn't. She observed, "You're paralyzed. How do you like it?"

Damn you! Brulk saw the enmity in her eyes, and he hated her in return. His hate gave him reason enough to live. She certainly enjoyed his situation. In his mind he struggled but without effect. In his mind, he could see his arms pushing her face away, but his arms hung numbly at his side. He felt weaker, dizzy.

She smiled through disfigured lips, as if she knew his thoughts. "You could learn something from this experience, Admiral Brulk." She shook him to keep his attention. "Being paralyzed the way you are is a bit like being a clone. You can think; you can want; but you can't do anything to help yourself. Neural mapping, ignorance, fear—they all paralyze just like the succinylcholine on that dart sticking in the back of your neck. Interestingly enough, if you live long enough, the paralysis wears off. We clones lived long enough to survive our paralysis. The neural mapping faded away, we got over our fear, and here we are taking your place."

Brulk felt a prod at his chest and saw the stump of an amputated forearm pass before his eyes. He fought to breathe, but his lungs merely spasmed a tiny bit of air. *I'll kill you.* His lungs burned. He could not close his eyes or ears to the taunts.

"If you could just survive five more minutes—a lousy five minutes—you'd beat the drug and you'd live. Good as new. But you've stopped breathing, Admiral Brulk. Your lips are blue. If you don't mind, I'm going to just sit here and watch you die."

I spit on you! Brulk willed the rest of his fading energy to spit in Tara's face, but he could not move. The screaming inside his head caused him to ache.

The noise abated to a soft doleful moan. Brigon looked south, past the immediate battle. He held his large pistol loosely at his side. The bandage on his head was unraveling. His headache was gone, his mind clear.

He studied the blue sky, expecting to see the contrails of attack air coming too late to relieve Sarhn. The sky was empty except for a line of mottled clouds near the coast. The sun felt warm against his face, a sharp contrast to the cold dampness of his clothes. He turned his attention back to the ugliness around him, the sounds of pain, and the smell of offal.

A thousand wounded old-order clones reclined among the dead, suffering, many waiting patiently for their turn to die. The healthier ones were too tired to revel in their victory—many too tired to tend to their own wounds. Their chests heaved from heavy breathing. Their hair was matted from sweat. Steam rose from their bodies into the crisp spring air.

Mostly, Brigon heard names called out, forced breathless calls—the wounded looking for comrades. He heard some quiet weeping as the living cradled their dead. The mourning was mixed with ebullience, even sparks of laughter, as pairs separated in the fighting found each other. Relief, nervous laughter, groans, and tears rose as a babble above the NewGens' silence.

The battle against the NewGens was over. The large NewGen cadavers were wrecks, stripped of body armor, broken and twisted. Across the asphalt and concrete field and the carnage, Brigon spied Eric wading through the morass. Eric personally inspected the dead NewGens, prodding their remains with the toe of his boot. Brigon hollered across the field, "Eric!"

Eric turned at the sound of his name. He shaded his eyes, raising the pistol with his free hand and looked back in Brigon's direction.

Brigon hollered again, "We've got to get everybody out from the open. The Ordinate still have air and space assets. You put five hundred rifles on the wall. I'll find Tara and the others. We've got to restore that sonic barrier and seal the gates."

Eric nodded, then turned to a group of exhausted clones. "You heard him: all of you, secure the walls." The clones who possessed the strength helped each other to their feet. They followed Eric as he retraced his steps back to the wall.

Andrea and Tara found the Ministry of Security operations center dark and deserted. As she tapped a wall switch, Andrea mused, "At least they turned off the lights."

The consoles emitted a low-volume chatter of excited inquiries. A moment of eavesdropping told Andrea everything she needed to know: the Ordinate knew that Sarhn had fallen. Various Ordinate commands concurred that they must first refugee-out the citizens. The commands were in a vigorous debate on what to do next. Andrea said, "They must lack the assets to counterattack. Otherwise, they wouldn't be arguing; they'd be on their way."

"They'll come soon enough," Tara agreed. "We'd better get ready to defend our city. Let's go. Ogorm, you stay here and mind the ops center."

Andrea and Tara left the Ministry building to return to the defensive walls. The full afternoon sun poured over Sarhn, melting the snow. Contrails of high-altitude reconnaissance craft streaked across the blue sky. Andrea noted, "They're watching."

Rivulets of water trickled down icicles that hung from the eaves of the fancy brownstone row houses. Many doors of the abandoned dwellings were wide open. Tara took a moment to peer inside a window through the lace curtains. She saw three plates of cold food at a small round table, two cups of cold gaval and one glass of milk. In the middle of the table, a calico cat sat on its haunches, fastidiously tasting the cold food.

As they approached the East Gate, they heard a shrill voice arguing. Andrea recognized the voice. "Carai? Sounds like he's in trouble."

Andrea detoured toward the ruckus. Tara followed. She came to a small plaza at the East Gate. The gate was open. In one corner of the plaza, several hundred Ordinate women and children huddled together, surrounded by angry clones brandishing weapons. Dr. Carai stood between the two groups, shouting fearfully, "You cannot . . . you must not shoot these civilians." He winced in expectation of a volley. He clutched the green case with the space comms to his chest. His parka lay folded at his feet. His knees trembled.

A voice yelled back, "Get out of our way, you animal, or we'll shoot you, too."

"No!" Carai closed his eyes tight and turned his head.

Tara ran ahead as fast as her limp allowed, until she stood next to Carai. She ordered, "Lower your weapons, all of you!" Then she poked one of the larger clones with her cane and demanded, "What's going on here?"

The clones erupted into a cacophony of accusations. Tara shouted back, "Quiet!" She waded into their midst and instructed them to address her one at a time.

Dr. Carai composed himself and stood back. Andrea went straight to Dr. Carai and asked, "What's the problem?"

He handed Andrea the green case and said, "I came into the city after the fighting stopped. I saw this group of women and children trying to get out of the gate. These clones were going to kill them—women and children."

Andrea looked at the Ordinate crowd. These anonymous figures, paralyzed by fear and confusion, stood against the wall like tentative deer. They were all strangely dressed, having taken flight from their warm beds into the cold streets. Small children buried their faces in their mothers' robes. The Ordinate made little noise except for stifled sobs and reassuring whispers. She could read the women's faces. They all expected to be dead within minutes.

Tara turned and said to Carai, "My people don't

understand but they'll obey." She walked passed Carai and Andrea and faced the Ordinate civilians. She pointed to the opened gate and said, "Get out."

As the crowd shuffled toward the gate, one woman held back. She was as pale as the wet snow she stood in. Her lips were dark blue from the cold. She wore a thin silky robe—peach colored and embroidered with an emerald dragon. Her naked legs trembled. She stood in thin wet slippers. The woman held a bundle in her arms wrapped in a blanket. She did not follow the crowd. She said meekly, "If you put us out here, we'll die. We'll freeze to death."

Most of the crowd paused to hear the result of the woman's request. Andrea interjected, "That's entirely up to you."

The woman ignored Andrea and continued to plead with Tara. "Please, let us stay. We'll work for you." The woman's voice had the edge of desperation. "It's inhuman to put us out."

"When did you ever think of us clones as human?" Tara asked rhetorically. The woman didn't answer.

Andrea noticed that the woman was soft, even plump. The round face had never missed a meal. The soft arms had never lifted a bundle bigger than the one she carried now. "What kind of work can you do?" she asked sarcastically.

The woman stammered, "I'll . . . I'll do anything you ask. We have no clothes, no food, no shelter. Please, let us back in." The woman slowly held up her bundle and unwrapped the blanket to expose a baby. The infant head, covered with fluffs of yellow hair, bobbled on its weak neck. Startled by the cold air, the baby began to bawl. The mother's eyes filled with tears, and she choked back a sob. "Don't make me watch him die out here." The child's unrestrained wailing echoed along the walls.

Andrea began to show her annoyance. "You'd be surprised what you can survive." She picked up the parka at Dr. Carai's feet and hurled it to the woman. "There, you won't freeze immediately."

The woman tucked her bawling infant back into the crook of her arms and she walked forward to gather up the parka. Without a word, she slipped her arms into the garment and bundled her infant inside the unbuttoned folds of cloth.

Andrea pointed through the gate to the forest. "Go out. Turn left. Follow the wall to the main gate. You'll see train tracks. Follow the tracks back through the forest for a couple miles. You can live in the clone precinct. You can eat the rations the clones left behind. You can wear the clothes of the clones you used, then killed. But whatever you do, don't stay long, and don't come back here."

The woman turned and looked at the tracks winding into the threatening trees. With slump-shouldered resignation, she began plodding away. The rest of the crowd drifted out the gate as well. Andrea called after the woman, "When your child grows up, you can tell him that the old-order clones treated you better than you treated them."

The woman did not respond to her taunt. In the parka, she soon became another shadow slouching out the gate. The group faded away. Tara watched until the woman in the parka disappeared. Noticing Tara's concentration, Andrea said, "You would have taken that baby, wouldn't you?"

The gate closed with a dull thud as Tara replied, "And you could have told her that the Ordinate have plans to refugee them out of here tomorrow, but you didn't."

Andrea looked askance at Tara and said, "I didn't like her." She took her green case and left.

chapter 17

The sun was low, yet the stones radiated the heat they'd collected during the day. The air was still. The city walls were quiet, except for the rapid drip of melting snow. A haze of smoke settled as a thin sheet above Sarhn. Small black birds with arrow wings dipped through swarms of midges. Contrails crisscrossed the sky. Looking past the forest toward the precincts, Andrea caught a glimpse of a hovercraft safely out of range of their Gatling gun. The sleek hovercraft slipped out toward the river, carrying the first load of Ordinate refugees.

Andrea worked alone on the flat round roof of a squat tower. Small mounds of emerald moss grew on the smooth pebbles near the drains. She set up her deep-space communications kit and initiated the auto-sighting program. While the small box calculated the exact aim for the transmission, she looked past it at the snow-covered plains. Patches of brown wheat stubble and fallow fields poked through the white blanket. The Cor sun settled over the flat slate-blue ocean. And she felt homesick.

The machine chirped. She had made a link with a courier at the Cor frontier. Andrea typed a brief message on the strange keyboard: *Old-order clones seized Sarhn today. Urgently need antiair and long-range cannon. Send shipments direct to Sarhn spaceport, coordinates: latitude 38.9762, longitude 6.5040.* She felt like adding a tag line—a challenge to K'Rin, but she refrained. She pressed the send button and the burst transmission lasted a millisecond.

Then she rested on her haunches to watch the blood-red sunset. *When I kill K'Rin . . .* Andrea closed her eyes. Reality mocked her. K'Rin was safely in another quadrant of the galaxy. So her sense of urgency waned. She felt impotent. Andrea squeezed her eyes shut, trying to lock out the onset of introspection. But her mind insisted.

Her natural, unreasoned and perhaps innocent anger began to fade. She almost mourned the loss of her anger like the loss of a reliable companion. Two months ago on Klamdara, the simplicity of her just anger kept her focused. K'Rin had to die. Her anger was as natural as breathing and as comfortable. *Can anger suffer from fatigue?* Now she relied more on discipline. Rational, disciplined anger was a poor substitute for passion, a dilution of herself. She felt smaller.

She wondered if given the opportunity she would go through with it—kill K'Rin. Of course she would. *There is no other way . . .* How she envied Tara—the spark in her eye as she watched Brulk die. Andrea had a brief vision that she was Tara and Brulk was K'Rin, a delicious moment that faded as soon as Brulk's eyes clouded. However, she also saw how Tara's countenance fell as Brulk slumped blue and lifeless onto the carpet. Would she feel the same way after killing K'Rin, sadness at the loss of the moment? *But it has to be done . . .*

Andrea heard a footfall rattle of the smooth pebbles and she stood quickly causing a moment of dizziness. She turned and saw Brigon standing behind her, alone. "I've been looking for you." Brigon's voice was a blend of complaint and relief.

Andrea said nothing, although she was happy to have her internal monologue interrupted.

Brigon seemed cross. "I tracked you down to the Ministry operations center. A woman on your team said you went to the East Gate with Tara. I went there. I found Dr. Carai; he said you'd retrieved your pack and gone back into the city center. There, Ariko sent me out here. Damn, but you're hard to keep track of."

Andrea didn't like the tone of his voice. She answered coolly. "I've been busy. We've all had a long day."

Brigon walked to her. "We need to talk." He sat on the ledge at the circumference of the tower roof with the last rays of the sun on his back. His mood brightened and he brushed some loose lichen from the ledge. "Sit, please."

She sensed, with some annoyance, that a rehearsed speech was coming. Nevertheless, she sat next to Brigon. Brigon pointed at the cityscape. Thin tendrils of smoke rose in the air from unseen cooking fires. The smells of bread baking and meat roasting filled the air. He said, "Last year, I would not have thought it possible."

Andrea tried to preempt any scripted remarks, saying, "Brulk is dead."

"I know." Brigon absolved Tara and Andrea by

adding, "Brulk needed killing." Then he said, "I've been thinking about the future, Andrea. I can see now that we are going to win our freedom from the Cor. Tara and Carai's plan—crazy as it seems—can work. We can make a life here." Brigon raised his swollen hand to touch Andrea's cheek.

"What?" Andrea mulled her own problems. *I had a life before K'Rin snatched it away.* She struggled to remember details about their little Cape Cod house—details that blurred.

Brigon put his injured hand on hers. "I thought the Cor Ordinate was the only constant in life—the ugly reality of life. I thought life was pointless. I planned to live in the wilderness, steal what I needed, harass everyone—my contribution to the cruel joke." He shrugged his shoulders. "But now, with the Ordinate gone, I can start over." He pressed down on her hand. "We can start over."

Andrea drifted back into his conversation and asked, "How?"

"We can live together for the rest of our lives. We can have our own children and . . ."

Andrea threw up her hands. "I can't talk about this, now."

Brigon's face flushed. "If not now, when?"

"Not now," Andrea replied emphatically as she stood up to leave.

Brigon grabbed her wrist and pulled her back to her seat. "Andrea, I love you."

Andrea pulled her wrist away from his grasp. "If you loved me, you would have helped me settle with K'Rin."

Brigon's voice rose in frustration. "If he comes here to do you harm, yes, I'll help you kill him. But you shouldn't waste yourself hunting K'Rin. Killing him won't solve the problem. I, too, had a score to settle for my mother's death. But I learned something this past year. I know how to get the ultimate revenge."

Andrea's eyes rose to meet his. "And what is the ultimate revenge?"

"To live well and prosper despite your enemies." Brigon pointed at the city again. "This struggle today wasn't about bringing the Cor down. This struggle was about raising the old-order clones up."

Andrea accused, "Easy for you to say. I helped you settle your score. Brulk is dead. You won't help me settle mine. K'Rin is still alive. We can finish this conversation after I've taken care of K'Rin. Goodbye."

Brigon stood up. His face reddened with disappointment. Andrea got up to leave, but Brigon blocked her way. "No, you stay and listen to me. You can give me a couple minutes."

Andrea set her jaw, but she stood silently, content that the rant would soon be over.

Brigon tapped her on the chest roughly. "You won't let the wound heal, will you? No, you *like* the festering and the pain. You *like* to pick that scab. Gives you an excuse to turn your back on the future. You haven't any room in your heart for me because you've filled it to the brim with anger."

Andrea glared back. Brigon stood close. She could feel his hot breath on her face.

"Do you think you're the only one here who has lost a loved one? The only one who feels betrayed? Look around you! You think you alone have a right to be bitter? In fact, bitterness is only a possession, and you're afraid to give it up. Why?"

"I don't have to explain myself to you." Andrea glared back.

"Someday, you'll have to explain yourself to somebody." Brigon stepped away and turned his back on her for a moment. His neck was red as he strained to control his temper.

Andrea had expected Brigon would be angry, but not this angry. She was surprised by Brigon's harsh words, but she would never let it show.

He turned again. His eyes burned with anger. His face was red from frustration. "I have had it with you, woman." Again, he tapped Andrea's sternum with his forefinger and said, "I'm tired of trying to wedge myself into your heart. It's too full of hate—no room for anything else. I see a new world opening up in front of my eyes. I see opportunities that I never imagined possible. I'd hoped we'd go after them together, but I was wrong. The only thing you are willing to embrace is death. I am such a fool. I thought your anger would burn itself out, then I might rush in to fill the vacuum. Well, I give up. I'm cutting my losses here and now. Good-bye, Andrea. I intend to leave Sarhn before the sunrise." Brigon turned and walked down the steps, never looking back.

At the drab spaceport at Qurush, the whine of hovercraft turbines continued into the night. They landed, disgorged passengers and left. Dispassionate New-Gens led stunned refugees to warm buildings lined with cots.

A disheveled Madame Prefect sat on a plain wooden bench in a communications shed. She wrapped herself in a rough gray blanket, clutching it to her neck. With a free hand, she held a cup of hot tea. Her hair was matted, her eyes dark, and her face pale. She listened to the sporadic reports from the high-altitude reconnaissance.

Dr. Sandrom stood by, still holding a hypodermic needle with the mild sedative that the Prefect had refused. A pair of NewGens stood near him waiting for instructions.

A colonel in a beige uniform approached and said, "Madam, we have assembled all the air and space assets necessary to obliterate the clones in Sarhn. You need only give the word."

"Obliterate how?"

"With quark munitions, of course," the colonel replied.

She dropped the blanket from her shoulders onto the floor. She stood up. The white fur coat she wore was wet and streaked with mud. Her shoes were soggy and her stockings torn at the knees. "You will do no such thing," she ordered.

"But Madam, we are just executing Admiral Brulk's standing orders for this contingency."

The Prefect practically spit the words, "Brulk, damn him, is dead. Now you listen to me. You will not destroy Sarhn. You will assemble every NewGen that you can find and make an army. Then you will take Sarhn intact. Do you understand me completely?"

The colonel explained, "Madam, if you insist that we *not* use our air superiority, then I must warn you that we'll need to expend at least sixty to seventy thousand NewGens to have any chance of success. We don't have sixty thousand NewGens here. Nor do we have the equipment here at Qurush. We would need to strip all the other cities' security forces of their weapons and transportation."

She turned to Dr. Sandrom. "How soon can we put sixty thousand NewGens in the field?"

The thin Dr. Sandrom stepped forward. He wore a simple white smock. His snow-white goatee and thinning white hair made him appear older than he was. He answered directly. "Three weeks, Madam, only if we recall the NewGens from the outlying cities *and* maintain our production schedule."

The colonel added, "In three weeks we can assemble the necessary equipment."

Madam Prefect looked menacingly over her shoulder. "Those clones in Sarhn aren't going anywhere. Okay. Three weeks it is."

One of the NewGens standing behind Dr. Sandrom leaned forward and whispered something in the doctor's ear. The Prefect noticed and she asked, "What did that NewGen say to you?"

"Nothing important, Madam Prefect." Dr. Sandrom gave the NewGen a disapproving glance. "The New-Gen simply observed that the colonel's aerial bombardment option seemed more efficient."

The Prefect blinked. *"What?* I thought they just did what they were told." She stepped back from Sandrom and the NewGen.

Dr. Sandrom showed his teeth through a reassuring smile. "I promise you, the NewGens never deviate from their mission statement. They are perfectly safe."

Andrea wandered the streets aimlessly all night. She sat on the wall in the biting cold and listened to the monotonous hum of the sonic barrier. She watched the stars slip in and out of thin clouds. Cor's mall-waxing moon lay a sheen on the black ocean in the distance. She pondered how at sea, the night was the master of its own darkness. And she wondered if she were ever the master of her own fate. Behind her the city bristled with incandescent light, trying to conquer the night.

The cold, more than fatigue, drove her indoors. She sought a deserted place to flop. Most of the clones had already commandeered the vacant apartments, so Andrea found her way back to the Ministry buildings and picked the darkest office, the Ministry of Support. The name Grundig glistened from a polished brass plaque.

The posh office had a long leather couch beneath a loud wall clock. She stopped the pendulum to stop the sound. Andrea found a man's full-length leather coat, new, hanging from a brass hook. She lay on the couch, using the coat as a blanket. She closed her eyes out of habit. Everything annoyed her, even the sweet smell of the fresh leather—these spoils of war. All night she heard Brigon's voice echo in her brain: *That black hole in your chest.*

She rose tired, leaden, dispirited, and she didn't know why. A bright sun poured through windows of cut crystal waking her. She opened her eyes to prismatic light around her. She listened intently and heard nothing. Her first thought was to find Brigon, but she quickly corrected herself: *He's gone, and probably doesn't want to be found—not by me.*

Andrea left the Ministry of Support wearing the leather coat unbuttoned. She walked through the old section of the city and stopped at an abandoned— she thought it was abandoned—café. Looking for something to eat, she found a pair of clones huddled under a large quilt behind the counter. Two groggy faces emerged, eyeing Andrea without the least bit of embarrassment.

"Excuse me." Andrea offered a perfunctory apology and poured herself a large beaker of cold, day-old gaval from an urn. She grabbed a handful of stale pastries from the glass case, and retraced her steps over the quilted clones. She found a cast-iron table and chair in the bright sunlight, where she drank the sour coffee and ate the sweets.

Pedestrian traffic increased as Sarhn awoke. The thin, dirty pedestrians wore new clothes. Andrea noticed the mismatched outfits. A younger pair of clone women had tried their hand at makeup or stacked their hair in awkward buns.

She was less amused by their almost uniform conversation. The rumor of Brigon's departure played heavily and the clones speculated about the cause. From fragments of conversations, Andrea learned key facts: Brigon left with four comrades at the break of dawn. The rest of the news was contradictory speculation. *Brigon went back to the mountains. No, he headed south. Tara sent him to reconnoiter. No, Tara didn't know he was leaving. He left in a bad humor. He seemed glad to be leaving.*

Andrea left her pastries and cold coffee to follow a group who was arguing about Brigon. One of the females, a short combative woman, challenged the others. "I got my information from Chana herself. Where did you get your information?"

Andrea caught up with the group and stopped the woman. "You know Chana?"

The woman turned. Andrea was perplexed at first:

the woman looked like Chana, except that her posture was bent from malnutrition. The wide sunken eyes framed by heavy eyebrows were Chana's: the dark hair, straight lips, and square jaw. A tattoo of black diamonds ringed the woman's neck. *Not Chana, but a sister clone.* Andrea asked, "Do you know where I can find Chana?"

Without identifying herself the woman said, "I know who you are." She gave the rest of the group a look of superiority and told them, "This is the other woman I told you about—Andrea, the Earth woman, Tara's companion—"

"Please," Andrea interrupted the woman. "You can tell them your story later. Just tell me where I can find Chana."

The woman stood with her mouth agape. Andrea sensed that the woman was drawing an unfavorable opinion of her, but she didn't care. The woman straightened herself, correcting her bent posture as best she could. "She took an apartment. I saw it."

"Do you know the number or the street?"

"No. The building is yellow stucco with white window frames—all curlicues. The roof is shaped like a big mustache. Fancy, across the street from the old hotel." The woman pointed. "About ten blocks that way on the wider street."

Andrea stood in the carpeted hall and paused to check her bearings. According to the frumpy man in the foyer, a CNA model had taken the third-floor suite and was rather pushy about the acquisition. "Like she owned the place," he complained. *That's Chana*, Andrea surmised.

At eye level on the large six-panel door, a brightly

polished brass plaque read, *Suite 300—Private.*
Andrea used the small brass knocker to rap an impatient entreaty—permission to enter. She heard
Chana's voice through the door. "Come in."

She turned the ornate knob and pushed the door
open. The short hallway was dimly lit with wall
sconces and it opened into a sunny room. "Who is
it?" Chana's voice inquired.

"Andrea Flores. May I come in?"

"I'm not late for my shift on the wall, am I?"
Chana stepped into the hallway. With the sun
behind her she was a dark shadow. She was trying
to manage the clasp on a thick necklace of blue
beads. Her face betrayed her disappointment. "Oh,
well. Come in." She disappeared around a corner
into the bright room and Andrea followed.

Chana walked to a gilt mirror over a credenza,
where she fussed with the necklace. She wore a knit
dress, dark maroon. The high-neck dress clung to her
broad shoulders, then swelled at her breast, coasting
down her stomach that carried the slightest bulge
from a large meal. The open back in the dress displayed lean muscles, pale skin, and an old pocked
scar. The dress exaggerated her ample hipbones. She
wore a dozen bracelets that jingled as she fussed
with the necklace. Her face looked weathered and
hard in stark contrast with the smooth dress.

A man's voice, from deep inside the apartment,
called out, "Chana, who's that at the door?"

Andrea looked through an opening to the next
room and saw a large man seated on the edge of a
rumpled bed, idly thumbing through a portfolio of
photographs. He wore a beige bathrobe. An aubergine
dress lay draped on a chair where he propped his cal-

lused feet. The man was clean and had wet dark hair, but Andrea found herself taking a careful look to make sure the man was not Brigon.

Looking back at Chana, she said, "Do you know where Brigon went?"

Chana gave up on the necklace and set it loose on the credenza. "He went south." She turned and flashed a coy smile at Andrea. "He asked me to go with him. He's hoping to link up with some of our wilderness clones who refugeed down there. Supposedly, there's an industrial city about two hundred miles down the coast, Qurush." She turned back to study herself in the mirror. "Why do you care?"

Why do I care? Andrea stood helpless, without an answer. Instead she said, "I'm surprised you didn't go with him."

Chana leaned back on the credenza with her hands and her rump. "I could have loved him, if he would have let me. He could have loved you, if you would have let him." She snickered. "Look at us now. Brigon's gone off to get himself killed. You're making inquiries, and I found myself another mate."

"That didn't take long." Andrea meant to insult Chana.

"Thank you," Chana replied. She cut her eyes to the bedroom. "I can tell that we're going to work out just fine. Can I get you some tea or some gaval?"

Andrea knew the offer was really an invitation to leave, and feeling perverse, she said, "Is the gaval fresh?"

"Of course."

"I'd love some."

Chana took a deep breath, exhaled her frustration, then led the way into a large kitchen. She poured the steaming gaval into two china cups, added sugar to each without asking. "Here." She handed a cup to Andrea.

"Thank you." Andrea took a seat at the wooden table. Chana continued to stand, sipping her gaval, watching Andrea over the brim of her cup.

Andrea said, "I didn't mean to hurt him—or you for that matter."

Chana winked in a mocking manner. "I'll be all right."

Andrea accepted the gibe. "You are a CNA model, right?"

"Yes."

"What were you—" Andrea tried to reel in the awkward word with her hands, "—manufactured to do?"

Chana answered without compunction, "The CNAs were—are, I suppose—the invisible domestics: laundry, cooking, and charwoman duties. Strong backs, small minds." She smiled and showed her straight teeth. "We were a fairly common model until they started canceling us."

She paused as if trying to decide what information to divulge. "My particular neural mapping was to cook. For seven years I worked in the hotel across the street." She parted the sheers on the window and pointed to a large establishment with a mansard roof. "Seven years. This apartment we're standing in belonged to the hotel manager and his wife."

"So you've been here before."

Chana lowered her eyes toward her cup. "Let's just say, the manager liked to get to know the help. He admired the culinary arts."

"I'm sorry."

Chana laughed softly at the situation. "Let's not

become chums, okay? We all have a past, and you are now part of my past. No offense, Andrea, but I'd like to keep it that way. Now if you'll excuse me, I'm going to find something else to do." Chana set her cup down with enough force to slosh some on the table.

Andrea left Chana's apartment for the quiet street. Although the sky was mottled with clouds, she saw the contrails, reminding her that they would eventually have to defend Sarhn. Brigon was one of the best tactical minds they had, and now he was gone. She blamed herself. Eric was a good fighter but a mediocre organizer. Tara had a knack for leadership, but no skills for planning a defense. Andrea put the heels of her hands to her temples and squeezed. *I've got to forget about K'Rin and Brigon and all of that—I've got to help the clones.*

She found Eric taking a catnap. He sat in a doorway of a storage shed near the main gate. A data card lay in his lap. The screen, crowded with cryptic notes, emitted a faint blue glow. He snored softly. He hadn't shaved—probably hadn't eaten since the battle the morning before.

Andrea shook him gently and said, "Eric."

He woke with a start, the data card clattering onto the pavement. Looking at the bright sky, he asked, "What time is it?"

"Midmorning." Andrea stood over him. Eric looked back suspiciously. She said, "Brigon's gone south toward Qurush, and you can't run this operation by yourself."

Eric stood on his own power. "There's no one else."

"I'll help." Andrea looked him over, head to toe. "You're a mess. Go clean up and eat a hot meal. I'll recruit some talent and meet you back at the Ministry of Security in two hours."

Eric's eyes widened. For a moment he was speechless. Then he smiled at the bad joke. "You and me? Work together?"

Andrea folded her arms across her chest. "Look, Eric. I'm not going to force myself on you. But the sad truth is that with just two semesters at the Academy and the Tenebrea field course, I'm the only person here schooled in matters of defense. Watching you make mistakes would just be too painful." Andrea caught herself. "I didn't mean it that way."

She looked Eric in the eye, and for the first time, she didn't see Steve looking back. She saw a tired man with intense eyes and stress etched over his face. "If we work together, we can organize these people to defend Sarhn. I doubt either of us could manage alone."

Eric closed his eyes in thought for a moment. Then he looked up and said, "Okay." Eric held out his hand. "We work together."

Andrea hesitated, then grabbed Eric's hand firmly.

Tara sat at the end of a long table. She called the meeting and felt unprepared. She told the small gathering, "I don't have an agenda. I just want to hear your thoughts."

She fought her rising tide of anxiety. The opulence of the government building bothered her—even more because no one else seemed to mind. She distrusted the clones' instant acclimation to bounty. Poverty was simple—fewer layers and variables—

and therefore easier to manage. On the other hand, Sarhn had so many relative levels of prosperity.

She had thought she would run Sarhn with the loose covenants that worked for them in the mountains. Now, she had doubts. Just looking at the room, the plaster relief ornamenting the ceiling, the cut-crystal chandeliers, the forest-green wallpaper, the chairs, the rollers on the feet of the chairs, the ball bearings in the rollers . . . . *It's as if poverty has no moving parts and prosperity has a million of them.* Tara was out of her depth and she knew it. The complexity of Sarhn was beyond her ability.

Who would help her? What advice could she seek? She looked across the table at Brigon's empty, deserted chair. Perhaps Brigon sensed the daunting nature of managing Sarhn. Perhaps he left to maintain the simple equilibrium of life in the wilderness. Tara looked at Andrea's empty chair. Eric sat across the table, but he worked on sketches of the walls, plotting fields of fire.

"Eric?" Tara asked.

He looked up. "Ordinate reconnaissance overflights continue. If they haven't bombed us by now, I figure they won't bomb at all. They must think they can evict us with infantry. Andrea is organizing everyone into cohorts of four hundred persons. This afternoon, I begin running drills for relieving units on the wall." Eric returned to his sketches.

Dr. Carai sat next to Tara. He was in better spirits. His fur was lighter after a hot bath. He had combed out all the burrs and knots. A stack of Clone Welfare Institute lab manuals lay on the table in front of him. He held one of the thick manuals in his lap, reading quickly, turning the pages with a repetitive snap. He muttered and wheezed, "Doable—most doable."

Farther down the table, the emaciated Hart worked with a data card, researching the city's inventory. He raised his eyes and announced to the small assembly, "In terms of food, we can definitely survive until the next harvest."

The dozen spectators in the room murmured approval. Tara coaxed, "Elaborate."

Hart pointed to his ledger with his bony finger. "The population of Sarhn is so diminished that we can survive on its supplies until the next harvest. Two years ago, the Ordinate civilian plus clone populations exceeded one million mouths to feed. My rough estimate is that we have about three thousand precinct clones that stayed behind when the Ordinate fled. Plus, we have sixteen thousand of our wilderness clones—a total of nineteen thousand mouths to feed. In other words, the total population of Sarhn is now two percent of what it was two years ago."

"That's good," Tara added.

"Not necessarily," Hart answered. "We can manage the problem of food easily. Even without the stored supplies, we can soon access the trout ponds. We don't have any livestock, so our protein must come from fish and legumes. The orchards—apples, pears, and pecans—have survived the winter and will produce more than enough by late summer. The rhizome plants are coming back. We can plant soybeans, oats, and wheat. Energy is no problem. The auxiliary nuclear plant inside Sarhn proper has another fifty years of fuel."

"Then what's the problem?" Eric looked up from his papers.

"The problem," Hart looked at his data card, "is that we don't have enough *people* to run a city. We have no surplus labor. We can grow the essentials, but the city will crumble around our ears. We can't manufacture clothing or any other household goods. I'm just a cabinetmaker, not a planner, but I can tell you one thing from my experience in the precincts and the mountains. Our well-being depends on a large, well-diversified labor force. We need more people. Even then, we'll need to trade with the other Cor cities to get the goods we can't make ourselves."

Eric chimed in, "And of course, the other cities are still controlled by the Ordinate."

Tara pointed her stump at Dr. Carai and told the rest of the room, "Dr. Carai says he can start hatching a new crop of juvenile clones in seven to nine months."

"Right," Hart replied in a helpless tone. "Juvenile clones that require food and will themselves put a strain on our limited labor pool. The fastest way to generate labor is to—" Hart looked around the table with his sunken eyes. He nervously licked his lips. "The fastest way to build a labor pool is to manufacture adult clones complete with the neural mapping, and—"

Tara Gullwing stood and smashed her cane on the table. The crash interrupted Hart's sentence. All eyes bounced up and saw Tara's red face. The scar turned purple. She pulled the thick cane off the table and said, "Damn you for even making that suggestion! Not while I live, will we manufacture and program adult clones. We are going to use the cloning technology one last time, then forbid the use forever.

We are not—*do you hear me?*—not going to become the Ordinate."

Hart was slightly unnerved by Tara's outburst, but he replied, "I accept your decision. We all do. However, you need to be aware of the consequences. Most of these fine buildings will fall to ruin."

"So be it," Tara interjected.

Hart continued calmly. "For generations, life will get harder, not easier. Our first crop of juveniles will have a good life. Then, their children will have less. Their grandchildren even less. In sixty years or less, our progeny will live in conditions no better than we knew in the precincts."

"Is that true?" Tara asked Dr. Carai.

"To some extent, yes." He chewed the end of his mustache. "Whenever a society suffers a sudden drop in population, the level of prosperity falls, too. Conversely, wherever the population increases naturally, the standard of living increases. Be careful. An artificial increase in population causes artificial, therefore, unstable results. You clones overthrowing the Ordinate is a prime example of the point."

"None of us are afraid of being poor." Tara felt some of her earlier anxiety abate. "As long as we're free, we can make do."

Dr. Carai wheezed, "I'm not afraid for you, but for your children. You need to teach your children and grandchildren something that sounds like nonsense but is very true. They must never be ashamed or afraid of poverty. If your progeny can hold on to that ethic, they will never be afraid or ashamed of prosperity either."

Tara sought confirmation. "So you agree, Dr. Carai, that we shouldn't manufacture adult clones."

Dr. Carai stood up to address the rest of the room. "I will not help you, if you try."

A misting rain fell over Sarhn. Andrea stood on the wallport watching one of the cohorts assemble on the cratered spaceport tarmac for a drill. Andrea wore her black Tenebrea uniform to conform to her formal military duties. The clones knew to obey the woman in black as they would Tara, Brigon, or Eric.

Andrea's hair was wet. A steady drip fell from her black ponytail. Along the granite walls, defenders stood shoulder to shoulder facing outward. She studied the thick encasement that held one of the sonic barrier transmitters snug against the wall. *Eventually, the NewGens will break down a section of the sonic barrier.* She speculated that the NewGens would target the wall that had the shortest distance of open space to the forest.

The sonic barrier with its unpleasant hum was temporarily off. Work parties slathered additional cement onto the encasements. Along the wall, work parties shoveled wet snow from the base of the wall. *Every marginal inch of cement might buy another hour.*

In the tree line, Ariko stood with a plastic poncho over his head, supervising the placement of traps. Throughout the forest, they fabricated primitive devices to puncture feet. They laid trip wires to set off explosives designed to splash nails and broken glass—anything to slow the NewGens down. She recalled her guidance: *We've got to cut 'em up good before they get to the wall.*

To her right, a group of engineers from the power plant manhandled a spool of copper cable. They measured the wall for a devilish device: raw cable draped over the walls, thirty inches apart. Each cable would carry a 20-amp, 200-volt charge—enough to kill a cow.

Ogorm walked up behind her. He had a rifle slung over one shoulder and a blowgun taped to the barrel. He had cut his blond hair to a military flat-top. He announced, "Hart found the propane you asked for—only about a thousand pounds left. We going to burn something down?" He raised his eyebrows in eager anticipation.

Andrea turned and brightened. "Much better, I hope."

Ogorm grinned. He clapped his hands together. "What are we gonna do with the propane?"

"I remember an experiment that the Army Corps of Engineers did at Aberdeen—not too far from where I grew up. The engineers used to clear minefields by firing small rockets over the area. The rockets let out a gas heavier than air."

Ogorm nodded, "Like propane?"

"Like propane. The gas spreads out, covering the minefield. Then gas mixes with the oxygen in the air. When the gas reaches just the right mix of air and flammable gas, it explodes. The overpressure detonates the mines. Anyway, the engineers wanted to see how the mine-clearing gas affected infantry and armor. They hauled in some old vehicles and tethered goats inside and out. Apparently the experiment worked exceedingly well. The overpressure ruined the armored vehicles and most thoroughly ruined the goats. The only problem is, I don't know how to make the gas explode at the precise air mixture, but I'll bet Ariko down there can figure it out."

K'Rin drummed his fingers nervously on the table. His staff noticed the uncharacteristic fidgeting and they traded glances. Kip sat on K'Rin's left, Bal'Don on the right. Commander H'Roo Parh took a place at the end of the table, where he studied the logistics matrix, trying to see how they could skim another million rations for the clones. He held another report: the damage to the *Tyker* and estimated time in dry dock: six weeks. His first tactical mission had been an expensive success—and barely a success.

A gentle voice piped through the intercom, "Sir, we are receiving General Kren-Shew's evening briefing on a twelve-minute lag from the Corondor theater."

K'Rin's drumming stopped and a large screen blinked from blue to a confident face: General Kren-Shew. The voice and lips were slightly out of synch. The bottom margin of the screen displayed statistics: Jod and Chelle casualties, munitions expenditures and other logistical data. K'Rin quickly calculated a ratio. The Jod continued to inflict casualties almost twenty times greater than they suffered. Unthinkable but fortunate. He had at best hoped that Kren-Shew would achieve a six-to-one kill ratio. Either Kren-Shew was a tactical genius or the Chelle leadership was even worse than imagined—probably the latter. Kren-Shew, a very sober individual, continued to make the same assessment at the end of every briefing. *Sir, they*—referring to the Chelle—*do not learn from their mistakes.*

The briefing began. Kren-Shew spoke to the current situation, starting with the enemy. "Chelle ground strength is estimated at one point six million. The Chelle have lost fifteen percent of their soldiers and thirty percent of their ground vehicles and tactical air assets."

Kren-Shew put a map with animated battle lines on the screen. Faded green lines showed old Jod positions abandoned in the retrograde. Gray lines showed current Chelle positions, thick or thin depending on Chelle troop concentrations. Bright green lines showed current Jod positions: a series of crescents bending back, inviting the Gray into carefully planned killing zones. Kren-Shew's voice spoke about the map and the lines moved on queue. "After repulsing four major assaults in two weeks, we successfully executed a theaterwide retrograde to prepared positions." The green crescents brightened.

"This morning the Chelle began a series of probing attacks in battalion strength. Judging by the diminished shelling, we estimate that the Chelle are conserving a dwindling supply of munitions." A long line of small red flashes appeared on the map. "By midafternoon we annihilated them. Small remnants withdrew to their lines. We captured and interrogated some of their stragglers. The situation is at present quiet. We anticipate a larger, but piecemeal attack tomorrow. We're ready." The map faded to the rear and Kren-Shew's face reappeared. He suppressed a thin smile. "Gentlemen, they still don't seem to grasp what we're doing. They think they're winning." Only thirty-five years of discipline and professional decorum kept Kren-Shew's sly smile from broadening.

K'Rin switched the screen off and raised the lights in the room. "In fifteen days, we recommission the dreadnought *Zat-Mar*. She's a bit underpowered; the crew is not used to anything bigger than a cruiser, but she's got all the firepower we need. I spoke with Captain T'Pan. He wants some time to incorporate the *Zat-Mar* into a few drills. Then he's going to chase the Chelle Fleet out of the Corondor system. Then Kren-Shew will have the bulk of the Chelle ground forces in a bag."

Turning in his chair, he told Kip, "Send my compliments to Kren-Shew and T'Pan. Include the report from the shipyard. Assure T'Pan that he will at last be able to take the offensive. Got that?"

"Yes, sir."

K'Rin rapped his knuckles on the table. "I know he's been itching to blow a hole through the Chelle lines. Ah, Kip, remind the General that T'Pan makes the decision when to commit the *Zat-Mar*."

"Yes, sir."

"What's next?" K'Rin looked around the table.

Kip said, "Bal'Don has the latest damage assessment from the privateers."

Bal'Don slid a piece of paper to K'Rin's place and said, "The good news is that more than fifty Jod merchants have taken your offer. Many of them are crews from the Parh Clan's mercantile enterprise. They want to know if they can operate in the Cor system as well."

K'Rin replied, "They are privateers. They can go

where they will. Let the bounty be the same for Ordinate shipping." K'Rin leaned over to address H'Roo Parh. "Your family always comes through for us."

H'Roo arched his thin brows. "With the frontiers closed, your offer was the best on the table, sir."

"So it is."

Bal'Don interjected, "Your offer may be too good."

"How?" K'Rin asked. He grabbed the piece of paper in front of him. "Look at these numbers. The privateers—I see that they're working in small packs and sharing credits—have destroyed over two hundred thousand metric tons of Chelle shipping so far. And we've lost—" he counted aloud, "—one, two, three merchants, two others in dry dock for repairs. The Chelle are sending more of their combat vessels to patrol their own space. I think the merchants are doing a splendid job wreaking havoc. I wish we could get fifty more of H'Roo's kin into service."

Bal'Don said, "Sir, you promised to pay the registry value for any Chelle ship destroyed."

"I know what I promised," K'Rin replied, annoyed.

"Well, sir. How are we going to pay them—the privateers?"

H'Roo piped up, "I can assure you they'll demand payment." His smile assured K'Rin and the staff that his comment was not insolence, but a jest at his own clan.

K'Rin hadn't seen a smile on H'Roo since Klamdara, and he paused to enjoy the moment. Then he said, "When we finish with the Chelle, they'll soon learn the price of peace is steep. We'll demand restitution for Heptar, the Fleet, and our dead. We'll clean out their reserves of platinum, palladium, and every other precious metal. Then, we'll use Chelle's bullion to pay the privateers for burning Chelle's shipping." K'Rin smiled broadly. "After the fact, we'll let the Chelle know how we spent their money. They will choke on that bone for a thousand years."

The double doors in the back of the room opened slightly and a messenger slipped in. He wore a tan uniform. He marched straight to K'Rin and stood at attention.

"What?" K'Rin could not avoid the intrusion.

"Sir." The young soldier stiffened. He held out a small data card. "You gave orders to interrupt you if we got any message from Cor. Courier just arrived with this message." He put the data card on the table by K'Rin's hand, then stood at attention.

"At ease," K'Rin muttered. He quickly took the data card and read it. He paraphrased. "H'Roo, this will interest you. Andrea Flores and her clones have taken Sarhn." In a more introspective voice, he added, "For better or for worse, she has always exceeded my expectations." Returning to the message, he said, "She says, H'Roo, you can deliver supplies directly to the Sarhn spaceport instead of dropping barges. She needs antiair and long-range cannon as soon as possible." He set the data card on the table and passed it to H'Roo. "Take care of this matter immediately."

H'Roo took the card. "Yes, sir. The *Tyker* is in dry dock for repairs."

K'Rin ordered, "Take a light cruiser and escorts from T'Pan's Fleet."

"But, sir," a voice from the end of the table objected. The officer wore T'Pan's sash, Fleet liaison.

"You just said Captain T'Pan must prepare to clear the Chelle Fleet from the Jod system. He will want all his assets."

"I understand." K'Rin pulled at his ear. "He'll need to succeed with one cruiser less." Turning to H'Roo, he said, "Commandeer a couple antiair batteries and a long-range cannon from the home guard. We cannot leave Andrea and her people exposed to bombardment from space or air."

Kip interjected, "With all due respect, sir, why not? We can finish the Chelle in sixty days, then turn all our assets against Cor. The rest of the command may not understand your decision to divert assets from T'Pan to relieve the Terran woman and a bunch of clones. Every clan has relatives on Corondor."

K'Rin responded with an icy stare. "That's my problem, not yours." He muttered, "Now, Commander Parh, you will leave as soon as possible for Cor. Understood?"

"Yes, sir," both Kip and H'Roo answered in unison.

"And Kip," K'Rin lowered his voice to barely a whisper, but a whisper that the rest of the room could hear, "never contradict me on the matter of Commander Andrea Flores-*Rin* again." He emphasized her adoptive clan ties.

"I'm sorry, sir." Kip's neck flared briefly. He pressed his fingers together, in an act of self-control.

K'Rin switched off his data card. Then Bal'Don raised his voice, "That, gentlemen, concludes today's briefing. I'll see all of you here tomorrow, same time."

Everyone rose sharply and stood as K'Rin left the room. Kip followed on his heels and caught him in the corridor as he entered his office. "Sir, may I have a word? In private?"

K'Rin ushered Kip into the office. "Don't sit. You've got only two minutes." He poured himself a glass of cold water, drank half, and poured the remainder into a potted plant.

Kip came to the point. "Don't be cross with me about Andrea Flores. I understand your position better, now."

"Do you?" K'Rin asked cryptically. "Sometimes, I'm not sure I understand myself. But continue."

"I understand your sense of gratitude toward Andrea—a sense of loyalty to a subordinate. As you point out, she did help rescue us from Klamdara." Kip pressed the palms of his hands together, a gesture of reason and compromise.

"Oh, spare me," K'Rin replied sarcastically. Then he said, "If I owed her only gratitude or loyalty, I'd be content. However, I owe her a blood debt. I am responsible for her husband's death."

"A blood debt?" Kip shook his head. "No, sir. I disagree. Steve Dewinter was just another clone. He would have been terminated long before had you not intervened."

K'Rin held up his hand. "You don't need to rationalize Dewinter's death for me. I've rationalized enough for both of us." K'Rin fixed his resolute eyes on Kip and quoted one of Jod's hallowed ethics: "It is better to endure an injustice than to inflict an injustice upon another."

K'Rin pointed to a glass case. His badge of office, the gold necklace, lay inside. The gold triskelion identified the Rin Clan. He said, "When Pl'Don stripped my father of his title and privileges and publicly humiliated our clan, my father infuriated us by calmly saying, *the shame is his, not mine.* I thought my father was naive." K'Rin stifled a pained laugh. "I was a two-ringer then, a pilot. My world was a cockpit—a simple set of rules: chief among them, kill or be killed. I was motivated by the practical considerations of survival, survival for me, my clan, and for Jod. I never wavered. I was always confident. Then, at Baltimore Harbor, I committed a grave injustice."

Kip argued, "There was no other way."

"No, Kip, I had options. Sacrificing Steve Dewinter was convenient. He was a clone that I smuggled onto Earth with two aging Cor Ordinate refugees. The old ones were marginally informative. But Steve was just a liability with no utility. So, when I saw the practical opportunity to use him, that is, sacrifice him for Eric who could be marginally more useful, I set up Steve's death."

"Sir, you made the right decision."

"I had no right to make that decision."

Kip insisted, "He was just a clone."

"He was Andrea's husband. He was the father to her child. By rights, Andrea can claim a blood debt."

Kip's voice strained with frustration. "The blood debt is an old Jod custom that applies to the Jod only. She has no standing."

K'Rin tapped himself on the chest. "My custom, Kip. My custom."

Kip squared his shoulders. He abruptly changed his tack, saying, "Sir, you are right: I don't understand your motives completely. Nevertheless, my job is to make your life easier. Therefore, I propose that I attempt a reconciliation between you and Andrea Flores."

"You? How?"

"First, we need to find out what Andrea will accept

to satisfy the debt. Therefore, I request permission to join Commander Parh on his next mission to Cor. I will take a small delegation of Tenebrea to protect my person. Commander Parh can arrange a meeting. I'll find out what she wants to reconcile this matter. I will explain as best I can what happened at Baltimore Harbor, and I'll extend your regrets. To satisfy our law, I'll ask her to recant her treasonous threats against your life."

K'Rin walked behind his desk. Looking down at the polished wood, he thought, *We must start somewhere.* "Tell her," he looked up at Kip, "tell her that I'll do anything she asks."

Kip winced and said, "Anything within reason."

"Don't qualify my words when you speak to her. In fact, I'll write her a letter for H'Roo Parh to deliver." He sat down at his desk and rustled through a drawer. He retrieved a small tablet of paper and an old ink pen. "Inform Commander Parh that you'll accompany him to Sarhn."

"Yes, sir." Kip bowed and started for the door.

"Kip. Thank you for your good counsel."

Kip turned and smiled. "Sir, it has always been my pleasure to serve you."

K'Rin was taken by Kip's unbridled elation at this insignificant bit of praise. As he began to write, he was moved to add, "You know I've always been stern with you only because I see a lot of myself in you."

"I don't mind." Kip's neck warmed to a sentimental rose.

"I want you to succeed—I really do." K'Rin raised his hand halfway between a salute and a benediction. "And if you succeed in reconciling Andrea to me, I will be forever in your debt."

Kip's smile evaporated into a thoughtful pause. "I'll do my best." Kip closed the door gently as he left.

K'Rin hunched over his desk. He looked at the blank sheet of paper. The pen felt thick between his fingers. *How to start?*

chapter 18

Tara brought Andrea into the Ministry operations center. She pointed at the floor-to-ceiling display. "All communications on Cor have ceased: microwave, laser links. All silent. The only feed from the lone remaining satellite is the weather."

With clinical detachment, Andrea said, "The Ordinate are getting ready to move against us. Show me your last week's data on the comm links."

At Tara's command, the wall image changed. The weather disappeared: cloud cover, precipitation, fronts, and a plethora of data that meant nothing to either Tara or Andrea. The map quickly reconfigured itself to show the natural and man-made features. The vast majority of the planet was emptiness: mountains, deserts, plains, and oceans. An irregular continent sat clumsily in an endless blue. To Andrea's eye, the landmass resembled Europe and Asia turned ninety degrees with Spain reaching toward the North Pole and Kamchatka stretching toward the south. A couple of minor landmasses seemed to float offshore like an afterthought, uninhabited.

On the continent, Cor had about thirty large cities, most of them larger than Sarhn. Each city had an irregular shape that conformed to the natural vagaries of the terrain. Most of the cities clung to the western coast, near a river or natural harbor. All of them remained in temperate or tropical zones. Sarhn was the northernmost city. Each city was color coded: a small enclave of green to mark the boundaries of the Ordinate living space and a large spread of brown to mark the clone precincts. Andrea noted the dearth of roads. In the southern hemisphere, the larger cities linked themselves with rail. For some reason, the capital city Sarhn preferred relative isolation, relying on air and ocean barge. Topography contributed to the isolation: mountains to the north and east, bogs and salt marsh to the south. Tara typed in a command and announced, "The Ordinate have rerouted their communications. The screen shows their microwave, laser, and land links superimposed."

A spider diagram of multicolored lines instantly linked the cities. The preponderance of the links terminated at Qurush, Sarhn's southerly neighbor.

Andrea pointed to the hub of comm links. "The Ordinate are staging out of Qurush. They'll come overland." She asked Tara, "What do we know about Qurush?"

"We've always known it was a small factory town." Tara cropped the map and zoomed into Qurush and Sarhn and the two hundred miles that separated them. The cities had neither road nor rail to close the two-hundred-mile gap. Andrea studied the inhospitable terrain to the south.

"I'll bring up the data on Qurush." Tara paused to

tap a few keys on her console. A chart appeared on the wall screen, and she scrolled through the text— mostly information about mean temperature, rainfall, and such. Tara stepped closer to the wall to read the information. She recited the key facts out loud. "Square miles—342.2. This is odd: current Ordinate population only 200—hardly any. Old-order clones—zero. Doesn't make sense."

Andrea contradicted Tara. "Well, somebody is occupying that 342.2 square miles of real estate. What about NewGens?"

"Doesn't say." Tara rubbed her cheek with the stump of her right arm. "I've already searched every database in Sarhn to find out how many NewGens they've manufactured. No data."

Andrea observed, "NewGen production must have been secret."

"Then we have no idea how big a force they plan to send against us—tens of thousands, maybe."

Andrea looked again at the wasteland between the two cities. She imagined Brigon slogging his way through the bogs and the slush. She imagined him angry—his physical discomfort adding to his anger. She imagined him walking into a hive of NewGen production.

The Jod ship settled down on bright spikes of flame—the largest ship that any of the clones had ever seen. The bulbous nose and markings of concentric circles—blue, violet, and red—convinced the nervous clones that the ship was not Cor Ordinate. Andrea watched with keen interest. H'Roo was on board. He had brought the heavy guns as she requested and quickly, too. She had so conditioned herself to be disappointed that the timely arrival of the Jod transport upset her prejudices.

Two clamshell doors opened. A small crew of Jod manhandled four large pallets onto a magnetic lift, gliding the cargo out of the belly of the ship onto the tarmac. The cargo was draped with a taut silver tarp that showed the outline of long barrels and bulky transformers. Three of the Jod wore the standard beige Fleet duty uniform. Two others wore the Tenebrea uniform, and Andrea believed she recognized the young faces even if she didn't recall the names. The five Jod worked silently, guiding the pallets around bomb craters toward a half-standing hangar. They left their cargo and returned briskly to the ship.

H'Roo squinted into the sunshine. Behind him the clamshell doors closed, sealing their ship from would-be intruders.

Andrea saw that he was looking for her in the crowd. She was wearing her black Tenebrea uniform, faded from use. Her belt was a coarse weave of hemp. An oily scabbard held a rugged knife. Her holster, strapped to her leg, held a gray revolver with a thick barrel eight inches long.

She stepped onto the tarmac to identify herself. "H'Roo Parh."

H'Roo turned and with his back to the ship, smiled warmly. He walked quickly albeit with some professional reserve to Andrea. He wore the black and gray Tenebrea uniform, sparked with the insignia of his new rank on his sleeves. On his chest he wore an embroidered crest, the Parh family's circle of dolphins instead of the Rin triskelion. Wearing his family crest was H'Roo's right, although he was the only officer in the Tenebrea to do so.

H'Roo held out his hand, but Andrea did not reciprocate. Awkwardly, H'Roo dropped his hand to his side. His countenance withered and he commented on her attire: "Your uniform is a bit shabby."

"It's gotten a lot of use." Andrea looked past H'Roo to the large pallets. "Thank you for bringing the antiair and the cannon. I think we're going to need them soon."

"K'Rin sends his compliments as well." H'Roo looked around at the damaged spaceport.

"Did you have any trouble out there?" She pointed to the sky.

"Not a bit. They scanned us, but they didn't engage this time. They did not threaten us from land assets either. I guess you stung them good." H'Roo grinned briefly.

"I think the Ordinate have mustered all their assets in one place to prepare an assault to take Sarhn back. My guess is that they don't want to show their hand yet. You won't want to be here when the shooting starts."

"Maybe I do." H'Roo looked around. "Where's Brigon? I thought he'd be with you."

"He left, went south."

"Why?"

Andrea pursed her lips tightly and replied with a shrug.

H'Roo furrowed his brow. "And Tara?"

"She captured this city. Now she's trying to figure out how to run it." Andrea glanced back toward the taller buildings in Sarhn. "She and Dr. Carai are going to build quite the little Utopia here."

"You disapprove?"

"Not really. We'll probably all be dead in six months, so why not let them have their fun. H'Roo, I'll bet the Ordinate are manufacturing NewGens at a rate sufficient to overrun our puny outpost."

"Maybe we can help." H'Roo held his hand up to shade his eyes. "Is there some shade close by where we can speak in private?" H'Roo kept his back to the Jod ship. He said softly, "Family business."

"Sure." Andrea took the hint. "Follow me. We'll have a bite to eat."

Andrea led H'Roo through a maze of rubble—stubby walls and piles of brick and charred timber. She said, "Give my compliments to the *Tyker*'s gunner. You cut the Sarhn garrison strength in half, and you managed to spare most of the city."

"You could come back to Jod and thank him yourself."

"An interesting proposition. I've been thinking of ways to get back to Jod." Her eyes smiled but her lips remained tight and cold. She turned a corner, leading into a bomb-damaged barracks. They walked through the roofless shell to another street and stopped at a small restaurant. Looking back through the husks of buildings Andrea saw the silhouette of the Jod ship, but she knew that no one aboard the ship could see her.

She led H'Roo inside. "You can speak to me in private here." Andrea took a table, brushing the crumbs off with the back of her hand.

Sitting at the bar, wearing an apron, was a middle-aged man, a burly clone, leisurely finishing his meal. Without turning his eyes from his plate to see who had entered, the clone said, "I'll be with you folks in a moment."

They left the door wide open and the fresh air followed them in. Before H'Roo sat down, he reached over the bar and helped himself to a bottle of water and a pair of glasses. The tablecloth was cornflower blue, matching the skimpy curtains that bisected the large windows.

"So what's on your mind?" Andrea asked.

H'Roo reached into his tunic and pulled out an envelope. The dark red seal bore the Rin Crest. "K'Rin asked me to deliver this letter personally. Here." He held the envelope over the table. Andrea refused to take it.

"Aren't you curious?" H'Roo's voice had a touch of tease.

"You read it," Andrea said with rehearsed nonchalance.

"Okay." H'Roo broke the seal and unfolded the letter. "It's written in K'Rin's hand." He turned the paper around to show Andrea the round cursive text. He says, "Dear cousin—"

Andrea looked away and muttered, "I resent him invoking family. He's a hypocrite."

H'Roo cleared his voice and continued reading, "I'm sorry I can't deliver this message in person—"

"He's never worked without a surrogate before," she sniped.

"—but I am tied to my desk, at present. I asked Commander H'Roo Parh and my Chief of Staff, Kip Rin, to make initial inquiries as to how we might be reconciled. We need to put aside this enmity between us. Put simply, what will it take to satisfy you? You can make any demand of me through

H'Roo and Kip. Signed, your cousin, Hal K'Rin, Headman of the Rin Clan, Counselor and Chief Executive of Jod."

"I'm impressed with all his new titles." Andrea's face was flushed. Her olive skin was darker, her lips almost purple. Her jaw muscles tightened. "His titles sort of dwarf the moniker of *cousin*, don't they?"

"K'Rin has always been a little stiff in personal relationships." H'Roo folded the letter and passed it to the center of the table. "I admit this letter is not the warmest communication, but Andrea, it's an opportunity. I think you ought to meet with Kip. I'll be there, of course. Kip will have three witnesses to our conversation."

"Witnesses? How dumb do you think I am?"

H'Roo shrugged, "Witnesses, bodyguards . . . you did threaten to kill K'Rin in front of everybody. I'd be nervous if I were Kip. You two never did get along. He takes your threats seriously."

"He should." Andrea looked at the letter as if it were diseased. "If K'Rin were sincere, he would have come himself."

H'Roo shook his head emphatically. "He can't. Just as he says in the letter, he's tied to his desk. The political situation on Jod is still uncertain. Some of the clans are grumbling about his usurpation of power, as they see it. Our food supply from Corondor is cut off, so the people are rationed. K'Rin has mobilized the reserves and has diverted much of our collective energies to restoring the Fleet. The cannon on the tarmac—I had to pull it from the home guard outside the city of Gyre, upsetting a lot of *my* kinsmen. You're not the only person angry with Hal K'Rin. The situation on Corondor is precarious. I think we're doing as well as expected on Corondor, but the Chelle do outnumber us five to two. K'Rin might as well be in a prison. Listen, Andrea," H'Roo folded his hands, "I think you ought to talk with Kip."

Andrea shook her head. "No chance."

"You can demand anything."

She raised her voice, "I want my husband and child back. I want my life back."

H'Roo shook his head and reiterated, "K'Rin can obligate all the resources of Jod. You can dictate the future for you and these clones of yours. Do you need aid in the form of food? Technology? Do you want your little wreck of a world to be included in the Alliance? Or do you want to be left alone? You don't need to decide the specific terms now, but you ought to accept the offer while it's good. If you refuse to speak with Kip, you may in fact jeopardize the marginal help you're getting now. Perhaps you could swallow your anger just long enough to help your friends here: Tara, Brigon, Dr. Carai . . . You'd be doing me a favor, too."

"How?"

"If you isolate yourself through your enmity toward K'Rin, I most probably won't get to see you again. I would," H'Roo swallowed, "miss you. I remember when you first joined us. I remember sitting with you for hours talking about your home-world."

Please don't get maudlin. Andrea blurted out an awkward observation to stiff-arm H'Roo's sentimentality, "I was afraid you were getting infatuated with me."

"I've always been fascinated by things exotic. I

suppose fascination and infatuation might look the same to a woman." H'Roo's eyes narrowed. "Was I ever rude?"

Andrea broke eye contact, a bit shamefaced. "No, never."

"Then I can reminisce without offending." H'Roo leaned over the table and cupped his hand over hers. "I remember Dlagor Island. I remember leaving you at Clemnos after you killed that Hunter. I left without saying good-bye." H'Roo's neck flushed slightly, but he quickly regained his composure. "I remember how glad I was to see you return. I remember Vintell and that hellhole Yuseat. I helped you steal the *Benwoi* to go back to Earth."

"Where you got yourself shot for your trouble." Andrea tried to move the conversation off H'Roo's sentimental memories.

But H'Roo continued. "I got to see Earth. I got to see your homeland and village with all the boats. You took good care of my wound. You dragged me here to Cor. I nearly crashed the *Benwoi*."

"I sank her."

"And Klamdara Prison. They'd all be dead if it weren't for you. In a strange twist of fate, you even caused Pl'Don to dispatch the *Kopshir*, else we'd have no dreadnought and the Chelle would whittle us down to nothing. You're a lot of trouble, Andrea, but I've never had such a good time." H'Roo poured two glasses of gaseous water from the bottle. He drank his. "If you won't help yourself, help your friends. Think about it."

Andrea rested her elbows on the table and cradled her head in her hands. She watched the bubbles in her glass expand from nothing and let go, rising to the surface and disappearing into nothing. She felt as pointless as one of those bubbles. Part of her wanted to share memories—share anything— with H'Roo, but she couldn't. She couldn't afford sentimental distractions. Then a thought struck her: *Perhaps K'Rin is the distraction. I'll never get close enough to K'Rin to kill him,* she thought. *Perhaps the best I can do is squeeze the old man to benefit Tara and Brigon. The Cor Ordinate aren't beaten yet. What would Tara say if she knew I turned my back on such an offer?*

She looked up at H'Roo. "Since I've nothing to lose, I'll speak with Kip. I won't promise anything, but I'll speak with him."

"Good." H'Roo stood. "I can take you back to the transport now."

"No, not there. Kip can meet me here."

"Why?"

"Don't take this personally, H'Roo, but I don't trust Jod integrity. I wouldn't want to get on the wrong side of a locked door, if you know what I mean. Kip can speak with me here, alone."

"All right. I'll bring Kip to you." H'Roo got up and looked back through the plate glass toward the outline of the ship. As he started toward the door, the disheveled attendant got off his stool and asked, "Can I get you folks something?"

H'Roo said, "She'll order for me. I'll be back soon."

Kip listened to H'Roo's report in stiff silence. H'Roo pointed through the rubble and through the shadows. He identified the small restaurant with the cornflower-blue curtains. H'Roo emphasized that Kip must handle the negotiations with delicate consideration for the wrongs Andrea had suffered.

Without moving a muscle in his face, Kip promised, "Utmost delicacy, I assure you."

"Don't expect too much from her. She's ready to listen. I believe the key to achieving the reconciliation is to convince her that K'Rin can help her friends here."

"The clones?" Kip asked.

"Yes."

"I see," Kip muttered with some bemusement. "We are to expect Hal K'Rin to serve these, uh . . . subspecies, and for that promise, the Terran woman will recant her traitorous intent of murdering him. H'Roo, you forget that Hal K'Rin is the just head of the Jod government, after all."

H'Roo uncrossed his arms from his chest and balled his fists. "Are you countermanding Hal K'Rin? Perhaps you'd better let me do the talking with Andrea. I think I can better represent K'Rin's interests."

Kip nodded to one of his cohorts. "Perhaps you ought to stay here and mind the ship."

"Oh, no. I'm going to attend this interview."

Kip shook his head. "As your superior officer—a captain and Chief of Staff—I order you to stay here and mind the ship. Somebody has to protect the ship, and I say that somebody is you."

"And if I refuse? Do you think you can court-martial me? My first witness will be K'Rin."

"No, I don't think we're going to have a court-martial." Turning his head he commanded, "Mat S'Kor."

H'Roo felt the blunt muzzle of a handlance in the small of his back. A voice behind him responded, "Yes, sir."

Kip approached and removed H'Roo's handlance and dagger from his utility belt. He stuffed the weapons into his own belt and said, "Trust me, H'Roo. This is for your own good. Andrea has a history of violence. After all, if she can't kill K'Rin, I'm probably the next best item on her list. I was part of the Baltimore massacre plan, you know. In fact, marking Steve Dewinter was my idea. I plan to tell her that."

"Why?"

"I don't plan to spend the rest of my life watching my back. I can't predict how Andrea will take the news."

"I can." H'Roo's jaw tightened.

Kip arched his brow. "Actually, you're right. She is overly invested in an effort to punish Steve Dewinter's murderers. We might be forced to defend ourselves, and frankly, I'm not sure whose side you'd join: hers or ours."

H'Roo glared at Kip with menacing silence.

"I thought so," Kip confirmed his decision. "Mat S'Kor, keep Commander H'Roo Parh on the bridge until we return. If he tries to escape, shoot him."

"You want me to stun him, sir?"

Kip pursed his lips at the notion, "No. If he tries to escape, I think it best if you kill him outright." Kip turned and left with three of his so-called witnesses, leaving the fourth to hold a weapon on H'Roo. "Tell the rest of the crew to prepare to depart immediately."

The door hissed closed, and S'Kor backed his way

to the door arming the lock, recording his palm print on the access pad.

H'Roo quickly discerned his predicament. Kip and three armed Tenebrea were on their way to assassinate Andrea. Kip had used him. He felt his own rage building, yet he forced a calm onto his face. He could not let his emotions show on his neck. Instead he leaned against the navigational console and said in mock dejection, "Well, that was pretty insulting—whose side would I join . . ."

S'Kor said nothing but held the handlance steady.

H'Roo continued, "So Kip and you four planned all along that you'd kill Andrea Flores."

The armed Tenebrea looked sullen, refusing to engage in conversation.

"When he's through with Andrea, he'll kill you, too. He needs accomplices, but he can't have witnesses."

"I must ask you to be quiet, sir."

H'Roo stood and took a tentative step forward, "You heard him. He's got to kill Andrea because eventually, she'd learn that he was as much responsible for her husband's death as K'Rin—probably more directly responsible. His idea, remember?" H'Roo inched closer and spoke in paternal tones, "I'll bet he told you that you need to kill Andrea to protect K'Rin. Am I right?"

S'Kor shook his head nervously, confirming H'Roo's suspicion.

"Right. But let us review the facts. You plan to say that you killed Andrea to protect Kip. And what will K'Rin do if he finds out that you assassinated the woman who saved him—saved all of you from Klamdara Prison? Saved you all from an ignominious death? In effect, she saved the Jod race from extermination at the hands of the Ordinate and Chelle. I'll tell you what my cousin K'Rin will do. He'll rip the enzyme out of your arm and leave you to die in a cell."

"No." S'Kor's neck flushed.

H'Roo stepped closer. "Is your assignment to murder me on my own bridge?"

"No! My orders are to hold you here. You might interfere, that's all. Everyone suspects that your loyalties to the Earth woman exceed your loyalty to the Tenebrea."

"Interfere with what?" H'Roo pressed. The barrel of the handlance was inches away from his chest.

S'Kor started to backpedal. He tightened his grip on the handlance. "Stand back. I'm warning you."

H'Roo studied the pair of eyes watching him. They darted back and forth, up and down, simultaneously tracking H'Roo's hands, shoulders, and face. H'Roo inched closer trying to trap S'Kor's eyes with his, to take them off his hands. "K'Rin will make sure your name is crossed from the book. You will never have existed and your parents will be forbidden to utter your name. Eternal shame. You are a lost soul." *There!* The eyes widened, transfixed.

H'Roo struck. He grabbed S'Kor's pistol hand. Stepping deftly inside the arm, he turned the elbow down and snapped the arm over his knee. The handlance fell to the floor and rattled away.

S'Kor howled in surprise and pain, but his soldier reflexes survived the shock. He punched H'Roo three times rapidly in the small of the back just above the pelvis. H'Roo endured the searing pain, keeping his grip of the arm and manhandling S'Kor off-balance.

S'Kor reached with his good hand and pulled his dagger from the sheath. H'Roo anticipated the move and purchased a grip on the wrist, turning the thumb out, pointing the blade away. Then H'Roo drove his knee into S'Kor's midsection, knocking the wind out of him. He let S'Kor fall into a heap on the deck. S'Kor struggled to his knees attempting to rejoin the fight, brandishing the dagger.

H'Roo found the handlance, turned the setting to stun, then fired a bolt between S'Kor's shoulder blades. S'Kor fell to the floor twitching and shaking although unconscious. H'Roo muttered to the unconscious Jod, "If anything happens to Andrea, I'll come back and kill you."

Then he dragged S'Kor to the door and used his palm print to unlock the door to the bridge. He took S'Kor's knife and put it into his scabbard. Then, he ran into the hall and slapped the comm console, but he bit his words. *Who else has Kip recruited?* He didn't know whom to trust. H'Roo ran out of the ship, his back throbbing with each step. He set the handlance to kill.

Andrea stood next to the large window. She felt the gauzy blue curtain on her cheek. In her mind she rehearsed the conversation that she, H'Roo, and Kip would soon have. Always, her mind flashed to the past, the Harbor massacre. With painful force of will, she banished those thoughts and contemplated the future. Given present circumstances, she couldn't lay a hand on K'Rin. She'd never get close enough to make him pay the way he ought to pay. *Unless,* she entertained a fantasy, *unless I lie to them, fake a reconciliation—then I might get close enough. Perhaps I could make him trust me—turn the tables on him. I could go back to Jod. I can see him reinstating me into his household, handing me back my ceremonial dagger. Then I use it on him.*

Andrea swallowed hard: *I can't.* She felt the awkward weight of scruples, and she felt like mocking herself: *what do you mean, you can't?* A sadness washed over her as she remembered being a young woman back on Earth. She wasn't the nicest person she knew, but she was honest. Now her thoughts had wandered off too far. She gritted her teeth and forced her thoughts to the present. Perhaps she should accept as a collateral consolation K'Rin's largesse for the benefit of Tara and her people. *It isn't enough!* She wanted drive her fist through the thick plate glass.

Looking up she saw four Jod walking over a mound of rubble. They stopped, looked around, and then proceeded, unsure of their way. *Can't be H'Roo.* Andrea looked closely. One of the figures was Kip. He wore an officer's tunic with rank on the sleeve. The other three wore standard issue field uniforms and utility belts, not rank. They were younger Tenebrea: enlisted. *Where's H'Roo?* She felt her hands sweat. She saw Kip point to the restaurant. The foursome stopped to confer. Then two of the enlisted Tenebrea walked away.

Andrea's head ached. What were the possibilities? She pulled her large pistol from her holster and checked her load. Then she pulled the hammer back until she felt and heard the click. At that point the cafe's lone attendant returned from the back room to take his perch at the counter. He scratched his scalp through his wiry black hair, yawning. *He looks like a CPP model—like Coop. Everybody looks like someone.* Andrea said bluntly, "You'd better get out of here."

The attendant, a large man, turned and saw her pistol and gave her a hard look. "You need help?"

"I might, but you'd better go. I don't want to shoot first. And if they do . . ." she gave no clue as to who *they* were, ". . . you don't want to be in sight."

The CPP model clone reached around the counter and retrieved an old revolver. "I'll wait in the back."

Andrea turned her attention to the window. She heard the swinging door to the kitchen flap.

H'Roo scrambled over the rubble. He paused once to catch his breath, bending at the waist, trying to relieve the pain in his back. He could feel the bruises above his kidneys. As he straightened himself, he saw four black uniforms a hundred meters away, in the shell of a building. They stood face-to-face. Kip was gesticulating, giving last-minute instructions. H'Roo raised his handlance and took aim, but he was out of range, without a clear shot. If only the handlance made more noise, he might warn Andrea. H'Roo ducked behind a ragged slab of concrete wall to collect his thoughts. He had to get closer, without being discovered.

He peered around the corner and saw the four Jod separate. Kip and one Tenebrea walked toward the restaurant. The other two split in opposite directions. He watched one climb to the second story of a damaged barracks building and settle into a prone firing position at a window. There, the Tenebrea screwed barrel lengths to his handlance, converting the short-range hand weapon to an accurate sniper's weapon.

H'Roo realized that a straight dash to the restaurant door would be suicide. The sniper would burn him, and Andrea would never know that he'd tried to rush Kip. She'd never hear the quiet whine of the sniperlance. He watched Kip and his accomplice approach the restaurant. His heartbeat quickened.

H'Roo lost track of the fourth Tenebrea. He presumed that Kip had ordered him to seal the back of the building. H'Roo watched Kip, flanked by a large Tenebrea, walk confidently to the front door of the restaurant.

H'Roo plotted a more circuitous route to a stump of stucco wall across the street from the restaurant's front door. He could stay out of the sniper's sights most of the way. He had to get closer. He had to try. *At least Andrea will know that I tried, that I was not one of Kip's assassins.* Nothing else mattered. He had to reach her with that truth, before they killed him. He remembered something Andrea told him, *Being dead greatly uncomplicates life . . .* At the time, he had thought her quip absurd. Suddenly it made sense.

The CPP clone hunkered down in the kitchen. He could see a fraction of the small dining area through a crack in the door. He laid his old revolver across his knee. He didn't understand the nature of the danger. But he knew about the Earth woman— everybody did. The clones believed she was some invincible creature, friend to Tara Gullwing and prized by Brigon, the clone child. He felt important to be helping her. After today, he'd have a story to tell that everyone would listen to time and again.

He watched every detail, almost preoccupied by the future telling of his story. Andrea squeezed her narrow body against the piece of wall that separated the large window from the front door. She stood with unnaturally straight posture. She held her pistol in her right hand across her chest.

The front door opened and two Jod in black uniforms stepped through in single file. They were hairless. Their deep-set eyes flashed over the multicolored rings that festooned down to the cheekbone. They seemed disappointed and surprised by the emptiness of the room.

Quick as a snake, Andrea raised her pistol and pressed it against the older Jod's head. "Don't even breathe."

The younger Jod just as quickly unholstered an energy weapon and put it to the back of Andrea's head. Andrea said, "You can burn me here, but I'll still get off one round and splatter Kip's brains all over the wall."

The CPP clone listened intently as the older Jod, the one called Kip, said, "Let's all be calm."

The CPP raised his own pistol and cocked the hammer gently. He looked down the barrel and put the iron sights on the younger Jod. The range was tricky, but he figured with careful aim he could plug the Jod in the forehead, perhaps knock him back hard enough to stop him from firing at Andrea.

"Where's H'Roo?" Andrea's voice was ice.

"I had to leave an officer on the ship's bridge. We are in a tactical zone, you must realize." Kip kept his eyes forward. The CPP saw fear and treachery in Kip's eyes, but the voice was steady. "H'Roo warned me that you'd disapprove."

"I do."

"We're in a bit of a—what is that colorful Earth idiom?—a Mexican standoff." Kip forced a smile. "Let me suggest that my man, Har-Por, put his weapon away. Then you can put your weapon down."

Andrea pressed the barrel of her pistol more tightly into Kip's temple. "Where are the other two I saw you with?"

"I sent them back to the ship." The smile left Kip's face.

"You're lying." Andrea clipped her words.

"This interview isn't going very well at all," Kip said flatly. "I'm supposed to be discussing your reconciliation with Hal K'Rin. You don't seem to be predisposed toward reconciliation—judging by the weapon pressed against my head."

"That depends," Andrea said, "on what you say next."

Kip said, "Har-Por, put your handlance back into your holster."

"No—on the countertop, here," Andrea countermanded.

"Do as she says, Har-Por." The CPP saw Kip's facial muscles twitch.

The younger Tenebrea obeyed the order, putting his handlance on the glass counter. Andrea backed away with her pistol covering both, "Now let's talk."

The CPP lowered his revolver and let the hammer back slowly. However, he kept his eyes glued to the crack in the door. He flexed his legs to work out a cramp that had begun to set in. Then he sat on his knees to be more comfortable as he thought, *This conversation may take a while.* He did not want to miss any of the details.

Suddenly, he felt a rough cord slip over his thick hair and down his forehead. An instinct told him to drive his hands between the cord and his throat. He barely got his fingers in as a violent jerk pulled him back. He tried to shout, but a thick, carefully placed knot crushed his Adam's apple. He could force no air out, nor suck air in.

The strength behind the cord was greater than his forearms. He sensed the bulk behind him. The cord cut into his flesh, through his fingertips and then into his neck. Panic grabbed as hard as the cord. He fought to hold on to his wits. He tried to recover his legs and press himself backward, but a knee planted in his back stopped him. He felt consciousness ebbing away, and with it his sight. The CPP fumbled with his quivering hands and found his pistol in his lap. With his bleeding fingers, he found the hammer, but he lacked the strength to pull it back.

H'Roo darted between piles of debris, working his way nimbly toward the restaurant. He caught a fleeting glimpse of three figures in the shadows just inside the entrance. H'Roo crouched by a stump stucco wall. He knew the sniper was less than a hundred feet behind him, probably focusing all his attention on the crosshairs in his scope—else he could not have gotten as close as he had. He heard Andrea's muffled voice. She sounded confident.

Risking exposure, H'Roo stretched his head out to get a better look. Andrea pressed her pistol barrel against Kip's head. Then, H'Roo's eyes fixed for an instant on the handlance pointed at Andrea's head. He pulled back to his cover where he held his breath for an instant. He expected a weapon to discharge any moment. He heard Andrea challenge: *That depends on what you say next.* H'Roo strained to hear more. Kip's voice carried through the door: *Har-Por. Put your handlance back into your holster.*

H'Roo stole another look. The Tenebrea inside lowered the handlance from Andrea's head. He heard her voice: *Now let's talk.*

No, don't talk—shoot the bastards! Now! H'Roo knew time was running out. If Andrea stepped into the doorway, the sniper would get her. He assumed the fourth assassin waited in the back.

Andrea leaned against the counter. "I read K'Rin's letter." She watched the two Jod standing in front of her. The usually loquacious Kip simply nodded. *He doesn't say anything. He didn't come to talk.* Andrea knew for certain she was caught in a trap.

She heard a scuffle in the kitchen. Her eyes cut backward to the kitchen door, then returned to the pair standing in front of her. Kip crouched and reached for his weapon, while Har-Por lunged for his handlance on the counter. In a single liquid motion, Andrea vaulted backward over the counter, crashing into racks of clean glasses. The whine of Kip's handlance echoed through the room and the mirror behind the counter shattered.

H'Roo saw the commotion. He saw Andrea dive backward. He heard the handlances fire. He stood and rushed the door.

As he filled the door frame, he felt a crushing blow to his back that staggered him. He fell facefirst at Kip's feet. The fourth Jod burst through the kitchen door firing a handlance that hit H'Roo's shoulder. H'Roo squeezed the trigger on his weapon and the fourth Jod crumpled, propping the kitchen door open with his body.

Andrea heard the crash through the front door and the exchange of handlance bolts. She heard Kip's voice exclaim, "H'Roo hit Ti'Pol!"

H'Roo! Andrea knew instantly that H'Roo had come to help her. She feared the worst. She crawled on her hands and knees through the broken glass to the end of the counter. She knew the two assassins would fire first at the place she landed. The half second they wasted on a bad shot might save her. She knew her revolver had a slightly faster rate of fire than the Jods' energy weapons. She looked over the counter at the spidering cracks through the mirror. Through the angled glass, she saw a blur of movement—two shapeless shadows separating, one to each end of the counter. One of the assassins would jump over the counter and land practically in her lap. The other, a short thirty feet away.

As the two assassins crowded the counter she caught a better glimpse in the mirror. They, too, took cautious glances, trying to find her reflection, but she squeezed herself into the dark shadow at her far end. She crouched, ready. At the other end of the counter she saw an arm decked with officer rank— Kip's—rise and drop quickly. A signal.

Har-Por scrambled over the counter. Andrea reached up and met him. She grabbed his wrist just above his grip on the handlance. She pulled him quickly over the counter as she fired a bullet point-blank into his face. His handlance discharged, blasting loose the clay tile on the floor next to her.

She pulled his bleeding and shivering body over hers to shield herself. She heard Kip's handlance whine and felt the impact of the bolt, stifled by Har-Por's body. Har-Por died instantly as his chest split open from the bolt of energy.

Andrea fired three rounds at Kip who stood at the other end of the counter. The first round plugged Kip's thigh, the second, his gut, and the third punched a hole through his chest.

Kip dropped to his knees. A dent and blood on the stainless-steel refrigerator doors assured Andrea that she'd knocked a hole through him. Kip inspected the hole in his chest. He coughed a little blood and shook his head, as if critiquing his own poor performance. Then he aimed his handlance at Andrea. Both he and Andrea fired simultaneously.

The bolt blasted Har-Por's torso apart and still carried enough power to stun Andrea badly. She felt herself go black. She held on to the pain, because she knew the pain meant life. She remembered that a slip into unconsciousness would probably be her last. H'Roo had saved her from her last encounter with a handlance stun. *H'Roo, I need you again.*

She slid herself out from under the burned and bloody mess that was Har-Por. Her vision remained blurred, but her hearing returned as the loud buzz in her ears faded. She heard a racket growing outside. She heard gunfire outside. She heard voices—the clones pursued a fifth assassin. The room began to spin, and she felt nauseous.

Then, she heard the hollow roar of the Jod ship leaving on a fast burn. She forced her eyes open and watched the prismatic light from the shattered mirror. *I must remain conscious*.

Then, voices clamored inside the restaurant, reverberating in her head. The voices chattered about the mayhem—the Jod bodies splayed on the floor. Then a voice she recognized commanded the others to be quiet. She muttered, "Eric?"

A face she knew leaned over her. The thin lips in the dark beard moved. "You're safe now."

Andrea struggled to her feet. Standing made her dizzy. Her hands tingled. Her pistol hung loosely in her hand but she didn't feel the grip or the trigger guard. She started to lower herself to the comfort of the floor, but Eric grabbed her arm and said somberly, "Someone you must see."

He helped Andrea over the counter. She saw H'Roo Parh lying on his back. His eyes rolled in their sockets. Andrea slid down the glass casing and knelt beside H'Roo. She touched his face with her tingling hand. "H'Roo?" she asked.

H'Roo turned his head in her direction, but his eyes did not focus. His lips moved and he whispered, "I didn't know." He breathed with painful effort.

Andrea looked up at Eric, inquiring with her eyes. Eric said, "He's hit in the back—lost a lung." Eric shook his head indicating the prognosis.

Andrea leaned closer, her face next to H'Roo's. She stroked his cheek gently, helplessly. "You came to save me again. You are a good friend," Andrea whispered in his ear. "My best friend."

H'Roo reached up with fingers spread to find her face. Andrea led his probing fingers to her cheek. She whispered, "I'll get him for this. K'Rin won't walk away from your murder."

"No." H'Roo struggled to issue the words. "K'Rin doesn't know. Kip's idea . . ."

Andrea looked at H'Roo's flushed face, his blind eyes unable to yoke or focus. She disagreed with H'Roo, but wouldn't trouble him with a contradiction. The whole assassination attempt had K'Rin's fingerprints everywhere: willing and unwitting surrogates. She put her hand on his chest just below his neck. "You rest."

H'Roo gurgled and spit a mouthful of red phlegm over his blue lips onto his chin. He strained to speak in a hoarse whisper, "K'Rin will atone." He inhaled painfully. H'Roo sagged, exhausted. His fingertips fell away from Andrea's cheek.

Andrea felt his big heart through the hot tingling in her hand. Her hand rose and fell with the shallow breathing—then nothing. Nothing but tingling. H'Roo's eyes stopped swimming in their sockets. They rested slightly skewed, unnatural. The gurgle in his throat stopped.

Andrea choked back a sob. With two fingers, she gently but firmly pressed H'Roo's eyelids shut. She closed her own eyes. *Don't go . . .*

She looked again and touched his cheek. She wondered if the painful tingling in her fingertips might animate H'Roo's dead flesh—a silly thought. His cheek was wet, she noticed—her tears. She thought she would convulse into tears for H'Roo, for Steve and Glendon, for the clones stacked in putrefying mounds in the mountains, for Brigon who must certainly die in the wilderness. She clutched two handfuls of H'Roo's black tunic and buried her face in her friend's broad but still chest to muffle her sobs as she could no longer hold herself together. She even wept for K'Rin, yet at the same time, blamed him for all her misery.

Then, Andrea felt a gentle hand on her shoulder, pulling her away from H'Roo's body. She turned and looked through wet eyes at the curious crowd in the restaurant. The faces were a shallow echo of her loss, some sense of condolence. Eric took her arm and helped her to her feet. He said, "I'll take a few men to gather wood for his pyre."

Andrea nodded her appreciation and walked away, shaky, but under her own power.

chapter 19

Andrea remembered little about the next couple of days. Mostly, she remembered that she had not known such grief since Steve and Glennie died.

Dr. Carai gave her a complete physical and discovered a mild fibrillation in her heart. Andrea thought perhaps her heart was really broken, but Carai told her that her body needed only a week to shake the effects of the energy bolt. He claimed that her heart was strong.

Eric quickly put the Jod antiair batteries and heavy cannon to use. His new crew shot down a pair of high-altitude reconnaissance craft. The overflights ceased instantly, and everyone's confidence increased.

She remembered how H'Roo's funeral pyre burned for hours, becoming a great pile of red embers. Then the kkona winds blew in a heavy storm. Lightning raked the ground. Torrents of cold rain fell, dousing the embers and raising a hissing cloud of steam. She stood and watched until the pile of ashes melted and ran in rivulets across the ground. Washed away.

She remembered Tara bringing her an alloy disk,

warped by the pyre's heat, burnished to a permanent oily finish—two dolphins swimming in a circle.

She spent hours sitting on the wall overlooking the flatland leading to the ocean. Alone, with her unsteady heart. She brooded over H'Roo's last words, *K'Rin will atone*.

She wore a thick plastic poncho that kept the cold rain out. She sat through five days of incessant rain from clouds so thick that she could not distinguish night from day. The snow disappeared, and the Sarhn River left its banks, flushing large slabs of ice into the ocean. The newly planted fields were all submerged. She imagined Brigon out there with four companions huddled under a tree on a hillock, watching the water rise.

Eric relaxed the drills during the deluge. Nevertheless, he remained in nervous anticipation of the NewGens.

Tara used the enforced inactivity of the rain to study the problem of the clones' future. She continued to shrink from the avalanche of details and decisions. With each passing day, she felt less competent in her role as the leader and she leaned more on others' opinions. She put the question to her intimates, "How do we organize ourselves?"

Eric became increasingly frustrated with the question. "I've got security. Hart manages the logistics . . ."

"No," Tara interrupted crossly. "I'm not talking about a military operation. I want to know how we manage ourselves when we get past the challenge of day-to-day survival. Right now, I don't need to motivate our people—I've got an army of NewGens out there to motivate them. But, what happens when the NewGens and the Ordinate are gone? I have no idea how one organizes a society, and I don't want to imitate the Ordinate."

Hart spoke for himself, "She's right. We need to grow or we'll wither and die."

Eric scratched his head. "Yeah, I know. Carai will produce the last crop—a crop of fertile clones."

Carai raised his wheezy voice. "I wish you'd stop referring to your kind as clones." He shook his head disapprovingly. "I've said it a thousand times. The technology—I should say biology—that created you was not cloning, but twinning. In fact, you ought to change your collective name from clones to a word that reflects the truth. I would call you Geminines."

All eyes turned for a moment toward the Artrix to consider his point, but they shrugged it off as unimportant. Eric returned to his argument. "I don't see what's so mysterious. We just replicate the Ordinate system. We follow their plan—except this time, we live in the city and they can scratch out a living outside the walls, doing labor for us."

Tara looked across the table. "What do you think, Andrea?"

Andrea looked up from the dolphin medallion in her hand. "Think about what?"

"About Eric's proposal—that we organize ourselves by following the Ordinate model."

Andrea spoke as one detached from the argument—without conviction, but with some introspection. "You would set into motion the cycle where two factions struggle perpetually—the slaves become the masters, the masters become the slaves. Eventually, the Ordinate would displace you. Perhaps you'd displace them again."

Carai echoed, "She's right."

Eric set his jaw. "We can break that chain of events. We kill them all."

Carai sighed. A high-pitched wheeze punctuated his dismay. "Actually, I recommend that you attempt to absorb them. I can make you a last crop of *twins* and restore their fertility, but unfortunately, your genetic diversity is lacking. As a species you would do well to absorb the Ordinate stock into your own or encourage immigration from the Terran system. Biologically, if you want to prosper as a people, you need two key elements: larger numbers and as much variety as possible."

Hart echoed, "True. Numbers and variety."

Eric rose from his seat and began pacing the floor. He began a litany of questions. "Well, who does the hard labor, then? How do we plan to absorb the Ordinate without finding ourselves at the bottom again? How much do we plant, manufacture. Who decides? Who raises the new crop? How do we put all these pieces together?"

Tara returned to her original question. "My point exactly—how do we organize ourselves?"

Dr. Carai answered quietly, "It just happens."

Eric raised his voice. "That's absurd. I don't know how you Artrix do things where you come from, but . . ."

Dr. Carai interrupted, "You, sir, came out of your artificial womb about ten years ago with your brain filled with information and images by so-called teachers whom you just defeated. On the other hand, I have been alive for two hundred years. I've seen how different societies work—or fail to work. You, my friend, would overengineer your little society and repeat the Ordinate's mistakes."

Tara grabbed Eric's right hand with her left to calm him. But she took his side. "We need to organize ourselves in *some* way. What kind of advice is, *It just happens*?"

Dr. Carai settled back into his chair. "Do you understand irony?"

"Yes," Tara answered, not amused by the question. "A sense of humor."

"Much more than a sense of humor. I'm telling you for certain that you cannot have a successful society without a strong sense of irony. You must expect the incongruity between what you might expect and what actually occurs." Carai ended with a jocular wheeze.

Tara looked down the table to see if anyone comprehended.

Eric shook his head. "Riddles? This is a waste of time."

"Cold, hard reality." Dr. Carai folded his hands and rested them on the table. "I'll try to explain. Your question—how do we organize ourselves—is slightly off the point. When you try to organize yourselves into a society, you are actually trying to organize intelligence—an immeasurably complex task. But even before we try to contemplate organizing intelligence, we'd better understand what intelligence is." He paused to see if Tara, especially, grasped the distinction.

"Go on," she said.

Carai cleared his throat. "Intelligence is either binary or analog." He addressed the whole table. "What do you say, Eric? Is intelligence binary or analog?"

Eric answered, "Binary. You gather the data, analyze the data—"

Tara interrupted, "No, Eric. I am a computer operator." She corrected herself. "I *was* programmed to be a computer operator; isn't that ironic? Machines gather and process data, but people don't always think that way."

Dr. Carai pulled at his mustache. "How do you know?"

Tara turned and looked long at Eric before she replied, "I'm not sure how I know, but I do. So many different stimuli can trigger a thought. One moment I look at Eric and I remember the first time I saw him."

She addressed Eric directly. "You were with a dozen other ERC models recruiting them into your little cabal. I just remember knowing that I wanted you. Why you? All of you looked the same, but I sensed something different about you. Even more now."

Eric looked at his hands folded on the table. "We've all changed some."

Tara reached over with her left hand and brushed a lock of Eric's black hair, "Now, I might look at you and speculate about the future: where we'll live, what kind of work we'll do. How do such thoughts pop into my mind? When I think about you, Eric, I know I am not gathering and analyzing data the way a machine does. The thoughts are too random."

"More than random," Dr. Carai pointed across the table, "all intelligence is analog. We absorb patterns of sound, image, touch, smell, and taste—all sensory inputs to the brain are analog—sight, sound, touch, even if at some point the information resided elsewhere in digital format. We absorb and process in analog. Do you agree?"

Tara spoke up. "Okay, intelligence is analog. So what?"

Carai nodded with satisfaction. "The consequences of this fact are enormous when you consider how to organize intelligence—that is, organize a society. If intelligence were binary then theoretically I could transfer all my information to you—teach you everything I know. In turn, you could teach me everything you know. We could continue to update each other with our experience. In effect, we could interact like machines. If intelligence were binary, then society would be mechanical, and we could engineer it. We could calculate optimum solutions and measure progress. We could truly apply the scientific method to social questions. I must say, it's a tempting point of view for a scientist like me, but the premise is flawed. Intelligence is not binary. None of us can ever transmit the totality of our experience to another."

"But that is how the Ordinate looked at things," Tara added.

"Exactly so. Their premise was wrong, and that error was the fatal flaw in their model." Dr. Carai nodded. "They transferred information to all you different clone models—programmed you according to function. They achieved some short-term efficiencies, but created for themselves a long-term catastrophe. What did you call their programming?"

"Neural mapping." Tara provided the Ordinate's technical term.

Carai raised his eyebrow. "But as soon as you entered the randomness of life outside the artificial womb, the neural mapping began to fade. Your analog intelligence created the incongruity between what the Ordinate expected and what actually occurred. You overthrew your masters, not because of flaws in the neural programming. You cannot engineer a society of analog intelligence."

Tara wondered out loud, "What about the NewGens? They seem binary, easier to control. The Ordinate think their NewGens are fail-safe."

"They aren't." Carai pursed his thin lips causing his mustache to rise. "Therefore, they are an incredibly dangerous phenomenon. They are animal; therefore, their intelligence, however focused, is analog. Even ants and wasps have swarm intelligence—enough to modify tactics. If ants and bees can learn, so can the NewGens. The NewGens will, given enough time, break out of their neural mapping just as you old-order clones did. The NewGens have the potential to escape the Ordinate leash and become an artificial species completely on their own. They could become to the galaxy what the slime cat is to Yuseat." Dr. Carai looked at Andrea with his soft eyes. "They will replicate themselves into perpetuity and eliminate all competition along the way."

Andrea muttered, "K'Rin sensed the danger."

Aside, Carai said, "Perhaps he did." Then he intertwined his long fingers, resting his hands on the table. "Let's get back to your immediate problem, Tara. Because intelligence is analog, society is organic. You don't engineer an organism; you nurture it. Individuals do not behave as parts of a well-ordered machine—like bits of data in an algorithm. No, they are analog and interact very much in the way that waves interact. Sometimes they cancel each other's energy; sometimes they create harmonics with peaks of brilliance or troughs of stupidity. Now if you have just one or a few individuals making the decisions—which is often the case when you have a few persons engineering the society—the peaks and troughs tend to be exaggerated."

Eric waved his hands to grab Carai's attention. "Slow down. I don't understand."

Dr. Carai chewed on his mustache for a moment. "Analog. Think waves. What happens if you have only two agents working on the ocean: let's say a steady wind and the tides."

Eric replied, "You get waves."

"And what happens when you have a strong wind and a strong tide working together?"

"You get bigger waves. I know that."

"Correct. Harmonics set in as the wind and tide work together. Now suppose it rains. You get billions of tiny ripples—tiny wavelets passing through each other."

Eric answered, "Absent heavy winds, the ocean goes flat. I've seen it before. Rain seems to flatten the waves."

"Billions of small harmonics canceling each other—creates a peaceful ocean." Dr. Carai smiled. "It is ironic, but you get a smoother, more peaceful society when you allow the greatest number of small, often conflicting decisions."

Andrea uttered one word, "Competition."

"Ironic, but individual competition begets peace, and peace begets prosperity. When you organize yourselves, try to maximize the randomness of your independent intellects. Adopt rules that protect the randomness. Accept the short-term chaos and competition, which is life itself. You'll need a few proscriptions, but the fewer the better. If you make too many rules, you are in effect trying to digitize the organic nature of society. You get poor results. If you tell persons what to do, you are in effect telling them what to think, and you frustrate the potential of analog intelligence."

The room was silent. Dr. Carai licked his lips. "Tara, learn to accept irony as confidently as you accept gravity. And don't try to make the most intellectually gifted among you the leader. Most intellectually gifted persons look at the chaos and think there's got to be a better way. They inevitably try to add structure—rules—to put some order into the chaos. They would make intelligence digital. Yet everyone recognizes that true genius is pure analog: the Artrix poet, Lingmeil; the Terran composer, Mozart. Another irony, analog intelligence is somewhat anti-intellectual. Most of us hate to admit that the best fruits of our minds are in great part serendipity—a happy confluence of events, an epiphany, a harmonic of intelligence—like when I stumbled onto the Quazel enzyme. I just happened to be at the right place at the right time asking the right questions." He looked at Andrea and wheezed a lighthearted laugh. "That's right, Andrea. The enzyme is not the fruit of my intellect, but the harmony of accident."

Brigon and his four comrades sloshed through the soggy plains. Snow turned to sticky mud. They followed the trail left by the two thousand or more South Mountain clones fleeing starvation just a few months before. The trail was littered with bits of rubbish—articles of clothing, empty bags, and the occasional charred remains of an open fires.

Despite the weather, they kept their spirits up by

talking about the old times. Soon, they'd find the large remnant of the clones, who'd be happy to have Brigon back as their chief. They'd develop a stronghold in the wilderness outside Qurush. They'd stay away from the battles up north, and regardless of the outcome, they'd live free. Brigon would fabricate new wilderness cloaks and they would take from Qurush what they couldn't find in the wilds. Just like old times. To reward their fortitude, the storms ended. The returning warm sun confirmed their optimism.

The trail led them over a gentle rise to a plateau. Brigon stopped. The air suddenly smelled foul. In the distance, the ground seemed to crawl. His instincts bid him to be wary.

"What's the matter?"

"I don't know." Brigon crouched. He wrestled his binoculars from the pouch and raised them to his eyes. In the middle of the plateau, the ground stirred with every kind of carrion creature. Rodents crawled over each other fighting for their share of the carrion. Birds with ruddy, featherless heads hopped about, too gorged to fly. Small slinky mammals darted between the large birds to snatch pieces of flesh and run away. Lizards and insects also attended the feast. And the feast was the remnant of the South Mountain clones. Brigon surveyed the bodies lying in a jumble—bones and scraps of clothing mostly. He saw a small bird pulling out tufts of long hair from a skull, probably to furnish a nest.

"Well? What do you see?"

Brigon just handed the binoculars to his interrogator. "See for yourself."

The man looked intently and muttered, "Damn." He put the binoculars down and looked at Brigon and the others. "Looks like someone herded them together, then butchered them."

Another took the binoculars, looked, and commented, "Must be a couple of thousand of 'em—dead. I'd say they've been dead for months."

Brigon pulled at his beard. "No fire tonight." He looked around for comment. No one argued for the comfort of a warm camp. "We'll move up wind from the stench before we settle into some cover."

Everyone agreed. They backed off the plateau and marched along the reverse slope in a wide arc that carried them west. They stayed in gullies and ravines. Periodically Brigon would sniff the air to judge their relative position to the killing ground. By nightfall, they stopped at a stream running through a thick stand of evergreens.

One of the men knelt down to take a drink. Brigon caught him by the hair before his lips touched the water. He said, "That water's coming off the plateau. If I were you, I'd settle for thirsty."

As night closed in, Brigon noticed the thin layer of high clouds overhead. The clouds reflected the dim yellow glow of artificial light, confirming what he suspected: they were close to Qurush. He told the other three to rest by the stream. He would use the cover of night to get close enough to the city to reconnoiter. He pointed to the pale glow on the underbelly of the clouds. "I figure they're less than ten miles east of the city. I'll be back tomorrow night. You can move about, but stay under cover and be here this time tomorrow."

The recommissioned *Zat-Mar* slipped into deep space outside the Corondor system. She looked like a ghost ship, with all her portals black except for the bridge. The ship's skin was dull and mottled from years of being mothballed. Acrylic patches covered dimples hammered into her by chunks of ice, rock, and tar hurtling through space. The half dozen figures on the bridge worked in hardsuits. They merely watched the ship's vital signs. They made sure the ship's sensors continued to feed information to the brains of the ship—a small destroyer bolted into the belly of the giant dreadnought where the *Zat-Mar*'s captain exercised command and control.

Captain Stem'Bar was an older Jod, retired and likewise recommissioned. He sat in the captain's chair favoring an arthritic hip. His uniform fit badly around his girth. He left the front of his old tunic unfastened. His jowls sagged to a pronounced dewlap and a permanent snarl. Although his eyelids hung heavy, his eyes sparked. Loose skin beneath his eyes obscured the indigo and yellow rings. Stem'Bar made no apology for his age or his physical unfitness.

He'd handpicked his crew—other old hands who had forgotten more during their retirement than most crewmen knew. He was instantly intrigued by Hal K'Rin's proposal—operate a dreadnought with a skeleton crew, no environmentals, improvisation every step of the way.

They slipped into their zone carried by their own inertia. Stem'Bar even improvised steerage, using puffs of compressed air to maintain the pitch and yaw of the giant ship. They applied total emissions blackout and full stealth. At a distance, they'd look like a chunk of space debris wandering. Surprise and timing would be everything.

The *Z-axis* maneuver was simple in concept, but difficult in execution. Captain T'Pan likewise encroached upon the Chelle Fleet's perimeter on the *X-* and *Y-axis* with tactical comms and sensors at full acquisition. The *Zat-Mar* would quietly approach the Chelle position from below—the *Z-axis*. They would take advantage of the Chelle's bias, or weakness, for linear thinking. Moreover, the Chelle had every reason to believe that the Jod Fleet had but one dreadnought. The Chelle would put their shields and weapons forward to face T'Pan's advance. Stem'Bar would sneak the *Zat-Mar* into a favorable range and rip the guts out of the Chelle's capital ships.

Captain Stem'Bar received encrypted targeting data from *Kopshir* on the low-frequency logistics channel, a ruse and precaution. The targeting officer relayed the data to the weapons suite, then reported with a gravelly voice, "We have a lock on three Chelle heavy cruisers—two tubes each, two fighter carriers, three tubes each, and six destroyers, one tube each." The order to open fire would come from T'Pan.

Stem'Bar rubbed his fingers into his palms. "Steady," he said as if talking to himself. "Helmsman, prepare to come full about."

"Yes, sir."

"Fire control—"

"Aye."

"We might have time to retarget and fire a second salvo. Plot accordingly."

"Ahead of you, Captain."

A hot-red light flashed on the forward screen. T'Pan's voice broadcast one word: "Fire." Captain Stem'Bar rose from his chair, watching the screen as the blue balls streaked through the blackness of space. "Helmsman, bring propulsion up to fifty percent. Reverse thrust and slow us down. Keep your distance."

In the distance, the black night burst into light. His barrage of torpedoes stung the middle of the Chelle formation of capital ships. A hundred thousand miles starboard, along the perimeter, the Chelle destroyers took the brunt of T'Pan's assault.

The targeting officer reported, "Second set of targets locked."

"Fire!" Stem'Bar stepped toward the screen shaking his fist. As his own weapons discharged, the computer alerted him that his ship had been scanned. Prudently, he turned and said, "Helmsman, take us out of here."

At three o'clock in the morning, K'Rin and his staff held vigil in the communications center waiting nervously for the history-bending verdict at Corondor. They listened to relays of T'Pan's tactical comms. K'Rin, Bal'Don and the others listened as if to a solemn rite. Without comment, K'Rin pieced the reports together and although the message was clear—complete victory—K'Rin did not allow any emotion to show. Bal'Don finally broke the tension, saying, "I would love to be in General Kren-Shew's command center today."

K'Rin looked at the clock on the wall. "His counterattack started five hours ago."

Soon, reports from the Corondor ground campaign filtered in. As T'Pan's Fleet continued to cut a deep wound into the Chelle Fleet, the Jod General Kren-Shew pressed a brutal counterattack, crushing the Chelle forward positions and sending over a million of the diminutive fighters into abject panic. T'Pan's briefing officer described the Chelle as "a swarm of ghost beetles fleeing a burning building."

The Chelle command quickly opened channels and declared an armistice. They powered down their weapons and shields, whereupon T'Pan ceased hostilities in a matter of minutes. Kren-Shew's forces didn't get the word as quickly and waded into the Chelle, slaughtering thousands as the Chelle were ostensibly surrendering. Kren-Shew sent a rather flippant apology that left K'Rin shaking his head. Having endured months of Chelle tenacity—almost suicidal tenacity—Kren-Shew and his subordinate commanders initially discounted reports of the Chelle's unilateral declaration of an armistice— whether accidentally or purposefully, K'Rin would never inquire. The Jod had buried more than twenty-six thousand of their brothers, and an armistice was not foremost on their minds as they attacked.

No one at Jod headquarters felt any compunction about Kren-Shew's tardy stand-down. When the Chelle sent a back-channel protest about the alleged slaughter of their ground troops, K'Rin sent a belligerent reply that their accusation constituted fighting words, and that he would like nothing better than an excuse to turn T'Pan and Kren-Shew loose. The next Chelle communication was a request for instructions on how to evacuate their forces from Corondor.

The Chelle evacuation from Corondor lasted three days. T'Pan and Kren-Shew allowed the Chelle to evacuate their personnel but none of their equipment from Corondor. Having retrieved their personnel, the Chelle retreated to their territorial space, where they assumed a defensive posture. Safely inside their boundaries, the Chelle broadcast a terse message to Jod, copied to the Terrans, Artrix, and Ordinate, reminding all parties that an armistice is not the same as a surrender.

K'Rin sent word to his privateers, telling them to get out of Chelle space immediately. He presumed the Chelle would use some of their liberated assets to protect their merchant marine. He also sent orders to T'Pan and Kren-Shew to keep up their guard. The Chelle still represented a considerable military presence. Until the Jod could bring another pair of dreadnoughts out of mothballs, K'Rin considered his forces disadvantaged. Boldness had served the Jod well, but at some point, boldness becomes bluff, and K'Rin still held to the Jod dictum: *Never bluff*.

So he ordered T'Pan's Fleet, now augmented by the second dreadnought, *Zat-Mar*, to stand ready at the Chelle frontier. K'Rin issued an unpopular order: that the Jod armed forces remain on Corondor— indefinitely.

Both T'Pan and Kren-Shew chafed at their orders for different reasons. Kren-Shew wanted to pull half his troops into a ready reserve on Jod. Still flush from victory, T'Pan wanted to pursue the Chelle Fleet. To Kren-Shew, K'Rin replied, "The Chelle are fixated on Corondor. If they attempt another ground operation, they will attempt it on Corondor. If you withdraw half your forces, you might as well send the Chelle an engraved invitation to return. Ninety days, General."

To T'Pan, K'Rin replied, "When we take another

pair of dreadnoughts out of mothballs, we can dictate terms. I'd rather show force than use it."

Bal'Don asked, "With four operational dreadnoughts, we'll certainly have the force to dictate terms, but what will the Chelle do then?"

K'Rin thought for a moment. A wry smile crossed his lips as he replied, "Officially, they will pretend that none of this ever happened."

Bal'Don's eyes opened with surprise, then settled on the reality of K'Rin's statement. He nodded almost apologetically for having asked the question. "Of course."

K'Rin shrugged. "We'll send them terms for their surrender and within a month, you can bet that they'll try to reestablish a diplomatic presence— without any mention of the war."

"Of course."

K'Rin smirked. "When we refresh their collective memory about this war that they started, the destruction of Heptar and our capital ships, the murder of the council, the invasion of Corondor, and the quarter of a million Jod dead, *they* will complain that *we* are holding a grudge." K'Rin smiled broadly now as if he finally understood a complicated joke. "They will lobby the poor Terrans and the Artrix relentlessly."

"When they make their bid for a diplomatic reconciliation, what do you plan to do, Hal K'Rin? Do we welcome them back into the Alliance . . ."

"Welcome them? I don't think so. They'll have to meet our demand for restitution first. Even then, my instincts tell me to quarantine the Chelle from the other major systems."

"Will they pay the restitution, Hal K'Rin?"

"I think so." K'Rin rubbed his scalp. "Ultimately, the Chelle are willing to give up their treasure, their time and energy, even their territorial claims as long as they can hold on to their righteous indignation and moral superiority. We'll let them keep their heightened sense of righteous indignation. In fact, the more we exact from them, the better they'll feel about themselves." K'Rin laughed out loud. "Moral superiority is an expensive commodity." Bal'Don and the staff joined in the laughter.

Hal K'Rin felt young again. He returned to his office, where he settled down at his desk and leaned back in his chair. A wave of self-satisfaction washed over him. At last, the parts of his life seemed to come together. Finally, the vagaries of life seemed to favor him. His father's soul might rest in peace. His reputation and that of the Rin Clan was restored. His own reputation—so recently suffering the calumny of Klamdara—was made whole. The Jod, pushed to the brink of disaster, had fought back and reestablished themselves as the dominant system in the galaxy. The threat of the Cor Ordinate clone armies was checked in time. K'Rin sensed more good news was coming. Tomorrow, H'Roo would return with news that Andrea accepted his offer for reconciliation. Then, his personal guilt would be erased. He felt a wave of gratitude that reinforced his satisfaction.

K'Rin searched his memory. When had he felt so good about life? Not since R'Oueu promised to marry him.

A brief knock on his door interrupted K'Rin's pleasant recollections. "Come in."

Bal'Don stepped into the room. K'Rin sensed from the pallor of his face that something was dreadfully wrong. Bal'Don said, "Sir, the supply mission to Cor has returned."

Brigon reached the outskirts of Qurush as the first pink light competed with the incandescent yellow of the streetlights. He found a perch on a bluff overlooking a fast narrow river. Through his binoculars, he watched the city.

Even at predawn, the streets bustled with shadowy figures. Qurush did not have an old city center like Sarhn. The whole city was a utilitarian apparatus, more like an oversized clone precinct.

He saw a large factory, acres of flat warehouse. Slurry pipes snaked around the building. One fat pipe led to the river and discharged an inky liquid. Periodically a company-size formation of men marched pale and naked out of the factory building to an adjacent facility, where they later emerged wearing simple tan uniforms and brown boots.

At the far end of the factory, hundreds of large men labored, pouring cement and raising iron girders. They were doubling the size of the factory.

As the light improved, Brigon got a better look at the denizens of Qurush. Under his breath, he muttered, "NewGens." He scanned the streets looking for any sign of Ordinate. He saw a few Ordinate officers, but he didn't see any sign of an old-order clone or an Ordinate citizen anywhere. He did see thousands of NewGens.

From hundreds of long barracks buildings, small fingers of smoke rose into the air. Brigon understood immediately. *A NewGen army.* He extrapolated a number by counting the barracks. He estimated ten square feet of living space per NewGen, thereby estimating four hundred NewGens per hut—at least sixty thousand, not counting the labor pool. Moreover, he counted the pale, naked NewGens emerging from the factory, escorted to the barracks. The Qurush factory was manufacturing clones at the rate of a hundred per hour.

Scanning the streets, he saw large cargo haulers in a long caravan. He counted fifty, but the column turned and disappeared among the buildings. The iron monsters sat on haunches of steel tread and they were piled high with provisions. Nylon webbing held the crates on board. Each hauler had a blunt cupola brandishing a four-inch thick barrel.

He saw flatbed trucks stacked high with pontoons. *Bridging equipment.* Sleek crawlers scurried to the front. *Recon. They're coming to take back Sarhn.*

Brigon experienced a new fear: he had nowhere to hide. Even if he could find a place to hide, he would live in abject loneliness. After the NewGen army exterminated the Sarhn defenders, the ever-increasing army would methodically eradicate every old-order clone on the planet. Brigon feared the prospect of loneliness more than the army of NewGen. He edged back from his ledge into the trees, then ran as hard as he could back to his camp.

"Where's Kip?" K'Rin's neck flushed amber as he struggled to control his temper. The two Tenebrea sat in front of him with downcast eyes. Each waited for the other to speak. The rest of the small crew of the transport, Jod regulars, stood at rigid attention with their backs against the wall of the dark room.

K'Rin reached down and grabbed hold of S'Kor's

tunic just above the handlance burn. He jerked S'Kor to his feet and repeated his question. "Where is Kip?"

"Dead, sir."

"How did he die?"

"The Terran female killed him."

"And H'Roo?" K'Rin shook the soldier like a doll.

"Commander Parh is dead."

"How did he die?"

S'Kor lowered his eyes, but K'Rin tightened his grip. Bal'Don stood behind S'Kor's ear and ordered, "Answer the question."

"I don't know, sir. I guess the Terran female killed him, too."

"That's impossible!" K'Rin roared. He shoved S'Kor back into his chair. He leaned over to put his face on the same level as the two Tenebrea. He stabbed at them with his forefinger. "I will give you one chance to tell me everything you know about the incident. If I suspect you're withholding anything, I'll hand you over for an interrogation—the *old* kind."

The second Tenebrea raised his face. "We were following Kip's orders."

"What orders?"

"He wanted to protect you from the Andrea woman. So—" he turned his chin down to evade K'Rin's angry glare, "he ordered us to assassinate her before she could assassinate you. Commander H'Roo got in the way."

K'Rin raised his fist and smashed the Tenebrea so hard that the soldier and his chair rocked backward and would have keeled over had not Bal' Don intervened to set the chair right. The other troops in the room showed no emotion as they witnessed this breach of decorum. Nobody stepped forward to restrain K'Rin, and it appeared that K'Rin was incapable of restraining himself.

Blood poured from the Tenebrea's broken nose. He didn't raise a hand to defend himself—he wasn't bound. Nor did he protest the blow. He lowered his face and said softly, "I'm sorry."

K'Rin raised his fist to inflict a second blow when he heard the young Tenebrea mutter. K'Rin checked his swing and asked, "What did you say?"

The bloody face looked up at K'Rin. The young Tenebrea's neck turned ice blue—not the color associated with fear, but heartbreak. In a slightly louder voice, he said, "I'm so sorry." Then he lowered his eyes so that he wouldn't see the blow he expected.

K'Rin calmed himself. He stepped away and put his clenched fists rigidly at his side. With his back turned to the beaten Tenebrea, he asked, "Is Andrea Flores alive?"

The Tenebrea answered wearily, "I believe so, but I can't be sure."

K'Rin spoke to Bal'Don, "Get them both out of my sight."

With a wave of a hand, Bal'Don echoed the order. The provost hustled the two Tenebrea from the room. Bal'Don turned and told the rest of the onlookers, "Dismissed."

The room cleared, leaving Bal'Don and K'Rin alone. K'Rin unfastened his tunic about the neck. He cursed, "*Damn* Kip."

Bal'Don said nothing.

"Now, she'll never believe me. I send my aide and

her only friend to intercede for me, and what happens? They try to assassinate her; they kill her friend. *Damn them!*"

"You must not let the men see you react so."

K'Rin pointed to the spot where S'Kor stood. "I should have killed the little bastard."

"No, I didn't mean your physical remonstration. Sir, a leader of your stature cannot be overwrought by guilt."

"How else should I feel?"

Bal'Don crossed his arms over his chest. "She is inconsequential. Let it be."

K'Rin grumbled, "Andrea has a blood debt against me. I am liable to judgment."

Bal'Don shook his head but said nothing.

K'Rin composed himself and explained, "Everything else in the world is working itself out, but me—" K'Rin put his hand over his heart, "How can I lead the Jod, when I, myself, am liable to a blood debt?"

"She can't touch you. She has no standing."

K'Rin's ire returned. "Oh, yes she does. By rights, she can judge me. Therefore, she owns a part of me that I do not want to part with. Whether she can touch me is beside the point; whether I even see her again is beside the point. The problem is, Bal'Don, I know the truth, and Andrea has the right to judge me." Then K'Rin looked vacantly across the room.

Bal'Don stepped into K'Rin's line of sight. "I think you can safely presume that she judges you guilty. No offense, sir, but her opinion is irrelevant." Bal'Don put his hand on K'Rin's shoulder. "Sir, you are the leader of the Jod now, the headman of all the clans. Nobody on Jod would dare judge you. That Terran female has no right to judge you. She is insignificant compared to you. The Baltimore killings are now ancient history. The matter is trivial compared to our present situation. You must put it behind you, absolve yourself of this trivial incident and focus on the future."

"So you would have me judge myself."

"As a matter of practicality, yes."

K'Rin set his jaw. "Any Jod who judges himself profanes justice."

Bal'Don stepped away. "Well, in any case, you don't have to go looking for trouble."

K'Rin smiled painfully at Bal'Don. "So you think I'm being impractical?"

"In this matter, yes."

K'Rin closed his eyes and said, "Good. Finally."

chapter 20

A week of cool breezes and warm sun dried the fields. The swollen Sarhn River retreated to its banks, but the water ran fast—two meters per second, judging by the occasional slab of ice passing down the channel.

The clear skies remained clear of reconnaissance. Eric became increasingly frustrated with the false sense of security in Sarhn. His defenders began to slack from their drills as they explored the unimagined opulence of a city provisioned for a population ten times their number. Other priorities began to whittle his force in half.

With Tara's blessing, Hart organized everyone who had agricultural knowledge. They tended the orchards and planted maize, soybeans, and vegetables.

Tara recruited any personnel with experience at the Clone Welfare Institute. She assigned them to Dr. Carai and his work. They found enough warehoused equipment to fabricate the artificial womblike incubators. Carai planned to hatch the new crops as helpless eight- or nine-pounders, so they did not need, nor would Carai allow the use of, neural mapping technology.

Eric found Andrea and Ariko standing on the wall. They took turns looking through a surveyor's optics, planning the placements of the rapid-fire lasers. Andrea wore a tight short-sleeved shirt. She had tied her long-sleeved jacket around her waist. She wore a brown cap with the bill turned backward, as she pressed her eyes to the surveyor's tool. The granite rock was warm, even though the air was cool.

Eric asked Andrea to intercede with Tara. "You've got to make her reassign everybody back to the wall."

"Me?" Andrea sympathized with his predicament but said, "I'm not getting between you and Tara for anything."

"Somebody has to."

Ariko put up his hands in mock surrender. "Don't look at me."

Eric fumed. "If Tara quotes that Artrix one more time—" Eric mocked Carai's annoying wheeze, *"It just happens*—I swear, I'll shoot the old fool."

"I wouldn't do that." Turning her cap around, she advised Eric, "You're doing fine. But remember: it is possible to overdrill your people. You can kill their initiative. They know how to get to the wall. They know what to do. The only thing you need to worry about is that they get on that wall when you tell them to. Even then, I don't doubt their courage for a second. Do you?"

Eric was not appeased, but he said, "They're good people."

"Keep telling yourself that." Andrea gestured toward Ariko. "Here's some news to cheer you up. I told Ariko, here, about that army engineer mine-clearing scheme. He knew exactly what to add to the propane."

Ariko bubbled with enthusiasm, gesticulating with his hand, mangled from other failed experiments with explosives. He said, "It's so simple—liquid propane and phosphene, PH_3. We've got a thousand pounds of propane, and I can make the phosphene in Carai's lab. When the phosphene mixes with the oxygen, it spontaneously combusts, which in turn ignites the propane. I know how to deliver the weapon, too."

Ariko grinned, looked around, and spoke softly, as if he were divulging a state secret to Eric, "I found a cache of five-gallon glass bottles, called carboys, that can handle the pressure needed to keep the propane in liquid form. We fill about twenty carboys and cap them. In one or two of the carboys we mix about a half gallon of phosphene. At the right time, we throw the carboys off the wall onto the stones below. The carboys break. The liquid propane turns quickly to a vapor heavier than air, then spreads down into the low ground around the wall. Each carboy holds enough liquid propane to generate 8,000 cubic feet of combustible propane-air mixture when it spreads. When the phosphene mixes with enough oxygen in the air, the phosphene spontaneously combusts, setting off 160,000 cubic feet of explosive propane gas in a huge explosion. The concussion kills anything in its midst."

Eric allowed, "That will clear the base of the wall in a hurry."

Andrea gave Ariko a congratulatory slap on the shoulder. "It gets better." Ariko smugly explained, "The propane explosion uses all the oxygen in the area. Any NewGens who run down to fill the void, are running into a giant CO_2 cloud. They suffocate."

The next morning, Eric walked the rampart of the heavy walls inspecting his troops. At the western corner, he found a foursome—two men and two women—lounging at their post, sunning themselves, eating a picnic lunch. The foursome saw Eric approach and they quickly got to their feet, brushing crumbs of food from their simple one-piece suits, half-pleased with themselves, half-embarrassed.

Eric scowled and prepared to curse them. But he didn't. He just walked to their post and stood in their midst with his long-range binoculars hanging about his neck. He said nothing, pretending that the four picnickers didn't exist. As far as he was concerned, they didn't. As far as he was concerned, he was standing among four civilians, who had nothing to do with security. The fact that they were on the wall with a mounted laser cannon was a coincidence.

"Uh, we were just having lunch." A male voice behind Eric volunteered the obvious. The voice was edged with concern.

Eric ignored them. He raised the binoculars to his eyes. To the left was the thick forest standing as a privet hedge hiding the dingy precinct buildings. To the west, he saw the orchards and fields. Farm hands worked in pairs in freshly plowed fields of wet black soil. The sun had already coaxed out pale green shoots of soybean and maize.

The fields sloped gently down to the banks of the Sarhn River. Black water cut a channel through winter's residual ice. On the far shore, uncultivated land rose in pastel green hills and patches of hornbeam trees lining streams. Eric raised his sights, following the land to the horizon.

Something in the distance caught his eye: specks bobbing on the horizon. Eric turned a knob to increase the magnification of the binoculars. The five specks grew into human shape, running toward Sarhn. At such a distance, the tiny shapes bobbed up and down. Eric had to presume forward progress. One of the figures staggered and fell. The taller among them stopped and hauled the weaker man to his feet. According to the ranging metrics in the binoculars, the figures were six miles out.

Eric pointed toward the horizon and said, "Strangers are approaching. On foot. I count five."

"Refugees?" a woman's voice inquired.

"I don't think so." Eric turned and gave her an order. "You go find Ariko, tell him to bring a couple riflemen to the main gate. You," he turned to one of the men, "assemble two dozen fighters from your cohort and meet us out there." He pointed in the direction of the specks. "You two," Eric turned to the remaining man and woman, "grab your weapons and come with me."

Eric ran the length of the wall and scampered down the steps, through the gate, and through the opening in the sonic barrier. His two troops followed. They ran to the edge of the fields where they commandeered a small tractor hitched to a small flatbed trailer. Eric shoved the sacks of seed corn to the ground. He motioned for his two companions to sit in the trailer. "Hold on. This is going to be a bumpy ride."

They drove west. At each rise in the terrain, Eric paused the tractor to take another look through his binoculars. The distant figures continued to race down the gentle slopes toward the far riverbank. They appeared exhausted but highly motivated. "They're armed," Eric reported.

The man in the trailer squinted at the horizon and said, "They sure are in a hurry."

Eric stood on the seat of the idling tractor, holding the binoculars to his eyes. "Yeah, but they sure as hell can't run across the river. Wait a second . . ." Eric strained his eyes, trying to give definition to the distant figures bounding forward. "That's Brigon!"

Eric dropped to his seat and drove the tractor as fast as he could. The bouncing nearly bucked the pair off the trailer. As they drove over the last rise, Eric could see Brigon without using his binoculars. He saw Brigon and his men toss their rifles aside and run abreast onto the far shore ice, completely disregarding the danger of the fast water and thin ice. As they ran, black cracks shattered the silver-white ice, crumbling the frail bridge behind them. They ran with reckless abandon, then tossed themselves into the frozen water.

"They'll drown in the fast water!" Eric yanked the wheel of the tractor and aimed for the bank farther downstream. As he drove he watched the five heads bobbing in the water. They swam clumsily in the icy current. Their progress was agonizingly slow compared to the swiftness of the water. One of the swimmers slowed to a stop and sank. A second began thrashing wildly as if eaten by the cold, black river. His thrashing stopped, and he floated downstream like a piece of driftwood. The remaining three swimmers inched their way toward the shore even as they slipped downstream.

As Eric drove to the shore to meet them, he saw one limp arm reach onto the ice floe, then Brigon's white face and blue lips. Brigon groaned as he pulled himself out of the water. Then the ice cracked, and he slipped in again.

Eric jumped from the tractor. He grabbed the end of the winch cable spooled over the front axle and ran down the bank putting a wrap of cable around his waist. He snapped off one of the many cottonwoods that grew along the bank. Fastened to the cable and with the cottonwood pole in his hand, Eric slid onto the ice on his stomach. He spread his weight as much as possible. The wet instantly soaked his clothes, gnawing his flesh. He slid quickly through the inch of cold water that pooled on the melting ice.

Brigon's hands and two other pairs of hands groped the ice shelf. The faces were so blue. The eyes were shut against the pain of the icy water. Eric could not distinguish them. He slid to the edge of the water and reached with the cottonwood pole. "Brigon!" Eric called.

A pair of eyes opened and peered out of the water over the ice shelf. Brigon grabbed at the pole with a hand stiff from the cold and cramped into the shape of a claw. He could not hold on. The pole was useless.

Eric shuffled himself to the edge and grabbed

Brigon's hand. As he did, he felt a dull quake and heard the hollow crack in the ice. He yelled to his help on the riverbank. "Start the winch!"

Eric grabbed a fistful of Brigon's clothes and pulled with all his strength. The ice shelf collapsed with a violent seesawing lunge, tossing Eric into the black water. He spasmed and lost his grip on Brigon. The ice water stung. He squinted his eyes tight against the pain as he let himself sink, groping around for Brigon. He felt a head below the water. He grabbed a fistful of hair and pulled it to the surface.

As their heads broke through the water they both exhaled with a groan. Eric knew he had Brigon. The others floundered about the floating chunk of ice. "Grab hold of me," Eric commanded through chattering teeth, and the other two drowning men obeyed. Eric held his breath as the weight of the three men forced him under. Then he felt the reassuring pull of the cable squeezing his middle, dragging them all through the crunching ice, and finally onto the dry bank.

Eric willed away the shock to his system. He forced his cramping arms and legs to straighten. Then he began peeling off his shirt. "Q-quick!" he stammered. "P-pull the-their shirts off. G-give the-them y-your shirts."

Eric peeled off Brigon's shirt and lay him in the warm sun. He rubbed his hands over his chest and arms to stimulate the blood. He felt every rib. Eric's people likewise ministered to the other freezing men, cradling their half-naked blue bodies against their pink skin. Brigon shuddered as he whispered in a hoarse, but steady voice, "They're coming."

"Who?" Eric asked.

Brigon pointed feebly across the river. "NewGen army."

Eric stood slowly and looked at the horizon. He didn't see anything, but he didn't doubt Brigon. "How m-many?" Eric shivered.

"Sixty thousand, at least." Brigon convulsed momentarily and Eric dropped to his knees and began kneading Brigon's cramping muscles.

The number shocked Eric, but he hid his fear. "How f-far back?"

Still hoarse and out of breath, Brigon answered, "Vehicular scouts—one hour. Main body—five days."

Eric looked again across the river. He let his eyes backtrack Brigon's path to the river, and this time he saw them: a small group of NewGens in green field uniforms. They sat on their haunches just below the ridge. A small dark-green armored vehicle lay squat on the ground behind them. They were tracking Brigon. Eric saw a glint, a reflection from the glass in their binoculars. Eric ordered, "Put Brigon and the others in the trailer." He directed the woman, "You drive. I'll sit with Brigon."

Eric performed an instant calculation. *We have six—maybe eight days to prepare depending on how they cross the river.*

The tractor retraced its grooves left in the soft soil. Brigon lay outstretched in the flatbed trailer exhausted. He propped himself up on an elbow and told Eric, "I must warn Andrea. She must get H'Roo to take her off this planet."

You poor devil. You ran all this way to warn her. Eric pondered how best to explain Andrea's situation. He said, "Two weeks ago, the Jod landed a transport in Sarhn and they offloaded long-range cannon that Andrea requested."

"Good, she can call them back."

"Brigon, the Jod used the supply run as an excuse to send a squad of Tenebrea into Sarhn. They tried to assassinate Andrea. H'Roo was killed in the exchange."

Brigon sat up. "Her own people? Why?"

Eric chided Brigon. "You were on Klamdara. You saw what she did. She threatened to kill Hal K'Rin."

The warm sun began to put more color into Brigon's skin. He turned from a ghostly white to a flushed prickly red. He hung his head, deep in thought. "But H'Roo gave her more of the enzyme. If they wanted her dead . . ."

Eric put his hand on Brigon's shoulder. "They were using her. They're using us, now." Eric blurted out the harsh reality. "Listen, Brigon. I lived with the Jod for a year. I know what they think of Terrans in general and clones in particular."

Brigon slumped on the wooden trailer bed where he was jostled by the ride. His exhaustion was compounded by defeat. His one hope—getting Andrea off the planet—was dashed.

For the rest of the ride back to the city, Eric pondered the news of the NewGen army. The calculus of battle favored a strong defense. Perhaps they might withstand the three to one odds. The problem was the inevitability of attrition. The Ordinate would simply manufacture replacements. Eric realized how small their numbers actually were. He sat with his legs dangling off the back of the trailer. Looking back at the river, he imagined the tactics required to repulse the NewGen attempt to cross.

As they passed through the orchards and fields,

the tractor driver told the farmhands the news. She told them to get back to the city.

A small crowd of agitated farmhands preceded the tractor through Sarhn's main gate. Eric saw Andrea standing near the entrance like a rock splitting the torrent of people. She raised her hand to stop the tractor. She found Brigon sitting with his legs dangling from the side.

Standing next to the trailer, Andrea was taller than the seated Brigon. Without a word, she reached forward and cradled Brigon's head in her hands. His hair was a mass of wet ringlets. His bushy beard felt rough. His face was thinner than she remembered, the cheekbones exaggerated, the eyes deeper. His face was burnt by sun and cold wind. White flakes of skin curled from the cracks in his chapped lips. He said nothing. His green eyes were clear, but his furrowed brow suggested he had a question that he was reluctant to ask.

Andrea pulled his face toward hers and kissed him full on the mouth. Brigon's large hands embraced her around her waist, pulling her slowly against his bare chest. Six weeks of living off the land had taken its toll. Brigon was gristle and bone—strong, but not in the sculpted manner that pleased the eye; rather, tough, even foreboding. His pants were tattered from the knees down. His leather boots were falling apart. But Andrea embraced his raggedness. She prolonged the kiss, then slowly parted lips to whisper, "I love you, too. On the wall, I should have—"

Brigon pulled her back to him and kissed her again. He told her, "I wish I was bringing better news."

*   *   *

Two short hours later, Andrea walked into the Ministry building with Brigon. His longer hair made a cap of loose tawny curls that covered his ears and exaggerated the thinness of his face. He had cropped his runaway beard to allow the shape of his square jaw to show instead of the round bush. His eyebrows appeared blond against his sunburned skin. He wore a new shirt and jacket, and he seemed strangely comfortable in this most uncomfortable situation.

They walked into the operations center. An animated debate fell to an awkward hush. Tara stood in the middle of a small gathering. She held her cane in the crook of her severed arm. She was flush with anxiety. Her eyes darted around the room. Eric stood by her side, likewise agitated.

Andrea looked at the familiar faces, most of whom diverted their eyes. She let go of Brigon's arm and asked, "Are we interrupting?"

Eric answered for the reticent group, "We were just arguing whether we should make a stand here at Sarhn or flee back to the mountains. Most of these people wish to flee."

Brigon asked, "What do you say, Eric?"

Eric glared at the others in the room. "I say we have no place to run. We stay. We hold Sarhn or we die here."

An anonymous voice blurted a challenge. "Staying is suicide."

Hart quietly added, "I won't go back to the mountains. I am tired of presiding over slow starvation."

Chana stepped forward from the pack. She asked, "But how can we hold out against sixty thousand NewGens?"

Brigon insisted, "We can make them pay dearly to cross the river. Then we fight from the walls."

Hart interjected, "We can't defend Sarhn alone. We must call the Jod for help."

A murmur of approval rose. The other occupants in the room quickly echoed Hart's suggestion.

"No!" Brigon shouted them down. "No Jod."

A dozen of the clones complained, "Why not?"

Brigon said emphatically, "The Jod tried to kill Andrea, they'll try again. We can't ask them to come."

The others in the room looked at each other with raised eyebrows as if to reiterate the question: *Why not?* Andrea saw the faces and interpreted them accurately. She grabbed Brigon's hand and squeezed it, whispering, "It might help if I were not part of these deliberations." She squeezed his hand again, turned and left the room. "You do what's best."

The room fell silent as she, the immediate object of their deliberation, walked through their midst and left.

Andrea left the Ministry buildings. The courtyard was filled with a thousand other clones waiting for news. The word had spread—a NewGen army was coming. Doom was coming. She saw the worry on their faces, not fear. Most of them stood as couples, arms entwined. From the cacophony of conversation, she discerned the consensus—they expected to fight, not flee. They expected to fight until the last man or woman died at the hands of the NewGens. They made private promises to die at each other's sides. Nobody wanted the loneliness of being the last survivor. Most of them were glad for the sixty days of living in Sarhn—the city they and the predecessor clones, their artificial twins, had built. However, no one wanted to live in Sarhn alone.

Andrea walked through the crowd. Many conversations paused as the clones acknowledged her. She was the Terran female who led the raid that crushed the Clone Welfare Institute, the one who galvanized Tara and Brigon, the one who brought the Jod help, the mysterious woman whom the Jod tried to kill. Many touched her as she passed through the crowd—friendly, reassuring pats. She couldn't return their smiles. She knew that upstairs in the council chambers, a small cadre of clones debated sacrificing her to the Jod to procure Jod assistance.

Andrea left the crowded courtyard and turned up an empty alley, thinking, *We cannot come this far and fail*. She returned to the squat tower on the west wall. Her one-way transmitter waited dormant. She flipped the small toggle switch and the mechanical brain adjusted the stubby transmitter. She knelt on the ground, sitting on her heels, as she typed a short message: *To Jod High Command. Sarhn besieged by sixty thousand NewGens. Send relief immediately*.

Andrea paused with her fingers above the small keyboard. She turned and looked back into the city and at the distant snowcapped mountains. *I might run from the NewGens, but I'll be damned if I'll run from the Jod*. She hit the transmit button and the machine discharged a burst of energy.

When Andrea returned to her small apartment, she found Brigon seated at a glass table studying maps. He oriented the maps, putting east at the top. For Brigon, the top was where the sun rose. Despite that foible, he understood cartography well. After all, he'd walked the land for all of his twenty-eight years. His memory supplemented the cartographer's marks with boundless detail. Without looking up he said, "Tara and Eric persuaded the others. They would not give you up for Jod's help. Eric especially."

Andrea raised an eyebrow. "Eric?"

"Yes. He was emphatic." He pointed to the colorful maps. "The terrain favors us. We can give them a good fight."

She said softly, "I already called the Jod."

Brigon lifted his eyes from the maps. His tight jaw relaxed. He lowered his eyes to the map and said, "Then we can't stay here. I'll take you north into the badlands. If we leave now—"

"I'm not running." Andrea stood straight and looked down at Brigon. "Eric and I trained this mob. I can't leave now."

"What about K'Rin and the Jod—the Tenebrea?"

"If we get past the NewGens, I'll worry about them. Besides, I doubt K'Rin is foolish enough to come himself." She saw the dread in Brigon's eyes.

Brigon reached across the table and grabbed her hand tightly. "Promise me you won't do anything foolish—that you won't get yourself killed."

She forced a smile and replied, "Only if you promise likewise."

While Eric's cohorts drilled, Andrea's cadre of engineers added to the traps and snares outside the wall, and Brigon led reconnaissance patrols to the

Sarhn River. He stayed in the shadows in the tree line overlooking the river trying to discern where the NewGen would cross. He watched the NewGen scouts drive up and down the ridgelines along the far shore. He carried one of Ariko's air rifles, and occasionally, when a target presented itself, he plugged a NewGen at a range of a thousand meters. The wounded NewGen would turn to face the direction of the bullet, stand there and bleed. Through high-powered binoculars, Brigon could see the consternation on the wounded NewGen's face. Other NewGens would gather around with their binoculars.

With each ensuing day, more NewGen vehicles arrived: some track, some with all-terrain tires. Most of the NewGen vehicles hid behind the natural folds in the terrain. As yet, Brigon did not see any bridging equipment.

On the fifth day, he saw a low cloud of diesel fumes, a dark yellow cloud spreading like a fog behind the ridge. *Here they come.*

Columns of transports lumbered into view. Then the NewGen army on foot spilled over the horizon like a thick sludge. It oozed over the soft green hills and down the gentle draws toward the Sarhn River, where it stopped at the ridge defining land and sky. Brigon slowly scanned the army counting the equipment. He saw dozens of small hovercraft barely a hundred feet above the ground, providing cover yet staying low and back, to avoid Sarhn's air-defense cannon.

Using air assets, the NewGen could shuttle men across the river, but not their equipment, and they would need their heavier guns to breach Sarhn's defenses. Therefore, they would have to build a bridge or march for weeks to get around the water obstacle. Brigon watched the NewGen drag stacks of pontoon boats forward toward the shore. *Their bridging equipment is in the open—their first mistake.*

Night fell. A large moon began to rise over the mountains covering the grassy hills with a blue light. To the west, the Sarhn River looked like quicksilver. Eric and Brigon assembled two large reconnaissance teams to leave the main gate to patrol the river. They wore dark clothes and soft caps. They smeared their faces with charcoal. Three large men pulled a cart with the 20-mm Gatling gun.

Andrea pulled Eric aside. In a low, tentative voice she said, "I've been meaning to speak to you."

Eric raised an eyebrow, causing the charcoal stripes on his brow to arch.

Andrea paused, then blurted out, "Thank you. Thank you for saving Brigon from drowning."

Eric was genuinely startled. He cocked his head as he processed the strange words. He shrugged and turned to leave.

Andrea followed him, grabbed his shoulder and turned him around. "I said, thank you."

"Unnecessary—Brigon already thanked me." He pointed with his thumb. "I've got to go." He walked with his rifle slung over his shoulder.

As he walked to his place, she followed. She turned him again, and said hotly, "Don't walk away from me when I'm thanking you."

"*What?*" Eric set his rifle butt on the ground. "What are you talking about?"

"When I say, *Thank you for saving Brigon*, you're supposed to say, *You're welcome* or *the pleasure was mine*. It's called manners, Eric—just plain common-sense manners. You know something, Eric, as much as I'm truly grateful—and I am—you sure make it damned hard to say *thank you*."

Eric frowned. "And you make it pretty damn hard to say *you're welcome*."

Andrea started to retort, but words failed her. Then the humor of their exchange grabbed her and she burst into laughter.

"*What?*" Eric protested.

Andrea shook off the laughter, swallowing hard to stifle another outburst. She patted Eric on the shoulder. "I'm not laughing at you, I swear. I'm laughing at us." She paused to collect herself. "Thank you, Eric. From the bottom of my heart, thank you."

He leaned away from her touch and said, "You're welcome."

Brigon walked over from his patrol to investigate the commotion. "What's going on here?"

Eric pointed at Andrea who continued to chuckle. "I think she's finally lost her mind." Eric grabbed his rifle and walked briskly to the front of the column, out of sight.

Brigon smiled, and turned to Andrea. "So?"

She shook her head. "Our little joke. You be careful out there." Andrea stood by the gate as the two columns filed through. "We'll debrief as soon as you get back."

Brigon and Eric led their recon teams through the main gate. Outside they prepared to separate. Brigon cautioned Eric, "Remember, we can't stop them from putting a bridge across. However, we can make them pay for the privilege. So, let's try to coax them into making their beachhead in line of sight of our heavy cannon."

"I understand," Eric responded. "We won't get too rowdy at our end."

"Good." Brigon took forty heavily armed men east through the precinct buildings. His people worked twenty meters apart, ducking furtively from building to building, anticipating trouble at every step. They worked their way to the slopes by the riverbank. Ogorm and a small cluster of burly clones manhandled the cart with the 20-mm Gatling gun. They carefully picked their way through pastures, staying in gullies, walking in shadows.

They found a place where the forest encroached upon the river, and they took positions in the tree line. Here, the river was narrow—an advantage for a river crossing; however, the water was correspondingly fast, compressed inside steep banks—a disadvantage. Melting snow in the mountains continued to swell the river.

Brigon wore the only pair of night goggles. He looked across the river. He saw pontoons waiting along the riverbank. Stacks of tactical bridge material lay on ground transports. Several hundred NewGen stood by the boats. Every third NewGen wore a helmet equipped with the bug-eye night goggles. They carried large automatic weapons, and they gazed over the river.

Despite the darkness and the green grainy distortion of his old night goggles, Brigon saw the NewGens clearly. They were all six foot tall, with broad shoulders, thick waists, and tree-trunk legs.

They had no facial hair. They never smiled, never frowned. Their faces were as expressionless as a death mask with cold black eyes that suggested a primitive intelligence.

Brigon turned to Ariko. "I want your sharpshooters to spread out and start picking 'em off. On my mark, you fire at will. Let's see if we can introduce some confusion in their ranks."

Ariko replied with a nod and crawled away.

"Ogorm, can your guys hit those pontoon boats with your Gatling gun?"

"Easily."

"Well, I want you to chew them to pieces. They can't build a pontoon bridge without pontoons."

Brigon cautioned the others, "The rest of you don't shoot. I don't want them to count our rifles. When Ariko starts knocking them down, they'll blindly return fire. So, keep your heads down. When the Gatling gun rips, the NewGen will send over their hovercraft. If they send three or fewer ships, we stand and fight. If they send four or more, we get out of here. We scatter and regroup in Precinct 15. Do you understand?" Up and down the line, hand gestures assured that they understood.

"Okay, then." He looked at his chronometer. He knew Eric was watching a stretch of river farther downstream. Brigon calmly ordered, "Ariko, commence firing."

Eight air rifles spit. Brigon watched the far shore. He saw one NewGen knocked off his feet, then get up to inspect his mortal wound. Others fell, never to rise again. The .52 caliber bullets struck hard. The group of NewGen raised no cry of alarm. Instead, they walked toward the river looking through their goggles. Ariko's men quickly reloaded and began sniping at will.

The Gatling gun burst into a long roar. The first rounds fell short of the pontoons, ripping a pair of NewGen in half, but the gunner quickly corrected. Brigon watched the result though his goggles. The Gatling gun ripped the thin aluminum hulls of the pontoons to shreds, knocking down the neat stack.

Instantly, the far shore erupted into a thousand flashes of light—the muzzle flashes of a thousand rifles all aimed at the Gatling gun. Brigon heard bullets whizzing by. Then the Gatling gun fall silent. He turned and looked at the gun placement. Three bodies lay draped over the berm. The Gatling gun barrels pointed harmlessly skyward. Three others lay back in the grass groaning.

Ariko's rifles continued to spit death. The NewGen barrage stopped the concentration on the Gatling gun and spread over the hillside.

In the distance Brigon heard the sound of hovercraft. He didn't need to see them to know that they exceeded five ships. "Grab the Gatling gun. Fall back!"

Just below the crest of the slope overlooking the river, Eric knelt on one knee. He knew better than to silhouette himself against the night sky. Looking back over his shoulder, he saw Sarhn's faint glow. Eric heard the hum of generators and the occasional rev of a large motor from across the river. Small lights blinked across the fields like fireflies in the grass. The main body of the NewGen army bivouacked on the other side. He wondered what they must be thinking, if they had any thought at all.

His fighters spread out, watching more than a mile of riverfront. He overlooked the very spot where he'd pulled Brigon from the freezing water. Everything was quiet.

The land sloped gently down to the shelf of ice and the water. On the other side, NewGen foot patrols walked the banks. A solitary flat-bottom boat motored in the fast channel. Occupants of the boat periodically used heavy yellow cord to measure the width and depth of the channel.

Eric heard an anonymous voice to his left. "I can hit him. Just say the word."

Eric responded urgently, "Nobody discharges a weapon. Keep out of sight."

Then his ears pricked at the distant sound of the Gatling gun. The ripsaw noise echoed far upstream. Seta—de!" Eric ordered. The faraway gunfire quickly ceased, and quiet returned.

The NewGen patrols turned and faced the source of the noise. They quickly resumed their tasks, measuring the river. Eric passed the word, "One at a time, each of you back away."

"But we didn't kill nobody," came an anonymous complaint.

Eric said, "When they cross here tomorrow, we'll kill plenty, then."

The patrols returned just minutes apart. The troops retired to clean their equipment and catch a couple hours of sleep. Andrea took Eric and Brigon to an all-night lounge near the main gate. She remembered the place from her first trip to Cor. The arch over the door displayed a set of carved faces, a sandstone version of the rake's progress. The servers were a weatherbeaten pair of clone women. They served hot drinks, tea laced with strong liquor that tasted like butterscotch.

Andrea listened as Brigon and Eric succinctly told of their night's work. Andrea remained concerned that the NewGens would attempt a crossing at two sites. She asked, "Are you sure you destroyed all their pontoons at the east approach?"

Brigon answered, "Pretty sure we got most of them. They don't have enough for two bridges."

"That will slow them down." Andrea surmised, "Then they can only ferry equipment and men across the east approach—where you were, Brigon. They'll build their bridge in the west." She pointed to the map. "The NewGen won't attack the wall until they get all of their armor across the river: they'll need all their firepower to take down the wall. We are going to let them put their bridge in the water."

"Why?" Eric asked.

Andrea replied, "We're going after their equipment. If your reports are right, the NewGens don't have much tactical bridging left. They may have unlimited manpower, but they have limited equipment. So, we attack them at their weakness. We'll let them get all their bridging assets into the water, then we use the deep-space cannon to blast them out of the water. They'll be forced to ferry their equipment upstream. They'll lose at least two days."

"Then what?" Brigon asked.

"If the NewGen learn anything tomorrow, they'll know better than to stay in the open. The NewGens will most likely use the forest as cover and move their armor close."

Eric mused, "Ogorm's booby traps will make life miserable for them."

"Not as miserable as an open field and a cannon." Andrea pointed to the map and a section of the wall. "Here. They can get within a hundred meters of the wall and still use the forest for cover. My guess is that they'll concentrate on these two sections of wall to make a breach by knocking out some of the sonic barrier transmitters. After the sonic barrier falls, they rush the wall. Then, it becomes a real slugfest."

Eric rubbed his chin through a two-day growth of black stubble. "These NewGen are hard to kill."

Brigon finished his hot tea in a last swallow and said, "I'll tell you what really bothers me about fighting NewGens—not that they're tough. The NewGens simply don't care. They just do what they are programmed to do. Personally, I find it disconcerting to fight a species that is both efficient and indifferent. You can see the void in their eyes." He asked rhetorically, "Do you suppose they have the advantage—by not caring?"

Andrea stood and backed away from the wooden table. She fought a yawn and said, "You can bet the NewGen aren't lying awake analyzing our motives. Eric, you catch a couple hours of sleep. Brigon and I will keep the crews busy putting the space cannon on the wall."

A thin fog spilled in from the ocean, frustrating the night watch. Brigon and Andrea stood on the wall. They heard the distant whine of hovercraft through the thin haze.

Andrea asked, "Do you think the fog will burn off in time?"

Brigon pointed to the stars. "I do." He held his binoculars to his eyes. "I saw some of their foot scouts about two thousand meters out. You can bet that they're watching us."

Andrea wondered what the NewGen were able to discern. Just fifty feet away, masons finished building a heavy crude wall with a firing slit to protect the space cannon and crew. They had poured a cement apron with six large bolts protruding straight up. Fat lug nuts sat next to the bolts. The sound of iron on stone seemed comforting. They fabricated a huge gin pole from three tall pines, stripped of their branches and bobbed at the top. Sap oozed from the wounds giving a pungent smell to the night. The precious cannon hung in a cradle of ropes waiting for the masons to finish the crude shield. Large insulated cables dangled from the cannon—tendrils that connected to four heavy transformers anchored in the middle of the street at the base of the wall.

Farther along the street, four cohorts sat on sidewalks with their backs against building walls. Many wore pieces of body armor they had scavenged. Some wore helmets. They held an assortment of weapons across their laps. They tried to rest, but Andrea saw their heads turn to face each other, engaged in low conversation, adding a soft murmur to contrast with the clicks and pings of the masons' tools. *They're nervous.*

She heard the dull scrape of the cannon's steel base as it scraped the mounting bolts and settled on the stone apron. Then quickly the crew took box wrenches as big as their arms and began seating the heavy lug nuts, synching the cannon to the base. "Good," she said loudly. "Not much time to spare, but you did it. Good work. Keep your wrenches, tackle, and gin pole ready. We may want to pull the cannon off the wall in a hurry."

An anonymous voice answered through the gloom. "Right."

Brigon wandered over to inspect the cannon. Andrea looked toward the mountains and saw their black silhouette against the first twilight. They poked their majestic heads high above the thin ground fog. The beautiful saw-toothed rock was still heavily snow covered. The white caps caught the first pinks of morning. The peacefulness of the moment mocked the anxious preparation for battle. The indifferent mountains would survive. Yet, somehow, she felt she would survive, too—not from indifference, but desire. *Desire.* Unlike the NewGens, she and the twenty thousand old-order clones did care. She believed that their caring—their desire—gave them an advantage. She thought that someday she and Brigon would wake up and look out a window at the mountains just to lazily enjoy the view. She *desired* it.

The first rays of sun poured over the mountain, casting long shadows and turning the fog from gray to white. Brigon returned and pointed through the dissipating fog. "Look!"

Andrea raised the binoculars that hung around her neck. She saw a dozen hovercraft sitting on the Sarhn side of the river. NewGen troops poured out, fanning to make a perimeter defense.

Suddenly along the riverfront, the NewGens set explosions to pulverize the remaining river ice and

to cut a kilometer-wide path through the cottonwood trees that lined the banks. Water and ice rose
eighty feet in the air and splashed down. Cottonwood sailed through the air like chaff.

"What was that?" Brigon asked.

With the binoculars still raised to her eyes,
Andrea commented, "They need to clear both banks
for the bridging equipment. And here it comes."

Thereafter, the river crossing unfolded like a bal-
let. The NewGens pushed forty flat-nosed motorized
pontoons into the water. Equidistant, they sped to
the middle, then turned like a wheel spoke. The skip-
pers managed their boats' power with great skill,
accommodating the different rates of flow in the
river. In the middle channel, the boats churned a
long white froth behind them—less so near the
shore. Others on the boats used long poles to fend
off chunks of loose ice.

In unison, each boat transformed. Metal decks,
the length of the hull, slowly turned perpendicular
to the river. NewGens with long poles tipped with
steel hooks grabbed the ends of the decks and
forced them together, while others scrambled to
bolt the decks together into a sectioned ribbon of
steel across the river. From every bridge section, a
pair of NewGen unwound a spool of thick cable,
carrying their ends to the riverbank upstream,
where they fastened the cable to large spikes
driven deep into the ground—all to stiffen the
bridge.

Brigon ordered, "Cannon crew, are you ready?"

"We have them in our sights," came the answer.

"Hold your fire until my command."

The first vehicles to cross the bridge were the

sleek scout vehicles. They raced to their defense perimeter. Then a long column of footsoldiers interspersed with supply trucks appeared and queued for the crossing. A truck mired at the far end, and the bridge quickly jammed.

"Fire!" Brigon hollered.

The space cannon let loose a bolt that fell short, gouging a trench through the NewGen forward defense, leaving a wide brown scar through the green turf. "You missed!" Brigon ran along the wall to the cannon. "How could you miss?" The gunner overcorrected and fired a second bolt that flew over the bridge and hit the far shore, ripping a hole in a column of supply trucks winding its way to the river. The gunner complained, "The aiming sights don't work!"

Brigon pulled the gunner out of the seat and took his place. The cannon used long-range sensors to plot target solutions, and those sensors failed at such short range. Brigon overrode the automatic targeting logic. He looked down the laser barrel, using pressure rings as a crude iron sight. He fired again. The bolt fell short and to the left of the bridge, digging another giant divot from the ground, but causing no damage to the NewGens' bridge. "Damn!" he yelled.

Brigon composed himself, gently nudged the barrel, and fired. He hit the river in the middle but downstream of the bridge. The NewGen reacted. Their hovercraft took off, spreading out. They raced for cover. The columns of equipment and NewGen scattered. Three trucks still remained trapped on the bridge.

Brigon bracketed his fire and loosed another bolt.

This blue bolt hit the bridge in the middle. Two pontoons and a supply truck disintegrated. Others nearby snapped loosed from the tethers and flew into the air, swinging in wild arches tethered to their cables. NewGen trucks, and bodies scattered over the ground and water.

Brigon lowered the barrel and fired again. He smashed another section of the bridge. He kept firing, methodically destroying their bridgehead.

While Brigon concentrated on the bridge, Andrea watched the surrounding chaos. She was the first to see the dozen high-speed attack craft streaking toward Sarhn in a tight formation. The two Sarhn antiair lasers began firing, immediately knocking down two of the craft. They fell from the sky, crashing behind the precincts. The formation didn't split as expected. They didn't react to the antiair lasers. They continued to race toward Sarhn.

Toward the cannon! Andrea realized.

She ran to Brigon, who concentrated his fire, destroying NewGen equipment on the far shore. "Brigon!" she yelled.

"Not now," he answered gruffly and fired another bolt.

"Air attack! Get out of there." She reached the cannon and grabbed hold of his jacket.

Brigon glanced through the slit in the stone wall to see the approaching aircraft. "I can't leave yet." He fired another bolt and blasted two armored vehicles slouching away. "I'm getting the hang of this cannon."

"Brigon!" Andrea's voice cracked with exasperation. "The *deal* is neither one of us is supposed to get killed."

"I can take half their armor." He squinted down the barrel.

Andrea said angrily, "Then we'll both die. Here. Together." She planted her feet. Then she caught a glimpse of the aircraft closing in. "Oh, screw this." She reached up and jerked Brigon out of the gunner's seat.

"What the . . . ?" Brigon's cheeks turned red as he picked himself off the cold pavement.

"You'd better start listening to me." Andrea pushed him with all her might to the edge of the wall. Then she grabbed his jacket and jumped, dragging him after her.

They fell twenty feet to a steep clay tile roof. They whacked the roof hard and tumbled down— the pair of them sprawled out, dislodging roof tiles as they slid. Andrea caught an iron chimney with her free arm. She held tight to Brigon's jacket with the other hand. She felt the strain in her shoulder as they jerked to a stop. Andrea knew that had her tissue not been augmented by the Quazel Protein, she would have ripped her shoulder out of its socket.

The wall above them shuddered from the impact of high explosives. The attack aircraft sped overhead beginning a turn for a return run. Bruised but alive, Brigon looked up and saw the black smoke billowing from the spot where the cannon had been. Only Andrea's grip on his jacket kept him from sliding the rest of the way down the roof. He gingerly turned on his side and found some finger holds. Looking up at Andrea, he tried to make light of his near disaster, saying, "From the first time I saw you, I knew you were my kind of woman."

"Oh, shut up." Andrea was genuinely peeved. She hollered to the street, "We need a ladder up here!"

With the bridge destroyed, the clone garrison enjoyed a short reprieve. The NewGens gathered and repaired four pontoons, then began ferrying heavy equipment across—first the armor, then the supply trucks. NewGen hovercraft, wary of Sarhn's antiair lasers, slipped in and out, quickly offloading fifty troops at a time. Slowly the NewGen spread over the fields.

The next three days were relatively quiet and sunny. However, the steady buildup of NewGen assets on the near shore cast a dark shadow that seemed to crawl toward the city. The orchards burst into bloom. The wheat and soybean fields sent up their first sprouts just to be trampled under foot and armor tracks.

Eric stood watch on the wall. Four cohorts sat or knelt, shoulder to shoulder, with their weapons resting on masonry. Using sandbags and loose masonry, they built gun emplacements for their heavier weapons.

The NewGen began filtering into the precincts, using the forest to encroach. Eric heard small explosions: the booby traps. But the occasional casualty did not deter the NewGens. They continued to fill the woods. He heard the motors of armored vehicles periodically rev. In his mind's eye, Eric could see the tracked vehicles lurching over a fallen log. Always the sounds came closer, but he never saw the enemy.

Ariko's snipers stood ready, but the NewGen did not give them a target. They remained deep in the foliage, preparing their assault.

Around noon, Eric heard a chorus of engines roar to life. "This is it!" he hollered up and down the wall. He turned and waved to Brigon and Andrea, each standing with a fresh cohort. Tara stayed behind to direct succeeding cohorts into position. He hollered down, "They're sending their armor against the south wall."

The iron beasts rolled to the forest edge, knocking down saplings. They fired at the wall. Eric ducked as a splash of shattered stone rained down. He peered over the stone edge and didn't see any infantry. His own gunners poured lasers and large caliber rounds onto the armored vehicles without effect. Wanting to conserve their limited ammunition, Eric ordered, "Cease fire! Cease fire!"

The clone defenders enthusiastically obeyed, ducking low to avoid the incoming blasts. Eric stole another glance, and saw the precision of the NewGen gunnery. They fired only at casements that housed the sonic barrier generators, blasting away the thick sheath of rock and concrete. A splash of sharp pebbles raked his face, and he lunged for cover. Blood flowed into his eyes from cuts in his forehead.

Brigon witnessed Eric's injury and ran up the steps. He scurried on his hands and knees to Eric's side. Eric sat up, blinking away the fresh blood.

Brigon asked, "How bad?"

"I don't know."

Brigon held up Eric's chin to inspect the wounds, three deep gashes running from his eyebrows to his hairline. "You're cut to the bone. Get out of here. They'll sew you up."

Eric touched the ragged, numb flesh on his forehead. "The NewGen are blasting out the sonic barrier with their armor. We can't stop them."

"At least we know what section of the wall they want to breach. We'll double our force here." Brigon sent Eric away and ordered two more cohorts onto the two hundred foot section of wall. Andrea's people carried wooden spools of cable to the wall— every odd spool had copper cable; every even spool had aluminum braid.

Suddenly, the cannon blasting stopped and silence returned with the suddenness of an explosion. The ubiquitous hum of the sonic barrier was gone—that annoying hum. How everyone wished they could hear it again.

Brigon looked over the wall and saw thousands of NewGen standing in the tree line. They began a slow run toward the naked wall. The NewGen in the front rank carried heavy stainless steel shields as tall as themselves. Brigon cried out, "Fire at will!"

The four cohorts of old-order clones fired at the oncoming horde, concentrating their fire on the first rank. Their volley staggered the line, but had little effect. Bullets splashed off the shields causing minor wounds. Energy weapons put dark scars on the shiny metal. The NewGen returned withering fire. They closed the gap between the forest and wall too quickly.

"Fire into their second ranks and deeper," Brigon yelled above the racket. The word quickly passed and the clones shifted their fire, decimating the NewGens in the rear. But the Sarhn defenders, too, suffered many casualties.

Under the hail of bullets and crimson lasers, the first wave of NewGen reached the wall and began climbing. The Sarhn defenders reached over to fire directly down on the climbers, striking their helmets and shoulders. The NewGen body armor buckled under the heavy fire, and the stricken NewGens fell to the base of the wall. If not dead, they rose and tried to climb again.

Unfortunately, to fire straight down the wall the clones had to expose themselves and they suffered heavily, often falling forward, their bodies mingled with the dying NewGen.

A second wave of NewGen reached the wall. They used the dead and dying as steps as they began their climb.

Andrea raised her fist and dropped it—her signal to toss the hundred spools of copper and aluminum cable over the wall. The clones quickly knotted copper to copper, aluminum to aluminum, stringing feeds to power cables dug out of the ground. A pair of women stood by the naked cable. Each wore thick rubber gloves. Each waited with a large alligator clip in her hand.

The NewGen grabbed the cables to help pull themselves up the wall. The wall was thick with the large figures hanging on, firing straight up as the clones fired down. A third wave crashed against the wall and began climbing. The first NewGen soldier reached the top of the wall, firing blindly only to have a rifle barrel shoved below his helmet chinstrap, a bullet and muzzle blast ripping the head off.

Along the wall, Andrea saw the NewGen helmets popping up. "Now!" Along the wall, the cohorts backed away from the naked wires hanging over the wall. Then Andrea pumped her right fist twice to signal the pair of women below.

Each crammed an alligator clip over the naked cable, then leaped back from the blue sparks. Twenty amps and two hundred and fifty volts pulsed through the wires, electrocuting the NewGen on the wall. The collective groan of lungs constricting was louder than gunfire. The shock threw some from the wall tossing them head over heels to the stony ground below. Several NewGen clung to the electrified cable, until the current burned through their spasmed muscles and bone. They fell backward, eyes wide, cloudy, and lifeless.

The smell of flesh burning wafted over the wall causing some of the clones to vomit. No fewer than six hundred NewGen fell from the wall into a heap, adding a layer to the dead already stacked below.

The NewGens retreated into the forest. The clones cut the power to the cables.

In the lull, Tara sent fresh cohorts to the wall. She was horrified by the scant numbers of the first four cohorts who retired from the wall without a wound. The healthy carried the dead. The wounded crept away into buildings to bleed and wait. The first battle for the wall had lasted barely two hours. At the present casualty rate, Tara calculated that they would all be dead in another four days.

Eric returned with his head bandaged, blood still encrusted on his eyebrows. He saw the concern on Tara's face and pulled her aside. She pointed to a group of wounded clones helping each other down a side street and she expressed her anxiety, "We're getting slaughtered, aren't we?"

Eric scowled, "We're doing the best we can."

Tara's face crumpled at his harsh retort. She quietly remonstrated, "I wasn't criticizing."

Eric saw the effect of his words. He set his gear aside and embraced her, squeezing her hard and whispering in her ear, "I know. I know." He turned to climb up the stone steps to the wall.

"Tara?" She looked up at him.

"Thank you," he said. "Thank you for . . . I don't know. Everything."

"You're welcome, Eric." Then Eric smiled fully and warmly at his mate and gave her a shy shrug.

"Well, I didn't want to be the first to die, and I got my wish. Now all I ask is that I not be the last to die."

After an afternoon of resting and waiting, Andrea took her turn at the wall. A red sun slipped into the ocean. Thin clouds caught the last luminescence. She saw a swarm of bats from the precinct rise like smoke, then head toward the river. The forest became a murky collage of shadows. The three-quarters moon had not yet climbed above the mountains. She took a bite of dried fruit, a mango, she thought.

Andrea stopped chewing for a moment and looked at the first stars. Part of her wished those specks of light were Jod transports. Part of her was glad that the night lights were the constant stars. The stars wouldn't help her, now. But she could trust them.

Psst! A voice farther down the wall alerted everyone. *I see something.*

Andrea turned to peer over the wall. The forest was thick with NewGens. All along the wall other clones passed signals: everyone saw the tree line fill with NewGens.

She tossed her last piece of fruit over the wall, muttered, "Night attack."

A woman to her right grumbled, "I hate the night."

"Cuts both ways," Andrea tried to encourage the woman. The foliage and dim light obscured her vision. Andrea put on a pair of night goggles and looked again. Many NewGens carried long wooden poles. They wore thick, clumsy homemade gloves—looked like mattress stuffing held together with tape. Andrea knew. *They are going to try to beat the electric cables.*

Andrea waved to Tara below. Everybody prepared.

Tank-mounted xenon searchlights lit the wall. The sudden flash of white light, bright as the sun, temporarily blinded the clones staring into the dark forest. Andrea ripped the goggles from her face and rubbed her sore eyes. She ducked behind her rock barrier, blinking away the pain.

Then, the NewGen tanks commenced continuous blasts from their laser cannons. They raked the walls—the crimson shafts of light crisscrossed, chewing away the rock as well as the cable. The defenders hunkered down and listened to the buzz of laser cannon and the crackle of shattering rock. The smell of ozone wafted over the wall. They marveled at the huge expenditure of energy. Andrea turned to the woman on her right and said, "Even Ordinate tanks don't have an endless power supply; laser crystals don't last forever."

Andrea reeled in one of the cables to confirm her suspicion. She pulled in a short strand of aluminum braid cut to a nub, still hot to the touch. *It's going to be a long night.* The NewGen lasers scorched the wall until one by one the crystals burned out. Then the NewGen infantry attacked the wall in droves.

Andrea ordered, "Kill their lights." In seconds, the defenders blasted every xenon light and stark black returned. The darkness favored the clones firing from the wall. They were small targets, whereas the NewGen horde crammed against the wall provided a large target.

The night was long. Muzzle flashes and crimson laser rifles punctuated the gloom. The constant clatter of guns and the dull thud of bullets smashing flesh and bone almost became background noise. The occasional grunts and moans of the wounded barely merited attention.

Fresh cohorts replaced exhausted and decimated units on the wall. Minutes turned to hours. The moon rose and filled the killing zone with pale light. The NewGens continued to pour out of the forest like waves rolling out of the ocean onto the shore. The NewGens remained as tough as ever to kill. Most of them did not reach the wall without some wound. With animal strength, they climbed the walls, using pockmarks and laser cuts for handholds. Usually during the climb they endured automatic fire.

The bodies continued to collect at the base of the wall creating a ramp. In places, the NewGen could race up the ramp of their own dead and leap onto the wall. The forty feet of sheer stone shrank to twenty feet. Many more NewGen were reaching the top. A few forced their way into the defenders' positions, creating havoc. Panicked defenders responded with erratic bursts of automatic fire, wounding some of their comrades in the process.

Andrea sensed the rising panic. The moon was in its descent. She worried that as more NewGen breached the wall, the night's advantage would shift to them. If one section of the wall collapsed, they were finished. She bounded down the steps. She corralled Ariko and eighteen others, waiting to take their turn on the wall.

"Come with me." Andrea ran to a stone building buttressed against the wall and opened the door. Inside stood twenty glass carboys, each filled with five gallons of liquid propane. Two of them were marked PH_3, the two mixed with phosphene. "Okay, line up and I'll give each of you one of these bottles."

They formed a line. Andrea pulled a simple glass-cutting tool from her pocket and etched a deep scratch around each container, handing it to a bearer.

Ariko asked, "Why are you cutting the glass?"

"We've got to make sure they break when you throw them over the wall." She etched the PH_3 carboys last. "Now listen carefully. Whatever you do, don't drop these bottles on our side of the wall, especially these two." She pointed to the PH_3 bottles. "We go to the wall. We spread out about thirty feet between us. When you see me throw my bottle over the wall, you do the same. Got that?"

They answered in unison, "Got it."

Then, with the heavy carboys on their shoulders, they shuffled toward the door. As they passed, Andrea told them, "After you toss the carboys, get everybody off the wall as fast you can. In about fifteen seconds, there will be an explosion that will kill everything between the wall and the forest."

"If we leave the wall, some NewGens might get in."

"Some of them will get in—not many. We'll take care of them after the blast. Let's go."

Walking slowly up the stone stairs, they announced loudly, "Explosives behind you. Explosives behind you." Andrea walked behind, ready to sprint forward to steady anyone that might falter with his dangerous cargo. She watched them spread out along the wall. Then she took one of the PH_3 carboys from a bearer. She looked right and left to ensure that her companions saw her. With all her might she threw the carboy over the wall. The others imitated her. She heard the reassuring crash of broken glass. "Everybody—off the wall!"

The clones clamored down the steps. Along the wall, NewGen heads peered over. The NewGens, many of them wounded, hauled themselves inside.

Outside the wall, the carboys shattered. The pressurized liquid propane tossed shards of glass into the closest attackers. The liquid turned instantly to gas, and the colorless, odorless propane spread, covering the ground between the wall and the forest. The NewGen never knew they were knee-deep in explosive. The phosphene mixture also mixed with the air's oxygen and reached the point of spontaneous combustion.

The explosion shook the ground. A giant flash of yellow flame lit the forest momentarily. A bluish bubble of flame rose high in the air. The sound belied the strength of the explosion—a dull, hollow *karumf!* But the overpressure killed two thousand NewGen in an instant. Another thousand lay stunned on the ground, dying.

Another cloud, colorless, odorless, also heavier than air, settled over the blast area: carbon dioxide.

Fresh NewGen rushed in from the forest to fill the void. They stepped around the bodies that littered the ground. They had unwittingly rushed to their deaths as they stormed into a giant bubble, void of oxygen. They didn't realize their predicament until they lacked the strength to run out. The NewGens fell asleep, as it were, on the battlefield. They would never wake up.

Without needing a command, the Sarhn defenders poured merciless rifle fire on the few NewGen lucky enough to get inside Sarhn and escape the propane bomb. The battle was soon over for the night.

Andrea found an empty building and took a nap on the floor nestled among exhausted clones. Brigon found her and brought her a breakfast, a sandwich of scrambled eggs and butter plus some gaval. He studied her for a moment to satisfy his own mind that she was well. Her black uniform was nicked and scraped from fighting, dusted by the dark residue of gunpowder. Her face was streaked where sweat eroded small channels through the dust and there was gunpowder residue on her skin. He noticed little crow's-feet at the side of her closed eyes. In her black uniform, she looked like a cat. She rested peacefully. He wondered if he ought to let her sleep, but he decided that she also needed to eat. He gently woke her, grabbing her arm.

Andrea opened her brown eyes, embarrassed to be found sleeping. "I should be up on the wall." She sat up and crossed her legs.

Brigon handed her the gaval. "Eric's got it covered. Everything's quiet for now. The NewGen haven't figured out what hit them last night." He handed her the sandwich. I figured you need to eat something."

"Thank you." Andrea ate quickly, as soldiers do. She chewed and swallowed. She looked around at the clones lying on the cold floor or lounging in chairs. She said, "I had the strangest dream last night."

"Tell me about it." Brigon held his cup of gaval nested in both hands.

Andrea shrugged. "Dreams are nonsense." She finished the sandwich and wiped her mouth with the back of her dirty hand.

"Tell me anyway."

Andrea paused to recollect the details. She started slowly. "I was on a sandy atoll—the place where we Tenebrea get our survival training. I had dug my solar still, put up shade, built a fire, and caught a fish. I had everything I needed to survive. All I needed to do was wait out the clock until the end of the exercise, except I couldn't remember if the exercise was for six days or six years. But, I was alone and I was restless. Then who should come walking into my camp but Hal K'Rin."

She paused to drink her hot gaval. "He looked different. The rings beneath his eyes were gone. He looked more human. And he looked confused. We did not exchange words; rather, we squared off for a fair fight."

"What happened?"

"I don't know. You woke me up."

Before Brigon could comment, the sound of gunfire split the morning calm.

Brigon and Andrea ran from the building and met Tara ushering another cohort to the wall. Tara looked more worried than ever as she reported, "Hart tells me that we're getting short on ball ammunition. He says we won't last the day."

Andrea joined the flow of people climbing the steps. When she got to the top she glanced over. She felt her blood chill. Each attacking NewGen picked up a corpse and held it as a shield to absorb the defenders' bullets. Upon reaching the wall, the attacking NewGens merely tossed the bodies onto the pile. Then they ran back to gather other corpses. They were finishing a ramp built from their own lifeless bodies. Andrea fired at a NewGen charging up the ramp to stack another body near the top. Her bullet passed through the NewGen's neck. He fell and slid backward, adding yet another body to the ramp.

She leaned over and quickly calculated. The NewGens' ramp already stood twenty-five feet high. In another twenty minutes, they would be able to charge the wall at a dead run. No vertical climb would slow them down. They'd run up the ramp of corpses and hop over the last two-foot lip. *In twenty minutes we'll be fighting hand to hand—outnumbered.*

The NewGen army had forty thousand more expendable soldiers. Now every NewGen they killed just became brick and mortar for their expedient ramp. Soon forty thousand NewGen would storm out of the forest, up and over the wall. *It is over,* she thought, *but there will be no surrender; the NewGens will take no prisoners.*

Andrea ducked back to think as bullets whizzed by. She looked at the old-order clones around her. They had fought well. They had suffered about two thousand dead, another two thousand wounded. In return, they had inflicted more than twenty thousand NewGen casualties. She felt bad for them. They might have pulled it off, if only they had enough ammunition.

She hollered down to Tara, "Get every last person with a weapon out here. Tell them to bring their blades."

Tara turned and ran with a limp back toward the reserve cohorts.

Andrea continued to fire from the wall until she exhausted her ammunition. She decided not to take any more of the ammunition for herself. Instead, she hunkered down and drew a heavy blade from the sheath strapped to her thigh. She looked up and down the wall trying to see Brigon. She wanted to see him, even if she didn't have the chance to say good-bye. She couldn't find him on the crowded walls, and she felt acutely disappointed.

Then Andrea heard thunder, earsplitting thunder as loud as the thunder from the kkona storms. She looked at the cloudless, blue sky. *Sonic booms. That's all we need.* She searched the sky horizon to horizon for signs of enemy aircraft. The thunder returned. She winced from the pounding noise.

Above the mountains, she saw streaks of light trailing thin threads of white in a giant arc. The fliers had passed overhead, cutting a tight turn—two-hundred miles is tight at supersonic speeds. *Three contrails, three ships. Out of range of our antiair lasers. High-altitude bombing?* She looked again. The single threads split into tiny filaments, tiny balls of fire flying toward Sarhn. Others on the wall were too busy fending off NewGen attackers to notice.

She saw the weapons heading straight for her, as if they had her and her alone in their sights. She sat with her back against the wall and gazed at the cluster of objects. *Imagine watching a meteor hit you in the face.* In the last moments the incoming missiles grew from tiny specks to large shafts. In a split second they passed over her head and blasted the forest.

The ground shook violently. The blast of scorching heat blew overhead. The clones on the wall toppled backward, many of them burned, others just bruised by their fortunate fall from the wall. Most, like Andrea, had their heads down and watched stunned as the fireball rose behind them and overhead. Another three missiles followed, pulverizing half the precincts.

Andrea looked up and saw no more missiles. She peered over the wall and saw the inferno. All the trees lay down, uprooted or snapped. A fire roared. She saw NewGen dead lying everywhere, their clothes on fire. The few that lived ran from the killing heat. She herself could not stand more than a couple seconds of the intense heat radiating from the forest, now a wall of fire. She left to find Brigon.

Feathery ashes fell like a sickly snow. The Sarhn defenders—Andrea and Brigon among them—scrambled back to the walls to find the NewGens gone. The forest was flattened and the helter-skelter tree trunks continued to smolder. Blackened hulks of NewGen armor lay beneath the burning trees. Using high-powered binoculars, Andrea saw a large remnant of the NewGen army reconstituting itself near the river. She guessed that the remaining NewGen still numbered in excess of thirty thousand.

Then a trio of Jod shuttles descended rapidly. Brigon calculated that the Jod ships would land on the pockmarked spaceport, in exactly the same spot Kip landed. Brigon turned to Andrea. "You stay here, out of sight. I'll make first contact with the Jod."

"No, I'm coming, too." Andrea watched the small ships carve a gentle arch through the sky. She thought she recognized the larger of the three shuttles; she thought she saw the captain's gig from the light cruiser *Tyker*, K'Rin's ship. She entertained her fantasy, *Perhaps he will consent to a fair fight. He did fight well at Klamdara.*

Brigon knew better than to argue. Instead, he told her flatly, "You stay behind me." Then he gathered several hundred of his battle-weary soldiers and ushered them to the rubbled spaceport to greet the Jod. He spied Eric and beckoned him to joining the welcoming party. They formed a thick semicircle around the landing pad.

The three shuttles landed simultaneously, kicking up a cloud of red brick dust. Andrea started toward the ships when Brigon grabbed her wrist. "No, Andrea. I want you to stay back in the crowd until we know their intentions."

"You may never know their intentions," she warned.

"Nevertheless, we're not going to do anything foolish, are we?"

"That's K'Rin's gig in the middle. He's here." Andrea looked at Brigon's hand gripping her wrist. Brigon tightened his grip and added, "A little prudence is all I ask. Let me speak with them first. I want you out of sight for now." He let her go and

Andrea stepped back into the protective folds of the crowd. Her face turned hard as flint.

Each of the shuttle bay doors opened and out stepped the Tenebrea in full battle gear. They wore black uniforms with cross braces and heavy packs. Each carried a helmet in the crook of his left arm. Each held a heavy weapon with a white-knuckled grip. The tension was palpable. Their Jod faces were austere, the rings beneath the eyes foreboding. They had come to kill or be killed.

After they had formed their dense ranks, an older Jod stepped from the middle ship: K'Rin. Andrea felt her blood rise upon seeing him. *I wonder how he explained H'Roo's death to the Parh Clan?*

Over his neat black battle uniform K'Rin wore a dark crimson cape bearing the Rin seal. He stood behind the ranks of Tenebrea, watching over their heads. Andrea could see his eyes searching the mob, looking for her face. *He knows better than to stand in the open*, Andrea thought. About eighty meters of rubbled field stood between the mob of Sarhn defenders and the Tenebrea's ranks.

A spokesman, Bal'Don, stepped forward. He surveyed the disorderly mob of battle-weary clones. He spoke loudly, and his baritone voice echoed from the walls of the nearby ruins. "Hal K'Rin wishes a private audience with his cousin, Andrea Flores."

Brigon stepped out in front of the clones. He kept a safe distance from Bal'Don and said, "We thank you for coming to our aid."

Bal'Don bowed slightly to accept the token of gratitude. Then Brigon added, "However, on your last visit to Sarhn, your agents tried to murder Andrea. We won't hand her over to you that easily."

Bal'Don pursed his lips. He looked over his shoulder in K'Rin's direction to receive a hand signal. He turned and said, "The private audience is a prerequisite to your receiving any more of our help."

Brigon bristled, "Then you may pack up and leave."

"No!" Andrea called from the back of the mob. She elbowed her way into the open. "No, Brigon. We can't survive another day without Jod help."

Brigon turned to push her back into the relative safety of the mob. He whispered hoarsely in her face, "He'll try to kill you. We'll wait for another time."

"Wait for what?" Andrea shoved Brigon aside. "At least now, I have them all in front of me. I don't have to worry about my back," Andrea said with false confidence.

Brigon grabbed her arm and pulled her toward him. "I won't let him kill you. I'll give the order to fire on them, I swear. I'll take him out first."

Andrea offered Brigon a bitter smile, "No, love. Don't interfere."

Andrea stepped twenty meters in front of the old-order clones. Her creased and worn black uniform had a film of red and gray dust on her shoulders. Her hair was oily from four days of ceaseless fighting. The white linen bandage on her arm, stained with blood, had slipped from the wound to hang loosely at her elbow. She watched the Tenebrea closely for any threatening sign, any shift in stance or weapon. The Tenebrea stood with pained discipline. She sensed that they all disapproved. *Disapproval of what?* she wondered.

Bal'Don turned and walked back to the Tenebrea

ranks. With a hand motion, the ranks opened like a pair of doors. K'Rin stood in the middle. His eyes widened slightly as he caught his first glimpse of Andrea.

Andrea studied K'Rin. She had expected him to be older, perhaps weaker. However, K'Rin appeared as he had the first day she saw him, large and formidable. Unconsciously she began kneading her hands, limbering the tendons for the fight she expected. Her hands felt clammy. *Damned nerves*, she thought. *I can't make a mistake now*. She felt a bead of sweat trickle down the back of her neck. She forced herself to take deep breaths—surreptitiously, because she did not want K'Rin to see her quiet preparations.

K'Rin turned away. He carefully unfastened the clasp at his neck and removed his cape, handing the heavy cloth to Bal'Don. Over his battle uniform, he wore a heavy necklace of gold, each link an emblem of the major clans, the sign of his office and rank. K'Rin carefully removed the precious necklace and draped it over Bal'Don's outstretched hand.

Still with his back to her, K'Rin unfastened the holster and withdrew his handlance. Andrea reached for her pistol. The ranks of Tenebrea stood frozen, gripping their equipment, probing her with their eyes. She saw the strain on their discipline. They wanted desperately to intervene. She thought: *K'Rin must have given them strict orders to stay out of the fight. Why?*

K'Rin carefully handed his handlance to another one of the Tenebrea. *He's smart. A duel with short-range weapons gives me at least a fifty-fifty chance of killing him*. She relaxed her hand from her pistol grip.

K'Rin unbuckled a small silver buckle and removed a slender belt that held his dagger. Andrea watched with interest. *He knows I can beat him with the knife. He will want to grapple: trust his Jod strength. He figures that after days of combat, I'm exhausted. Well, I saved something for you, old man.* She began rehearsing her moves. She must not let him get hold of her, whereas she must land many blows to his neck and head. *So be it.*

K'Rin turned and faced her. He held out his empty hands to advertise his lack of weapons. Then he started across the disheveled tarmac, stepping over chunks of asphalt. Andrea became increasingly aware of the space between them. She adjusted her stance slightly, finding her center of gravity. She decided she would let him make the first move, let him close the crucial gap. With her greater agility, she'd evade, then attack. Evade and attack—that must be her strategy. As he walked toward her with a deliberate cadence, she felt her heart beat faster.

He stopped just out of arm's reach. Then, K'Rin knelt down on one knee and bowed his head. His neck turned a bluish purple, and he did nothing to suppress this manifestation of his emotion. Andrea backed away a half step. The neck color pulsed—purple in blue—in time with the beating of a Jod heart.

"Andrea, cousin." K'Rin did not lift his eyes. "I am responsible for your husband and child's death. You have a just blood debt against me." He looked up.

Her entire body was coiled, ready to strike at K'Rin's head. *What?* She was as stunned as if she'd been hit by a handlance. She felt her fingernails digging into the palms of her fists. The silent voice in her soul screamed at her. *Make some sense!* She had thought that a stand-up fight with K'Rin would finally make some sense of her chaotic life. *But this?* K'Rin helpless before her was a contradiction beyond her imagination: she didn't understand and instinctively despised the contradiction because it sapped her strength. Her arms fell slack at her side as she muttered incredulously, no longer believing her own words, "And I intend to kill you."

K'Rin said, "It is your right."

"Get up, you son of a bitch." Andrea felt dizzy with confusion. "Defend yourself."

"No, cousin," K'Rin's voice was deliberate and loud enough for all to hear, "to satisfy the blood debt, you must either forgive me, or kill me in front of these witnesses. No Tenebrea will lift a hand to stop you. Neither need you nor your friends fear retribution." He continued to kneel and bow his head, eyes fixed on his own black shadow.

Andrea backed away dumbfounded. Breathing was painful as her chest constricted. *You must believe that I won't kill you.* She took her eyes off K'Rin and looked at the Tenebrea standing in ranks. They carefully controlled their emotions. She looked over her left shoulder and saw Brigon and Eric. Tara had squeezed between them. Dr. Carai stood behind her. A growing multitude of the old-order clones gathered in silence. She read Tara's face easily: Tara needed the Jod forces to achieve her goals, her eyes pleaded for the Jod's life, yet she did not intervene. Brigon's face was harder to understand. His eyes were afraid, even sad, as if he were resigned that she would make the wrong choice. Yet he, too, would not intervene. *Why?*

She looked back at K'Rin. *And you, why did you take away my Steve and Glennie?* Her lips moved, but she made no sound.

K'Rin lowered his eyes and said in a low voice only for Andrea. "Forgiven or not, I am sorry. I resolve never to make such an error again. If you forgive me, I am obliged by the ancient code to obey your lawful and moral orders—even if you tell me to resign my office."

Andrea could barely breathe. She looked down at K'Rin and a flood of memories collided in her skull. *I ought to kill you.* But she didn't want him dead. The stark contradiction pressed a nerve behind her eyes. *Why can't I kill you? Could it be as Eric suggested that you and I are too much alike? How can that be? When did I become like you? Or when did you become like me? Are you so much a part of my life that I'm afraid to cut you off? Could it be that I have empathy for you? Impossible! You used me so badly. You are responsible for killing my beloved and my child—my family.*

Andrea remembered back when her own people railroaded her out of the Academy, an acute embarrassment for K'Rin. She remembered bracing for his admonition and he said *institutions shoot their wounded—families do not. Can it be that I am part of your family? Do you love me as kin?*

Oh, Steve and Glennie! Her memories became a flood of anguish and anger. But the anguish wasn't hate—just pain. And the anger wasn't hate, but disappointed love. *Where is the hate?* Andrea searched her treasury of memories and the hate was gone. *The anger remains, but the hate is gone. I want him alive . . . but why? Can it be that I love Brigon or that I still love Steve and Glennie, or—* Andrea glanced over her shoulder at the old-order clones, those clones whom she once discounted and with whom now felt such a bond. More than a bond. The overwhelming realization made her blush: *I am loved. What irony—love pours itself out on the unlovable.*

Andrea felt her chest tighten as if her heart might not beat again. She tried to say the words, but she could not find enough air in her lungs. Instead she reached out and touched K'Rin on his hairless head.

K'Rin winced ever so slightly, not expecting an unseen touch but some word. Andrea backed away. The touch was not repugnant to her. She fixed her eyes on K'Rin's bowed head. She took a deep breath, steadied her voice and whispered, "I forgive you."

K'Rin bowed lower. "Thank you, Andrea. Thank you, cousin."

She bit her lower lip and let K'Rin speak.

Without raising his eyes, he said, "I am your servant." Slowly the purplish tones disappeared from his neck, fading to red, and then red faded to the natural pale white.

Andrea watched wide-eyed still trying to comprehend this new turn in her life.

"Tell me what you would have me do." K'Rin looked up. His eyes were clear and Andrea knew that he meant every word. She remembered H'Roo's face and his last words: *K'Rin will atone. But what pain could he endure to satisfy me?* Andrea looked into K'Rin's eyes and saw a gnawing pain trying to purge itself.

"No." Andrea shook her head. "No, sir. I release you of any obligations to me. Instead, I ask a favor."

K'Rin's eyes brightened at the word *favor* as if the request confirmed the forgiveness. "Anything."

"You can't undo what you've done, but you can help these old-order clones. I free you, so you can help them defend their freedom." Andrea pointed toward the raggedy mass of people—a collection of faces straining to hear the low whispers at the center of the tarmac.

"We will fight by your side until the regiments from Corondor arrive three days from now."

She said softly, "Now, get up."

K'Rin rose and waited to be dismissed.

Andrea's curiosity prompted her to ask, "Hal K'Rin, what did you expect would happen here today?"

K'Rin stepped forward. He lowered his voice to protect the privacy of this part of their conversation. He said, "Andrea, I never, never underestimated you."

"What does that mean?"

"It means, cousin, that I *hoped* you would forgive me. I *believed* you would forgive me. I know I sound presumptuous, but this simple declaration is meant to be a compliment. Now, you have proven to everyone else that you are better than I."

Andrea looked over K'Rin's shoulder at the anxious gathering of Tenebrea. She said curtly, "I'll send Eric and Brigon to coordinate with your staff for the defense of Sarhn." Then she turned and walked back to Brigon. K'Rin likewise turned about and rejoined his ranks.

The clones were craning their necks to see and

hear the results of the meeting. Tara reached out with her good hand to welcome Andrea back into their midst. Brigon asked for all of them, "Andrea, what happened out there?"

Andrea put her hand on his chest. She saw optimism in his eyes, infectious optimism. She wanted to respond in kind, but she felt her sudden desire for optimism recede into a long-forgotten vulnerability. She looked up at Brigon and said softly, "Now, we have a future."

Authors' Note

We would like to take this opportunity to present two worthy organizations that help children in need: Camp Heartland and Half the Sky Foundation. Camp Heartland is the world's largest camping and outreach program for children affected by HIV or AIDS. Half the Sky Foundation was created by adoptive parents of orphaned Chinese children to enrich the lives of and enhance the outcome for babies and young children in China who wait to be adopted.

By purchasing this book, you have already helped these children. The proceeds of this collector's edition go to these two charities.

To learn more about these charities, visit my Web site, *www.roxanndawson.net* or go directly to *www.campheartland.org* and *www.halfthesky.org*.

Visit
❖ **Pocket Books** ❖
online at

---

www.SimonSays.com

Keep up on the latest new
releases from your favorite
authors, as well as author
appearances, news, chats,
special offers and more.

SIMON & SCHUSTER
A VIACOM COMPANY
www.SimonSays.com

Pocket
Books

2381-01